Destiny Skye

Nancy Thorne Hinkel

Karen,
Happy Reading!
Nancy Thorne Hinkel

Copyright © 2012 Nancy Thorne Hinkel
All rights reserved.

ISBN: 1-4681-8361-3
ISBN-13: 9781468183610
Library of Congress Control Number: 2012900586
CreateSpace, North Charleston, SC

Dedication

My treasured friend, Mary, who is never timid to ask,

"Okay, so who's here?"

And then she sends them all home with me.

chapter 1

As soon as I step onto the first of four creaky wooden steps leading into Suggs General Store, Mama recognizes the sound of my Birkenstock. "Hi, sugar," Mama's lyrical voice sings the words. She's rocking in her favorite chair, a large box of snap beans splayed over her tiny lap and light, ethereal music playing throughout the store. The countertop is hidden by stacks of fresh sweet corn ready to have their husks pulled off and silks cleared away. Fuzzy ripe peaches are proudly displayed in a large ceramic bowl begging to be carved and tossed in sugar and spice. Mama has just turned sixty-two years young. Seeing her in a sundress, her deeply tanned skin glowing and glossy, wavy brown hair bouncing against the nape of her neck, one would think she is much younger. She gives me one of her signature beaming smiles. Mama radiates God's love, sharing it with all who enter the store, including me, her daughter of forty-three years, Emileigh Louise.

Tahlulah Bell Suggs took over the general store when I was a mere eight years old. Daddy ran off with a faith healer and his daughter, Yolanda. None of the local women had heard of Yolanda before her daddy drove into town to cure what ailed us. We didn't recollect anything needed to be cured. Despite our good health, they came to lay hands on us. Yolanda was perky of spirit and body. Daddy put his faith aside, succumbing to the whispering promises of the devil, and took up with them—particularly Yolanda. She must have had some touch. He went off never to return, with nary a word. Daddy left Mama in a lurch. She put the house up for sale, and once it sold, she bought the decrepit general store. We lived in a small, tidy apartment in the back. Mama put our lives in the hands of the Almighty and her energy into the store.

"Hi, Mama, is it hot enough for ya?"

"Oh, sugar, do you know how many times I hear that phrase in the course of a summer's day? I've got some nice snap beans, corn, and barbecue for dinner. Are you stayin'? I hope so. You know how I love it when you do. The girls will be over later. They say there are strange sounds emitting from across the lake. We are plannin' on investigating tonight."

"Sounds? What kind of sounds? Animal sounds? Whatever else could it be?"

"You'll have to be here and listen for yourself."

"Mama, after just how many glasses of wine would these so-called strange sounds be heard?"

"I don't rightly know. We don't count while sitting on the dock; it just ain't done."

"Is Louise bringing her party barge over for the investigation, or are you ladies skinny-dipping with the moonlight guiding your way?"

"Like I said, sugar, you'll have to be here to see."

"Or to keep a watchful eye on y'all. Are those binoculars I see on the porch? You've been spyin' again, haven't you? Don't tell me it was a bird you were watching. That dog don't hunt."

"All this worry about tonight and you haven't come over here to give your dear mother a hug or a kiss. What is this world comin' to?"

As usual, she's right. I give her a gentle hug, catching a whiff of her lavender and thyme lotion in the process. Mama keeps me in her embrace until I have at least three kisses on each cheek. She is a lot of things; lacking in affection for others is not one of them.

The general store smells of freshly brewed ice tea and Grandmama's angel biscuits. Mama usually puts either a vanilla bean or a cinnamon stick in her tea. That's about as exotic as she gets in the kitchen. The smell of tea and the glorious angel biscuits baking asking to be topped off with sweet peaches dripping in syrup mixed with fresh pine scent from outside is the quintessential smell of summer to me.

Mama's eyes are the color of root beer, dark brown with caramel highlights; a bubbly effervescence shines out with love and light. Her lashes are naturally long and luxurious, beckoning strangers to gaze a bit longer than comfortable. When I was a youngin, Mama taught me how to give butterfly kisses with those long, flittering lashes. Those special, gentle kisses always made me giggle with glee. Tahlulah Bell Suggs is truly a beautiful woman inside and out. It's easy to see why the menfolk of town don't put up arguments when asked to make a trip to the general store. Daddy destroyed Mama's trust in men, especially when it came to ever wanting one beside in her bed. She still flirts, tossing handsome men her best come-hither looks. I've never known if flirting is for business reasons or natural instinct. When Mama took over the general store, it was in pretty bad shape—a shambles really. She didn't have a nickel to spare. We've managed over the years without putting much into it besides elbow grease, a lot of sweat, and the help of our good friends. It's nestled on a hill amid tall pines. The dark brown exterior, forest green tin roof, and cobblestone foundation speak to an era of yesteryear. The wooden screen door always squeaks, bounces twice, and doesn't quite shut when someone enters. Inside, you can see Mama's touch everywhere—polished wide plank oak floors and rows of various everyday goods, groceries, local creative wear, and objects of art all where they should be. In one corner stands an upright bass next to a piano, a fiddle, a guitar, and a tired old banjo—all ready to be strummed, picked, bowed, or played. They are quite frequently by the locals, who once upon a time had ambitions of grandeur to perform on stage. Across the street is a flat grassy spot in an otherwise very hilly area. We have a dock there with a magnificent view of the hills surrounding the lake. It truly looks as though God etched out the lake with his finger and anointed it with vast blessings.

"There's an old car at the pumps and a guy wearing a suit. You reckon he's a lawyer or something?"

"You know what happens to curious cats."

"Just remember who has the binoculars at the ready when you say stuff like that!"

Mama smiles as she reaches to take payment from the stranger pumping gas. I hear her talking: "You stayin' near or headed far?"

The man doesn't respond despite Mama's best efforts to have a polite conversation. He is ruggedly handsome and wearing a tailored suit. A bit refined for these parts, I think. He tips his head in a quaint gesture while uttering a thank-you. A gleam in his eye twinkles as he notices Mama's form. He lingers for a moment, and his head tilts slightly to the left, as if he wants to say something; instead, he smiles. Glancing upward, he spots me standing behind the screen door and pauses as a questioning look overtakes his handsome face. My pulse begins to race. The mere glimpse from a man has never affected me before, but his stare is intriguing and intense. He heads south in a vintage pea-green Land Rover. As he pulls away, I find myself hoping he'll stop another day.

My mind is set on a long, cool shower, as this is an exceptionally steamy summer day. A sprinkle of baby powder afterward may help keep me fresh. I find a bottle of powder that had previously been opened by a customer. I'm unable to call Mama; the words are stuck somewhere between my head and tongue. Pushing through the odd feeling, I reach for the baby powder. Suddenly, my legs begin to wobble. Sprawling on the wide planks of the remedy aisle, I look as though I'm in some strange, contorted yoga position. Downward dog isn't supposed to feel like this. Hearing me tumble to the floor, Mama quickly comes from behind the counter. Placing her long, elegant arms around me, her head resting ever so lightly on my back, she says, "Baby girl, don't go there again." Her soothing, melancholy voice is relaxing. Cradling me in her arms, she begins to hum the familiar sounds of comfort and peace. Able to push off the floor and sit up, I see Mama's eyes full of compassion. Her inward light leaps forth, calming the torment within my heart. "Hush, little girl, don't you cry, for God's got love in an endless supply. Yesterday's pain has gone by and by, bringing you closer to joy in your life. Don't let the devil dance on your soul. Pick up your spirit. Know you are loved. You never walk alone, for your path is from above."

It's as if she channels the Holy Spirit, passing on blessed assurance in times of despair. She guides me back from wherever I'd been. It's a journey I'd rather not take again, but I have found myself dealing with more frequently. She shepherds my quivering limbs over to a chair by the counter and pours a cool glass of iced tea. One thing I love about Mama is her uncanny way of knowing when and when not to change the subject. I guess seeing the one and only product of your womb crumple to the floor is enough of a clue. The subject won't be swept under the rug but dragged out into the light of day and examined fully. I hope it will be after my head clears and not before. Grief strikes at the strangest times and in the most unlikely of places. On a hot sunny day in the midst of the remedy aisle, the old familiar storm within strikes me like a hammer hitting a nail, pounding it into my heart. I hope grief is found to be the underlying cause of the condition.

Handing baby powder to Mama with a sly grin, I say, "Maybe if I use something more age appropriate these spells will go away."

Lighting up with laughter, she exchanges the glass of iced tea for a large glass of pinot grigio over ice. "Come with me." Mama hangs the "Gone to the Lake" sign on the handle of the screen door. "Let's sit on the dock and dangle our feet in the cool water. This old bottle of wine needs to be finished."

"Old bottle, my foot, Mama. You just opened it."

"Yes, sugar, it's always music to the ears when a pesky cork gives up its hold and pops out. Such a delightful sound, ain't it?" Her eyes beam as she delicately fills our wineglasses. Relief pours over her as she watches my countenance return to normal. "I think we need to gaze upon the water and dream."

"Oh, Mama, dreams used to be so easy. When Josh died, so did all of our dreams."

"You need to begin having your own dreams." She holds my cheek tenderly. "If you let others help you release some pain, we can make room for new dreams. We both need dreams. When the stars come out tonight, I'll say a prayer to each bright star twinkling in the heavens above to lift our spirits and allow us to build new dreams."

The night sky takes over, casting purple hues across the rolling hills. Melodies from the store begin to carry down on heavy, humid air to the lakeshore. Those good ole boys, the Ramblers, are at it again, welcoming the cool night air with songs of yesterday. Their harmony of instrument and voice ushers stars to pop out of nowhere, creating the perfect venue for Mama's promise come true. We learn at an early age to wish upon a star. Those early lessons are cherished as we grow older. The simplicity of youth is what I long for in life. After all life's experiences, education, trials, triumphs, joy, and grief, I still find my heart happiest when I'm sitting with a cool drink in my hand and a friend at my side wishing upon the stars. Speaking of friends, Mama shoots up from her spot on the dock. The regular crowd has arrived: the Suggettes, a self-given name to the ladies who surround Tahlulah Suggs. As loud as they are, Mama and I instantly know dinner has long been forgotten. Luckily, no one has to drive; everyone lives within a stone's throw. Summer is a time of long, lingering evenings filled with wine and laughter. Scientifically, it has been proven beyond a shadow of a doubt if you ever find yourself in medical peril, a girlfriend holding your hand is a bona fide healing touch eliciting a faster, deeper, and healthier response than either a husband's or sibling's grasp. Don't ask me how they know this, or who they are, but it's the truth according to the local women. If a friend has healing power in times of peril, just imagine her power in life without a trauma at large.

Mama is known as Tah to her friends. She has been through everything imaginable with her closest friends, yet Tah remains the only one unmarried. She is without anyone 'cept the likes of me for family support. I assure you, I'm a piece of work in progress and question vehemently my ability to support her, although Mama will argue till she's blue in the face with a contrary opinion.

chapter 2

Three of Mama's friends are known as the Suggettes, a friendly group of ladies who can gook down yesterday's vintage with the best of them. My name
is a blend of each of theirs: Emileigh Louise. Because Mama is somewhat of
a legend around these parts, the land and buildings we own are referred to
as Tahlulahville.

Emily Cantour Dupree runs the local swap shop called "From Swags to
Witches." She isn't tall but gives the illusion by touting long, willowy limbs
attached to a slim, fit body. Her hair is silk spun of a translucent blond,
which neither reflects light nor absorbs it. Her aura is a bright blue hue.
Emily's skin has never seen a blemish nor held a tan. Her eyes are light gray,
and with her alabaster skin and light, flowing blond hair, she looks colorless,
almost like a haint. She reminds me of a figurehead who guides tall ships
safely into harbor placed just above the waterline, facing what is coming
with a sense of adventure and strength. Emily is married to a contractor who
thinks it his job to single-handedly keep women of all ages, shapes, and sizes
feeling as though they are the most beautiful of God's creatures. In plain
words, Grayson believes he's a gift to women. Emily is quick to let him know
otherwise. About a year ago, there was some scuttlebutt about him lovin' and
leavin' a trollop who lives up the road a piece. Emily commenced to question
her, and the tart confessed she'd heard rumors about Grayson and thought
it would be funny to see him squirm on Facebook. Emily let the social networking young bitch know in no uncertain terms it's a wife's privilege to see
her husband squirm. Furthermore, she let her know Grayson is a flirt and no
more. After the escapade, Grayson was seen around women less and circling

the golf course more often. Grayson and Emily Dupree have a rather testy and tumultuous relationship. Moments of extreme passion are matched by lowly times of disdain.

Leigh Riley writes a special column for the town paper. She's a tall, sturdy, attractive woman of few words in person, but she has uncanny insight and is long-winded in her opinions in the written word. She anoints herself with humility, having a strong, healthy contempt for any injustice she observes. God pity the fool who crosses Leigh. When Grayson was wrongfully accused and only after Emily had her peace, Leigh wrote a diatribe about Facebook and its evils. Local folk thought it deserved a Pulitzer Prize, but what do we know about social networking? A cork heard being popped, and we come running clutching our plastic wineglasses. Sunday morning finds most of us sitting in a pew giving thanks, grateful to be. Electronic social networking should be left to those who think they know better; we do our networking the old-fashioned way, in person or in prayer. Leigh's husband, Steve, is as manly a man as they come. Long golden locks frame his weather-worn face. He has a soft, deep voice that makes us lean in to catch his words. The two of them are an odd pair. Their love is apparent and their adoration for one another a delight to behold. Both are fiercely independent, yet seemingly of one mind. Physically, they appear incompatible, but their happiness abounds. Steve has always been Mama's right arm. She may not trust a man in bed, but she trusts Steve with any confidence, need, or woe.

Louise Tromble is Mama's friend who dances closest to the edge of sanity. She is actually perfectly sane but does keep us wondering. She sees things from a deeply spiritual and spirit-filled perspective. Louise knows things. She keeps them to herself mostly, but on the odd occasion or with enough coaxing, the doors to other realms are slightly cracked open for us to hear about and look into if we open our minds enough. None of us to date has dared look into Louise's other world, but she is hopeful one day we shall. Until that day, we are all content to hear about it and have a healthy respect for her containing what she sees in this world separate from what she sees around us. It's a precarious balancing act Louise must carry out each day and night. I'm amazed at her ability to juggle all she sees. Because of Louise, we are aware we are never alone. She has a wonderful sense of humor and knows she must laugh at herself; it does help keep her grounded. I've a firm notion she laughs at us as well, wondering why we can't visualize or hear what she does. If Louise is around, the day always holds promise of entertainment. Tall, attractive, candid, and gentle, Louise is full of life. Cook is her husband. It isn't just an odd name; it's his life's passion. If Louise were the entrée, Cook would most assuredly be the dessert. If I were to undress any man who lives nearby, it would be Cook. He is definitely eye candy for any woman to fantasize about. More than his overpowering good looks, the way Cook treats his admittedly eccentric wife inspires me to dream. The mere placement of his large hand spread out on the small of Louise's back, his gleaming green eyes guiding her to his side, gives you the impression they are caught up in a romantic tango. One can only imagine the passion they have in private. Louise and Cook are most generally together except when she ventures down to Tahlulahville. Cook will meander down making certain "his girls" have something good to eat before heading home.

Being Emileigh Louise Suggs, I'm an honorary Suggette, having the privilege of always being welcomed among them. The Suggettes' undying spirit is contagious. The hope within them is omnipresent, and when they're together, their undying faith is able to move mountains. Louise is quick to point out to those willing to listen that all of us have the opportunity to have a spirit dwell within us, simply by asking. She follows with "And I've seen it."

Louise strolls my way and refills my glass of wine. She sits down on the dock next to me. She strikes a match and lights two candles. The glowing candles, placed in front of my crossed legs, light up my face as the flames flicker spastically in the gentle summer breeze. Lapping water against the side of the dock has a hypnotic effect. Twinkling above is a bright canopy of stars. As she sits down, Louise caresses my bare arm with her tender touch. "Tah said it happened again today."

Huge tears fill my eyes and begin to spill onto my cheek. Nodding once in acknowledgement, I try ever so hard not to make a scene in front of Louise. Emily and Leigh appear out of nowhere and sit next to us. After finding her way amongst the Suggettes, Mama puts her arms around me. Not another word is spoken; there is no need. Mama begins to hum "Twinkle, Twinkle, Little Star." Singing the words louder and louder, we are like a coven of witches poised over a cauldron stirring a potion and chanting. Unceremoniously, we cast our clothes off revealing not nakedness but bathing suits; the Suggettes are many things, one of which is always prepared. We hold hands and jump into the cleansing, cool water below. A husky male voice with an odd accent yells, "Aren't women wonderful?" We laugh singing and splashing.

Agreeing wholeheartedly with the passerby, we respond, "These women most especially are wonderful; we are the wild, wacky women of Tahlulahville."

From down the road, there is only one word in response, "Aye." An engine sputters to life; as it pulls away from the edge of the lake, each of us looks at the others with a ruminative expression.

"Girls, girls, girls, time to come ashore and get dried off! Your men are here to cook for you." Grayson announces as he, along with Cook, and Steve arrive with food, drinks, plates, and a grill. They are a welcome sight. It's late, but none of us care. The guys must have found themselves alone and hungry. We're in the mood for some fun and still have our investigation to begin.

Emily hears the call of the men and lets out a sigh of relief. "Guys, your timing is impeccable. My stomach is beginning to rub blisters on my backbone. I can only imagine how y'all feel."

Cook chimes in, "Tah Bell, we were listening to the Ramblers drudge on about love and such when I saw a bounty of good-lookin' food just begging to be devoured. I hope you don't mind Steve and Grayson helped me gather all the food to bring down and prepare for our lovely ladies."

Mama tries real hard not to snicker; thinking back, it did kinda look like a setup with food displayed to prepare and make into a delectable presentation for dinner. She tells Cook very casually, "Darlin', if you're so inclined to cook those vittles for the likes of us, please feel free anytime, but most especially now. I don't know how it got to be so late. We haven't had a late-night picnic in a long spell. We'd best put off our investigation till tomorrow night. Any of you boys been keepin' an eye on the till at the store?"

Steve replies sarcastically, "Yes, Tah, we've done our best to clean you out, no worries."

Giggling, she proclaims, "I really should get a lock on the door, but who needs high tech at this stage of the game."

Steve tells Tah once they finish collecting everything for dinner they'll ask the Ramblers to pack up so they can cut out the lights for the night. None of us feels inclined to lend the guys a hand. Tah looks content knowing her friends have taken charge, giving her the night off to enjoy spending with the girls. The guys are wonderful men; they know how to please without being near, and that's a special gift. The Suggettes treasure them all, even Grayson and his sometimes roving eye.

chapter 3

IT'S THE WEEK of July Fourth; lots of vacationers are in town as well as the usual weekend crowd. Mama and I have our hands full but find the magnitude of people stimulating and the constant rush to the register a bit head spinning, albeit profitable. Church has let out, and that only means one thing besides more business to us. Reserves of patience will be tested, for Beulah Bell will likely make her weekly appearance, gracing her daughter's store. Grandmama is the epitome of a Southern belle mixed with a bit of old time Appalachia. She was raised not far from the foothills of Moravian Falls, between Boone and the Tennessee border—far enough away to miss the open heaven influence the rest of us have supposedly been blessed under. She's tough as nails and finds praise overrated. Here she comes barreling down the road. Her Mini Cooper screeches to a halt, creating a plume of dust that covers the folks wearing their Sunday best. Boy howdy, she's in a mood this week. The preacher must have been goin' on about "love thy neighbor" or some such ridiculous concept according to Grandmama. She bounds up the four steps into the general store with the energy and fortitude of someone a third her eighty-three years. Taking off her white Sunday gloves adorned with pearl accents, she greets us in a huff, "Afternoon, Daughter, and to you, Em."

"Grandmama, how are you doing this beautiful summer's day?"

"No need to sugarcoat your words, dear. It's hot as Hades with too many damned folks milling around these parts. That so-called preacher who televised how we have, what is it he said, an open window or door to heaven with sinner and saint alike seeing angels floatin' about all while they are gettin' visions or some such nonsense—that son of a bitch should be shot. No offense to the Moravian faith, they're good Christian people who're payin' a price with this news. Open whatever! Should be open season on those money-grubbing TV evangelists. They ain't got a clue about the history of these parts. They've ruined our area, all these sinners coming here to see something so they can believe. Well, I never! If they gotta see a miracle to get faith, I have a hard time believing God would want 'em."

"Oh, Mama, hush! Didn't you just come from church? I'm full of thanks. The store has never done better; most local folk need the influx of tourist money to make ends meet. Sinner or saint, both are welcome. Please, Mama, lower your voice."

"Well, it still ain't right; I pay taxes. Peace and quiet ought to be enforced. These here city folk come in and take over like we ain't anything but yesterday's news." Without missing a beat, Grandmama, spouting the same vehement attitude, turns to me and quizzes with no emotion, concern, or empathy in her voice or demeanor, "Em, how old would that child o' yours be now?"

Every year between the first of July and the fifteenth, Grandmama storms into the store repeating the same inquiring sentence without any thought of consequence. Each year, it pierces my heart. I suppose she thinks it's her way of recognizing her great granddaughter. Who knows? Maybe it's painful for her too. I've never spoken about my feelings, but perhaps the heat of day or the harshness of her tone sets me a blaze. "Grandmama, she would have been eighteen this year, starting college in the fall, ready to begin a wonderful new journey in life." I can feel my cheeks heating up, turning bright shades of red, and sweat beading on my upper lip. Personal embarrassment aside, my tongue unleashes, spouting words locked away for years; it feels good, really good. Still it's my Grandmama. I've always made every effort to be civil and respectful, even though she hasn't been known to do likewise. In a lowered voice, attempting to have a tiny bit of decorum, I skillfully choose my words as best I can, all while smiling courteously so other folks know things are fine and they can resume their shopping. Looking Grandmama straight in the eye, it's difficult, but I manage, feeling a deep confidence swell from within. "I will thank you never to bring my sweet baby up again, unless I do first. My loss to this day is very painful and traumatic. It isn't that I don't think of her; I do every day and wonder 'what if.' You come storming in here complaining about everything under the sun including the sun and the heat, making folks who are here to spend their hard-earned money think twice about taking their wallets out, and you turn and without missing a beat bring up something so painful for me to hear from eighteen years ago using a tone like it doesn't matter. It matters; it shall always matter, and I will forever love that little one with all my heart, just like her daddy, whom you despised and made no secret about it. They're both gone from not only my life, but Mama's, yours, everyone's. You'll never have a chance in this life to make peace with my husband, so I suggest you do so with yourself and the Lord before it's too late."

Mama quickly comes between us to intervene; she acts all a dither, talking about customers who need to be helped and reiterating our private lives should be kept private. Grandmama whirls around. Her dainty purse strikes the black-eyed peas, and cans hit the floor and go spinning and rolling down the aisle. Grandmama is both shocked and insulted by my unlikely response. True to form, she storms out of the store, her dignified appearance a bit off kilter. She has yet to utter a response; normally, it would be a most welcome silence, but to Mama and me, it just means a storm is brewing.

"Baby girl, you just trounced on a hornets' nest, but I'm proud of you. You've got gumption."

"Those hornets will swarm and sting, but eventually return to the nest. I wonder what will happen next." "You spoke your peace; now let it pass. Just look at all these wonderful customers beggin' us to take their money! Besides, something tells me we'll find out very soon how it made Mama feel. She doesn't contain feelings very well."

All sorts of folks are pickin' and grabbin' goods off the shelves. The colorful locals got an earful to share around our picayune little town; that's for sure. Grandmama slams her car door, shooting a dismissive, electrically charged grimace in my direction. Disarmed by her departure, I notice the green Land Rover I had hoped to see return is parked near the street directly in front of the store. Someone with a deep, masculine voice clears his throat over in the wine and beer aisle. I feel drawn, almost summoned. Trying to act disinterested, I meander over, helping direct folks to what they need along the few steps it takes to reach the spirit aisle. Each step takes me closer to the gent, who clears his throat once more. Lord, have mercy! It's all I can do to contain my laughter; it's like trying to keep lava from spewing out of a volcano. I have never! Where is Mama? She has got to see this! It's a gift of sweet charity, especially after confronting Grandmama. The guy who wore the suit the other day pumping gas certainly isn't suited today, on Sunday of all days. Instead, he dons a tartan kilt with all the Scottish regalia this girl from Western North Carolina has ever seen. What a sight to behold in the middle of Suggs General Store! An absolutely gorgeous hunk of a man squatting down, looking at the meager wine selection with a bewildered expression. I've always fantasized about what swishes around under those kilts. Perhaps today I'll find out. As if by magic, the kilt slides up his thigh revealing tight, taut muscles, but nothing more. Focusing on one sensitive portion of his kilt, I try to raise it a few more inches telepathically. It took ego to walk in here dressed like a Highlander—or at the very least balls. He isn't going to walk down the spirit aisle without me finding out more, no, sir, not today. He sees me staring, fixated on his kilt. I pray the smirk I am so desperately trying to suppress isn't noticed. He rises and keeps rising; he's a mite taller than I reckoned.

"Aye, lass, could you please give me a bit of help? I seem to be at a wee loss as to what to take to a pig-pickin' for drink. I haven't ever been to a pig-pickin'."

Oh my goodness, a thick, luscious Scottish accent. Who wouldn't help? Yes, he seems at a loss as to what to wear as well. I draw closer smelling a delightful, subtle blend of light musk and cherry pipe tobacco. His eyes are begging me to come near and administer assistance. As I do, his strikingly good looks send me awash. Testosterone is practically dripping on the floor, turning my legs into spaghetti.

Words fumble out while I unsuccessfully try to remain aloof. "Hi, um, I'm Emileigh. My mother owns the store. You say you're going to a pig-pickin'? Whereabouts?"

"Oh, on the other side of the lake. I'm renting a house there. Some local folks I've started to do business with are cooking; they've suggested I should be in charge of drinks. Obviously, I haven't a clue. If I were home, I would, but things here are so different—nice, don't get me wrong—just different."

Doing my best to conceal the sudden moistness beading above my lip and elsewhere, my concentration drifts. Struggling to reply winsomely, I say, "We get that a lot from folks, but, um, you don't look as if you are trying to fit in. I mean, well, your outfit is…" My voice trails off, and I am grateful he interrupts me before I have to find words that aren't so audacious.

"Yes, it is. Some lads and I are playin' the pipes later. Everyone thinks we should look the part, but, miss, the heat and this wool don't agree. After you help me with drink, will ya please show me if you have some powder; even baby powder would help."

Baby powder, if he only knew—maybe he does. Maybe he can smell a bit on me. But he has other ideas of where to dab it. His words send my mind reeling, conjuring up all sorts of less-than-Sunday-appropriate thoughts and desires. "I'd be happy to help you in any way I can, Mister…What did you say your name is?"

"Well, I beg your pardon, Miss. It's Ian Duncan MacDougal. Ian, if ya please."

Good grief, did I just say I'd help in any way? Ian is the perfect name for him. "Why, it's ever so nice to make your acquaintance, Ian." The words harmoniously slip out with a mighty polished Southern inflection, reminiscent of the Old South. I look smack dab into his big, sparkling puppy-dog brown eyes, which consume my every thought. Deep-set crow's feet show he smiles often. Long, full lashes surround his brown eyes, which are sprinkled with gold flecks, beckoning me to delve deeper, pulling me as if by a spell closer to his chiseled face. He chuckles a bit at my reply. "Aye, and it is doubly my pleasure to make your acquaintance. I couldn't help overhear your conversation with your grandmother. Sorry to eavesdrop. Sorry more for your losses."

"Oh, I'm the one who is sorry. We shouldn't have aired our dirty laundry for the whole store to hear."

"Life takes roads we least expect. You are young. The journey certainly isn't over. So those drinks, lassie, where should we start for thirty-plus folks of various ages?"

"Follow me, Ian, and we'll get you all set up like the locals do it. Yes, sir, I'll take good care of you."

Fate would have it that just as those words come out of my mouth, the Suggettes, in all their glory, come streaming into the store, mouths agape as they spot me with Mr. Ian MacDougal in his kilt. I find it impossible to stop smiling. Their staring drills holes into both of us. I need Mama to intervene again but doubt she can hold it together any better than Leigh, Emily, or Louise are able to do. Oh, it must be Sunday, 'cuz here's the cherry on top!

Grayson, Steve, and Cook walk over to their wives, unable to take their eyes off Ian's kilt. Looking up at the ceiling as if expecting God to be hovering there laughing, I pray, *Please, God, don't let me say anything foolish, nor them.* I know that happens to be asking a lot of the almighty. My heart is pumping fast, skipping beats, and my hands are shaking like a schoolgirl's on her first date. To my astonishment and in all probability more to theirs, the Suggettes and their men keep their tongues at bay; however, all eyes are locked toward our direction.

Ian is open to buying whatever and however much I suggest of it, which tells me two things. One, he is alone in whatever adventure brings him and completely lost as to how to entertain, particularly in Moravian Falls, and two, he has some money to make certain his guests are well hydrated. White wine in copious amounts for the girls, beer for the men, sweet tea, lemonade, and soft drinks for children, and water for all—yep, that's what he needs. Ian seems pleased to get help. As he loads the car, he grabs a water bottle for himself. "Emileigh, thanks so much for your help. You've been great!"

I find it hard to stop looking at him. He is the most gorgeous man I remember ever seeing.

"I should get some ice as well, to be certain there is enough to last the evening."

"Absolutely, we are running low, but expecting a truck with more at any moment. Can you wait?" I ask, hoping against hope he says yes, so I can rest my eyes on this Scottish rogue awhile longer.

"No, I'd best be getting back. Guests are due to begin arriving. It would be less than welcoming if I'm not there to say hello."

"No one else can greet them?" It's a difficult question for me to ask him, but I just want to know if he's here alone. I also know it doesn't mean there is no one at home. After all, Ian is quite a catch, from what my eyes can derive.

"No, lass, I'm alone, but I tell you what, if you're able, will you come over later when things calm down? If the ice shows up, bring it along. I mean, I'd rather see you. We can deal with the ice situation."

"The store is open till five on Sunday. Given how busy we are, I should stay until then. Mama is alone. It wouldn't be right to leave. Where are you renting?"

"Do you know the Sutherlands' place—almost exactly across the lake from here?"

"I do indeed. It's a gorgeous spot and home. How about I head there around five thirty and drop off the ice. Call if you find you need something else in the meantime."

"You'll stay awhile, won't you?"

"I can stay for a bit, but I do have plans back here tonight. Kind of a tradition, you know."

"I see. Any time you can spare will be a delight, and I'll make certain you get home, no worries."

Ian opens the door to his Land Rover, takes a long sip of water, and winks in my direction. Any time I can spare will be a delight! Who has ever said anything like that to me? It's 1:30, and the store is still packed. I'm not sure my feet are even touching the ground. As I come bouncing up the steps into the store, Emily, Louise, and Leigh are ogling me. Louise, as only Louise can, is the first to set aim on interrogation. "So, who is the guy in the skirt?" She blurts it loud enough anyone who has seen Ian and been in the store a while bursts out in a fit of laughter.

I try to be coy, but I don't pull coy off well; it's more Mama's forte. "Why, whatever do you mean, Louise? 'Skirt'? I did have some dealings with Ian, but he was wearing a kilt."

Leigh has been silent; she hasn't said squat up to this point, but when Leigh opens her mouth, especially in a crowded situation, we all know to listen with an attentive ear. "Emileigh Louise." Chills begin to go down my spine—my first and middle names are being used by Leigh!

"Yes, Leigh, I'm all ears."

"Good. Then out with it. I'm a reporter. I want to know who, what, where, when—the why I get. Just look at him. Ian, you said, right?"

"Leigh, the store has ears too. Can we do this later? Besides, I don't know enough right now to give an in-depth interview with the likes of you."

I figure the reply is enough to satisfy Leigh; she'd give me the benefit of the doubt and settle into the summation. There isn't much information to jot down in her vast memory banks at this time anyhow. It might be enough to quell Leigh's curiosity, but Louise and Emily look like two cats perched above prey, ready to pounce. Emily peers in my direction. Luckily for me, someone needs to find a paper towel and lickety-split, as her toddler has just spilled juice all over the inside of her SUV. The moment I return, Mama has obviously said a word and shooed the Suggettes off for a moment or two. Cook grabs the phone to lend a hand.

"Suggs General Store, how can we help you? No, she can't right now. Can I take a message?...Uh-huh...Okay, I'll tell her. Ian, right?...Yup, five thirty at the dock. Anything else you need?...Emileigh, ice, and baby powder...I see, I'll give her the message. Good day, Ian." Cook normally has a soft voice, but now it seems to be a decibel or two above his normal speaking range. His jovial face is full of mischief; there is a hint of a smile to his words as well. "It was for you, Emileigh. A guy named Ian. Said he'd pick you up at the dock at five thirty. If you happen to have a couple of bags of ice, that would be great. Oh, and baby powder too." A pin could have been heard hitting the wide plank floor and bouncing to rest. A collective gasp, audible to every ear, releases as an adolescent, "Ouuuuhhoooo!" sweeps the store from aisle to aisle.

Oh, Ian Duncan MacDougal, what have you done? You can't put the cat back into the bag, can you? You certainly cannot put the Suggettes off now. They swim as one, in long, fluid movements toward me like piranha circling raw meat. Louise is always the first to sidle up and test her observational skills with short quips.

"Pick you up, eh? This is skirt boy talking, right? You sure he is okay to go off with? Where is he taking you, little Miss 'Oh-I-helped-a-guy-named-Ian-wearing-a-kilt'?"

"Well, if you must know, I said I'd drop off ice for him since we're out and he asked me to stay for a little while at the party he is giving at the Sutherlands' house. He is renting it. That's all I know, so y'all are just gonna have to find some other widow to harass, at least until I do know more."

Mama gets the drift of what is happening; she is pleased by my actions and shoots a quick glance at the clock. "Sugar, if you want, I can handle the customers. Sounds like you've made plans."

"Oh, Mama, get a grip. Delivering ice is hardly plans. I'll stay, have a drink, and see who is gathered, and then come back for dinner with my favorite people. Ian already knows I want to be here tonight."

"He does, does he? And he is okay with that? I like him already, baby girl."

chapter 4

THE ICE FINALLY gets to the general store at three. The afternoon is quickly going by, and I'm getting the nervous Nelly jitters. I haven't been out with a man in a very long time. I've never been fond of those early days of getting acquainted. Ian does make it a bit easier than other men I've known. He puts himself out there and seems to be kind, generous, confident, and thoughtful. I keep reminding myself it's only a drink, and he may be married and is just being kind. Even if he isn't married, it doesn't mean he is anything but kind. Oh the mind can be a cesspool of illusion and brimming with hope at the same time. The deluge of customers dwindles as the clock ticks closer to five. I'm kicking myself for agreeing to go over to the Sutherlands' place, but here I sit waiting for the clock to strike five, wanting to put the closed sign in the window. Finally, it happens. I dash into the apartment to freshen up and gain a minuscule iota of composure. Fear, trepidation, and disillusion I think must certainly be stamped in dark ink across my forehead. The reflection in the mirror says quite the opposite. Thoughts of Ian pop into my head and remarkably have a calming effect. I'm excited to see him again. I suppose the fact Mama's friends were jesting about him means they were giving their thumbs-up of approval. I could tell Cook was a little relieved to know where I'd be. He is the rescuer of the group. Looking tired and drawn, Mama comes into the apartment. It has been a busy day for all of us, but most especially for her. Putting her legs up on the foot stool, she leans back in her favorite rocker and lets out a sigh.

"So, Em, how did we do today? You getting ready to go across the lake with that fellow?"

"We did really well today, Mama. More business than Wal-Mart, if you ask me. I'll be gone for an hour or so. It'll give you some time to rest and get ready for dinner."

"I hate to even bring this up, but we'll need to restock before opening tomorrow. Think we can do it early in the morning?"

"Sure, we need time to enjoy ourselves too, Mama. Let's put up the sign tonight for a 10:00 a.m. opening."

"Good idea, baby girl. Will you put it up?"

"Sure. You okay, Mama?"

"Just bones wore out. I didn't eat a thing all day, and Cook said we aren't to lift a finger tonight. Don't think I could if I had to."

"Good to have caring friends, Mama. You stay put, and I'll get you a cool drink. You sure you're all right?"

"Course, girl. Get going. You don't want what's his name to wait."

"Don't have to tell me twice. I'll just grab the bags of ice and leave."

"Emileigh, enjoy yourself. Please, girl, have some fun."

"Okay, Mama, I'll tell you all about Ian's party when I get back. Love you!"

"Back at you, sugar, and don't forget Ian's baby powder."

I heard the smirk in her voice. It carries me with a happy heart across the street where I see a boat heading straight across the lake. An old woody sprays water with a deep growling engine steadily churning its way toward the dock. Blowing in the breeze at the back of the boat fly two flags: a proud American flag on one side and the flag of bonnie old Scotland on the other. There he is—Ian—an Old-World charmer at the helm of a classic beauty donning a wide, bright smile. I have to pinch myself. No, it isn't a dream. Somehow, reality is even better than any dream I could have come up with, so far. For the moment, this magnificent view I have before my very eyes finds me suddenly and unexpectedly enjoying today in ways I never would have thought possible just a few short hours ago.

Ian docks the boat with ease. He leaves the wheel, drops the bumpers over the side, and casts a line to me. Then he grasps the wheel, brings her in, and turns the powerful engine off. He's taken his kilt off. He now sports a bathing suit with a polo shirt and deck shoes.

"Hi, Ian. Where's the kilt?"

"Too hot. I'm not one for changing clothes much during the day, but I had to relent today. Besides, my guests were giving me a hard time." Ian turns from me to appreciate the lake view. He raises his arms to the heavens as he takes in its splendor. Overhead, puffs of white and light-gray clouds pepper the sky, assuring hues of gold, red, and lavender are to follow. The humidity of the day, with its weighty air, has settled into the hills, sinking among the pines like heavy fog. Birds are soaring, dancing in flight on the light winds aloft. There is both sadness and an inviting call to the evening. Another day is drawing to a close, using the sky as its palette to bid farewell. Ian spins around and looks thoughtfully into my eyes. "The view is breathtaking, something I want to carry with me the rest of my life." Swept away by his words, I'm unsure if he is referring to the lake view or me. After hopping onto the dock, Ian picks up the bags of ice and tosses them into an ice chest at the back of the boat.

"Are ya ready, lass, to cross to the other side?"

His question sounds like something Louise might say. "I'm anxious to see the house you're renting and meet your guests."

"Aye, let's be off. Let me give a hand to you, and, lassie, I'm happy you want to join us this evening. Whenever you want or feel you need to come home, just whistle, and we'll fire up old Bessie."

He offers his hand to help me down into the rocking boat. My hand slips into his with ease. He has a firm but gentle grasp; his skin is soft against mine. My hand feels small in his. Taking the first step down, I slip and find myself falling against his chest. "Oh, Ian, I'm such a klutz. I'm sorry."

"Nothing to be sorry about; the first step is wicked getting into this old tub. I brought you a glass of wine for the ride; it may make you a bit more at ease."

Ian has thought ahead, and of me. I feel special for the first time in a long while, having someone new in my life. I hope he is in my life; he is for the moment anyway. My heart floods with gratitude. The engine comes to life, and we cast off, heading across the lake. He is in no rush and enjoys the short ride. The Sutherland cottage is more of an estate. It's a large post-and-beam home with tennis courts, a pool, a boathouse, and a smaller, separate guest cottage. I've never been inside, but I've seen it many a time from the lake.

"Ian, are you renting the main house or the guest cottage?"

"I'm renting the main house; no one is in the guest cottage while I'm staying here. I've still got almost two months left on the lease. I just got here a couple of weeks ago. Still getting my bearings and figuring out the lay of the land."

"What brings you to our little neck of the woods? Seems a bit off the beaten trail for someone from Scotland to spend a good part of the summer here."

"The more I travel, the more I like to be off the beaten path. After all, I'm just a country boy at heart. Don't care for big cities. The allure which so many crave isn't there for me."

"I'm not very good at geography, but I'll ask where in Scotland are you from?"

"I was born on the Isle of Skye, outside of a wee small village. The family home is on a loch, or lake, much like this. I stayed there until a short time ago and decided to come to the States with a plan to subsidize life back home by earning money in real estate. Mainly in developing land. It's pretty much all I know to do. With the recent downward trend in real estate here, it's the perfect place to put money, a gamble of sorts, especially since I like those, as you say, off-the-beaten-trail areas. Enough of me. What about you?"

"Oh me, well you've pretty much seen my life in action. There isn't much more than meets the eye."

"I like what meets my eye. Is there someone special in your life?"

"Besides Mama and her friends? They're about all I have. If you're referrin' to a man, no, there isn't anyone. I reckon we all know each other too well around here to think of anyone as special. You know, we all have history."

"Since we seem to be revealing our weak subjects, consider mine history. So about my guests, they're all locals. In all probability, you know them better than I do. I've just met them."

"Who are they, Ian? You say you buy land or real estate. Are these folk's owners or realtors?"

"A blend of real estate agents who either have land listings or in some cases folks I'd like to know more about before doing business with. There are also a couple of attorneys, some business owners, developers, contractors, logging specialists, people who can benefit from land sales or development of land. Most of them know each other, so it ought to be interesting to be an observer. I don't do well in crowds; thirty people to me is a lot to deal with. Two others who will be greeting you are my recently adopted sons. I'm sure they will be soaking wet from the lake and eager to meet you. We're here."

The hum of conversation stops as all eyes fetch a long look at the two of us. Ian is right. Most of the guests have familiar faces. I hadn't thought about that when Ian invited me here. For some odd reason, I imagined they'd all be from out of town like he is. One word springs to mind, *awkward*. Ian helps me off the boat and asks someone to grab the ice chest for him. He makes a gesture to me and takes my hand while assisting me to the dock. Still holding my hand, he makes a statement to his guests, but a louder one to me. I like what the unspoken word conveys. Intrigued by the mysterious stranger, I find myself desiring to delve deeper. Two huge and overly exuberant Labradors round the corner of the boathouse and veer straight toward us. They are not disturbed from their course by people leaping to safety, spilling drinks, or dropping plates of appetizers. Guiding me behind him just in time, Ian lets the dogs leap on him, begging for attention.

"Are these your adopted sons?" The moment the words came out of my mouth, I cringe, hoping I haven't insulted him.

"Yup, these buggers are Bear and Moose. Bear is the black one and Moose the chocolate."

"Did you bring them with you or..."

"They kind of appeared about a week ago, and as of yet haven't been claimed, despite my putting word out. They are good guys, but if they are too much, let me know, and I'll put them in a crate."

"No, no, no, you can't crate a lab when a lake is in view. They teach us all how to play, and to put them in a cage is punishment."

"Good, those are my sentiments. I just want you to be comfortable."

Louise's voice is still in my head: "Is he all right for you to be going off with?" My heart says, "Yes"; my head says, "Slow down, silly girl, slow down.

I should have known better. Just think of her, and Louise calls. "Hi, Louise. Y'all gettin' ready for dinner over there? Do you need anything?"

"Em, you okay?"

"Louise, tell Mama I'm fine. Most of the folks here are locals, even the dogs. I'll be back before you can skip a rock six times on the water, ready to eat and give you all the details."

"Is skirt guy still...ummm, you know, skirt guy?"

"Louise, I don't even know what you're asking, but he is wearing a bathing suit now and right next to me. I must go."

"Is it one of those long, mid-thigh suits or a revealing Speedo? I'm betting a Speedo; take a picture with your phone Em, pllleeeeaaase!"

"Bye, Louise!"

It is obviously apparent by Louise's call that I don't have a life. It has morphed into something comfortable and predictable that doesn't live but survives. I guess the same could be said for them. But I do love Louise. She does have a way of making me laugh.

"Lass, everything okay on the western side of the lake?"

"Gads, you know they are checking up on me, Ian? I am ever so embarrassed. Lordy, can you believe them?"

"Oh, Em, lighten up. They care, and I probably looked pretty strange, like a serial killer in a kilt."

"Actually, killer wasn't referenced; Louise was more interested to know if you are wearing a skirt or a Speedo."

Those words create a roar of the most genuine laughter I've heard, putting me instantly at ease. We walk together over to where the guys have been roasting a pig all day. It smells heavenly. Ian has never been to a pig-pickin', so he is going to have his taste buds tickled for certain.

"Ian, how long before y'all eat?"

"Oh, I dunno. Not to worry, lass, I was in charge of drinks, remember? Speaking of which, you are getting low on your wine. Let me refill it for you, and I'll grab a Heineken. Stay for this glass, and then we'll go. Let's mingle, for a half hour or so."

"I may grab one of those coconut-crusted plantain shrimp with fresh basil and mango chutney. Have you ever tried these?"

"Lass, you just spoke Greek to me, but if you say they're good, I'll give one a try."

Grasping the shrimp between two fingers, he lifts it up and peers at it cross-eyed, before placing the tender morsel in his mouth. "What a delicate fusion of marvelous flavors! Can you make this?" As he goes about shoveling more shrimp into his mouth, a pleasant expression of joy overcomes him.

"Yes, I can. You'd be surprised at what I can make."

"Sounds like a challenge to me, but I bet you can't make haggis?"

"No, I don't think anyone should!"

Ian brings his beer to his lips after the same bellowing laugh bursts forth. He is virtually ignoring all his guests and spending each moment alongside me. "I suggest we circulate a bit and take a quick tour of the house." He obliges with ease. Our tour complete, he walks me to the dock and reluctantly helps me into the woody. We had a plan. I don't want to overstay my welcome. I also feel like he needs to return and attend to his guests. It is a business affair after all, and I, well, I am a diversion.

Bessie comes to life, set to blast through the waves and churn up water. The day has been a busy one for boaters; the water shows the effect with high waves and white foam. Ian becomes quiet and distant, maybe lost in thought as we leave the dock. About halfway across the lake, he turns to me. "You mind a bit of a ride, Em?"

"No, don't you have—" Realizing I'd just stepped over my bounds, I retreat. It's still rather early. "They won't even be thinking of eating until half past seven or eight."

"Good. I wish…" Ian's words trail off—a thought better left unspoken or a private wish he kept under his breath.

"Ian, do you want to eat with us. I know you have a full house across the lake, but you're welcome to stay."

"Oh, lass, you're a kind woman, but not tonight. Some other time, perhaps, I'd love to."

"Then, well, you seem distracted. I don't know you very well…Actually, I don't know you at all, but are you okay?"

He responds very slowly. Ian turns the boat toward the dwindling sunlight and with a twist of the key brings the noisy engine to a halt.

"I guess I am a bit melancholy, if men get that way."
"I'm a good listener."
"On the way over to the party, I mentioned I'm not good at history. Well, what I meant was my history, not the kind you learn from a book. Everyone here is cordial, and I suppose since they surmise I'm only here short term, no one inquires about my life."
"I would think everyone would be mesmerized seeing how you are from so far away."
"No, I figure they are acquainted in some manner, and I'm a seasonal resident. I'd like to tell you a bit, if ya don't mind."
"Please do. I'd love to hear whatever you'd like to share."
"My home is on a large estate, as I mentioned, on the Isle of Skye in a small town. Some there call me a laird, an old Gaelic term for lord. It simply means I run the estate, as a MacDougal has for many generations. It's a rite of passage. You certain you don't mind listening to this?"
Sitting in the bright sun watching it play in Ian's hair, I notice there is sadness to his voice.
"Ian, I'd like to hear what you have on your mind."
"My father died in a car accident when I was twenty-two. I was far too young to take over the estate, but being the eldest, it was deemed necessary. Not only does being laird mean I'm in charge of the house, but many farms, businesses, and tenants who dwell on the acreage. The estate has thousands of acres. A vast number of people's welfare fell in my hands and their well-being on my shoulders. After my father died, as most young men do, I didn't doubt my ability to handle the business transactions and maintenance of the estate. Father took such precious care, making it look easy. Parents often don't show the struggle they go through; they want you to live your life and be happy. Young people are always a bit cocky thinking the world will always be at their beck and call. I found the work to be a daunting task, extremely overwhelming. What I didn't expect with a new title was how the opposite sex suddenly found me attractive. Women were doing very strange things to get my attention. One day, I thought I found love. Molly and I married, and soon afterward, she got pregnant. The estate is extremely remote. Medical

care isn't a few minutes up the road. It can take hours, depending on the time of year. Molly's due date was very near. I was out on the estate tending to an erosion problem. Keep in mind, there weren't cell phones at that time. Even now, there isn't reception in many places. Coming home late, I found Molly in bed, suffering greatly. Calls were made by staff for help, but no one came in time and I didn't have a clue how to help other than to make her comfortable. I sent someone after a midwife who lives an hour away. Molly went in and out of consciousness. She began bleeding horribly. With no help around, I found myself having to deliver the baby while watching Molly slip away. She died soon after delivery, so did my son. Both gone. I just stood by unable, unknowing how to help or how to get help there sooner. After the funerals, I fell into the abyss of a deep, dark depression—drinking too much, sheltering myself away from everyone and everything I used to love or care about. Lack of attention quickly drove the estate into ruin; people were suffering because of my failure to run the business. It didn't matter to me; nothing did. I was alone, with my wife's and baby's blood on my hands. Then one day, something happened. I looked out a picture window facing the loch. It's an ever-changing view. On this particular day, the water was golden; the light from the sky piercing through the clouds was very peculiar. Words don't do it justice; it was simply heavenly. My heart melted, literally. It was as if God reached into my chest, took my hardened heart, and healed it by massaging it ever so lovingly. I felt forgiveness toward everyone, but most especially toward myself. Forgiveness is a gift you give yourself. Never did I know that; I'd never felt it. For over twenty-five years, I suffered, mostly because I couldn't forgive myself and get on with life. A quarter of a century, lost. I vowed to make a difference, to help the estate get back on track, especially for all those who dwell there. I promised myself I'd fall in love completely. I loved Molly, truly I did, but I never gave her my whole heart. There is a huge difference, as I am certain you know. The day after I made the vow, I left the estate. I haven't been back. The memories are still painful; I have to know I've made up for all those lost years wasted in that huge house before I return. I'm doing well now with God's grace and help; I've been around the world buying this, selling that. I also made a vow to God if He would have me, I would serve Him, and hopefully, we'd put things right in my life. I know I was bursting with promise and potential as a youth. I used to beat myself up about lost potential, but I have learned a secret. Potential can be rediscovered and retooled to be even better after some life experience; so can love."

Ian's words put me on an emotional roller coaster. I have just met this man, whom no one would ever guess has had such a tragic adult life. I look at his chiseled face—the double, deep-set dimples; cleft chin; full lips; and large, hauntingly loving brown eyes. His skin is tanned and dark; his hair has glistening soft black curls mixing with highlighted silver traces. He speaks so humbly about his life, speckled with hints of shame, now seemingly filled with purpose and promise. I dab a multitude of tears off my cheek, speaking for the first time since hearing his story. The boat drifts ever so close to the western shore. Mama is probably sitting on the dock with her binoculars in hand.

"Ian, I am so very touched you shared your life's story with me. I am also very sorry, for Molly, your baby son, and all the years of torment your soul's journey has taken you through. I don't understand why you felt so compelled to tell me this today of all days, but I don't need to know why. That part of life is yesterday. Memories have their place; it's true. Grief teaches lessons after the initial shock is over. So, Ian, please know, the man before me today in all his glory, be it in Speedo or tartan plaid kilt, is the man I'm glad to know. I am honored to hear a piece of your past, but it's just the cast which has molded you into the man before me today."

I want to kiss him, to make him understand how much I care. I can't bring myself to be vulnerable, yet. I find myself on my feet moving toward him, resting one hand upon his shoulder and the other clenching the chest hair over his heart. He looks up at me and stands up right into a hug; our eyes connect with a long, lingering stare. Ian stares, and breathlessly whispers, "I'd best get you back to Tahlulahville for dinner, and then I have to get back to my guests."

"I guess if you must, Ian."

I feel like I've disappointed him, or it may be sadness for his past. The first pangs of falling in love are beginning to stir. I want to be the one he takes back to his home in Scotland, to make him laugh again on the shore of the loch. I shake off my fantasy while watching Ian confidently maneuver Bessie.

The rest of our short journey is spent in silence. I don't know what Ian is thinking about, but I am at a loss for words. He skillfully brings the boat to the dock where Grayson catches the line from him. The Suggettes, all present, are lounging on lawn chairs wine in hand, full of vim and vigor. Mama sits with a big ole Cheshire grin, hastily kicking the binoculars farther under her chair. Obviously, they've been tossed away quickly in an ill attempt to conceal their whereabouts. Standing on the dock, Ian offers his hand to guide me safely off the boat; weakness takes me by surprise, and I find letting go of his grasp difficult. He goes straight over to Mama and her friends to say hello, giving a cheerful greeting to all.

"Thanks for sharing this lovely lady with me for a little while today." I don't know how he does it, but Ian seems always to have the right words for everyone.

Emily speaks up as she raises her glass in salute. "So, did y'all have a good time? Can you stay, Ian, or must you get back?"

"Oh, I must go back. There's a house full of guests I've totally ignored while Em has been with me. I hope to see all of you very soon."

Ian slips his hand into mine as we retrace our steps back to the boat. Behind us, there is a chorus saying good night. "I appreciate you listening to my story, mostly for just taking it all in without a bunch of questions. Although I feel a bit daft divulging the past."

"Will I see you again?"

"Wild horses couldn't keep me away. I've got business appointments taking up most of the next two days, but how about dinner Wednesday?"

"Wednesday at six thirty here okay? Does everyone still say 'lass' in Scotland as much as you do?"

"Aye, it's a date. And no, they don't. I use it a bit more around you, because it seems to fit. Remember, we're playing the pipes tonight. I hope you hear them. The last song will be 'Ashokan Farewell.' I dearly love the softness of the notes; it's a haunting melody. Tonight, it will be my song to you. Not farewell, just good night."

"Oh, Ian, no one's ever...I'll be listening, I promise."

Both of his warm hands tenderly caress my face. His ring finger slips gently onto my neck, feeling the fast pulse beneath the skin. Ian keeps his hands there a good length of time. Taking one finger, he traces my jawline. I find myself transcending deep into his eyes, wanting more. In a low, soothing, almost hypnotic voice, he says softly, "I'd take you and kiss you right now in front of all your loved ones, but if I were to start, I'd never want to stop. A first kiss shouldn't be rushed or witnessed. Good night, my lassie. I'll call you tomorrow."

Ian's cell phone chimes in, ruining the mood of a romantic good-bye. He peers down to see who is trying to reach him. With one look, he turns it off in a huff and angrily slams it shut. I wonder who was on the other end and what it would take to upset him so much. Bessie rumbles to a start. Ian turns toward me, forcing a smile as he waves.

chapter 5

BESSIE SLIPS SLOWLY from the shoreline, her rumbles of power softened by distance. The ceaseless constant dribble of questions emanating from behind me are growing louder. My senses are in a heightened state, my cheeks flushed as I remember Ian's last words. Oh, how I'd rather face a herd of stampeding horses than turn around and face those questioning eyes. Steve walks up to me and hands me a glass of wine. "Emileigh, come sit with us. It looks as though you've had a good time. We're all very glad to see some happiness find its way to you."

Steve softens the blow of facing everyone. He is a kind and gentle man, who, by all accounts, has had many opportunities to be otherwise. Steve and Leigh have three children, who are all grown and have kids of their own. He's always had money, which he inherited from his parents. He found out quite early that having more than enough money is really a double-edged sword. Steve's had to fend off those who want to use his money for their own desires, taking advantage of his good and kind nature. Yet, he is emotionally near for those he genuinely cares about. He'd give those few the shirt off his back. Over the years, he's had to develop a hard shell to protect his soft heart from being torn apart. To his credit, Leigh is a tower of strength and does not spend their savings foolishly or overtly. She has a knack for making more, finding ways to celebrate with those less fortunate or donate anonymously to causes that touch her heart.

"Hi, Steve, I did have a good time, and I know everyone is full of questions. I'm a little apprehensive about ploppin' down and spillin' my guts. I'd really like to sit and absorb it before getting into it with everyone."

"That's a tall order, but we'll see if Cook can give you a task that needs to be done in preparation for dinner. I'm sure you can slip up to the apartment to freshen up."

"Let me talk to Cook and see if he needs anything from the store. How does Mama seem to you? She was really worn out earlier."

"She's tired, but it was a hell of a day for the store. I got the money out of the register to take to the bank in the morning. Em, I've never seen receipts this size for y'all before. We should think about a couple of days off for her after this week is over. This is your biggest week of the year, isn't it?"

"It's the make-or-break week for us. I'm with you; maybe we should talk to Leigh or one of the others and have them take a minivacation to rejuvenate. I'd like that for Mama regardless. Can you talk to Leigh about it for me?"

"Absolutely, and not for nothing, Ian and you would have more time as well."

Steve shoots me a big grin along with a wink.

Cook is busy chopping, dicing, sipping, and tasting by the grill.

"Hey, Cook, I'm headed to the store. Is there anything you need?"

"Glad you're back. Yeah, can you get me some fresh basil, pine nuts, and garlic...oh, and a lemon?"

"I don't know what you're fixin', but I'm standing next to you when you do. Back in a jiffy. If anyone asks, I'm just freshening up. I probably should grab more wine too. You guys set tonight?"

"Grayson and Steve brought some scotch and cigars for later; in the meantime, we have our usual."

What a relief to sit down in the apartment alone and away from chatter. I've been out of my comfort zone today; being with Ian took a lot out of me. But to come home and face the Suggettes and Mama, yes a break is a great idea before dinner. I wonder what Ian is doing right about now? I'm sure he is busy with his business acquaintances. Lathering up a washcloth,

I peer into the mirror, still not believing what transpired today. Never ever underestimate the magic a day holds, Emileigh. The smiling face reflecting back looks years younger. I'm bolstered and armed to face the interrogation down at the dock and really ready to eat. I'm starving!

"Hey, Cook, I think this is everything you asked me to bring down for dinner, right?"

"Perfect timing, just what I need when I need it."

"That's me! You're constantly full of new ideas. Some of the combinations you put together I would never think of."

"Well, it's a holiday week in the midst of summer. Some people celebrate with baubles and trinkets; I celebrate with food."

"And you always have an anxious, captive crowd awaiting your next array of creative delights."

"You make dinner sound like a commercial for the Food Network."

"With you, who knows?"

Cook flips his grilled vegetables and sprinkles a bit of lemon juice over top. He winks, grinning from ear to ear. "I'm not ready for my first show yet, sweet pea. Practice makes perfect."

"You can practice all you want on us. Your kids arrive tomorrow with grandchildren in tow, right?"

"Yes, indeed. Tonight is the calm before the storm; I think Emily and Grayson's kids come tomorrow as well."

"Good times for all of us. I can't wait to see them. It's been too long."

"Steve said you needed a bit of time to yourself. Well, we obliged. We cain't stand it. Get yourself over here, Emmy!"

"Mama, so how about you first, and then we'll just go around the table."

"No, sugar. Leigh may very well want to hear about Ian first."

"Em, the most important thing is what did you think?"

"Oh, Leigh, Ian is what y'all might refer to as a complicated man. Any one of us with a history could be called complicated. He told me a little about his past. He comes from a large estate on the Isle of Skye, manages it financially by buying and selling real estate here in the States—"

Unable to contain her impatience listening to my dribble, Louise chimes in with her otherworldly encounter. "I'm sorry to interfere, but can't help myself. Y'all know me; I see something, sometimes I just have to blurt it out. This will sound weird, but there is some very sad attachment to Ian from the other side."

Grayson has no patience for Louise and her sensing things. He grabs his beer and heads up to the store, and as usual, the other guys also excuse themselves when Louise's visions commence.

"It feels like female energy. Whoever it is chooses to be earthbound. She must be a depressing drag on him, a constant draining energy. Who knows? Maybe she is alive, but it doesn't feel like that. She has had a dramatic effect on Ian. Too painful and sad, I have to get away from her before I get pulled into an emotional vat." Louise is not always right, but 80 percent of the time, she is close, if not exactly hitting a bull's-eye. Some may say her visions are the devil's magic, but I believe her visions are from God to help us cope.

"Sadly, Louise, you're right. Ian explained briefly about his wife and child. They passed away years ago after she had just given birth. I don't think anyone could ever get completely over seeing such a tragedy happen before their eyes. Do you?"

"I can't imagine! Oh, the poor dear man! Has he remarried?"

"No, he's alone."

Emily begins to squirm a bit in her chair. Something said obviously isn't sitting right with her. I remain as elusive as possible. Talking about Ian when he is just across the water seems a lot like gossip, yet I want to share some things about the extraordinary man who has walked into my life. "Let's all just cut to the chase here, ladies. Yes, he has a past, and don't we all; what I want to know—what we all want to know—is, did he kiss you?"

"Mama, usually it's Louise who makes me blush, not you. In answer to your probing question, no, he did not."

"Okay, he is a gentleman. Did you kiss him?"

"You raised me to be a lady, Mama. No, I did not, but—and this is a huge but for me—I desperately wanted to."

The men spin around from the grill, and the ladies drop their jaws. Yes, this is out of character for me. Pressing my memory banks, trying to recall a time when I have made all of their expressions at once fill with surprise, joy, and wonder, I cannot recall a moment when all of them were at a loss like right now. Grayson appears from the store and is moving rather sheepishly. I'm not sure if he is being nonchalant because he's figuring out if Louise is still gazing into her crystal ball or if he heard the last bits of conversation and is stunned too. Cook sees Grayson and announces that dinner is ready for the brave to try. When he talks like that, he has tried a new recipe and secretly thinks it's fantastic. It's a great segue leading us from the silence of my revelation. If they only knew what I am really thinking, oh their expressions would be much different! Conversation over dinner ebbs and flows, much the same as it would at anyone's dinner table. There are a few smatterings of specific questions regarding Ian, most of which I either choose not to answer or simply don't know the answer to. More laughter and reminiscing occur, which place me in a more comfortable position. Just as we are all finishing our most delicious meal, Emily begins to clear the plates, and when she comes to my end of the table, she drops a bomb. She'd been quite out of character at dinner, quiet and contemplative.

"Em, we don't really know anything about this man. You know what he has told you, but it seems off to me. The enormity of it all—the huge extravagance and the lavish, extroverted persona leaves me wondering."

"Wondering what, Emily? Must you pour cold water on the first day I've had where a dream may be beginning to come true? Some people have big personalities. Isn't it nice to have new blood visit and someone intriguing to get to know? Why must we tear down instead of build up? Jesus, being positive is difficult enough; maybe I should just live in a cardboard box."

"The situation and Ian, they don't seem real. I think you are overreacting and a tad defensive to my voicing concern for your safety."

"Emily, he has half the town's businesspeople over at his house for a party for him to get to know them and them to get to know him. He is here to help the community; no matter what his situation is, he can and wants to help ours. Tomorrow, I'm betting most of the town will know of him."

"Perhaps. We'll see. Or next year at this time, will we be remembering skirt boy and how he took the town for a ride along with our savings?"

All too familiar with her propensity to overanalyze and her speculative nature, Grayson steps in and reassures his wife. He asks her to keep her concerns to herself for the time being. "Emily, unless you have something more substantial to go on—evidence if you will—we owe it to Em to back off and let her enjoy life. She was with Ian for a mere couple of hours, and listen to us, half of us want them to bed down together and some want him rail ridden out of town. Maybe we all fear change a little, but Em is smiling brighter than I've seen in a long time. Let's not be the ones to take that away or diminish her hope—our collective hope."

Mama's eyes fill with tears hearing Grayson respond like his old self to his wife's rant. It's hard for me not to hold a little resentment when spoken to in such a manner. Mama sits with my would-be aunts and uncles; I know that every word spoken is out of love, so forgiveness is easy, but timing is everything. Louise and Cook say they are going back to their cottage to get a really awesome bottle of red wine and the party barge. They want dessert out on the lake. We all agree, it does sound perfect. The sky has turned to coal; stars like diamonds are appearing. This day of days is over, and I am anxious to hear the bagpipes breathe to life on the opposite shore.

"All aboard! Let's get this party started!" Louise makes no bones about enjoying being on the lake instead of beside it. Cook has a couple of bottles of wine and peaches. Looks like dessert is gonna be drunken peaches. We all board the familiar craft, and Louise points her toward the opposite shore. She must be reading my mind, again.

"Ladies, we still have our investigation to do, and now that the lake has calmed down and resembles glass, we can sneak about easily, as long as we don't break out laughing or singing too much. Tah, did you get the binoculars?"

"Of course, I'm not a newbie at this espionage game, Louise."

"I can verify that. Mama should be working for the CIA of Moravian Falls."

"May I have your attention please? I'm your trip coordinator, Cook. Please keep hands and feet inside the boat at all times, unless you want to take a dip. Then inform your trip coordinator, *moi*, and I will get permission after a lot of begging and pleading from the admiral to park the barge for your entertainment pleasure. This is also the correct procedure if you are female and have to pee. Gentlemen, you are on your own. We do have a variety of drinks; I'm sure one of them will be to your liking. Right now, I'd like to draw your attention to the culinary lesson of this passage. We shall all be making our own drunken peaches. If you please, each tenderly, so as not to bruise the little sweet ripe peach, grasp hers or his in one hand. Then with the other hand, take a knife which I have placed by your plastic parfait glass. Carefully, cut the peach into small pieces, keep the fuzz on them, and place the pieces in your glass. Of course you know this, but don't use the pit or cut too close it. Alrighty, looks like you are doing a swell job. Have some of you done this before? Now, I've previously uncorked a wonderful red wine; let me fill your parfait glasses with the wine. I'll sprinkle a little cinnamon and powdered sugar on top, just a tad. If you are crazy and prefer not to have my added delight, simply say no. Enjoy your journey. The admiral will now stop the engines so we can enjoy. Please have a safe and pleasant journey. Cook out." It doesn't take a brainiac to conclude Cook is a nut job, at the very least dramatic, but we love it. Just as Louise cuts off the engine, the boat begins drifting ever so slightly and an odd sound is heard coming across the water.

"Holy crap, Tah, do you hear that? What the hell is it?"

"How can any of us not hear it? Good lord in heaven! Sounds like a trapped animal!"

Steve hears the sound as well and cannot resist saying, "Y'all know, it is summer. Maybe it's an animal in heat."

"Steve, we've lived here all our lives and never heard anything sound in summer or any other time of year remotely similar; it can't be that." Emily is right. We would have heard this bellowing sound before.

Just as we are digging into our mighty fine drunken peaches and getting a handle on where the sounds are emitting from, it dawns on me. "You know, Ian and some of his friends are going to be playing bagpipes tonight; you reckon we are hearing them set up?"

Louise gobbles the last of her peaches and leaps to the helm. "I'm on it, y'all. We have to see skirt boy play the pipes. Let's get close enough to hear, but not so close as to be recognized."

"Yeah right, Louise; that'll work."

The sarcasm spews out of my mouth, but I want to do just as Louise does. How often in our little neck of the woods does this happen? Grabbing the binoculars, Mama is in her element. "There they are! Looks like four of them on the little grassy knoll in front of the dock. Got them kilts on. They're carryin' pipes, so we must be hearing whatever amount of air escapes as they get ready to play. Get ready. They're all set and looks like...yup, here we go. Oh and two labs are there. Wait a second. Now they are skidoodlin'. Guess them pipes are scary." Louise takes us in a bit closer. The sound is eerie and lonesome but beautiful. They play five songs—songs I have never heard before, but now adore.

"Tah, what is happening now?"

"Well, honestly, I don't know. It looks like Ian...Yes, it's him by himself. He is turning around on the knoll, facing...Oh good Lord!"

"Mama, what? Facing what?"

"Y'all hush your mouths now."

"Facing us, baby girl. Ian is facing us. He's up on that knoll looking right at us. Oh shit, how'd he hear us?"

"Mama, it could be we cheered and clapped too loudly at the other songs."

"Louise, you may as well go in closer. Our cover's been blown. We've been identified."

"This must be it."

"Must be what?" Leigh asks in a whispery voice.

"Ian said the last song tonight he is playing for me."

Louise drives the boat in very close to shore and turns off the engine. Ian stands as if at attention. The sound of the pipes begins low, and the "Ashokan Farewell" flows over the water to my ears. It's a beautiful, sad, almost spiritual song and lifts me up. We are so close I can hear Ian take deep breaths to continue playing. His arm is squeezing the bag against his body, and his fingers flawlessly control the notes. I'm at the front of the pontoon boat, on my knees, wishing this song would never end, but it does come to a solemn ending. Ian doesn't move from his military stance. He gazes across the water and into our boat.

"Ian, that was simply beautiful! Enchanting."

I spoke loudly enough for Ian and his guests to hear. After each of the other songs, there was mild, guarded applause, except from us. We tend to be overly exuberant, but after this solo, there was total silence. Emotionally, everyone was moved literally beyond words. The gentle lapping of water against the sides of the boat is the only sound heard. Taking his bagpipes off, he cups one hand over his mouth so we can hear him easily.

"Aye, Emmy, as are you. Good night."

"Shall I take us home, Em? You ready?"
"Yes, Louise. Let's take it slow, okay?"
"Anything you want, anything, sugar."
"Em?"
"Yes, Emily?"
"About earlier, what I said. Let's wipe the slate clean. Ian may very well be the real deal."
"Done. I love you, Emily."
"Me too you."

Cook hands the guys a very appropriate single malt scotch along with a fine cigar for the ride home, and we pour a nightcap of wine to which there is a toast: "To better days and paths of joy."

The day, as long as it's been, finds my heart filled with joy. I am looking forward to the emerging promise a new day holds. I don't reckon it's possible to have better days, but I'm open to the possibility. Today has been magnificent. I have so much to be grateful for. As the thought rolls around my head, shooting stars fly through the night sky.

"Star light, star bright, first star I see tonight. I wish I may, I wish I might, have this wish I wish tonight." The ride home is quiet; we are all tired, ready to sleep with starry wishes swirling around and dream sweet dreams.

chapter 6

THERE'S A RED bell hanging on top of the door; it rings to let us know when a customer walks in. The bell ringing is all I hear as I open the door. "Good morning, Mama. You up yet?" No response. Panic waves flow over my body. "Mama, sleeping in, eh? On a Monday of all days! What in tarnation has gotten into you?"

Mama rolls over, wiping sleepy seeds from her eyes. "Sugar, you here already?" Her old clock radio shows an unusual number for her to see in the morning: 7:00. "How on earth did this happen? Oh heavens to Betsy! Three hours till we open. You reckon that's long enough to get restocked?"

"We can do it if we get moving. I'll start the coffee and make a list of perishables we need to order. I don't think Monday morning on a holiday week will find us scrambling to help customers anyhow. Everyone from three counties was here yesterday."

Walking around the store, I see Ian everywhere—things he touched, the look of him in his kilt, the boyish charm oozing from every pore of his gorgeous body. Maybe I should put together a basket of goodies and fresh produce to take over later.

"Is the coffee ready yet, Em? My peepers don't want to open this morning. Heaven's sake, let's get these ceiling fans going. It's already steamy. I don't want to open the front door, people see that, and they think we are ready for business."

"The air is heavier outside anyhow, Mama, so it's best to leave it shut until a breeze kicks up. I've been thinking—"

"'Bout your fella, Ian, I bet."

"Uh-huh, what do you think of putting together a Welcome Wagon gift basket for Ian and taking it over to his place?"

Blowing on the steaming-hot coffee, Mama walks to the front of the store. She loves to have her first cup while gazing upon the lake. "Welcome Wagon, are they still going around? Grab your coffee. Let's sit outside before starting."

"Em, looks like you won't have to go far with the basket. A green Land Rover just pulled up. Isn't that old car what Ian is driving?"

"Oh my, I can't let him see me like this. I wasn't expecting—"

"Darlin', remember, God don't make junk."

Those words don't exactly put me at ease. God don't make junk, but in the morning, I'm too close for comfort. I had rolled out of bed, dressed, brushed my teeth, scooped my hair into a ponytail, and drove to the store. A little makeup will polish even what God made.

"Baby girl, he is still down by his car. I waved. He's on his cell phone, I think."

"Mama, please tell me you don't have your binoculars out already."

"No, I left them in the boat last night. Besides, I don't need them. He is right in front of me. Hey, look who else just drove up—Cook, Steve, and Grayson in Steve's la-di-da turbo-charged vehicle. Whatever possesses people to put that kind of money in a car? What is a turbo anyhow? I know he has money, but really."

"Mama, if you have to ask, then a turbo is out of your league. You've ridden in his car. It's so luxurious and refined. He buys it, and you ride in it. Seems like a good deal to me."

"Since you put it that way, you're probably right. Why should I care anyhow?"

"Morning, Steve, Cook. How are you doing today?"

"Em, I'm here too!"

"Sorry, Grayson."

"We're great. Just going to get some coffee and breakfast sandwiches at Orgasmic Delight—the place that just opened up."

"Cook, it's called 'Organic Delight,' but they could quite possibly do a better business with your name." "Okay, okay. Anyhow, we are going to eat there, grab some breakfast for y'all, and come help restock before you open. We figure with five—six, if Ian stays—we'll have you all set in no time."

"Laws a mercy, y'all are wonderful to think of Mama and me. Did you call Ian to come help?"

"No, but we did invite him to breakfast with us when we saw him."

"And is he going with you?"

"Yup, but we'll bring him back too. Where do you reckon he got that wreck of a car? Think he brought it with him?"

"I doubt it, but I think suits him."

"I'm beginning to think you'd like anything connected to him."

"Is Steve going to the bank after breakfast?"

"He's got the deposit all set; we'll get the money in the bank as soon as they open. I guess we're bodyguards; the deposit pouch looks mighty full."

"It is; please keep a watchful eye on it. I'm not sure what good sixty-plus-year-olds are at bodyguarding, but do what you have to, Cook."

"No worries. It's safe with us. Besides, Ian is a kid in his early fifties. We'll rely on skirt boy if anything physical happens."

Ian waves as he is gets into Steve's Mercedes. If Leigh, Louise, and Emily had known they were all going to breakfast, the guys would have had a laundry list of questions to ask Ian. Mama and I head back into the store to begin restocking. Time is wastin', and knowing those boys, they'll forget about time and get here much later than anticipated. Between seeing Ian and the hot weather, I decide walking into the cooler is a good place to start. It's already a welcome relief inside. Mama gets some boxes of light goods out from down in the basement and begins working on the shelves. Music plays through ancient speakers mounted on the shelves behind the checkout counter. The blades of the ceiling fans wobble, chattering the glass globes covering the bulbs.

"Mama, did you hear the bell?"

"I'll see who it is, sugar. Probably the boys back with breakfast. My belly says it's hungry."

"Holler if ya need me or breakfast is here!"

"Ely, son, we aren't open yet. Will be in a bit. What's the matter with you? You gonna be sick? If you're ill, I'll get you something."

"I ain't sick Misriz Suggs."

"Well then, like I said, we don't open for a bit. Come back then."

"No, I intends to stand right chere and make you do what I want."

"Ely, what in heaven's name has gotten into you? You know better. Speak to an elder with respect!"

I slide my head out of the cooler to see who it is Mama is talking to. Ely's hands are in the oversized pockets of his worn-out jeans. He must not realize I'm in the store. Startled by my sudden appearance, he looks back and forth between Mama and me. Sweat seeps through his tattered T-shirt. Just as I step behind Mama, Ely pulls out a pistol, pointing it directly at Mama's forehead.

"Ely, think for a minute; you don't want to do this."

"Miss Emileigh, gets back in the cooler. Now or—"

"Or nothing, Ely, I'm going. Don't hurt, Mama. Please don't hurt her. We know you. Why—"

"Misriz Suggs, close the door to that there cooler." Ely's hand begins to tremble.

Having a second to ponder the situation, she goes ahead and does as he asks, "Okay, Ely, now what? Emileigh can't stay in there too long. Let's get to the heart of why you came here today. What is it you want?"

"Money, open the cash register. I knows you gots scads of it in there, 'cuz of how busy you was yesterday."

"That's right; there was a lot, but it's down at the bank. Come here, I have fifty dollars in bills and coins here. You can have it, but it ain't enough to do anything with."

"I don'ts believe you. You ain't been nowheres this mornin'."

"You've been watching me? I haven't gone anywhere. I have friends who help, and they are due back at any minute. Put the gun down, Ely; let's chat about why you need the money for a second."

"Misriz Suggs, you ain't gave money to no one. You is just makin' that up. Now give it over to me. I ain't gonna ask you again."

"I cain't give you what I ain't got, son. Come over here, and have a look-see for yourself." Mama is as cool as a cucumber though there's a slight shakiness in her voice. I wish I had my cell phone. I also wish the guys would get back. Ely is only sixteen; as far as we know, he has a good home.

"No Misriz, I won'ts. You shut up. Hears me out. I be needin' that there money to gets out of town."

"Pointing that thing at me ain't going to get you anywhere but in trouble and incarcerated. If you hurt me, they'll hunt you down and drag you back to stand trial. If you stop now, it goes no further."

"You'll tell my mama! I knows you will!"

"Yes, I will, for your own safety, unless you tell me they are hurting you, and then I promise to do something different for your sake as well."

"No one cares 'bout my sake!"

"Ely, don't you dare, don't you dare point it at your head." There is a click and then silence. The gun must not be loaded. Mama pulls the door to the cooler with both hands. "Ely, put the gun down on the counter. I ain't gonna tell you again." Tears stream down his face. The gun is still pointed at his temple. Sobbing uncontrollably, he reluctantly lays the pistol on the counter. Mama grabs it, drops the pistol in the cash register, locks the drawer, and then puts the key to the register in her pocket. "Ely, come sit over here with me. Why did you do this today?"

"Emileigh, call his mother. Don't bother telling her why, just ask her to come down to the store. Is that okay, Ely, your mama coming here?"

"Yes'm. Mama. She's gonna kill me. What did I do? I am sorry, Misriz Suggs."

"Now, Ely, plenty of time for all that later. Have you been doing drugs or somethin', tryin' them or whatever?"

Ely pauses for a moment; he won't look Mama in the eyes. "Yez'm I dids at a party last night. Never had done none before. I's jess' been…well, all dem kept on tellin' me to. So I thought it'd be a…whatcha-call-it? Oh yeah, an 'scape."

"You can't find an escape or joy by doing drugs, I promise."

"Mama, shouldn't we call the police too?"

"Oh, please don't! Please don't! I's sorry, honest I is."

"Ely, there are consequences for actions in life. There are consequences for my actions too. If I didn't know you, I'd say, 'Yes, the police damn suredly should be here.' Em, wait on that call. We should keep the guys outside too when they get back. You wait outside for them and bring breakfast in for Ely and me to share while we chat and wait on his mom. We are all promised joy in life; that doesn't mean it's handed to us, but you sure can't steal it. We'll save the lecture and lesson for later. I think you're gonna be spending a lot of time at the store and seein' the likes of me for a good long while. You knew the gun wouldn't go off, didn't you?"

"No, Misriz. I don't know nothin' 'bout guns. I know'd it gots bullets in it, that's all."

"Well, then we are glad the safety is on, else you'd be gone. Ely, I'm disappointed you took this way to show your desperation, but still, there's somethin' deep inside my gut that says you knew I'd be kinder than most folks around here. Most of them have a weapon; the minute you showed yours, you'd've been blown to kingdom come. So, yes, I think you subconsciously or knowingly picked my store to get help. And for that possibility, we'll try and make something good come of this, but you are going to have to be the one to do the work. First thing is for you to tell your mama when she gets here, also what you did last night. It ain't gonna be easy, but ownin' up is the huge first step in healing, got it?"

"Yes, Misriz Suggs, I gots it."

The guys drive up the same time as Hannah Stiles. Wondering why Hannah is at the store before opening time, they stop and jaw a bit. Hannah tells them about the call to come down straight away. Of course, all the guys take a look at each other, guessing as to why we'd call Hannah. They walk her up the steps to the store. "Mornin', Hannah. Ely is inside with Mama. The guys have brought breakfast; you are welcome to share."

"You call me to come here immediately and want to share breakfast?"

"No, there is more. Please come inside. Mama and Ely will explain."

I grab breakfast from the guys and ask them to have a seat on the porch while I go inside with Hannah. Ian looks at me and instantly knows something is way off. "Guys, I'll be right back to explain. Please just one minute."

"Should we go, Em?"

"Oh, please no. We really need you here. Something has happened, but we're just fine. One minute. Sorry, Ian. Please stay if you can."

"Aye, I've got till noon."

"Good."

Mama looks like a wet rag. Not many folks have a gun shoved in their face early in the morning. Now she has the auspicious task of telling the boy's mother what he threatened to do. I'm relieved to drop off the breakfast and head back outside with the guys.

"Y'all know Ely Stiles?"

"Sure do. He asked me for a job awhile back as a gopher on one of my construction projects."

"Well, Grayson, he just tried to hold up the store at gunpoint."

"*What the hell?* Where is the bastard?"

"He is inside with Mama and his mom. Mama isn't going to press charges, but honestly, I think her sentence is going to be tougher on him than jail."

"Oh, I really think with a gun used, the police need to be here."

"No, Steve, he is bawling in there, depressed, scared out of his mind, and he tried drugs for the first time yesterday. Besides, if it's his parents' gun, they'd be in a lot of trouble."

"He needs to be drug tested at the hospital. One of us should go too."

"Good idea. Let's see if Mama suggests going down to doc's for a drug test."

"And a shrink."

"One step at time, fellas. Ian, I'm sorry you walked into this today. Did you enjoy breakfast with the guys?"

"Em, you're talking about breakfast as if nothing just happened."

"I have to. It's over; I'm shaking like a leaf, and we still have to restock the store."

The guys stand up when Mama and the others come out of the store. "All right, y'all. Here's the story. This goes no further than us and your wives, guys. Ely here is gonna make amends to Em and me by working here part-time this summer and after school in the fall. We'll also have a Bible study from time to time. We're going down to Doc's for a checkup and drug test. Ely will also be getting some counseling along with his parents. Not another word is to be mentioned about this incident unless Ely or I bring it up. Understood? Good." There isn't a moment to respond. "And another thing, Em, here is the key to the register. Give the gun to Steve. Steve, you lock it up somewhere or do whatever with it. I think it's mine to do with as I please given it was in my face. I want it gone for good, ya hear?"

The three are very slow to get into Hannah's car to go down to the doctor's office. All of them look sheepish and drawn. Grayson, Cook, and Steve stare at Ely as if he were scum.

Grayson claps his hands rallying the troops. "Guys, roll up your sleeves. We've got some work to do."

"Whether Ely knows it or not, he is one lucky kid. Tah has strong morals and will probably give him the best shot at a better future." Cook shakes his head listening to Steve before he chimes in.

"His future was already brighter the moment he put the gun down."

"Em, are you really all right?" Ian asks.

"For the moment, I'm fine, especially with you here and asking."

"Then, lassie, let's get this store up and running."

The five of us working together make light the work. We don't want Mama to come back and have to do anything today. The store opens on time; everything isn't where it should be, but we haven't had one customer either. Cook thought the store should open on time or surely someone would come by with questions. For the first time since Ely walked into the store, I begin to feel a bit wobbly. Enough time has passed for adrenaline to wear off and reality to set in.

"Um, Emmy?"

"Are you getting ready to head out and go to your appointments?"

"Actually, I think I'd rather stay here with you today."

"You have business to attend to, Ian. Babysitting me isn't going to take care of it for you."

"No, but to be honest, if I were to go, I doubt I'd hear a word anyone says to me. My thoughts would be centered on you and your mum. I'll make some calls; most of the information can be faxed or e-mailed to me, and I can review it right here with you."

"A lovely thought, but I just met you yesterday. I'm sure one of the others will be in and out, and once their wives hear, they will be here for sure."

"True, we met one day ago, but we saw each other before then. From the first moment we saw each other, you can't deny there was a connection.

Please let me do as my heart instructs and just be next to you. Let me in, Emmy. Let me care and take care of you, if only for today."

I don't know what to say. Ian certainly wears his heart on his sleeve. I'm being obstinate, but I also feel like Play-Doh and want him to be here. Ely scared me; I thought Mama was gone. The courage within her surprised me, but her compassion toward Ely was pure Mama.

"All right, Ian, I'm tired of trying to act strong. The morning's events are starting to take a toll. Your company is most welcome, but hands off the register. It's an oldie, a bit quirky and takes a familiar touch."

"The blasted buggers aren't my thing anyhow."

A wave of relief sweeps over me knowing Ian is here. I guess I should eat. Breakfast missed me in the commotion. The Suggettes are sure to appear soon. I hope, for Mama's sake, they'll come one at a time. Knowing them, they'll be travelling in a herd, sounding like wild elephants trampling up the steps.

chapter 7

LOUISE WALKS THROUGH the screen door, scanning the store for Mama. Her face is pale and drawn. "Emileigh, oh, sweetheart, no one should ever endure such a day. Ian, I'm glad to see you here. It has been helter-skelter at our house. Harper and Tyler are due in at the airport; Tess is driving in and due anytime with Annabelle and Morgan. The house needed to be cleaned, and then I hear from Cook about Ely!"

"Louise, have you heard from Mama?"

"No, I haven't. Are they still at Doc's?"

"That's where they were going when they left here about quarter to ten. It's one thirty, and I'm getting worried."

"You able to stay here for a while, Louise?" Ian asks.

"For a bit. Cook is home waiting on the kids to arrive so I could come here and check on Emileigh and Tah."

"Good. Emmy, I'm gonna take a quick trip down to where this doc's place is and make certain your mum is all right."

"Ian, you don't have to. I can go."

"No, you need to stay here and rest while it's slow. Where is the office?"

Scribbling down directions to Doc's office, Louise also gives Ian her cell phone number so he can let us know what he finds.

"Ian, thank you."

"Nonsense, it's the least I can do. Need for me to bring back anything?"

"No, I haven't exactly been thinking about needs."

"You've got my number if you think of anything you need."

Bearing the same expression Louise had when she arrived, Emily and Leigh take a seat. There's no need to beat around the bush; they want to hear what transpired. As I describe to them how from the cooler I could do nothing but listen to Mama's strength, while feeling mine seep out and freeze, the Suggettes gasp. Mama's compassion for Ely even in the midst of being terrorized in her own store was inspiring. The fear of losing her in the blink of an eye, my ear to the door of the cooler, unable to help, only listen, was horrifying. Ely had trapped me inside intent on separating us, but Mama and I are two birds of a feather; each gathers strength from the other.

"How are you, Em? I mean, how do you feel? Okay?"

"I admit to being shaky both inside and out. But I think mostly because I haven't heard from Mama and it's worrisome."

"She doesn't go off and not call."

"Hush, we don't need to heighten Em's worry by voicing our fears."

"Well, it ain't like we don't think it; may as well spew it out."

"Emily, Leigh, please don't start now. Bickering doesn't help. I know y'all are as concerned about Mama as I am. Ian went to see if he can find her. He'll call as soon as he knows anything. Where are Grayson and Steve?"

"Grayson is home with Samantha and Dylan. They're here for the rest of the week. They got home...oh, I'd say an hour ago or so. We are all supposed to have a dinner together this evening, remember?"

"I totally forgot. What about Steve?"

"He's out on an errand of mercy Grayson and Ian sent him on this morning."

"Errand of mercy, Leigh? For who?"

"You'll see when he gets back; the guys have cooked up a security plan for Tah."

Finally, the phone rings. "Ian, have you seen Mama?"

"Aye, lass, she is with me. She's fine—tired, as you'd expect. We're on our way back to the store. Should be back in a few minutes."

"Are you certain she's all right?"

"Trust me, Em. I promise, she's fine."

Ian certainly is proving himself worthy of trust in a short span of time. He's revealed himself to be a true gentleman filled with good intentions and delivering on them. Today should wipe away any trepidation Emily has regarding him. The Land Rover's coughing and sputtering engine pulls into the parking lot. Ian opens the creaky, unoiled door for Mama. I can't wait to give her a big ole bear hug.

"Oh, Mama, are you all right? What took so long at the doctor's?"

A figure timidly moves around the back of the car. When he gets near Ian, I realize it's Ely. "Why is he here? Ian, why did you bring Ely back here, especially with Mama? What were you thinking? Oh wait, you obviously weren't thinking!"

"Baby girl, settle down. Ely is here at my request. His folks need some time to talk about things. I thought we could all use this time to just be—no judgment, no worries, just some chill time."

Meekly, I apologize for coming down like an ax on Ian. "I'm sorry for jumping all over you, Ian. It's been an emotional day, which isn't an excuse to give in to my feelings."

"Oh, I would have said a lot worse. Water under the bridge. What time is the store closing tonight?"

"Not one minute past five. Did you know we're supposed to have dinner together tonight, Mama? We should pass, don't you think?"

Taking a moment to consider her possibilities, Mama comes to a quick decision. "That I don't have one thing to serve should be a hint to pass, but I think it best to celebrate life with those I love."

"Celebrate life? Really? After what you've been through?"

"What better day to do it? Besides, Ely has a lot to celebrate today, as do we—the joy of being."

"Aye, Mrs. Suggs, I totally agree. I have leftovers coming out of my ears from yesterday's party. I have no intention of letting them spoil. Do you want to come over, or shall I bring them here?"

"Perfect, everything except the Mrs. Suggs part...That has to go. Tah or Mama, take your pick. Would you mind bringing the food here? I'm plum tuckered out and want to put my aching feet up."

Ian puts his hand on Mama's shoulder as she sits down in her favorite rocker facing the highest hill on the lake.

"I'm not ready to call you Mama, so Tah 'tis. We'll go across the lake and retrieve the food, right, Em? Has Steve come back yet?"

"Haven't seen Steve, but the gals are inside. I'm surprised they haven't run down to see you."

"All in good time, I'll head up with Ely, and we'll make peace, right, Ely? Meantime, y'all go over and pack up the food. Take your time; the store ain't even closed. We do any business today, Em?"

"Misriz Suggs, is it all right if I stay on the porch while y'all jaw?"

"I reckon so, Ely. Em, how much business?"

"We've had very few customers, but, Mama, you sure you want to close up tonight?"

"Yes, Em. Like you say, it ain't busy, and I've been gone all day. You deserve some time to relax after the day we've had."

Mama looks at Ely while she sends us on our way. She, by all appearances, seems to have regained some momentum and her usual composure since talking to us.

"Emmy, grab your bathing suit. Let's go see how Moose and Bear are."

Ian and I rumble off down the road; the car feels every nook and cranny in the road, jumbling us head to toe, flattening our backsides. I'm glad to finally be away from the store. A black cloud has been hanging over it all day. It is freeing sitting next to Ian, sensing his desire. He drives the junkyard reject one hand on the wheel, the other on the stick shift. Just to be sitting next to him elevates my mood.

"Ian, where on earth did you dig up this old car; it's somewhat of a relic, isn't it?"

"Some call it junk; I call it a classic. Could use some new shocks. I'll show you where I got it. The car should look familiar to you. When I came to check on rentals, Beth, my real estate, agent was kind enough to give me a tour. Wait, I've got an idea. First, I want to take a little detour and show you a parcel of land I want to explore; it's on the market."

"Okay, but walking land this time of year isn't usually done. Ticks, snakes, all kinds of critters hanging out waiting to crunch and munch—gives me the willies just thinkin' about it."

"We'll just drive by, Emmy. No crunching or munching on you today, unless I do it."

Struggling not to react, I focus on the road before us. "Right up this hill and 'round the bend; see, it has a full view of the lake. There's select timber to harvest, which will more than pay for the land. I don't understand landowners, but it's my gain. Selective timbering will open up nice areas for homes or cottages to be built."

"You think long term at all possibilities, don't you? It's lovely land up here. Opening it up will make the view spectacular and let in some needed light."

"You've read my mind."

Suddenly, I'm plunged into a foreign world, dropped in the midst of a romance novel. The robbery attempt is a far-gone memory. Mama was right; she knew I should get away for a while and spend some time with Ian. I can't help but wonder what the two of them discussed earlier.

"Nice to hear you like the land. Walking the acres tomorrow will help me to really see if it's worth the asking price. What is it you call them, 'critters'? That's it; critter protection will be enforced after your alarming revelation. I got the car from a guy who lives in this tiny little place, right over there."

"Ulysses Bucknell?"

"Do you know him?"

"Oh, Ian, everyone knows him; he's a bit mad."

"Mad or not, when Beth was driving by, I spotted this old beauty. Beth didn't mention he's mad, 'course she wouldn't since I was interested in renting the house a few doors down. Ulysses needed some money, and the car needed work. He hasn't been able to do anything for…well, I don't know how long. From the looks of his place, times have been tough for a number of years."

Stuffing and springs are popping up in the seams of the leather seat. I want to slide over and be closer to Ian but can't. He seems so passionate about his newly found treasure. "Ulysses lost his wife, Peg, a few years ago. They were quite a pair, full of life. They led a simple life, but a good one. He's never been the same since."

"Oh, I understand as you do, lass, how devastating losing a spouse is on the heart and soul. As for the car, we struck a deal. I get to fix the car and use her while here and then give it back to him when I leave. I let him use it on days when I am traveling or have other transportation. Let's take him some leftovers and give him the car tonight. I won't need it tomorrow; we can take the boat over to Tah's."

"Do you look for ways to enrich lives at every turn in the road?"

"I was born into good fortune, abused it, and now strive to pass it on. We all deserve kindness. Bear and Moose were his dogs. He came over and saw them early this morning. We figure they followed the car over here; anyhow, I paid him for the dogs as well. He isn't able to take care of them properly, and while I'm here, he can still see them anytime he wants. Speaking of my beasts of love, watch out! Here they come running!"

Bear and Moose are happy to see Ian. They leap and bark, carrying on with each other. Off they go, running to the water's edge, each giving a look back to ask permission for a dip. "Aye, lads, in ya go. We're on our way as well, right, Em?"

"Well, I don't know…"

"Yes, you do. I'm getting a Heineken for myself. What can I get you, a white wine?"

"I thought you'd never ask. Large, please, with ice."

"Go change, lass. There are guest rooms on the second floor…well, you saw it the other day. Bathroom, bedroom, make yourself at home. Here's your wine. Don't let those boys of mine drive you crazy. Those buggers are a rambunctious pair of Indians."

Wine has never tasted better nor been needed as much. The bedroom is sensory overload for me. It's so lavish. The room wasn't decorated by Ian, so it's difficult to sense his style. Given the classic boat and the classic junker he drives, he does have his own style, but I'm not certain there is a label for it.

"You look comfortable, more at ease than last time, definitely more than earlier today."

"Coming here is especially relaxing tonight. Today's been a beast."

"Some nibbles for you. I don't think you've eaten much today; the huge glass of wine will just go to your head."

"Would that be bad?"

"No, not from where I'm sitting, but we have to get dinner. Before you get too cozy, let's take a swim. It's always refreshing, and the boys love company."

"Can we dive off the end of the dock? Is it deep enough?"

"Yup, kerplunk to your heart's content."

The water instantly melts stress away. Ian peels off his shirt, revealing a sculptured body. "How is it, Emmy? Feel good?"

"Oh, yes, just what I needed."

Ian doesn't know it, but seeing him half naked is really what I needed more than the swim.

"Think we can outswim Bear and Moose?"

"They live for the water and look right at home next to you. Give it a try."

"All right then." Ian takes a few strokes, turns around, and heads toward me. In an instant, he's beside me. "Come over here." He puts his well-toned arms around my waist and his head next to mine and whispers, "Put your arms around my neck."

"Ian, I don't—"

"Yes, you do. Come on now. Trust me. Put your arms around my neck."

As I do, my heart leaps, and my pulse takes off. How I desperately desire this, but at the same time, it's too soon. Ian senses my nervousness. He holds me as if I am a fragile china doll, delicately but firmly.

"I'm not going to hurt you, Emmy. I simply want to feel you close to me, just hold you. I have fought this all day watching you cope with the emotions of the morning. Your mum told you she wants to celebrate life today. Let me help you in some small way celebrate too, okay?"

"Ian, I'm not sure. I haven't been with anyone since Josh, not even a kiss."

"And how long has that been, Em?"

"Four long, lonely years."

"Oh, then you know a smidgeon of how nervous I am; it has been twenty-five years, Emmy, twenty-five *years*."

"How can that be? You're full of love, so sure of yourself. How can that be? Oh, Ian, the thought breaks my heart."

"Enough of yesterday. Follow your heart, lass; it's beating ever so close to mine in so many ways."

Ian reaches down and lifts my legs; he whispers in my ear again, persuading me to put them around his waist and hold him tightly. This time, it's easy for me. He begins to move back and forth and then spins around in a circle, slowly and easily. "Remember how I said a first kiss shouldn't be rushed? I'm going to kiss you and hold you like this forever." He takes my face in his hands. His lips come up to my left cheek and then the right; over my eyes, he kisses tenderly and sweetly. My lips grow hungry for his and part slightly in anticipation. His full lips finally touch mine; they linger for a moment. Pulling back slightly, he looks deeply into my eyes and I into his. Drawing me closer for another kiss, he parts my lips with the tip of his tongue. We grasp each other tightly, and he begins to probe more deeply, sweetly becoming more passionate. Ian stops and pulls away with a laugh. He nuzzles my neck with soft, easy kisses and then rests his head between my breasts and chuckles.

"What is so funny, Ian? Am I that bad?"

"You must like it on top."

"Like what...holy crap, Ian, what are you saying?"

"Where did you learn to kiss? Some odd prep school? I mean, I know it's been a long time for me, but I've never been kissed like that before."

I'm unsure what to say, so I figure less talk is better. Not a word is spoken as I smile and pull him closer for a lingering kiss the likes of which will surely rock his soul and mine. His rigid body molded to mine I feel the depth of his desire. Our heartbeats are audible and quivering limbs teased to the extreme when Bear and Moose suddenly have had enough of being ignored. At the same time, both dogs jump on us, and we fall deeper into the water laughing and desiring much more. "Emmy, we better get dressed and start to gather the food."

"It would be easy to stay here, but I have a feeling lots of folks gathering at Mama's will want to meet you. No doubt the Suggettes will be wondering what has taken us so long to return."

"Oh, I think they have a good idea!"

Ian tosses me a towel. Moose and Bear are next to us, shaking themselves dry and looking quite pleased with their swim. They soak the two of us. "Em, I'm going to jump in the shower to rinse off the lake water. Feel free to join me."

"I'll use the guest room, even though your offer sounds mighty enticing...another day; we haven't much time before the others get hungry."

I can't stop my imagination from wondering how lathering his body with soap in a hot, steamy shower would feel. Someday soon, I hope to know. There is so much food to take across the lake—all of it neatly and easily stored in containers. Ian takes out some of everything and piles it high upon a plate for Ulysses. "Em, I'm going to run a plate of food and take the Land Rover over to Ulysses. I'll be back in a few. Look and see if we need to take anything else with us, if you don't mind."

We have enough food to feed an army. A few pieces of Ian's favorite treasures are scattered around the room but few if any pictures from home. His belongings are probably placed to make it feel more like his home. "Are ya ready to fire up Bessie and go feed the ranks?"

"I'd rather be staying here with you, but let's go make some hungry folks full. What about Bear and Moose?"

"They'll be fine inside, unless you'd like to take them with us."

"I'd like to, but there are going to be so many of us, it may be a lot for those guys to handle."

"Sorry, lads, another time...You be good."

The evening sky is full of light, wispy clouds, feathered out above with paths of golden hues between. It has been an eventful day, one full of life and friends to see. I think of days gone by and memories flood my mind. "Em, you've grown somber; the day weighing on your mind?"

"I guess, also a few things, like why did you come to the store this morning? I thought you had appointments all day."

"The morning appointments were postponed until another day. When I saw a few hours to spare, I couldn't help but see your face on the boat last night as I played. I found myself driving to you. That cannot be all to still your mood."

"No, you've mentioned a couple of times about leaving. When are you going?"

"The beginning of September, I'll be headed to New York."

"You're going to New York City?"

"Nowhere near. I'm headed to the Finger Lakes."

"All I ever recollect hearing about New York is snow, all the time snow."

"Oh, then you have been caboodled, lass; it's beautiful. September, from what I've been told, is exquisite."

"So, you're going there to buy real estate? Will you be coming back here?" I had been dreading asking Ian this question. But my heart is quickly becoming entwined with his. The thought of him leaving at this early stage of our relationship, even if his departure is two months away, seems unbearable to comprehend. "I'll have to come back as business develops or changes here, but not for any lengthy time…well, as I see it now. My life is flexible, Em. I never write anything in stone."

I feel teased and toyed with by his last statement. If Ian is genuine and cares for me as much as he seems to, why isn't he more open about where we stand. Maybe he is as unsure as I am.

"Emmy, there you go quiet again. I'm trying to be honest with you, but if you close off, we can't make much headway."

"Headway? You're leaving in a little less than two months. What would you have me do? Surrender my heart and then have it broken for two months of fun?"

"I never thought I'd be falling in love and have to make changes to my plans. I have to make progress financially for those to whom I'm responsible. I'm not asking you to do anything I am not asking myself to do, Em."

"Falling in love? Are you, Ian? My heart, your heart…they've been broken before, and that pain, I can't…no, I will not bear again, especially for a few minutes of happiness. I want love, but long term. I am also aware nothing is ever written in stone, especially where love is concerned. I have ghosts who pull me back emotionally; they do it every day. It's difficult to press on to something new. Even though my heart tells me I must, I feel I'm unfaithful to those ghosts if I try."

"Aye, those aren't the ghosts making you feel like that. The ghosts who haunt your dreams and memories love you; they'd want you to be happy, not alone, even if love doesn't last forever. Those feelings of being unfaithful are Satan's tool to make you depressed and to keep your thoughts in the past. One cannot live in the past; it's impossible. The past is over, in a way, dead. God gave us eyes in the front of our head for a reason, so we don't look back. The only way to live is now, in this moment. It's all we have. I want to share whatever moments I have with you, and yes, I am falling in love with you."

"You are? Still, Ian, I don't know. Give me some time to think."

"No, I won't. React with your heart, not your head. If we're meant to be together, it will work out. You can go with me, or I can change my arrangements. But, for the time being, I'm New York bound. I've got to go there in a couple of weeks to look for a place to rent. I think I'll be there about a week. Come go with me. Let's have our own miniadventure."

"What about Mama? She needs help."

"You're giving it some thought? Ely can stock, and your mum is quite good at taking care of herself. Come on, Emmy, join me in Naples."

"Naples, where is it?"

"It's in the Finger Lakes region. Come on, take a chance."

"I can't look at you and refuse. When do we leave?"

"Whoa, lass, that was fast."

"You said to react with my heart; I did. You told me you're falling in love with me, and I never thought I'd hear anyone say those words to me again. I do want to spend more time alone with you."

"Well, how about going in a couple of weeks? Your mum needs some time off before we go, and then there is Ely. We should be sure of him before we go; otherwise, neither of us will feel good about leaving. You'll be in charge of the store when she is gone, I trust?"

"Look who is the one slowing down this fast-paced relationship; our trip is getting delayed more and more. I'll put Ely through his paces and make sure he knows what Mama and I expect from him."

Ian stops Bessie when we are almost at the dock. He turns to me, takes me in his arms, and presses his lips to mine in a passionate kiss and embrace. "You have just made my heart leap, Emmy. Working alone is all right, but having you beside me, if even just for a week, will be sheer joy. I promise you'll have a good time."

"So, Tah, what you reckon Ian and Emmy will be up to while we are away?"

"We goin' somewhere?"

"Yeah, thought we should head to Beaufort or Oriental for some crab cakes and to set a spell by the ocean."

"Beaufort? Really? Oh, I'd prefer Wilmington."

"Why there, when there is so much we could do elsewhere? How 'bout Myrtle Beach?"

"And get caught up in all that nonsense, no thank you. Good food, sunshine, the smell of the salt air, sand beneath my feet, I don't need entertainment or hoards of people."

"Then, Tah, why Wilmington?"

"'Cuz I know the best place for crab cakes 'n' beer, the ocean is there, the inlet too, and besides they may be filmin' something we could watch and see iffin we spot a person of interest."

"Alrighty then, let's go next week for four or five days. Maybe Emily or Louise would like to join us as well. The guys can help Em out with the store. What you say, Tah? I need it; you sure need it. Let's do it, a girls' vacation!"

"You make the arrangements, let me know the days, and count me in."

"Em...did you hear? Your Mama and me, we're headed to Wilmington!"

"Really, Mama? That's great."

"You okay with Ian by yourself for a few days?"

Mama's smirk is wide and proud; she let the cat out of the bag for my would-be cousins to hear. Louise and Emily are quick to chime in on the announcement. Not only are they glad to hear Tah is going away for a few days, but they are hell bent on joining to make sure she enjoys herself.

"Excuse me, Misriz Suggs, but when y'all go, will I still have to come and work at the store?"

"Ely, of course. You will be needed to help Emileigh. She'll keep you busy. Another thing, Ely, this 'Misriz Suggs' business, we have to do something about that. It makes me feel old and like a stranger to you. You figure out what you'll be comfortable callin' me from now on, pass it by my ears, and see if it meets approval, okay?"

"Yes'm."

Ely turns and walks away from Leigh and Mama. He kicks a pebble and nearly slams into Grayson.

"I's sorry, Mr. Grayson, sir."

"Ely, watch where you're goin', son."

"Yes, sir, Mr. Grayson, I'll do just that. Pardon me, sir."

"Did you name that rock Grayson?"

"Sir, what?...I mean, pardon?"

"Ely, look up at me. When you talk to someone, look at them, not down at the ground. It shows you respect the person you're talking to, but more important, it shows you respect yourself. That's better, chin up, and shoulders back. How 'bout no more 'sir' either. It makes me feel like I'm about to be shipped overseas. Been there, done that."

"But, sir, I mean, Mr. Grayson, that ain't how I done been raised."

"Time for a change, it's time to grow up, Ely, at least around me. I don't know what Tah Bell would say, but 'round me, just call me Grayson."

"Tah Bell? What is da Bell fur, Grayson?"

"It's her maiden name; we like the sound of it."

"Me too. It makes me think of angels, you know, from the movie, I can't recollect the name, but you know a bell rings an angel gets wings?"

"*It's a Wonderful Life*."

"That's it! Oh I love that movie!"

"You are an odd egg, Ely. Things come out of you I don't see coming."

"Louise, who is the yummy hunk with Emileigh?"

"You mean skirt boy? Ian Mac-do-something-or-other."

"How ever did they get so chummy without word from y'all gettin' round?"

"It appears somethin' heavy happened over yonder, don't it? Em don't set snares for men like some women, but he does look like he fell into a trap, don't he?"

"He looks like he has had to shake off a few before too. Let's go over, and you introduce me, Louise."

"Let's not and wait till it ain't so obvious as to your motivation. It don't appear he is shaken' Emileigh off, so put your claws back in, Samantha."

"Fine, Louise, I'll just get my mama to do it."

"Let me know how that works out, Sam."

"Steve, where have the likes of you been all day and evening?"

"Leigh tells me y'all are going to Wilmington next week for a few days."

"Whatever does that have to do with where you have been? I heard you went on a mission of mercy. What's the mission?"

"Ian, Grayson, and I decided you need a security monitoring system, in case of emergency, like, well, you know..."

"Mama, won't it be wonderful? We'll rest easier, and so can you. I'm staying at the apartment until you get back from your trip. When can it be installed, Steve?"

"Actually, I went ahead and set it up for next week regardless if you were going to be here or not. Felt it should be done as soon as possible, given the day's events."

"Careful, no more talk about today. Were any of you going to consult me on this expensive undertaking, or did you just think I'd pull the money outta my ass to pay for it?"

"Not that we wouldn't like to see that happen—hell I'd pay to see it happen, Tah—but the system is a gift from all of us to you; there is no turning it down, painful as it might be. You can keep your money where it is."

"This is way too much, even for all y'all to chip in. I can't allow it."

"There ain't no allowin', Tah; it's already been paid for as has the monthly monitoring for a year."

"You think you know people, and then they raise the bar outta reach. I love y'all for thinking about me. I am touched, really touched, and appreciate it beyond belief. But one of y'all is gonna have to teach me how to use it. I ain't no good at anything other than the rotary phone."

"We'll teach you, Tah. No worries. The new systems are really are very simple to use."

"Can't be simpler than a knife and fork. Where is dinner?"

"Call the tribe together for a blessing...we are ready to commence the eatin'."

Ian is fresh blood in the neighborhood. With the Suggettes and their children around, plenty of questions keep being tossed in his direction, mostly about Scotland. "Ian, I see a few of the guys up at the store wanting to play some tunes. Let's go up for a minute."

A look of relief comes over Ian's face as he takes my hand. "Thanks, lass."

"Did you hear him, oh to be called, 'lass.' Isn't that the coolest?"

"Tess, what the hell are you talkin' bout? It sounds kinda queer to me."

"Oh, Tyler, anything with an ounce of class sounds queer to you."

"Come on now, y'all, you're too old for sibling rivalry."

"Yes, Mama."

"Besides, I like his accent, it evokes a certain...I don't rightly know, Old-World charm. It will do you two some good to hear."

"Mama, I said I thought it was the coolest, remember?"

"Uh, yes, you, Tess and Samantha, stay clear of him, ya hear?"

"Why's that?"

"For one thing, you are way too young for the likes of him, and another, don't y'all agree Emileigh deserves some time in the sun?"

"Yes'm, he's interesting to us."

"He is foreign. Perhaps if you paid more attention to your studies in college, you'd be going to those foreign lands and seeing up close the wonderments you are dreamin' 'bout."

"What is his full name, Mama?"

"Oh, it's Ian MacDougal...Ian Duncan MacDougal, I think."

"Mac Do Good, if you ask me."

"Tess, no one is askin' you anything."

"Shut up, Tyler."

"Misriz Suggs, I dun think I gots a name I'd like to call you. Would you like to hear it?"

"Let it fly; I'm all ears."

"Well, um, it be 'Ma Bell.' You reckon it'll do?"

"Oh, Ely, I think it sounds mighty fine to my ears. You have the soul of a poet, young man. You did good, real good, son."

Ian and I arrive back down at the docks and see Mama and Ely talking. Mama is in tears when she tells us Ely wants to call her Ma Bell. All I can think of is a telephone company, but with Mama's espionage capabilities, I see why she may like it as a code name. It isn't until Grayson explains by whispering in our ears how Ely feels about bells and angels that I too understand and become teary eyed. We have all had a day, but Ely has done a 180 in my eyes. I set up my cello on the dock facing the water; Ian grabs a guitar and begins to tune it.

"I didn't know you play the guitar."

"And I had no idea you play the cello."

"I haven't for years…well, ever since Josh died. We used to play a lot together. I tried afterward, but it was too difficult emotionally for me to continue."

"And so why choose tonight?"

"You are falling in love with me, and I with you. The last song you played last night keeps repeating itself over and over in my head. I'd like to try to play it—in a way to say good-bye to my ghosts."

"You can play from memory?"

"Hold off on any compliments until after it's over."

Most of the ramblers had been setting up at the store to play, but Ian and I convinced them to come down to the shore and play for all of us. Drawing the bow across the strings feels somewhat foreign, and I seem to be unable to form a quality sound. I'm hitting wolf notes. Ian gently touches my shoulder and whispers in my ear, "Remember, play from the soul and through the heart." The moment I hear his words, the notes strike a reverberation felt deep within my body. I have regained the energy it takes to play with soul. Ian begins to strum the guitar next to me, and we flow into the farewell song together, facing the lake as the light of day dims in the distance. When the song is over, Ian lightly caresses my neck with his hand, and I let the cello fall onto my chest. Behind us, Samantha, as only a younger person can, breaks the somber moment, "How about something a little more upbeat?" No longer than it takes the words to come out of her mouth, the Ramblers begin to play "Thank God I'm a Country Boy."

"Sun's comin' up, got cakes on the griddle." Music is playing, and everyone is singing at the top of his or her lungs; even the surrounding camps join in. It's a moment to embrace. "Life ain't nothing but a funny, funny riddle."

I look at Ian; he winks back. It's funny how the answer to a riddle can fall into your lap at the most unexpected moment.

chapter 8

"ELY, YOU GET over here right this damn minute, ya hear? Do you have any idea what time it is? Land's sake makin' us come all the way here with all these here people to pick up the likes of you and make sure you get home. You just wait..."

"Evening, Hannah. I reckon time slipped away from us. We've enjoyed Ely's company tonight."

"I'll bet, Mrs. Suggs. I'll just bet..."

"Good night, Ely. We'll see you between nine thirty and ten in the mornin', right?"

"Yes, Ma Bell. I'll be here. You can be sure of that."

"Did I hear you right? Did you just call Mrs. Suggs 'Ma'? Did she make you do that?"

"Mama, Misriz Suggs asked me to done figure out 'nother name to be callin' her."

"Tahlulah Suggs, is that right?"

"I don't like to be addressed so formally by someone who's gonna be spending a lot of time with me. I asked Ely to come up with something he could live with to call me other than Mrs. Suggs. I mean no offense to you."

"You should have asked me first. I am the boy's mother."

"Hannah, what has gotten into you tonight? I do apologize for Ely's sake."

I could tell Mama was struggling to hold her tongue. Hannah arrived with a corn cob jammed up her behind. Ely cowers over to the car like a whipped puppy.

"Tahlulah Suggs, I want my gun back."

"Is that you, Peter?"

"You know it's me. I want my gun back this very minute."

"Peter, if I called the police this morning, your gun would be in their hands and you'd be in a mess of trouble right about now. You hear me? It's mine, already gone from here, never to harm anyone or anything again. You understand me?"

When Peter hears Mama explain his gun would not be returned, he hits the gas so hard the wheels spin in the dirt. He certainly has heads spinnin' down at the dock to catch sight of the commotion. Pressing his young face against the rear window glass, Ely's fearful expression pleads for help.

"God in heaven, what have we done?"

"Mama, what do think will happen to Ely? You think Peter is gonna take this out on Ely's hide?"

"I'm inclined to say we just witnessed something that explains most of this morning's events. Poor boy, we should probe a bit deeper into his home life first chance we get."

As the dust settles in the parking lot, Mama stands transfixed on the taillights of Peter's car as it disappears down the road.

"Mama, I'll go relay your good nights to everyone. You just go on to bed. We'll clean up, and what we don't get tonight, I'll do in the morning." There is a loud sigh from her room.

Steve's voice jolts her out of the apartment. "Ladies, where would you like these?"

"Over by the sink or anywhere you can find a spot."

"Tah, what was all that with Ely? Were we supposed to have fetched him back home earlier?"

"I am as bewildered by the explosion of temper as you. Ely was supposed to have spent the afternoon and evening here while they talked. To be honest, I'm afraid for his safety now. I'm at a loss as to what we should do."

"Mama, at least we know the gun—or the one gun—is out of Peter's hands. And I am staying here at the apartment until the security system is installed and you are back from Wilmington."

"That'll be mighty nice. I must say good night, Steve and Ian. I am mighty tired and ready to hit the hay. Thank you both for everything today. I am so blessed. See you tomorrow, I hope."

"Sweet dreams, Tah. You need anything, call us."

Ian saunters up behind me as I'm washing dishes and loading the washer. He puts his hands on my hips, slowly wrapping his arms around my waist, pulling himself as close as he possibly can. His warm breath makes the hair on the back of my neck rise. Rose-petal kisses touch my skin, sending shivers over me. Dropping the dishes, I raise soap-lathered hands and fondle his curls. With one twist of his wrist the button opens on my capris and he slips them down. Ian's warm hands move over my hips. He grasps them and spins me around. My hands grab the edge of the counter for balance as his skillful fingers probe deeper and find a welcoming moistness inviting his touch to linger. His supple lips nibble at the buttons of my blouse opening them with ease. He nestles his mouth over each breast breathing deeply, nibbling and exploring their shape with his tongue and lips, bringing them to peak in pleasure. I shake my head and force myself to push him away. He resists. Ian bends me back over the sink with his hand spread over the small of my back. He pushes my legs apart his desire swelling tossing my capris aside. I lift my legs clasping them around his hips. Using all my strength I pull up to gaze into his lust filled eyes.

"Ian stop, Mama is a few feet away. I just can't, not here, not now."

Cued by my reluctance to pursue our desires, without missing a beat he pulls away and changes the subject. Ian's heart is still beating furiously. His raspy voice forcing words to dampen his arousal. The instant change of tone and thought takes me by surprise.

"Emmy, you play the cello beautifully. I'm glad to hear you play. I don't know how you play a song you've heard once from ear."

"Oh, Ian, your flattery will get you no further tonight. I know I massacred the song, but I also know I gave it the fighting Irish try."

"Irish, lass?...Remember who you are talking to, a proud Scot. It sounded well played to my ear."

"Is there anything left down by the lake to bring in? I'm with Mama and ready to turn in. It's been a long, stressful day."

"Come with me down to the dock, and let's take a gander. I think everyone left after Ely's dramatic exit."

"A gander? Is that what y'all call it over yonder? Shall I come as I am or pull up my britches?"

As always, the cleanup is the last thing any of us ever has to worry about. It gets done with a collective effort. Ian walks over to Bessie and looks forlornly toward the darkened house across the lake. "Sadly, it's time to say good night. It has been a day, hasn't it? Your first holdup, our first kiss, and dinner with everyone under the sun including the robber. You know this place, for being off the beaten track, sure has more than its share of intrigue and mystery."

"I've lived here all my born days, and until the likes of you showed up in the store wearing a kilt, no intrigue except for faith healers and tourists ever came this way. You seem to have stirred up something in the community, Ian. You certainly have within me."

A wide smile crosses Ian's lips. He is pleased to hear he's had an effect on me. "I'm only interested in what I stir inside of you, Emmy. Do you want me to stay over here tonight? Are you and your mum going to be all right?"

"Kind offer, but we need to know we are okay on our own. I'll have my cell phone on all night and will shove something in front of the doors. I'm not worried about Ely, but his stepfather is another story. He seemed revengeful tonight, but maybe he was just drunk."

"Oh, now that makes me feel real comfortable. I'll be sitting up all night with worry. Where are your mother's binoculars? I may need them to keep an eye on you...Do you want me to bring Moose and Bear back for good ears to hear if anyone comes by?"

"Ian, kiss me and go home. You have a full day of appointments Tuesday, and I know we will be busier than beavers."

"Oh now, lass, you are a tease...asking me to kiss you and mentioning beavers in the same breath...Be still my heart."

"You are such a romantic, Ian...Nice to know guys aren't all that different no matter where they are from. You just sound so much better sayin' it."

"Come here, lass. I can do better than just say things and sound good."

A quick wave and a dashing smile, and he leaves, taking part of me with him. There is no sound except the deep growl of Bessie in the distance. It has been quite a day. I realize nothing that commenced earlier has really even been digested. We flowed through the day doing what needed to be done. With everyone gone, the quiet of the night takes over and the mind has time to reflect and absorb. I am scared. I wasn't until Peter and Hannah came back for Ely. I think it best to call one of the guys before turning in, probably Steve. They live closest, and Steve already keeps the most watchful eye on us. Plus, they have no kids visiting to worry about interrupting. The person I'd really like to talk with is Louise. She may have a cosmic hit on Ely's home life.

"I have to say, Em, it seems like old times wakin' up with you here. Thank you for staying with me. I did sleep much better without one eye open and both ears alert for trouble."

"No one should have to live like that; I wouldn't have slept for worrying about you anyhow, Mama. Guess we sure are cut out of the same cloth. I suspect today will be busy. Folks will be gettin' geared up for the holiday. You heard from Grandmama?"

"Oh Jesus, Em, can't we have a cup of coffee before going there? She was fit to be tied on Sunday. Don't that seem like eons ago, baby girl?"

"Well, I'll be a blue plucked duck in Chinatown. Will you come see this?"

"Oh, don't tell me something else happened!"

"It has, and he is over yonder at the dock. Do you believe your eyes, Mama?"

"Lord have mercy, the boy is smitten. Are those his dogs with him?"

"Moose and Bear. He calls them his newly adopted sons."

"Well, don't just stand here gazing at him, girl. Fetch a cup of coffee for skirt boy. He does look cute all stretched out on the chaise with those dogs at his side, doesn't he?"

As I'm preparing cinnamon toast and a large mug of coffee and grabbing some dog biscuits, the phone rings. The lilt in Mama's voice suddenly drops off, changing to a serious tone. It must be Grandmama. Perfect timing!

"Ian Duncan MacDougal, did you and the dogs sleep here all night?"

"Morning to you as well, lass. Yes, the lads wanted to go for a boat ride. The three of us figured a campout sounded like fun. We found ourselves parked here and set up camp."

"I brought you some toast and coffee. Okay to give Moose and Bear a biscuit?"

"Do you see them? You cannot possibly think you can bring their favorite snack and not give it to them. Look at those faces. They are begging you for those biscuits, and then they'll want your undivided attention. Oh, this coffee hits the spot."

"Ian, why sleep here all night?"

"I got home and just couldn't stand being across the lake in case something happened. Once you told me of your concern about Peter, well, I had to be near."

"Such a gallant and sweet gesture. I bet your back will think twice before camping out on that old chaise again. What time is your first appointment?"

"Beth is picking me up at nine. I'd best get back with the boys. Time to get ready."

"What a wonderful surprise it was to look down at the lake and see you. Thank you so much for caring and thinking of us, Ian."

"Em, you don't have to thank me. But if you must, perhaps some beautiful woman can think of another way of thanking me—maybe a stolen kiss or two on the lips."

"Not stolen, not earned, believe me, the pleasure is in giving. You have a wonderful day."

"Aye, no doubt after seeing you. Be careful, Emmy. Call if you need anything." Ian's morning kisses taste like honey. They've put a spring in my step. There go my boys, all three of them, Moose and Bear sitting in the back with their muzzles over the edge, and Ian waving good-bye. With a full and grateful heart, I head back to the store.

"Mama, who was on the phone?"

"Never mind that. I saw you kissing Ian."

I'm forty-three years old, and I still blush when caught kissing by anyone, but especially when Mama spies it happening. "Oh please, it was very discreet. Just a have-a-nice-day kiss."

"Ayah, it looked like more like three or four have-a-nice-day kisses. Y'all seeing each other this week?"

"Mama, nothing gets by you, does it? We have a dinner date tomorrow. Don't know where we are going to go. I never even thought with it being the third and all. The summer tourists usually take up most of the reservations. We may not find a place, 'cept the Country Time Bistro. I ain't in the mood for smothered chicken and tater tots. Where you reckon we should go, Mama?"

"Why don't you take a little drive up to Boone or Blowing Rock? There are a lot of inns there with great views and scrumptious food."

"I'll see what Ian is thinking before I make any suggestions to him."

"I bet he already has it all planned out. He seems like that kind of guy to me."

"Five will get you ten."

"You're on, baby girl."

"Now back to the phone, who called?"

"Well, if you must know, it was that dreadful stepfather of Ely's."

"He has a lot of gall calling here. What did he want?"

"Wanted to let me know he still expects to get his damn gun back. Steve is coming over. He said he turned it into the police department early this morning and has a receipt for it. If it was registered in Peter's name, I reckon I'll give him the receipt, and if he has the balls, he can go get it down at the station."

"Mama, I don't want Peter Barbour asking questions about the gun without Steve or somebody else close by. That man, he...well, something ain't right, never has been, but it seems turned up a notch since Ely's trouble. You think he put Ely up to robbing us?"

"Who knows? Maybe the full story will come out someday. Steve sounded as though he'd hang around here off and on today. Mostly to help and to keep an eye on Ely, but if what you say is true about Peter, then I'll ask him to be here more on than off."

After riding his bike right up close to the store, Ely leans it against the steps. He is early and looks very weary. "Mornin', Ely, you certainly are early. I thought we said between nine thirty and ten."

"I didn't rightly know how long it would take me to get here on my bike, so I jess' got up an' left. It be all right to be here early?"

"Ely, did you sleep in those clothes? Come over here, let me look at you. Why in heaven's name are you wearing a long-sleeve T-shirt in the middle of summer?"

Ely's clothes are soiled and torn. His face is plastered with dirt except for lines where tears have streamed.

"Oh, Mama, he can't greet customers like this. He needs a bath and fresh clothes."

"Ely, you gotta go home and take care of yourself, then come back, you understand? I can't have you pumping gas and stocking the store like this."

"Ma Bell, please, I jess' cain't go back home. I ain't allowed there right now, not when I's posed to be here with y'all. Please, I'll go down to the water and try to clean up a mite, okay?"

"No, Ely, that won't do. Tell you what, go in the bathroom and wash at least your hands and face. Have you had breakfast?"

"No, Miss Emileigh, I ain't ate."

"Okay, then after you clean up a mite, you can take breakfast down to the dock and eat. Take this with you too; I want you to start to read some. It's a good book; it'll keep you glued to every word on the page. When you eat and read one chapter, come on back up here, and we'll see what the day brings."

"Yes, Miss Emileigh. Thank you, miss."

Ely scampers down to the dock after washing off a few layers of filth from his face and hands. His entire demeanor changes the moment he is here, giving my CIA-worthy Mama reason to speculate as to what his situation must be.

"Mama, have you ever? He is just filthy, looks like he has been rolling in dirt all night!"

"Well, we know he went home with Hannah and Peter. If he had been missing, Peter would have said something to me on the phone earlier. He never even mentioned Ely, which I found odd, but then he may not be a hands-on dad. I'm gonna call Emily and see if she's going to be at Swags to Witches today."

"Whatever for, Mama?"

"I'm sure we can run over there early and get Ely some clothes to wear. Not much needs to be stocked here this morning. You can handle it if I'm not back in time to open, can't you?"

"Of course I can."

Mama dials Emily's number and gets Grayson, who quickly hands the phone over to Emily. Ely looks comfortable down at the dock sitting at the picnic table reading and taking a bite or two—a far cry from what he was doing this time yesterday.

"Emily, Tah here. You running the store this morning or is one of your helpers?"

"Morning, Tah, actually Dylan and I are headed over there to open for the first few hours. There are a couple of repairs that need to be done; for some reason, my contractor husband never gets around to doing them, so Dylan offered to help. Why? You need something? Everything okay?"

"Everything is fine, no worries. Ely is here, and well, we need a wardrobe fix. Got anything casual for someone his size?"

"Why on earth are *you* buying him clothes? Tah, you've lost your marbles."

"Long story, I'll tell you when we get there. Can you open up early so I can get back here."

"Head on over, I'm sure we can find something around to fit him."

"Thank you, sis. You are a dear. See you in a few."

Mama and Ely head off to Swags to Witches. Once again, I find myself happy to have a moment of solitude. It isn't quite nine, so I decide I'll get a quick call into Ian and wish him happy hunting with his real estate agent. "Hi, Ian, just me. Thought I might catch you before you leave with Beth to walk the property. Remember, watch out for critters! I'll be thinking of you today. Call if you get a moment. Let me know how it's going." Simply hearing his voice mail message is enough to last me awhile.

"Good morning, Tah, how are you? Ely, my goodness, young man, you are in need of some fresh clothes."

"Dylan, I hear you're contractor for a day."

"You work with your daddy, Dylan?"

"No, I'm just here visiting. I work for an investment banker in Charlotte, but I tell you what, I'd rather do this for a living. You're, Ely, right?"

"Yes, sir, I is. Guess everyone thinks I'm a mess."

"Not nearly the mess you were yesterday."

"Yes, sir."

"You boys go outside for a moment; I want to talk to Tah alone. Tah, why didn't you send him back home or call his mother and tell her he is totally inappropriate to work like this, and on his first day, really!"

"Emily, you are awfully hard on Ely."

"Hard on *him*? Are you crazy? He held you up yesterday with a loaded gun, threatened your life and the life of your daughter, and *then* tries to off himself. I think the boy needs a little tough love, and you're showing him a feather not a rod."

"Emily, please, another time. Right now, he needs clothes and for reasons I don't want to discuss with you right now. As for the rest, let's just see what is really going on. I don't think any of us has the full story. We shouldn't jump to conclusions about Ely. It's true we know what he attempted to do and failed, thank the Lord. Now let's build up from there, okay?"

"Tah knows best."

"Oh, Emily, just once without sarcasm. This is trying enough on me without petty snipes. I know you're being protective, but let's put our heads together later and try to piece this together."

"Okay, Tah. One thing though, I can't have him try on clothes as nasty as he is. He'll have to take a shower first. Dylan can take him to the cabana by our pool, and he can use the bathroom in there. In the meantime, we can find something for him."

"Dylan, come here, son. Show Ely the shower in the cabana. Tell him to scrub up good and wash that mess of hair too. Give him this plastic bag for all his clothes, shoes, underwear…all of it, you understand? We'll find some clothes and have you take them to him. Don't forget to show him the soap and where the bathrobes are...and, Dylan, he doesn't have a choice in this."

"Okay, Mom, I'm on it."

Pulling into the parking lot is a car a lot like Peter Barbour's. In all the fuss to get Ely tidied up and fitted with clean clothes, we forgot about Peter. I quickly press Steve on speed dial—one ring, two rings. *Come on, pick up the phone!* The one thing I didn't want was for anyone to be alone here if Peter Barbour drove up, and here I find myself situated exactly to suit my worst fear. Four rings, five...

"Steve, thank God! It's Em."

"What's wrong?"

"Get here fast! Peter Barbour just drove up, and I'm alone."

"I'm there in one minute already on my way."

Peter gets out of his car and is carrying something. My heart pounds wildly. I call Grayson's cell and just leave the phone open by the cash register. Hopefully, he'll hear and come as well. Peter opens the door with commanding authority, storming in loudly and abrasively questioning me. "Where is that mother of yours? And Ely, that damned kid, where's he? Answer me, bitch!"

Trembling and fearful of saying something to antagonize him, I try to emulate Mama's cool presence when confronted by angry customers. "They aren't here, Peter; they've gone to pick up supplies. We aren't open, so please leave."

"Oh, wouldn't that be peachy keen, if I just tucked tail and left?"

"What do you want? Hasn't your family caused enough trouble in the past twenty-four hours? You wanting to add to that, fine, just know the police are on the way and so are my reinforcements."

"Ain't you a tough, girl? You've been watching too many cop shows, callin' for reinforcements, my ass. I just want my nine-millimeter pistol back, nothin' more. But if that ain't happening, I figure you owe me—oh, say, about five hundred bucks to start and you're such a pretty thing, we'll go from there. Move, girl! Get it now!"

A loud ruckus in the parking lot tells me Steve has arrived. In through the door come my knights in shining armor, Steve and Cook. "Morning, Em.

Peter, what's going on? Peter, the store isn't open, especially to guys yielding baseball bats."

"Since my gun was stolen by Tahlulah Suggs, it's the only thing left that'll pack a punch."

"No more guns, that's good to hear. Your weapon, if it was yours, was stolen by your stepson and then recovered in an armed robbery and suicide attempt by my mother, Mr. Barbour."

"She still has it, and I want it."

"You're mistaken, Peter. The police have the gun. Cook and I took it down there this morning, explained to them Mrs. Suggs isn't pressing charges, but wants the gun in their hands. If you wish to go down and collect the weapon, here's the receipt. Feel free to try."

Grayson's car pulls up; he is in the store within five seconds, huffing and puffing and ringing wet, fear in his words. He heard every word Peter spoke. "Em, you okay?"

"Yes, Grayson, I guess."

"I called the police; they're on their way."

"Damn you, Grayson Dupree. None of you have seen the last of me. You wait and see."

"Threats aren't the wisest choice for you to be using right now, Peter. You'd best pipe down and realize we are all trying our damnedest to give you a break."

"You don't like my threats, Grayson; well, try this on for size!"

Peter Barbour storms out of the store violently swinging the bat, breaking the plate-glass window into millions of itty-bitty pieces just as the police pull in and witness his temper tantrum.

"Emileigh! Emileigh!...Steve, Grayson, give me a hand; she's down. Take her into the apartment. I wondered how much more she could take before something happened. Steve, can you grab a cold face cloth for her? That's my girl. She is coming around now."

"Welcome back, Em. Drink some water; take it easy. Cook is on the phone with Louise; she's on the way. We didn't call Tah, but Grayson is calling Emily to try and speed them up to get back here."

"No, no, please stop, Grayson. Y'all are here. I'm okay; it was the window breaking, I heard it shatter, and I guess thought one of y'all was hurt."

"You sure, Sugar? I've got Emily on the phone right now—"

"Please, Grayson, we can tell Mama when she gets back. Right now, we have to do something about the window. And the store, oh my, it's a mess! Glass is everywhere."

"Well, missy, just so happens I know a contractor. I'll make a couple of calls and take some measurements, and we'll have you right as rain by sundown, at least with something temporary."

"Oh you're a lifesaver. Where is that horrible Peter Barbour?"

Grayson stands in front of the store his shoes crackling on shards of glass. The huge plate-glass window left jagged broken pieces hurled throughout the store, large bits still clinging to the window frame. He looks down to the gas pumps watching the police talk to Peter.

"He's right where he ought to be, with the cops. I wonder if he is asking them for his gun back. You think he's that dumb? Rest easy. The guys and I have some cleaning up to do before Tah gets back and has a store to run. Em, you are under strict orders to take an hour of chill time; here's your phone. You want something to eat or read?"

"I'd love a cup of tea and some toast. I have a good book right here, but I don't think I can read right now."

Grayson turns from me for a second to face the kitchen where Cook is looking for boxes to hold the pieces of broken glass. "Cook, the lady would like a spot of tea and toast. Em, your book may be the exact escape your mind needs right now, since skirt boy isn't here."

A cheery Cook responds to Grayson's request. "I'm on it, my lord; the lady shall be served in the single beat of a heart."

"Good grief, y'all have the worst British accents I've ever heard."

"Me thinketh the lady doth protest too much, my lord, but oh look, a hint of a smile hath returned to the lips of the fairy princess."

"And now you sound like drunken leprechauns. You guys should brush up your foreign accents if you plan to use them."

"Grayson, you see what happens, don't you? Our fair maiden swaps spit a few times with skirt boy who dwells from across the big pond and suddenly she becomes a linguistic critic."

"What is it he says, oh yeah, 'aye,' she is getting big for her britches."

"All right, y'all. Now you're getting too personal, talkin' 'bout the size of my britches. Go get busy. I'll be out in a few."

Steve walks down to where the police are still talking to Peter. I'm certain he wants to give our account of what transpired. In the midst of the chaos, Louise plows through the parking lot, quickly scooting past the police and into the store. "Cook, where is she? My Lord in heaven what is happening here?"

"Weasy, settle down a bit. Things are tense enough for Em. She's fine now; we have her resting in the bedroom for a while. We'll sort through the glass and get things cleaned up. I'm sure she would love to see you, honey."

Another car pulls into the parking lot, and Leigh comes up to the door, taking the steps two at a time. "Tah, Tah Bell, you here? Cook, Grayson, where is Tah and Emileigh?"

"Morning, Leigh, Em is in the bedroom with Louise. Tah is over at Emily's."

"Leigh, we're in here. Come on in…How did you know, Leigh?"

"There is a police scanner at the paper. I heard the call to respond to Suggs General Store and shot like a bat outta hell to get here. Emileigh, are you hurt? Did that bastard touch you?"

"Oh, Auntie Leigh, no nothing happened. He broke the window, and I passed out, no big deal."

"What is it with you Suggs? It is a big deal. I should get Tah back here pronto!"

"No, let's just let them deal with what they are doing and then face the music."

"Em, it will be music of a different kind. She'd want to know. We owe her that."

"We owe her peace of mind too. Wait for the police leave, and then we'll call."

"Emileigh, you and I need to have a talk about these episodes of yours after we get back from Wilmington."

"Good luck getting her to go there now. If she goes, I'm going to New York with Ian after y'all come home."

"Good grief, did the earth suddenly start to revolve faster or what? Things certainly have picked up pace around here!"

"Mama needs to go to Wilmington. We'll work it out so there are plenty of folks around, and the security system will be in next week. I hope and pray the police keep that wretched Barbour down at the precinct. Wouldn't that solve a lot of worry here?"

"Will y'all give the guys a hand? I really don't want Mama to see the store with shards of glass all over the place."

Louise and Leigh reluctantly leave my side and start sweeping up the store. All the shelves within ten feet of the broken window have to be emptied and cleaned. One of the police officers comes into the store and asks me for a statement. Not knowing if any charges will be filed against Peter Barbour as a result of my statement, I'm uncertain if it's wise to speak with the officer.

"Can I come down to the station later and tell you what happened, Tommy?"

"We find it easier for people to make a statement at the time of the event, while their memory is sharp, aware of small details they may later forget."

"Will he be kept in jail or just fined or something?"

"It isn't up to me. I'm just here to get the facts so justice can be served to you and your family. Emileigh, you know me, maybe not personally, but please trust me, having me take down in writing what happened is in your best interest. You may not see him do any time, but it may make him pay back for the window or set the basis for a restraining order. Besides Chief Hobbs will tan my hide if I don't get somethin' written down in print from you." Tommy's words give me the impression he is looking out more for his best interest than mine.

"Well, we certainly can't have that happen. All right, since Steve already told you what he knows, I will too. But this has nothing to do with yesterday, does it?"

"I'm fully aware of what happened yesterday morning concerning Mr. Barbour's stepson; it may have to come out if a judge gets involved, but still, since Mrs. Suggs and you have declined to file charges against the minor, we have no recourse; he'll be fine."

One of the most uncomfortable of situations is to recall every frightening or painful detail. I find giving the officer my statement very troublesome—not only to me personally, but because it has cause and effect on Peter's life, Hannah's life, and poor Ely's life. Still knowing what I am doing may in fact protect Mama and myself from future harm, or perhaps one of our dear friends or customers, I realize my emotions have to be set aside and proceed according to what the law requests. Tommy witnesses my signature on the written statement.

"Ely, how do those clothes fit you?"

"Oh, Ma Bell, do you have anything with long sleeves? I ain't fond of short sleeves."

"Nonsense, it's hotter than Hades, and you want long sleeves? No, son, not today. Come on out here and let me see how you look. It's just you and I. No one else in the cabana, you shy thing."

"Yes, um, but I ain't wantin' to. You understand, Ma Bell?"

"An arm is an arm. My old arms are all freckled and wobbly, kind of comical to look at really, but I still flaunt them in public."

"Oh, Ely, look at you all cleaned up and with combed hair! Why, land's sake, you are a good-lookin' young man. Now, what is so...Oh you poor child, what? Who?...Emily! *Emily...*"

"Mom is in the store, Miss Tah. Shall I get her for you?"

"Dylan, don't come in here. Get me a first-aid kit, and yes, get your mom."

Dylan grabs the poolside first-aid kit for Tah and rushes into the store for his mother. "What in tarnation is it, Tah? I've got customers. Dylan is not exactly versed in all my wares. Why the big tears?"

"Oh my Lord! Ely, how did this happen? You must tell us, son. We just want to help."

"Iffin I tells y'all, my mama...he'll hurt Mama again, and I cain't let that happen, Ma Bell. My mama is scared to death of him."

"Him who? Your stepfather? Is he the one who did this? Are these cigarette burns, Ely? Looks as though you have rope burns on your wrists."

"Yes'm, last night he got real mad at me, said I did wrong, said I deserved to be punished. He took me outside, you know, away from Mama. He pulled off his belt, and well, y'all guessed it fer sure."

"Yes, you did make mistakes, but no one has the right to punish you like this. Did he hurt Hannah?"

"I don't rightly know; he done strung me up in the pottin' shed till daybreak. When he untied me, I jess got on my bike and rode to the store."

"Okay, let me put some ointment on these burns and on your wrists. Emily, do you have a long-sleeve T-shirt so he can cover these and not be ashamed?"

"I'll get him one of Grayson's. It'll be way too big, but won't pull on his wounds."

"Do you know where your stepfather is right now, Ely?"

"No, sure don't. Don't want to neither."

"What about your mama? Is she at work?"

"She lost her job about a month ago, Ma Bell. She's most probably home."

"All right then. Let's just get you back to the store and figure out what we should do in everyone's best interest, mostly yours."

I never thought the store would clean up so quickly. The police cruiser finally drove out of the parking lot, which is good for many reasons, not the least of which is business. The police ended up taking Peter with them and impounding his car for reasons that weren't disclosed. Grayson summoned a few of his guys to come and measure, placing a screen where the window was. A screen may actually be a nice relief to some of the relentless heat we've been having. The guys worked furiously fast. Grayson has several options in mind for a new window and is checking prices along with availability. Cheapest and quickest is my motto. There are three messages from Ian on the phone. My heart leaps in anticipation to hear his deep, sexy voice.

"Hi, Emmy, I got your message; I just wanted you to know Beth and I are watching out for critters, minding the snakes and really enjoying walking this lovely bit of land. It truly is special, and I plan to make an offer on it. You must be busy, so I'll try back next time we have a signal."

"Hello again, dear one. Sorry I've missed you once more."

"Well now, lass, seems you are avoiding me." His voice is filled with laughter and cheer. "You said something about being busy and beavers last night, so you must be tangled up with one thing or another. Wish I was available, but just firmed up dinner plans with a developer. Give me a ring when you are free." Pressing the phone close to my chest, I pray he is near when I call back. I don't want to mention the morning. Gads, what will he think, two days in a row something dramatic happening! When and if Leigh writes about this in the village paper, all the townspeople will be flappin' their jaws a mile a minute. Leigh will most likely listen to our requests to keep the story under the rug.

"Hi, Ian, thank goodness! No more telephone tag. How is it going?"

"Oh, lass, it goes much better since I hear your voice. Beth is pulling up comps on the land I'll be placing an offer on. I cannot wait to show it to you…if you're not afraid of critters grazing on you."

"No, Ian, after my morning, I think it would be almost a relief."

"What's going on? Busy?"

"A little more than business. Peter Barbour came here while Mama and Ely were gone. He ended up breaking the plate-glass window and then walked right into the arms of the police."

"Are you all right? Do you want me to come over?"

"I already have too much help, if you get my drift. I'm down at the dock taking a break, enjoying hearing your voice."

"Oh, my sweet lass, if you are certain you don't need me now, how about I swing by with the lads later, and we'll go for a boat ride. Say about eight? I have an early dinner, and this guy wants to cut it short."

"How nice it is to have something at the end of the day to look forward to? See you later."

"Call me if you need anything. Business is one thing; you're quite another."

Ian's attachment is overwhelming. I'm thoroughly enjoying the attention, but at the same time, it's early days. Our relationship seems to be flying at warp speed.

Louise walks out of the store with two large glasses of lemonade. Each step she takes is precise and observational. With all the spirits sensing her openness, she must feel besieged by otherworldly encounters. "Thanks, Louise. That will taste mighty good! I just got off the phone with Ian."

"Did you tell him about this morning?"

"Just the short version. He is quite busy today but is coming over with his dogs for a boat ride later."

"Skirt boy is a good thing for you! I just spoke with your mama. They are on their way back. Ely has burns on his arms from his stepfather. That son of a bitch tied him up and left him in the potting shed all night. Tah is beside herself."

"No wonder Ely was a mess this morning. Did you tell Mama what happened here?"

"'Bout like you did with Ian, the bare essentials so she doesn't freak when she drives up. She'll see the window missing, but isn't the difference amazing from just an hour ago? Grayson sure has some good guys working for him!"

"I think most of the work was done by y'all; glass was everywhere."

"And then there is you, Em. What am I gonna do with you?"

"You gonna work on me, Louise? Your third eye spazzing out again?"

"Well, my dear, since you asked and you know better than to ask a crazy lady like me what she sees. Hell, I could tell you there is a marching band behind you practicing the 'Star-Spangled Banner' for Thursday's parade, and you'd believe they're there in some realm doin' just that. I'm growing concerned about these spells you pass off as nothing. You been to see anyone or just dealing with it by the Suggs pick-yourself-up-by-the-bootstrap-and-march-on kind of way?"

"Some of both, but really, they will pass. I suspect loss has taken a greater toll on me emotionally, and now is effecting me physically."

"Usually, if something tackles you physically, there is an emotional or spiritual component as well. Do you want my take on this, plain and simple, no frills?"

"I guess I'd better hear it."

"It ain't rocket science, sweetie. We are spiritual beings first; in fact, the majority of who we are is a spiritual being. Spirit is energy—some say light. You have a lot of energy to disperse as you wish. All of us do. We shoot it or beam it into each thought, good or bad, about everyone next to us or in thought, everything past, present, and future...Beams are shooting out of us all the time. Are you following me, Em?"

"Yep. Like you said, it ain't rocket science."

"You also have a vessel harboring your spirit, and it requires a certain amount of energy to run properly. We all tend to shoot off more energy than is healthful for us to sustain a healthy body. There are vampires out there feeding on our energy. You know, those who take and never give. Extending yourself for the higher good makes God smile. If God is smiling, you are gonna get it back tenfold, I promise. But this is where telling you something is difficult, because I love you. The past and its ghosts take energy, and as much as they'd like to give back, they can't. Those who have gone before still love us and we them. We must focus on sweet memories, not on the regrets or guilty feelings. Em, you have to choose love and life. Live in this moment, not yesterday, last year, twenty years ago, or ahead. Ian will help a lot. I can see how his vitality and care gives you energy. He exudes light. Your next question to me, I can already hear...Yes, give him your heart, Em. I know you can't give all of it to him yet; some will always be with Josh...but he is one lucky man to have my Em. I see good things for you both. Don't hold back. We all deserve love, and you, my dear, are our treasure. Love will make you strong again."

"Ian...well, I'm a bit leery to give him any more of my heart. Everything is moving so fast with all the recent calamities at the store; I honestly want to take a step back. Knowing he is only here for a short time, I find myself wanting to spend every moment possible at his side but also wanting to protect my heart."

"A protected heart is not a full heart."

"Well, hells bells! If that ain't perfect timing! Look who pulled into the store!"

Honestly, none of us present knew what to say between Peter Barbour's escapade and Ely's tortured arms. Some may perceive mayhem walked through our door yesterday and has stayed for twenty-four hours. I choose to think of it as being chosen. Sometimes you think, *God, this has been a horrible day!* because another person's trials are placed at your feet, but oddly, I look at it as a gift. God must love me and trust me to help deal with whoever's dilemma. With every trial comes victory and much greater joy than ever could be anticipated. Ian is the polar opposite to any burden placed on our doorstep. Friends who love and cherish us help us deal with the ups and downs of life. We can face a lot and come up smiling. Life is a mixed blessing. Lots of people use that saying, but few really know the repercussions of dealing with both at once.

"Mama, how is Ely doing?"

"I think he finds relief in having someone know pieces of what's goin' on. You and I need to talk, Em; we need a united front in dealing with the next step."

"Man, everybody wants to talk today. I ain't too sure what you have in that noggin of yours. You like the screen Grayson and his guys put up?"

"Tah, it can be changed. I could put plywood up, but it would darken and heat up the store, probably draw a lot more attention from passersby."

"No, Grayson, it's fine. You should go home. Your kids are there, and I know how much you value your time with them."

"I'm not going until I know you are well. Besides, I have a couple of calls to make, and I can place them as well here as home."

"Cook, you still here too? Louise, you too? Oh now, come, y'all, go home. You have kids and grandkids waiting on you, I'm sure."

"No can do, Tah. We are having lunch, all of us, down at the dock. I'm in the midst of creating gourmet hot dogs, slaw, and chips. How's that sound, Ely?"

"Oh, Mr. Tromble, sounds mighty fine, mighty fine."

Mama asks me to go back into the apartment for a quick chat. She calls Hannah to make certain she is unharmed and to tell her she doesn't want Ely to go back there tonight. Hannah is shy to relinquish Ely for the night, but after some old-fashioned persuasion, she caves. Mama suspects she was beaten last night, but until someone sees her, it makes our next step vague and uncertain. "Where should Ely stay?"

"He can stay here, but I'd rather he didn't, since we don't know if Peter is going to be held in jail or released. I don't want him coming here and being able to get his hands on Ely."

"Hannah, how did she sound?"

"At wits' end, grateful Ely is out of harm's way. Something is definitely going on in that house, but it isn't our responsibility to find out what. Somehow, we've got to get the authorities involved."

Leigh sticks her head in the door and asks if she can come in to join our conversation. She's dressed comfortably in shorts and an embroidered T-shirt reading "Our Write to Read" one of the *Gazette's* promotional flops.

"Grayson is gonna come in after his call. I'm gonna ride over to Hannah Stiles's house, just to check on her. Hebron says Chief Hobbs is going to hold Peter overnight, until they have more time to investigate his story. They also tell me unless y'all file charges or Hannah does, they'll have to release him in the morning. Anyhow, there will be time to visit with Hannah for a chat. If she is being abused, as we all suspect, it's the perfect night for her to go to a halfway house. That's a big if, but one worth trying, don't you agree?"

"Oh, Leigh, yes, and who better to speak with her than you. She'll give an ear if not both to you, I'm sure."

"Don't know if that's the case, but we can all put our best foot forward here to resolve this drama quickly and with a positive outcome."

"Come on in, Grayson. We're just talking about Hannah and Ely."

"Long day so far, eh? And we haven't had lunch! Ladies, I know this is going to take you by surprise, but I'd like Ely to stay with Emily and our family tonight."

"Grayson, you have your kids at home with you. Emily won't go for this."

"Well, he and Dylan seem to have a developed a mutual respect for one another."

"There must be more, Gray—"

He interrupts Mama before she can inquire more. "Of course, there is, about a month ago, Ely asked me for a job, and I, well, I wasn't very kind to the kid. He looked a mess, spoke poorly…even a gopher has to have some intestinal fortitude, which I didn't see in him. Now I find out his mom was fired at that time, there's no money, and both are being abused by his stepfather, who probably drove him to get money. I'm betting he wanted to protect his Mom. Long story short, I feel guilty. The boy needs some positive male influence. Look at the difference in him in just a day. He is a good kid. I want to do this for him, just one night, and then we'll see. Emily isn't all kittens and puppies by the idea, but she also saw him today and knows he is basically a lost young man…If we leave it up to the system, who knows who he will turn out to be in a year? Sound like a short-term plan to y'all?"

"Saints be praised, Grayson! You're a quick answer to a prayer. Yes, a thousand times, yes. I'm betting Ely will love your pool. I saw him eyeballin' it this morning. You going to ask him, or shall I? He is still working here till about three, but we can work around that seeing's how he isn't going home."

"Let's have lunch, and bring it up together. I think if he knows his mom will be fine tonight, he'll have a peaceful night. It may give Hannah a chance to make some plans for the two of them. I think Ely will be dancing a jig if it all comes about."

After finishing lunch, the Suggettes return home. The store, which is full of customers, feels more like it should. Most of the angst is gone merely with the knowledge that Peter Barbour is behind bars and unable to harm or threaten anyone. It gives a lift to the atmosphere. Even Ely is happy helping customers—or at least trying.

"Ely, one last thing for today and then Grayson will be picking you up, okay?"

"Yes, Miss Emileigh, what you be needin' me to do?"

"If you'd please do us a favor, when someone comes to the gas pump, and let's say they are older or have a bunch of youngins in the backseat, offer to pump the gas for them so they don't have to get out of their car. Also ask them if they need anything from the store. Tell them you'd be happy to get it for them. You understand?"

"Yes, miss, anything else?"

"Take their payment inside for them, and if they're paying with cash, of course, give them the change, if credit, let them sign. Now here is the good part. If they offer you a tip, kindly accept; that's yours for being a good servant."

"To keep? Just mine for helpin'?"

"Yes, Ely, but now, if you are stocking the store early in the morning, don't break your neck to run out and help someone. Stocking comes first, got it?"

His smile bursts forth with excitement. "Got it, Miss Emileigh. Do you mind if I takes the book you gave me to read over to Grayson's tonight? I'll bring it back, promise."

"Ely, be my guest. I guess you like it, eh?"

"Yes, miss. Never knowed a book could be so thrilling; just thought movies was like that."

"You have a huge new world at your fingertips—huge. Off with you, grab yourself a drink while you wait on Grayson. You did very well today."

"Thank you, Miss Emileigh. Good night, Ma Bell!"

"Good night, son! See you in the morning. Sleep well."

The day seems like it has lasted forever, and yet in some ways, it has gone by in the blink of an eye. Mama and I decide to have a light salad for dinner and copious amounts of wine. Closing the store at five is earlier than usual during a holiday week, but the locals understand. If there is something someone needs, they all know to head down to the dock. We are right here to get it for them.

Promptly at eight o'clock, there is a familiar rumble in the distance. I see Bear and Moose sitting proudly in the back, Ian stoically at the helm heading at a fast pace toward our shore.

"Mama, Ian is almost here. You gonna be all right by yourself for a few hours?"

"Who says I'll be by myself, young lady? You know summer nights always bring company. Steve and Leigh are headed over to set a spell on the dock."

"Mama, leave the binoculars up here, please."

"I make no promises, baby girl. You just have fun; we'll probably see you later if not sooner." She snickers gleefully at the prospect of spying. I suspect by Mama's last statement the binoculars will be in full working order and glued to her eyeballs with her trying to catch a glimpse of something noteworthy.

"Ian, what a sight for sore eyes you are! Hi, boys! Enjoy your ride over?"

"Good evening, lass. I have a few goodies here for you and a nice white wine. Hop in. The lads and I are ready to escort you on the evening's journey."

"A journey on this little lake? Y'all been in cahoots, haven't you? Where are you guys taking me?"

My fingertips scratch Moose's brown head, and his tail begins to wag in a circular motion, like the blade on a helicopter. Bear comes over and nudges me to pet him, practically spilling my wine.

"We are searching to find peace at the end of your day. How does that sound?"

Shooing the dogs off, Ian puts his arm around me and gives me a swift kiss to the cheek.

"It was a quick journey. I've found peace right here next to you."

"It has taken years for us to find one another and miles of life to live through. Do you even want to talk about your day? I know bits and pieces. Cook and Grayson called me a while back."

"You know, since they've filled you in, I'd rather just sit and enjoy you guys, the view, and the wind in my face. Are you getting along well with Cook and Grayson?"

"Ya, we play well together—Steve too, all good men."

As we cross over to the northern end of the lake and back down to a small cove with no cabins or homes, Bessie slows down. Moose and Bear bark with excitement. Not much conversation unfolds except a few insights concerning his real estate searches. Ian anchors the boat offshore. The quiet is rejuvenating. Ian must know I need solitude. "Okay, lads, off with you! Into the water like good boys! You too, Emmy! Time to kick up your heels and splash away."

"Um, Ian, I didn't wear a suit, nor did I bring one."

"So, lass, you are in a bit of a conundrum, eh? Sorry, but only swimmers get a ride home—your choice."

"Ian Duncan MacDougal, you wouldn't!"

"Hummmm, try me, lass."

"Just so we are clear on this...if I don't swim, we don't go home?"

"No, you're off a wee bit...you don't get a ride home. My lads, they do. They are in the lake; I'm about to go in—with the boat key, I might add..."

"No, no, no, I get it. I'm already in the boat, Mister Smartypants, and if I stay put, then of course I'll get a ride home."

"No, look at them. The lads don't agree. The three of us can and will make you walk the plank."

"Then I'd be swimming."

"Then you'd get a ride home, so maybe in a roundabout way, you're right, you will get a ride home...just with wet clothes, or you could make another choice and have dry clothes. Would you like me to wait for your answer?"

"No, but I'll make you a deal."

"Oh, this ought to be rich...make away."

"I can't believe I am saying this...I'll skinny-dip if you do, and Lord help us if there are binoculars fixated in this direction."

"So, we are in an 'I'll show you mine if you show me yours' dilemma? Who goes first?"

"Are you agreeing, Ian?"

"Oh, lass, yes, of course. What red-blooded Scot wouldn't?"

"Okay, then here is the plan..."

"Really, a plan to skinny-dip?...Oh for the love of..."

Ian rips off his shirt revealing a toned and muscular chest, kicks his sandals off, and slowly, while staring at me, takes off his trunks. He throws them at my feet, steps onto the ski deck, and lifts his arms to the heavens, which thankfully were twinkling with stars and no moon, and dives into the lake smack dab between Bear and Moose. "Next...into the loch, oh, lass, come here! Be with me!"

"I'm with you. The tan line you've got is the difference between night and day."

"Aha, so you noticed! I do rather glow below the tan line."

"I took lengthy note and very much like what I see."

chapter 9

"ELY, YOU GOT a minute?"

"Sure, Grayson, what be on your mind? Did I do something?"

"No, son, I just want to tell you Leigh Riley went over to see your Mama earlier today. She tried to talk her into leaving your stepfather or pressing charges against him."

"Really? Did Mama get mad at her? She must know I jawed off about him. Bet she didn't care much for Misriz Riley bringin' it up."

"She isn't mad, Ely; fact is, it appeared to Leigh your Mama had some fresh bruises on her face. She's okay, just outta sorts, ya know?"

"You sure, Grayson? Maybe I'd best get back to her."

"No, not yet, Ely. She is too afraid to rock the boat and press charges against Peter. You need to muster up strength of mind to resolve the situation. This maybe the most important decision you will make for some time."

"Me, I doesn't know much, Grayson. Makin' decisions…I'd be afraid to do the wrong thing."

"Son, fear is no reason to stand still and do nothing. Doing nothing is giving someone else power. Is your stepfather the one you want making decisions for you and your mother?"

"No, sir, I reckon he be crazy."

"Okay then, are you man enough to take control and press charges against him for hurting you?"

"Well, I…dunno. What will happen to Mama and me?"

"I can't be certain, but what happens if you do nothing? I promise you, all of us will do our best to make sure y'all are taken care of, somehow, somewhere. Do you trust me on that, Ely?"

"The last couple of days has showed me y'all ain't like any other people I ever seen or knowed or even dreamed about—you know, like too-good-to-be-real people. Y'all make me feel like I matter. Mama, she tries, but with my stepfather, she done changed."

"You do matter; allow me to take you to the police or to child protective services to file a statement saying what he's done to you. They may want to have a doctor take a look at you, which is a good thing, but I'll be there if you want me."

"Right now?"

"Yes, Ely, it needs to be done soon, so we can keep him in jail if possible to protect you and your mother."

"Oh, Grayson, I..." Dylan walks over to his father and taps him on the shoulder while looking at Ely. "Dad, sorry, but I overheard. Can I go with you?"

"That's up to Ely."

"Hey, Dylan, you thinks I should be doin' this?"

"Sure do, and since I saw you this morning, I'll attest to it as well."

"Well, all right then, let's get it over with. Do I gots to tell them everything?"

"The more you tell them, the better the decision they can make regarding your stepfather. Tell them as much as you can and be very honest."

"It is kinda late. Can we do this tomorrow?"

"I know it's late, but if we don't do it tonight, he'll be out tomorrow."

"I guess we'd best go."

Heavy gray clouds are rolling in, promising rain. These parts need some; it's been a long stretch of dry weather. Tonight has been full of promises and surprises. "Lads, in ya come. No one had to walk the plank after all." A serendipitous look grows across his stunningly handsome face. "Time to leave for home, storms a-brewing."

"Whose home, Ian? You are taking me back, right?"

"Oh, lass, if I must. 'Tis nice you have dry clothes to wear for the ride, eh?"

"You played a game of dirty pool, Mr. MacDougal."

"Maybe, but you didn't seem to mind once in the water; fact is, I think you enjoyed yourself, didn't you, just a tad?"

"I plead the Fifth."

"Lass, you're in a boat flyin' the saltires, the flag of Scotland; Fifths can't be pled. Come on now, tell me the truth, you did enjoy yourself?"

I stand up, weaving as the boat rolls. My hands planted firmly on my hips and lips pursed, I say, "I just don't want to spur you on, Ian; you have a side to you, a rather obnoxious side, I want to keep at bay."

"Oh you say obnoxious, but I heard the hesitation in your voice and see the twinkle in your eye. I think you meant to say playful side…and you, Emmy, have forgotten how to play."

"Hummm, we shall see, skirt boy; we shall see."

Ian is right, but I can't allow him to know. He's cocky enough without flaunting his correct assumptions in his face. I did have fun, more than I am even able to express and am a bit afraid to try to. I'm not certain why I feel guilty enjoying myself, even if skinny-dipping isn't my usual form of entertainment. It certainly let me see Ian's form, sending wild, uninhibited stirrings to burn within, which until very recently, have been hibernating. He's a very unusual man. Ian fills my heart with promise and allows dreams to enter my soul. I thought dreams were a thing of the past. There sits Mama, binoculars in one hand, wine in the other. Steve and Leigh are flanking her with equal amounts of libations gripped in their palms. Bear and Moose jump onto the dock, greeting everyone with sloppy Labrador kisses.

"Y'all seem to have passed the lab test. Havin' fun tonight?"

"Seems we have a nice breeze to enjoy before the storm comes through. Don't y'all like the energy a storm kicks up?"

"Evening, everyone. Mind if I join you for a wee spell?"

"We'd love to have your company. Join us in a glass of wine?"

"Oh no, Tah. How about a scotch with me, Ian?"

"Ah, yes, usquebaugh, the water of life. Impossible for me to turn down scotch. My visa would instantly be revoked. Pour a double if ya don't mind, Steve."

"And what have the likes of y'all been up to?"

"Oh, just a little of this and that—nothing really."

"Actually, we've been in the water, as you can see by the lads."

"Oh, all y'all have?"

I want to die. My cheeks must be crimson. Ian has no sense of humility; he just blurts it out, proud as a peacock. I know he is trying to get me to loosen up, but with Mama? Oh how she must be enjoying herself. She can be coy and usually is just to infuriate me or weasel more information out of whomever she is passively interrogating.

"Yes, we went skinny-dipping; are you happy now?"

If I had only thought one minute before blurting it out! Ian hadn't said we went skinny-dipping, and no one knew I didn't have a suit along. I fell into my own mother's trap. "I can speak for all of us, Em; *yes,* we are happy now. Would you like to divulge any other state secrets while you're at it?"

Ian glugs down his scotch. "Leigh, oh, Mama...oh good grief."

"Aye, lass, you've got me blushing now. How about another scotch, Steve?"

"Yes, I think another is in order after Em's revelation. Well done, Ian. Evidently, Emmy is drawn to men wearing skirts." A boyish grin spreads across his face, as if he's found the map to the Holy Grail.

"Baby girl, you went skinny-dippin'? Oh how fun. I ain't done that in eons with a man. I don't rightly think Leigh, Emily, and Louise count as a thrill to skinny-dip with, but a man, 'specially one the likes of Ian—now, that's a titillating thought."

"Mama, you with a man?"

"Course, contrary to popular opinion, I'm not a prude, and it's one of the privileges of livin' lakeside. Don't look all astounded. It's natural; suits are unnatural."

"Mama, then by your analogy, clothes are as well."

"I like the tone of the conversation, don't you, Ian?"

"Aye, I may be dating the wrong Suggs!"

"*Dating*, you think we're dating?"

"Emmy, what would you call it?"

"Well, I hadn't thought...Tomorrow, I thought that was our first date."

"Okay, lass, we can consider it our first, if you like, but given the last couple of days, beware tomorrow."

"What have you got up your sleeve? Where y'all going for dinner?"

"I have a lot up my sleeve, Tah, but like any good magician, I know the magic cannot be revealed until it's time. I have a plan, but I also need some help. Think you can spare Ely in the morning for a few hours? I'll pay him for the hours he's with me."

"Can you pick him up and bring him back?"

"Absolutely."

"Okay then, but know this, he will be drilled with a batch of inquiries upon his return."

"Thank you, Tah, and if you didn't interrogate him, I would be disappointed in both of you. I don't think the lad will crack, even with the likes of both Suggs cross-examining."

"This sounds interesting. You need more help?"

"Hummm, Cook is already joining me, but if you'd like to add some muscle Steve, come along."

"What about Grayson?"

"He has store duty, tomorrow morning."

"Y'all pardon me, speaking of Grayson; Emily is calling."

"Okay, Leigh, what is this about store duty?"

"Tah, we aren't leaving you and Em alone till we know where Peter Barbour is going to be tomorrow."

"Oh, what welcomed news! Mama and I are truly blessed."

"The dreadful events have given everyone pause for thanks. Those special people in our life, who touch our inner being, we must all take care of one another every day in every way."

"Amen, brother Steve. You may want to slow down a bit on the scotch; you're growing too sentimental." "Emily said Dylan and Grayson are down at the police station. Ely is filing a complaint against Peter Barbour. What a courageous young man!"

"I find it hard to believe he is actually going through with it."

"Time has come for me to go across the lake. If I had known I was going to be over here all the time, I would have rather had a home nearby. Off with us lads, into Bessie."

"Not yet, Ian, we have to toast Ely's decision."

"Here is to happy new beginnings, strength, and faith to guide him and to Ely's first step toward being a man."

"To Ely!"

"Here, here! The lad has promise. I really must be going...Emmy."

"What time tomorrow, Ian?"

"How is six thirty?"

"Perfect."

Ian takes my hand and guides me to Bessie. He stands just looking back at the store. Moose and Bear are whining, ready to leave and have dinner. "You should sleep well tonight, Emmy. I'll see you in the morning when I pick up Ely. Good night. Sweet dreams." He kisses me like he wants the world to know. With one step, he's at the helm. Bessie roars to life. Leigh, Steve, and Mama wave and holler their good-byes. I wave, sad to see Ian head the boat toward the opposite shore and disappear into the darkness.

"Morning, Ely, Grayson. Can I get y'all anything?"

"Got any coffee left?"

"Sure. What about you, Ely? Need something to drink or eat?"

"Naw, Miss. I's good. Misriz Dupree stuffed me up to my gizzards this morning."

"How did it go at the police station, Ely?"

"Mornin', Ma Bell. It went fine. They said we'd be hearin' from them soon. I reckon my stepfather is in trouble worser than he'd a thought."

"Is that true, Grayson? Have they charged him?"

"I haven't heard yet; they are going to hold him until the district attorney studies the pending charges, and that's an ever-growing list. Some prescription drugs were found in his car, which didn't belong to him. The gun he was so hell bent on getting back was stolen three years ago and used in a previous armed robbery. Ely should probably tell you the rest; it was eye-opening to me. He really opened up. I'm proud of him. Enlighten Tah and Emileigh."

"I done lied to y'all, for Mama's sake, ya know. My stepdad, he's who gave me some kinda drug. He made me take it; I didn't want to. He had to force it in me. I didn't go to no party. Never have been to no party. That drug, it weren't to get high off of. It was a bar...a barbit-somethin' or other. Anyhow, it made me sleepy and not thinkin' right. He done gave it to me late Sunday night. That be what the police found in his car. Then the next mornin', he told me to take his gun and come down here to y'all's store and get money or else Mama was gonna be hurt real bad. I didn't want to, honest. Said he'd seen how busy you were Sunday and had been watching the store."

"Oh that gives me the creeps. Go on, Ely."

"Well, y'all know what happened. I thought when you didn't give me money, he'd probably kill Mama. I didn't rightly know but what he'd kill me."

"When you pulled the trigger, you really meant to kill yourself?"

"Yes'm. I guess I couldn't live knowin' Mama got hurt or dead 'cuz of me, and I couldn't face goin' back. After y'all sent me home, he strung me up...You know the rest. The police said it was a good thing you took me to the doctor. That there drug should show up. The police said it gave them a good time line and validity to my story."

Ely's detail of that night brings chills to us. If Mama had responded hotheaded, who knows if Hannah or Ely would be here? Realizing Ely did indeed try to kill himself, fearing his actions would probably cause harm to his mother, made me sad. Oddly, there is a misguided sweetness to it as well. Ian is right; Ely shows promise.

"Ladies, looks like you have my undivided attention for a while, at least until we know if Peter Barbour will be released from jail. I've got some calls to make, so I'll go on down to the dock. Surely is a beautiful start to the day. Good day for a date, eh, Em?"

"Does the world know about my dinner with Ian? Good grief, it's just a dinner, Grayson."

"Uh-huh, and I'm Spiderman."

"What does that mean? You claiming superhuman powers?"

"Never! Dinner is never 'just a dinner,' not when help from all corners is needed."

"Well now, we'll just see, but you're making me nervous as an old bitty hen with no rooster in sight."

"Don't go gettin' all...Oh, look who is coming in his beat-up Land Rover!"

"Ely, did Mama tell you you're gonna help Ian this morning? That all right with you?"

"Yes, miss. What we doin'?"

"You've asked the fifty-million-dollar question. You make sure to inform us later! See you after lunch."

Ian jumps out of the Land Rover spouting hellos to everyone. He's in a playful, high-spirited mood. There is an in-depth discussion between Ian and Grayson on the dock. Moose and Bear hit the water with a thrust of energy, which remarkably resembles Ian's.

"Good morning, my bonnie lass! How are you this glorious morning?"

"I'm good, Ian, but shouldn't you be sayin' those flirtatious words to my daughter?"

"First rule for a first date: butter up the mother. It's an unwritten international rule of first-date satisfaction."

"You expectin' to be satisfied on your first date with my daughter, Mr. Ian Duncan MacDougal?"

"Oh, Tah, I'm often pleased, rarely satisfied."

"You seem to have a thirst for, let's say, life, that's unquenchable, am I right?"

"The lady wins the prize! It's been a long while since someone took my breath away as your daughter has. Unless you dream and keep building those dreams, you mire down in muck. Why settle, Tah? Between you and me, that beautiful daughter of yours is a stretch for me, but I intend on reaching for the brass ring."

"Word of warning to you, she's all the family I have and I'm overly protective. You take care of her, ya hear?"

"The lady of the manor is given my solemn promise to be a protector of hearts and dreams. You shall not be disappointed; no harm shall ever come to Emmy as long as I have anything to say about it. Do I have your blessing?"

"Ian, I ain't never been asked to bless a date; you're a piece of work, a one-of-a-kind piece of work."

Tah takes the end of a broomstick, acting as though she is knighting him Sir Ian. "You have my blessing, my prayer, and my wish for happiness."

"Aye then, I've won the mother over, eh?"

"Ayah, Sir Ian, you've perpetuated my approval; winning my daughter over is another story. No brass ring will win her over either, if you get my drift."

"No rush. I'm taking one step at a time. Ely, ready to hit the road with me?"

"Lookin' forward to it, Ian. Check your messages every once in a while; we're expecting news about Peter Barbour and I want you to be up on his status."

"Yes, Tah, Grayson filled me in a bit. Will keep a watchful eye on my phone. Ely! *Ely*! Let's get a move on; we've got lots to do, and the sun is getting high in the sky."

"Yes, sir, on my way. Your dawgs, are they goin' with us?"

"You afraid of dogs so close to you?"

"No, sir. Love 'em. Never had any, but always did want one."

"Hop in, Ely. They are sure to make you want one even more...Oops, almost made a fatal error, Ely. Forgot to say good morning to the one I should have gone to first. Where is Emmy?"

"She up in da store, Mr. Ian, lookin' kinda nervous, like a twittering bird."

"Aha, a good sign. I'll be right back. Don't you move. You're trapped anyhow, with two dogs on your lap."

Ely's laughter urges the dogs to keep licking his brown, freckled face.

Ian bounds up the stairs shouting my name with a chuckle in his voice. He emanates joy and strews lofty vibrations. "Oh, sweet Emileigh, did you sleep well last night?"

"I did. You're certainly full of yourself this morning!"

"No, full of expectation. Doing for others puts joy in my heart, and preparing for our date, well, it's the most gratifying of gifts!"

"Sounds like you have high hopes for tonight."

"Only to please you and hope those efforts make you feel as special as you are to me."

I don't know how to respond to Ian. "No need to tell you to enjoy your day. Y'all have fun doin' whatever you're plotting. I can't wait till six thirty."

"Until then, lass. Dress casually. I don't go in for frills and such; just be comfy."

"Sounds good. Can't wait to see you later."

"Aye, we'd best get going."

He bounds down to the Land Rover whistling a happy tune. I hear it take off with two barking dogs and a giggling Ely.

"Morning, Leigh. Heard any news from the police?"

"Lots, Em. Tah around?"

"I'll get her; she's out front watering plants."

Leigh's voice is enthusiastic; I hope she has good news. It might be the reporter coming alive with a hot new story.

"What's going on? News about Peter, I hope?"

"Y'all can rest easy. A long list of charges has sprung up; some of which are: child endangerment, assault, assault with intent to harm, kidnapping, illegal drug possession, battery, and illegal weapon possession. He has two previous warrants for his arrest in South Carolina for armed robbery and assault. Tah, he's being held without bail; he's already confessed to the previous charges—no one knows why—but he'll be put away soon. Hannah and Ely can go on with life. In fact, there is a substantial reward for his arrest in South Carolina, money a family who had dealings with him are offering. It should go to Ely, so they can put their lives back together. Hannah came in, and the police interviewed her and filed an extensive complaint, which will undoubtedly lead to more charges. Tah, you did well by Ely; you're a hero in my book."

"Praise the Lord! What good news! I can't wait to tell everyone. I'm no hero, Leigh. We did this together. Strength in numbers, ya know. Ely is the real hero; his actions have brought peace not only to his family but to all of us. I must tell Em; she'll be thrilled."

Leigh's good news spreads like wildfire among the Suggettes and beyond. Ian's vivacious energy spread to all of us once we got the news Peter Barbour could no longer be a threat. There'll be court proceedings, but with him being behind bars and having already confessed, it gives us peace. Thanks be to God for speaking to us and letting us know the right thing to do.

"Louise, I was just thinkin' about you. How are those children and grandchildren of yours doing?"

"Good morning, Tah. Ain't today a relief? The news about Peter Barbour, jumpin' Jehoshaphat, what a drama unfolding! My gazing ball is shining bright with activity; something is definitely in the air. Everybody at home is just fine, mighty fine actually. I missed you and thought I'd drop by. We are having dinner with Harper, his girlfriend Isabel, and her family tonight."

"Is there something you see in the gazing ball we should know about Miss Weasy?"

"I can honestly tell you it isn't the usual, you know, so-and-so is here to say hello, blah, blah, blah, so much more I'm havin' trouble keepin' up with it, but all good. It's like the heavens are pouring out blessings, you know, after the trial and tribulation...I guess we are catching the victory wave."

"Well, that's all good and fine, but I was really meaning is there something with the dinner tonight? Might there be an announcement of some sort?"

"I'd never let the cat out of the bag prematurely, Tah. Tight lips where other people's news is concerned."

"But you sense something?"

"Where are Ian and the boys?"

"Changing the subject is a surefire form of acknowledgment, but I'll be patient. Ian is off with the boys doing predate stuff. He is overzealous but seems to be having fun. Em is a basket case of nerves. It's really quite cute; she must really like him!"

"Gotta run. Can you put this on my account? I ran out without my wallet or pocketbook. A houseful has a way of making me a bit spazzoid."

"Consider it done. I want to know about your dinner tonight. Call me later."

"And I want all the juicy details about skirt boy and Em, toodaloo."

"Mr. Ian, why you pullin' over here. Is we there?"

"No, just wondering, do you know how to drive?"

"Heck no, Mr. Ian. Ain't nobody trusted me to sit behind a wheel."

"Well, I think it's about time. It's Ian, not Mr. Ian."

"Really, you'll teach me?"

"We're on back roads and this old beauty is a good car to learn on, but you have to be patient and listen to me, okay?"

"Yes, sir, Ian, I'll be right careful."

"Now, this has a clutch and three gears. I like three gears because they are taller, and once you learn, you'll find you aren't shifting all the time and she acts like she is younger and feistier. So put your foot on the brake, the one in the middle, and press the clutch to the floor, the pedal on the left. Turn the key, and let's start her up. I'll show you where the gears are located."

"Oh, this is cool. Can I punch the gas now?"

"Hold off on hitting the gas. Slowly let out on the clutch and gently press down on the gas at the same time…easy does it. Perfect, don't hold the clutch in; let it all the way out. Stay in your lane, push the clutch in, let off the gas, and pull down on the gear shift.

"Am I doing all right, Ian? I'm really drivin'!"

The store is full of happy customers excited about the Fourth. Most everyone here has family visiting or are vacationers. The atmosphere is relaxed compared to the previous couple of days. I'm counting the hours until I see Ian. Not knowing what to expect is exhilarating and a bit scary. I haven't been surprised much in life, except by bad news. Life has always been more or less predictable; recently, with Ian, I find the path isn't ever clear. Just when I think I know a little about him, he totally surprises me, to the point where I can't imagine what will happen next.

"Ely, you see those cars beside the road up ahead. I want you to slowly pull in behind them and then stop."

"Okay. Ain't that Mr. Tromble's car? Is he helping you too?"

"Yes, Cook and Steve are going to lend us a hand. We have lots to set up, but it should be fun."

"Are you doing all this work to have a date with Miss Emileigh?"

"Yep, you'll learn; women have a way of making you do the oddest things. By the way, you did excellent driving here; we'll give it another shot when we take you back, if you like."

"Are you kidding? I love the Land Rover; she's awesome."

"Aye. lads, thanks for helping Ely and me. I've got a back full of gear that has to go up this trail to the clearing. It is about a half-mile hike. It was supposed to have been mowed yesterday."

"What the hell, Ian? There is a ton of...a refrigerator? Have you gone mad? We should have brought the four-wheeler."

"Nonsense, Steve; it isn't a full-size refrigerator, just a battery-operated one. We can get it all up there in...two trips, tops. The hard part is gonna be setting it up and the decorating."

"Decorating? Oh, now, Ian, I ain't...I mean, it's a bit out of my comfort zone. You gonna spread fairy dust and gnome bits about?"

"No worries, I'll take care of the decorating. I want it to be perfect for Emmy. Probably won't bring out the gnome bits this time; they're a mite rancid. A word to you men, not one word to any of the ladies. You are being sworn to secrecy; that includes the likes of my four-legged boys."

"Aye, aye, Captain, we shall vow to keep the women from knowing. Remaining illusive may be difficult with Weasy!"

"Cook, she is your responsibility. If she thinks she knows something, you must look innocent at least until Emmy is with me. Ely, you're gonna be hit the hardest with questions from Tah and Emmy. Think you can keep a tight lip?"

"Yes, sir, we guys gots to stick together."

"That's a trooper. Aye, looks like we have another helper. Mornin', Grayson. Off store duty so early?"

"We got the good news. Ely's statement was the final blow to Peter's freedom!"

"Looks like you can go home tonight, Ely. Thought I'd lend a hand. How much stuff can you fit in this old heap, Ian?"

"It was a bit of a tight squeeze, but it's all for a good cause."

"Oh, hey, Ely, you met Harper the other night, didn't you?"

"Yes, Mr. Tromble. I said hello, but we didn't jaw or nothing."

"Well, he asked me to tell you he'd like to represent you and your mother."

"What do that mean, sir?"

"Should you need an attorney, a lawyer, Harper would like to take care of you."

"Is we gonna need one? We cain't afford to hire anybody iffin we do."

"It's a wise idea to have someone knowledgeable involved whether or not you need an attorney. He can access information to make certain you and your mom are looked after from a legal standpoint. And about paying for Harper's services, he said he'd do it pro bono."

"What does that mean, Mr. Tromble?"

"Free, no charge to you or your mother."

"Really? Why, I mean, Mr. Tromble, I honestly ain't never thought there was people as nice as y'all. Mama and I, we just never had folks show so much care. Somehow, we'll repay y'all. It may not be with money; we done never had none of that, but somehow to be sure, we'll show our thanks."

"You just did, Ely. You just did."

The Land Rover pulls up watchfully to the front of the store, and Ely jumps out of the driver's side with a wide grin on his youthful face. Ian pops his head into the store still carrying the same exuberance he had earlier. Whining can be heard from inside the car as the dogs peer toward the lake with forlorn looks.

"Ely, thank you for your help. Couldn't have done it without you."

"Thanks for teachin' me how to drive, Ian. Can we be doin' it again sometime?"

"We'll see. You did well, but you need lots more practice."

"Afternoon, Tah, Emmy, I brought Ely back fat and happy, but maybe a little worn out."

"What have you guys been up to?"

"Well, Ma Bell, that's fer us guys ta know and y'all not to, leastwise not yet."

"Hmm, sounds like a good coaching job to me."

"What did I tell you, Ely? They'll be questioning you right and left. The brotherhood demands you be strong."

"I will. Besides, I only have another three hours here, and then I can go home to see Mama."

"I'll leave you ladies to carry on with the running of the store. I've got lots to do and miles to go before six thirty."

"Bye, Ian. I'm very curious about our date. I'll see you later."

The looks Ian gets from Moose and Bear persuade him to open the door so they can take a quick dip. He stands on the dock with arms folded, looking across the water, lost in thought. It's apparent Ely won't be coerced into revealing Ian's plans. It's fun to pick on him, hoping he'll spill the beans, but I'd rather see firsthand what Ian has been up to. The hours drag by, but finally, the clock's hands approach six thirty. Mama is down at the dock with the Rileys and the Duprees. The Land Rover comes to a halt beside the road; he waves to them and pulls into the store's parking lot.

"Come on in, Ian. Would you like to have a drink before we set off to our mystery destination? Oh what a lovely bouquet, for me?"

"You like the flowers, eh? Sorry, they're for your mum. Let's be on our bloody way out of binocular range, if you know what I mean."

"Flowers for Mama? I can't wait to see her face!"

"Lass those shoes won't do; you need something you can walk in easily."

"These are comfortable sandals, Ian."

"You have a bit of a trek ahead of you."

He heads down, bows, and hands Mama an aromatic bouquet of jasmine, lavender, foxfire, and juniper. "For land's sake, you've gone overboard. Tell us where y'all are headed."

"Guys not a word to Tah, understand? This is Emmy's story to tell if she chooses."

In a gallant gesture, he bends a bit at the waist, takes my hand, and opens the car door, promptly tossing me a blindfold and asking me to slip it on. Refusing to protest, I reluctantly place the blindfold over my eyes.

"You know, I've lived here all my life and can pretty much tell where we are going just by the roads we travel."

"Already thought about your keen sense of direction. I won't go directly to our destination. Maybe throw you a curveball to confuse and bewilder you."

After attempting to map our location in my mind, I realize I have no earthly idea where we are or where we are headed. Anticipation grows within me. "Okay, lass, here we are. Well as far as the car goes. Now we have a short hike."

"Can I take this thing off now, Ian?"

"Hmm, it would make the walk easier, but I'd rather you don't peek. Mind wearing it? Take my hand; I'll guide you safely."

"I do mind, but I wouldn't dare mess up your reveal. It makes me nervous imagining what you have devised."

I have never been a pushover, but Ian's playful spirit is contagious. I have no intention of spoiling his planning. Besides, he has to be very attentive when I'm blindfolded, and I find it quite alluring.

"All right, lass, stand right here for one moment while I take care of something. Don't touch the blindfold. No peeking until I come back and take it off."

"Okay, Ian, but it was hardly a simple walk; we went straight up for miles."

"It wasn't so far; maybe it seemed like it because you didn't see anything. Just one moment, be patient."

I hear the familiar sound of a cork being loosened from a bottle of wine a few feet away. There is loud, trickling water and faint music playing. As my curiosity grows, it is increasingly difficult to stand here blind.

"Emileigh, welcome to my newest property. Let's get this silly blindfold off. Quit squirming and turn a little to your left."

Before me is a beautiful Polynesian canopy enhanced by white mosquito netting. Inside is a futon with what looks to be a hundred silken pillows tossed about, each having a vivid print of various reds and greens. Candles glow in every corner; music softly plays in the background; flowers are scattered throughout; and a huge oriental rug is tossed upon the grass with rose petals strewn over it. There is also a fire pit, and the smell of splendid food lingers in the evening air. Behind the canopy lies a small pond fed by a waterfall, above a waning, bright blue sky with gold and lavender highlights. Ian holds my shoulders and turns me around. We are high above the lake at the south end with a full view of the lake; it's breathtaking. "Oh, Ian, this is beautiful, stunningly beautiful. I've never heard of a waterfall anywhere near.

The effort, the care you've put into this…I never…I don't deserve this; it's overwhelming."

Tears of joy and adoration cascade down my cheeks. The sheer beauty of this spot and knowing Ian was thinking of me as he created it for our first date are unbelievable. As he folds me in his strong taut arms, my heart leaps with joy.

"So you like it, lass?"

"Like is an understatement. I'm in shock. May we sit down?"

"Sorry, seeing you stand there, speechless, I forget my manners."

"How did you do all this? I truly don't deserve…You said this is your property?"

"Well, the current owner accepted my offer on it; legally, it isn't yet. We have permission to be here this evening. Isn't it special? The area claims to have an opening to heaven; this must be the center, don't you agree?"

"Oh, it must be. Ian, I'm overwhelmed; no one has ever…"

"They were fools not to."

"I smell exotic aromas coming from these covered trays and casserole dishes. What have you been up to?"

"Oh, Cook and I came up with a few Polynesian delicacies we thought you'd enjoy." He winks as he hands me a glass of chilled wine with ice cubes. Being pampered has an odd effect on me. It makes me feel quite out of place. The food is mildly sweet and spicy, containing a mixture of fruits and herbs. The perfect delights on a picture-perfect evening. "Emmy, you seem to enjoy everything."

"I most certainly do; you've made me feel so special. This ought to send those spells of mine away for good."

"Spells? What spells are you talking about?"

"Oh, I figured Mama or Louise would have told you. They are nothing really I just seem to be having moments where I black out for a couple of seconds; they'll pass."

"No one told me. When was the last one?"

"When Peter Barbour broke the window."

"You mean hours prior to me practically throwing you into the lake?"

"Oh, I was all right then, Ian; they only last a moment or two. It was hours before we went out."

"I can't believe you!"

I've spoiled Ian's mood. He's become agitated and protective. "Ian, what is bothering you so much? Those spells slow me down, but here I am. I refuse to live in fear or let them dictate my doings."

"What bothers me is you jumping into the lake, at night, without me knowing about the episodes. You could have had one in the dark water of the cove, and I wouldn't have known or been able to help you."

His big brown eyes are filling with tears, and suddenly, it dawns on me what is bothering him. Ghosts are haunting him. "Ian, oh, Ian, I'm not Molly. I'm right here with you. I'm sorry; it isn't right to bring this up now of all times. We've recently met, and I didn't feel it necessary. I know it isn't any excuse but…"

"No, lass, you're right. It just seems like we've known each longer than we actually have. I've fallen in love with you. Have been really since the first time I saw you. I was pumping gas, and you were standing behind the screen door peering down at your mother and me. You took my breath away standing filtered by the screen in the morning light, the hint of a smile on your face. I haven't been able to get the picture out of my mind. Now since I've gotten to know you, the feeling grows every moment of the day. Hearing you have something physically happening makes me protective. Have you had it checked out? Why didn't you tell me?"

"Louise seems to think I need to gather some of my energy back from places I waste it. I didn't tell you because I was scared to; thought it may frighten you away."

"Louise may be right, but she isn't a doctor. Promise me you'll see a doctor before we head to New York."

"Or what? I don't go with you?"

"Why must you go to such a negative extreme? You can't frighten me away. I just said I love you. I want you to enjoy the trip, and yes, partially for me to feel assured I'm not doing anything to harm you. Why is going to the doctor a problem for you?"

"Oh, Ian, that's a long story. I've fallen through the cracks with medical doctors a lot; maybe it's a lack of faith in them. I will go for you and Mama. The others will appreciate it as well."

"Good, and one more promise."

"What's that?"

"Promise me, if you have another one of these bouts, you'll tell me. No secrets, I don't do well with secrets."

"Neither do I. You have my word. Now can we get off this subject and go back to those three little words you said a short time ago?"

"What words are those, Emmy?"

"Oh, something about being in love with me. Hold that thought. Before you do, turn up the music, Ian. I love this song. Do you shag?"

"I beg your pardon, lass?"

"I've been with a lot of guys who say they can, but once we start, you know right away they weren't exactly tellin' the truth 'cuz they weren't very good at it."

"A lot of guys, lass? How many and who were these guys?"

"Oh you know, back in school at parties and such."

"Emileigh, are we talking about the same thing?"

"Carolina beach music, you know."

"Ah no, I don't. Guy from Scotland here, remember? Shag, where I come from, is well, to put it bluntly, sex."

"What you must think of me...A shag is a dance to beach music. Oh, Ian, I am mortified. Did you think...Oh, I can't even look at you."

A belly laugh erupts from deep within him. Ian's eyes are bright and playful. I burst out laughing as well while falling into his arms and placing a tender morsel in his mouth. "I guess we have a wee bit of a language barrier. So, lass, back to my feelings for you. I do love you, more than anyone I've ever loved; it's all so sudden and unexpected. Our meeting is a gift too wonderful for anything the two of us could have arranged, don't you agree?" He strides over to the wine bottle, fills both glasses, and sits down next to me. Wrapping a tanned muscular arm around my shoulders, he proposes a toast. "To us, may every moment be blessed and full of joy."

"Ian, I'm afraid to say...I don't want to waste time just because I'm fearful. Do you understand, Ian? Oh, please say you do."

"Of course I do. I need to hear the words, but I only want to hear them when and if you're certain. Until then, I'm at peace just being by your side. Remember, like playing the cello, from the soul through the heart." His lips come to mine in a tender, loving display of patience and care.

Passion from deep within stirs, but I hasten to respond. I kiss him back softly. Facing my fear, unable to keep my true feelings silent, with a trembling voice, I say the words I thought had been banished from my life. "Um, Ian, about those three little words, the ones you mentioned before."

"Yes, lass?"

"I love you. You had me loving you back at the store in your kilt squatting down looking at wine. You stirred my heart and gave me dreams of hope, love, and endless possibilities."

"Keep dreaming, Emmy. I'll do my best to make them all come true."

chapter 10

MY EYES OPEN to see Moose and Bear staring at me, their muzzles on the edge of the bed, tails wagging a hundred miles an hour. I look around at mildly familiar surroundings, and suddenly, it dawns on me this is Ian's guest room. The dogs start to whine and quietly bark as if talking. Ian walks into the room with a bright, charismatic smile.

"Aye, lass, you finally woke up! Would you like a cup of coffee here, or will you join me in the kitchen?"

"Ian, before any coffee, I'd like to know what happened last night. I don't recall coming here or anything after eating and drinking way too much."

"I think you just solved the mystery of lost time. We polished off not one or two but a few bottles of wine. Your beautiful peepers closed, so we came back here, and I put you to bed. I called Tah and explained to her I'd have you home this morning, simply to put her mind at ease. Her inquisitive nature wasn't satisfied with my explanation. I amused her and said you were sleeping soundly in the guest room."

"Mama's imagination will have a field day, but thank you for calling her; she does tend to worry. I'm assuming nothing more happened last night? No fondling? I mean, if it did, I'm sorry; I don't remember."

"No, lass, I'll say I was hoping, but you've been riding an emotional wave the past couple of days. You relaxed, had a bit too much to drink, and then…well, I won't ever take advantage of a situation. I hope when it happens, you'll remember. Guess it's the ego in me."

"Coffee sounds great. I'll meet you in the kitchen in a couple of minutes."

I want to burst out of bed and hug him. Ian seems happy to have me around. Last night was so special, our declarations of love for each other, his more straightforward than mine. Oh why did I drink too much and end up here? Not the most romantic of gals, I'm left to imagine what might have been.

Standing in the kitchen wearing jeans and a T-shirt, leaning down to pet Moose, Ian is a view to behold. Throwing my arms around Ian's neck, I lightly kiss his face all over. "Easy, lass, you'll make Moose jealous. That's generally his job, but I like the way you do it better."

"I should hope so, MacDougal."

"To what do I owe this smothering of kisses?"

"Because I adore you. The thought it took to set up the perfect location for dinner, and then I spoil—"

"Whoa, lass, you didn't spoil anything. I completely enjoyed myself and our time together. Do you know when you drink too much, you sing off-key?"

"I've got news for you: I always sing off-key."

"The walk down the hillside was challenging to say the least; you might have done better wearing the blindfold."

"Are you going up to bring stuff down today?"

"Yup, soon as I take you back to the store, I'd better clean the area before critters take it over."

"I'll call Mama after breakfast and ask if she can handle the store for a couple of hours. Let me help you gather everything and bring it down the hill."

"Not necessary, Emmy, I'm fine taking care of it and remembering you there with me."

"My motivation is purely selfish; helping gives me more time to spend with you. Besides, it's the Fourth of July. Mama closes up early; usually, the store is dead 'cuz of the parade later on."

"All right, I'd love your help. Maybe when we finish, we'll take Tah to the parade."

"First things first, MacDougal, I'm starving. Where do you keep the frying pan?"

"Ma Bell, ya here?"

"Mornin', Ely! You could've taken today off. It's usually slow; I yawn more times than customers come by. Oops, there's the phone. Back in just a minute. Good morning, Suggs General Store."

"Mama, how's it going?"

"Baby girl, I think that's a better question for you. Y'all have a good time last night or what?"

"Oh, Mama, I can't wait to tell you about it. Ian, he did as he told you; he had magic up his sleeve. I never, well, if I start, I'll want to tell you everything and I'd rather do it in person. You think you can handle the store for a couple hours? Ian has a lot of stuff to collect, and I want to help him."

"Ely is here, we'll be fine. Why don't you just forget about the store today? I'm thinking of closing about one or two anyhow. I can't wait to hear about your date with Ian. Hang on to him, baby girl."

"You've been closing early or opening late a lot lately! We aren't going to make our numbers this week of all weeks. Time to worry about that later. We want to take you to the parade, Mama, so close at one and we'll pick you up. Are we still having dinner with everyone before the fireworks?"

"Of course, girl, I think Louise and Cook have an announcement, so be sure you two are here."

"Love you, Mama. See you in a few."

"Love you more, baby girl. Can't wait to hear your story."

"Ma Bell, was that Miss Emileigh?"

"Sure was. Since you're here, I gave her the day off. How is your mama?"

"She's doin real fine, Ma Bell, real fine. Seems more at ease, like she used to be. How was Miss Emileigh's date?"

"Glad to hear Hannah is more herself. If y'all need anything, let me know. If things pick up around here, I may be able to use her help here at the store; you reckon she'd like that, son?"

"Oh yes, I do, I do, indeed. Can I tell her?"

"Why don't you let me call her? She can help while I'm away. Em can use an extra pair of hands. About Em's date, sounds like it went very well. I don't know any of the details, but she said it was magical."

"That sounds about right. Ian sure has good ideas. You shoulda seen what he did."

"Not another word, Ely. Let Em tell me, okay, son? I want to hear her words."

"Yes'm, I do too. I bet they be good words."

"Go see who drove up. See if they need help. I gotta get something out of the storage room."

"Morning, Misriz Tromble. Anything, I can do fer ya?"

"Hey, nothing, thank you. I'm looking for Tah. She about or Em?"

"Ma Bell is in the storeroom; Miss Emileigh ain't workin' today."

"Oh, you hear any news on the big date?"

"Not much yet, but we are expectin' to find out when Miss Emileigh comes by later."

"We are, are we, Ely? You fit in pretty well here."

"Misriz Tromble, you believe in angels?"

"Of course, doesn't everybody? Why do you ask?"

"Oh, it probably sounds dumb, I jus' gots this feelin' and cain't stop thinking about 'em."

"Well, Ely, have you ever asked the right person. Tell me more; I'd love to hear."

"Folks say you gots a gift of some sorts. I only listen with one ear when people ain't talkin' to me, so I may not've heard right. But you see or know things most folks don't; you know from the other side of this here life. Is that right?"

"In a manner of speaking. It isn't like I live there, but I do occasionally get visitors who have crossed over and sometimes hear things about the future. Enough of my gift, what about you? Tell me what is happening; give me all the detail you can."

"Oh, it ain't like your things. You seem so sure. I don't understand things I've not ever heard before."

"Ely, no one starts as if knocked on the head and instantly understands. I've had this since I was a child and thought everyone had the same connection, until I was mocked and shunned because kids thought I was nuts. So, I kept it quiet; still do for the most part. It isn't a trick. It's a gift, not something you turn off and on. It is always on; you just learn how to ignore things. Maybe I can help you tune in better."

"Well, you know life for me and my mama has been bad since my stepfather came into our lives. Now that he's gone, well, my heart is just so full of thanks, mostly for y'all, your care and help. Y'all could've turned your backs and like you said those kids did, shunned us. All of y'all could have done that. Most would have. I see Ma Bell…I've always been told angels ain't people, but, Misriz Tromble, she and all y'all must be. I gets this voice in my head, and it talks way better than I can, so I know it ain't me."

"Mercy, what does the voice say to you?"

"Mostly, it says to be thankful, grateful. I am, but then it tells me stuff, easy stuff like what to do for a customer or something. When I do what it says, those people say, 'How'd you know?' But, really, that's only happened maybe twice. Then I hear what sounds like singing around Ma Bell, beautiful voices, and see a gold light. Ain't that weird? Almost like God is makin' Himself known."

"You are unusual, Ely. Most people, when things go right, forget about God and lean on Him less, but not you. So now that brings us to Tah. Angels can take human form from time to time, even walk into the life of a person for a piece of time. Who knows? Maybe that's how Tah held it together when you were robbing the store, and maybe it was an angel who kept that gun from going off when you tried to pull the trigger. Stranger things have happened, especially when God has something powerful for you to do. I believe He does for you, Ely. You know the saying, 'to those who are given much, much is expected'? Well, most folks think the saying is for those rich or powerful people, but I think it can also mean for those who have endured many trials and have kept faith, or even found faith through them. People who go through a lot, as you have, our heavenly Father expects them to do much for Him as He will for them. As far as seeing gold around Tah, that's her aura. She is golden. You see someone like that, you run to them, Ely. They are special."

"An orrahh, she done got that. Wonder if she knows. What abouts the music?"

"I suspect you have a bored angel around you, who is striving to get your attention."

"What?"

"A bored angel. You've been bored, right?"

"Yeah, but I never thought an angel would get bored."

"Think about their life, Ely. They can't do what they want; their commands come from higher-ups or from those they serve."

"Really, Misriz Tromble? They jess' don't fly 'round helpin' folk?"

"How would you like to sit or hover around and wait on your person to even become aware you're there? You'd get bored and play tricks, especially if it may get the attention of those you are sent to keep watch over. You see what I'm saying, Ely?"

"I guess you mean I'm supposed to be tellin' my angel to do things?"

"More ask than tell. Just ask him or her to help you understand things from God's perspective."

"I ain't never asked an angel to do anything, ever. I can't imagine how bored mine must be."

"Weasy, that you? Come on up here and sit with me. I want to hear about Harper and your dinner with everyone last night."

"Ely, that's my cue from the queen bee; she wants to hear my news. I think you've gotten an earful of preachin' this morning. I need to see Tah. You reckon I ought to just be sly and talk angels to her?"

"Works for me, Misriz Tromble. Sure do."

"Well then, Ely, call me Louise or Weasy. Forget all this formality, if you please; you'll have my angel laughing so hard he isn't likely to be watchin' out for me."

The walk up the hillside to the clearing is easier without a blindfold. Views along the short hike are magnificent in the bright morning light. Listening to Ian sing some Celtic song that sounds like gibberish to my lazy Southern ear, makes me long to see where he is from. He doesn't speak much about Scotland or his home, but hearing the notes dance from his lips and the glee in his voice, I sense a longing for his roots down deep within. Maybe someday I'll share time with him on the Isle of Skye. It sounds so romantic, vast and dramatic. I'd like to meet some of his family to gather the full sense of Ian MacDougal.

"Ian, this is a beautiful sight in the morning. I can't believe you're about to own this property. When do you close on it?"

"Oh, nothing is written in stone yet, but we're hoping for late August, before I leave for Naples. Let's take a moment and have a drink before we demolish our little fort."

"Sounds good to me; the walk made me thirsty. We certainly have a lot to take down the hill."

"If we're smart, which is a stretch for me, we can make a sled and pull most of it down with a rope."

"I can't help but get a tight knot in my stomach when you speak of leaving for New York. It sounds final; from there, you will undoubtedly go to another location taking you even farther away."

"Lassie, come here. Sit next to me. Do you remember last night I told you I love you?"

"Yes, and I, well, I didn't say it nearly as elegantly as I'd hoped…I get tongue-tied around you, but I do love you; that's why the thought of you leaving, well, it just makes me sad, wondering where we're headed."

"Emmy, I don't walk away from love, especially yours; it's too precious. Your tongue sounds like it is becoming less knotted. Maybe I can help with that, and as far as where we are headed…I can help with that too." Ian takes me into his arms, lavishing me with kisses and once again unleashing the passion hidden deep within. His touch causes me to tremble with expectation; suddenly, he pulls away, gently grasping my hand in his. "I get a thrill looking at you. There have been so many empty years on our journey bringing us together. I want you, to make love to you, but not here, not yet. Probably sounds strange coming from a guy; if I were a younger man, I wouldn't think twice."

"You've had many more lonely years than I, waiting awhile longer, well, Ian, it just builds anticipation. Never in my wildest imaginings would I have believed my love could grow so swiftly and be returned with such intensity. Waiting to love you with my body as well as my soul is a treasure of its own; anticipation is a wonderful thing."

"Looks to me like we just got those kinks in your tongue worked out. Now let's get loaded up and start sliding our little fort down the hill. We've got a parade to see."

I don't want to take down the netting or stow away all the pillows. It is so picture perfect, lavishly set amidst the backdrop of a waterfall and the lake, our little private nirvana situated unexpectedly in the middle of no-where yet under an open door to heaven. There is a large part of me wishing Ian hadn't pulled away, a part wishing here, among this hidden paradise, he would have taken me and found those secret places within, which bring forth the sweet joy of ecstasy. I surprise myself by desiring Ian so intensely after quelling my feelings for him earlier. Life takes unexpected turns, and this turn came blindly raging into my life wearing a skirt. How many times do I have to pinch myself to make sure it isn't all a dream?

We grab the ropes to our makeshift sled carrying the makings of a temporary paradise. As we pull our hefty load, Ian begins bellowing out another Celtic song, inspiring me to muddle through the lyrics, slaughtering Gaelic words half spoken in Southernese. Our laughter far outweighs any lyrical impediment. He glances at me with a wide grin, impish charm oozing from every pore. Mama has it right; I should hold onto to him. I intend to do just so.

"Ladies, how is everyone this afternoon? And where are all your men? This looks like a hen party. Am I allowed?"

"Afternoon, Ian, Emileigh, the guys all have a golf date. It is a Fourth of July ritual; they should be done in an hour or so. Y'all had lunch?"

"We've eaten already. Ian, come on sit down; you should fit right in with us. You do wear skirts from time to time."

"Aye, Louise, that's right, and so far, I'm the only one present who has done so. As for the lunch question, I cannot speak for Emmy, but I'm hungry."

"Me too, Mama. Y'all got anything fixed or should we go get something?"

"Unless Ely is up in the store knockin' it all back, there's plenty. Fix yourselves a plate and bring it down. We've all got hives waitin' to hear about your date last night. Oh and while you're up there, go ahead and close up the store even though it's only noon. Ely can stay or go on home; it's up to him."

As Ian and I walk up to the store, we hear the Suggettes laughing behind us. No doubt they are full of intrigue and wonder. The ladies have quite the imaginations, and by this time of day, they've no doubt come up with a vast array of scenarios concerning our date that would make the devil himself blush. I prod Ian to flow with their fantasies and play with them a bit before revealing the true elegance and splendor of our date. He agrees a lot faster than I would ever have anticipated, leaving me to laugh as I speculate what the true effect wearing a kilt has on a man.

"All right, ladies of Tahlulahville, I understand you have strong urges to hear about last night. Ask away, lasses."

"Strong urges maybe taking things a bit far, skirt boy. But since *you* brought it up, what ahhh...what...ahhh...did y'all do?"

"Oh, Louise, you of all people should know! We had dinner."

"Okay, Louise will play with you till Sunday, but the reporter in me is more interested in detail than outline. Where did you have dinner?"

"Hmm, if I tell you it was more of a picnic on Traverse Hill, will it help?"

"Picnic is good. Where on Traverse Hill is there a picnic area?"

The Suggettes look back and forth at one another bewildered. Their chops ready to gnaw on any detail.

"Ah, Leigh, the magic starts."

"Magic? What the hell are you talkin' about? All I hear is magic this and magic that."

"Mama, he is trying to tell y'all about our date and answering your questions."

"And I asked one, what the hell is this about magic? We've been waitin' all day to hear, and I don't want to hear, 'Oh we had dinner, a picnic, and magic, good grief!"

"Oh come now, Tah, I told you I had magic up my sleeve, remember? It's just an expression; don't you fret so much. I'm not into black magic."

"Okay, skirt boy, I don't recollect anywhere on Traverse Hill where you can set up a picnic."

"You ladies are getting a bit hostile. Maybe we should break out more wine. Emmy, why don't you tell them what will tickle their ears and put their minds to rest."

"Okay, but I'm not certain I can put their minds to rest. It was so special words cannot convey the thought and care Ian put into the date."

"Emileigh Louise Suggs, we are about an inch away from pandemonium. You'd better spill it and spill it fast. Hell, Leigh is salivating. Somebody give her a napkin."

"She'll just take notes on it. Maybe that's a good thing. Here, Leigh."

"My goodness, y'all are so impatient. Don't you know anticipation is the best part?"

"Ahem, so I've been told, lass."

"Knock it off, Ian; you'll only feed the vultures. Obviously, we had a good time. We are here with you answering questions about our date, which I may add really is none of y'all's business, but since Ian and I are so good-natured we decided to tell y'all about it. First off, when we left here, Ian blindfolded me."

Emily jumps off her floral-patterned pad on her redwood rocker, shaking and pointing her finger at Ian. "He blindfolded you? Why on earth did you go with him? After all you and Tah have been through the past few days, Ian how could you make her do such an awful thing? Are you really all right, Em? You can tell us." She slinks over to me wide eyed and troubled.

"Oh for heaven's sake, do you think if I wasn't all right I would be sitting here in front of Ian saying he blindfolded me? Relax, Emily. Ian blindfolded me to surprise me. After we parked the car and walked up the hill to where he is buying some property, he took off the blindfold.

"Walk up a hill, buying property...are y'all—"

"Hush your mouth, Tah; let her go on...Em, please."

Ian sits silently across from me with the widest Cheshire grin on his face. The Suggettes are in their glory—protective, unashamedly inquisitive, and curious. The night was magical; my words did not have to be embellished one iota to convey our date's uniqueness. Fact is, my words in their simplicity don't do Ian's efforts justice. As he sits there, I find myself not looking at Leigh, Mama, or Louise, but at Ian, staring into his eyes, reliving and relishing last night. "So you see, the night was special from the moment Ian picked me up until, well, until right now."

"Did y'all buy it? Tah, do you really think skirt boy did all that on Traverse Hill and buy the land as well?"

"No reason to doubt. I don't think they're pullin' our chain. Just look at them. They can't take their eyes off one another."

"And, ladies, with the cat out of the bag, the details of our date so eloquently shared by the lovely and talented Miss Emmy, I must bid you all ado."

"Ian, you don't have to go, do you? What about the parade?"

"I'm afraid I must go. The parade is almost over; we've missed it, but what a lovely day to sit lakeside and take in nature's beauty. How many men get the opportunity to sit with five beautiful women? I have some calls to make, and my boys need a swim for certain. Are we having dinner here or would you all like to come across the lake?"

"We done missed the parade? Oh and I do so love marching bands!"

"Oh, Ian, we'd love to come over, but another time. All the kids and grandkids will be here shortly. You are coming back, aren't you?"

"If Emileigh is here, so shall I be?"

I don't want him to leave and yet I know he'll be back in just a few hours, which gives me some time to reflect and remember. Our adventures seem to come quickly and gather steam between visits.

"Emmy, I'll be back about five. I'll come with the boat, so we can go up the lake and watch the fireworks."

"Sounds perfect. Come back anytime. You don't have to wait until five unless you want to."

"'Tisn't a matter of wanting to, Emmy. I have to clean out the Land Rover, take care of the lads, and make some calls. If it were up to me, I'd never leave, but that's for another conversation, another day."

"Calls? Today, it's the Fourth; no one will be around."

"It is a holiday here, not at home. I've been neglecting some folks who need to hear from me."

Delicately taking my hand, he guides me over to the Land Rover, where he places an extended kiss on my parted lips. I could get used to this, but not with the present audience awwing in the background. Do those women have no shame?

"Guess they don't need binoculars."

"Yeah, look who is leaving me to face them. Look at them, unabashedly twistin' and turnin' to get a better view."

The snoopy-nose Suggettes have become more explorative in their quest for juicy details about our date. I understand their intrigue, but I just want a moment or two of solitude to soak it in for myself. I beg off to go up to the apartment to gather food for the evening.

"Y'all reckon Em's all right. She is elusive with her answers. That ain't exactly like her."

"Tah, you let her be. The girl has love written all over her. I am sure she is feeling all sorts of emotions, not the least of which is surprise. Ian waltzes in here like lord of the manor; we have all taken to him like a bee to honey. Ever wonder if he is too good to be true?"

"Emily, don't go down that road again; it's closed. Emileigh has had quite a week. We've focused so much on her while Louise is sitting right here with the biggest news tucked away, waiting for a moment to tell us. Come on now, Louise, tell us about the Tromble news."

"Oh, Leigh, I should really let Harper tell you tonight like we planned, but he knows I'm too proud not to say anything to y'all; besides I'm about to explode. Harper and Isabel are getting married!"

"Hallelujah, those two are a couple meant to be hitched if ever there was one."

"When are the nuptials taking place?"

"They want a fall wedding; both are trying to come up with a date in October, but haven't settled on a specific day. Harper wants to be married outside by the lake; Isabel really wants a church wedding, so obviously they have details to iron out."

"Or Grayson's gonna have to build an open church by the lake. Wouldn't that be something?"

"Emily, don't go there; let them come up with the idea."

"Yeah, but all those antiques I've got in the store and some of my gorgeous fabric strewn about with flowers, and oh, this could be fun!"

"Emily, it isn't your wedding, or Sam's or even Dylan's."

"I know, I know. I just love weddings. Who knows? The way Ian and Em are headed, we could be planning two this fall."

"Quiet, Emily Dupree. This news ain't about those two, and I refuse to go there; he is from freakin' Scotland."

"Oh, Lord, have mercy! Do you hear the ruckus? The boys are back, drunk as skunks at two thirty in the afternoon. How you reckon the golf game went? Do you hear them? Bet they are celebrating a wedding too, or do men do that? No they probably mourn them. Hang onto your hats, girls; it's gonna be a long, bumpy afternoon!"

"That's what I'm talkin' about, why I don't have one of those."

"One of those what, Tah? Men?"

"Ayah, one of them. I'm goin' to help Em with the food. Y'all take care of your critters on two legs. Don't let 'em go swimming till they sober up a bit, and for heaven's sake, help them get that way before your grandchildren show up."

"Okeydokey, Tah...we heard you."

Mama and I work side by side in the kitchen like two well-oiled machines. Cook comes gliding across the floor and gives both of us a smooch on the cheek. He was at the golf club bar, hole nineteen, a bit longer than he was driving balls on the course, judging by his appearance and affectionate state. We've seen Cook stir up some amazing dinners while inebriated, so we welcome his culinary expertise in any condition. Carrying food down to the dock is another story, we tell him to scurry down and we'll bring the fixin's for him. Mainly what everyone is looking for now are munchies and drinks. The wine is flowing, the beer is foaming, and the tykes are happy with lemonade and sweet tea. As we carry our supply down to the dock, I hear Bessie's engine rumbling toward shore. My heart takes flight. Ian is on his way.

"Harper, I suspect your thunder has been stolen. Everyone has already heard about you and your lovely bride-to-be."

"No worries, Grayson. I know this crowd. Good news travels fast. I'm just lucky it wasn't printed in the paper before I asked Isabel! I see Emileigh and Ian are becoming the next item up for inquisition."

"Oh, I think it best to let the girls speculate on those two. Must be like trying to spawn in a fishbowl around here."

"Ha, yes, but would we really want it any other way? We are some lucky men. These women are pretty special."

"Damn straight, gentlemen. You up to something, or just sayin' it loud enough so we hear ya?"

"I would be remiss if I didn't say a little of both, my dearest."

"Grayson, you are good."

"Yep Harper, it has taken years of experience to pull it off with ease. Live and learn, young one."

Cook takes a spoon and raps it against his beer stein. He seeks the attention of a rather rowdy and rambunctious crowd while he must steady himself by holding onto the picnic table. Most of the little ones are tired as the sun has set and the fireworks are about to commence.

"Ladies and Gentlemen—and you too skirt boy, whatever you are—I have an announcement to make, one I'm certain you've all heard, but I must say again, because I am so proud—we are so proud. The Tromble family is proud to announce a new daughter, Miss Isabel. We welcome her with open arms and hearts to our quirky and loving family. We pray Harper and Isabel enjoy all the joy and happiness this world has to offer, years of love and adoration, and see their wishes come true. Of which Louise and I are hoping for at least five grandchildren. No pressure, kids, just know, ticktock."

The gang erupts with congratulations and well wishes. Ian grabs my hand and guides me to Bessie. Unceremoniously, we jump aboard and set off to the north end of the lake. Midway, Ian slows the boat down. "Emmy, we are out of binocular range?"

"Oh, yes, everyone is so caught up in Harper and Isabel's news they aren't interested in us. Why do you ask, Ian?"

"I'd like to watch the fireworks from my house with you. Are ya up to it?"

"Why, Mr. MacDougal, I like the way you think. I'm a bit weary of so many people; I'd like to spend some time with you alone."

"Ahh, that's my lass. We'll sneak down on the western shore and leave the lights down low."

"Ian, you're a trip. Mama isn't so bad, is she?"

"No, she is that good. And tonight, I don't want to worry about who is seeing what."

Ian pours me a glass of wine. As we maneuver closer to his home, he becomes somber. We've both had a long and full day. The quiet is serene. Moonlight reflects on the lake, my mind is focused on this moment and the man I love. The past has melted away, and today is a midsummer's dream.

"Aye, there are the lads. Out ya come. Say hello to Emmy. What can I get for you?"

"Only you sitting next to me. The fireworks have started. Come here and enjoy them."

The fireworks are amazing. Ian holds me tightly by his side, and we both get caught up gazing toward the sky, our faces illuminated by the cascading color. Moose and Bear lay dreamily at our feet. After passionately kissing me in the warm moonlight, he leans in and whispers, "Emmy, let's watch the finale from my room."

Moose and Bear scamper ahead; Ian leads me by a willing hand up the stairs and into bliss.

chapter 11

"STUART, HOW ARE you? Everything on the range well?"

"Oh, MacD, good to hear your voice, boss. It's been awhile. Everythin' out on the range is going fine. One of our stags found comfort and warmth with many of the ladies last winter, lots of wee kids on wobbly legs finding the hillsides a bit challenging. It's here at the house where a change has just blown in, and I figured, you should know."

"Out with it, man. Should I be worried?"

"No worries, mate. Your mum has landed and is clearing the cobwebs, not with a dust broom, but her decibel level. Even the spiders are retreating. I try to explain you are running things from the States, but she seems hell bent on changing everything. MacD she hasn't been here in almost thirty years. She remembers me as an ornery teenager tagging along with my dad. I doubt she hears the voice of a man when I talk. Can you give her a call to put her mind at ease?"

"I'm a bit dumbfounded, Stuart. She seem all right of mind to you? Last I talked to her, she was living with some gent in Sydney."

"Aye, the way she flits about, you'd think her half her age. She is a force, like you. She came alone, so I don't know what happened in Sydney. I think if she hears the voice of the laird, she will calm down. You don't mind her being here, do you?"

"No, it's her home. Plenty of room for everyone to scatter if they hear her coming. I'm actually glad to hear she's home. I'll call her later. Been thinking of doing so anyhow. I've met a girl. I'm certain Mother will not approve, but I adore her."

"You gonna bring her home to Skye?"

"Aha, Stuart, let's just say, if you see me with Emmy strolling up the lane, don't be surprised, and if you do, much more is in the air than simply a trip home."

"Well now, it's about time. Glad to hear the good news. Convey my happiness to her. Hope to see you both soon. Let us know if or when you decide to come. We'll throw her a huge party."

"That's my man. Will do. I'll call you soon. Let me know if my mum gets under your skin or anyone else's. Hide the checkbook. We've got enough problems without Mum's help. Talk to you later."

"Who is Stuart?"

"Oh, lass, I didn't know you were there. Stuart is my gillie back home."

"Gillie? What is...or who is he?"

"My right arm, he tends to the estate, mostly the range and the wild-life, checks on the ecology, runoff, keeps poachers away or turns them in to the law. I don't know what I'd do without Stuart. He is the main reason there remains a MacDougal name on the postbox."

"What does he look like?"

"Stewy? Let's see...a gum ball basically. Bald, his face is round and would crack if he showed too much emotion."

"Remind me not to have you give anyone a description of me! Did I hear your mom is there?"

"You do have good ears. Evidently, she came roaring back to the estate. She has been somewhat of a globe-trotter since my dad passed away. Maybe she's finally home to stay. We MacDougals seem to take a long time getting over our grief."

"It means you have porous hearts; people you care about become part of you. Are you going to tell her about me...us?"

"As far as I'm concerned, especially after last night, there is no me with-out you. The porous heart you spoke of is filling with a Miss Emileigh Louise Suggs. Yes, I'll tell her all about us. But, Emmy, she is a lot like Tah. She is protective. Unlike Tah, she is kind of a hard nut to crack. Once you do, she is on your side for life, so beware, love, she isn't an easy person to get to know."

"I can do it. Besides, she's in Scotland, and I'm in North Carolina. I'm not too worried about running into her anytime soon."

"Aha, you are in North Carolina with her only son; don't be too sure about your last statement. Enough about my mum. How about a morning swim with the lads before I escort you back to the store?"

"If that includes breakfast afterward, I'm in."

"It can include anything you'd like afterward or during, anything at all, lass."

I'm beginning to think a morning swim means more to Ian than a few strokes in the water. Never has a man's touch turned my entire being to jelly, leaving me a quivering mass of happiness and joy and desiring more.

"Tah, you up and about? I'm just gonna grab a cup of coffee."

"Steve, what brings you about so bright and early today?"

"Just got an e-mail from the installers for your security system. They'll be here early on Monday. They estimate two days of installation, so by Wednesday, you should be taken care of where they are concerned. I'm here to put in a couple of deadbolt locks on the doors."

"Oh, Steve, I ain't used a lock in all these years. Do you really think it's necessary?"

"It makes no sense to go to the expense of putting in a state-of-the-art security system complete with video surveillance of the gas pumps and not at least put a lock on the door. We'll put keys somewhere down by the dock. I'm sure you'll lock yourself out. Leigh said she wants a key, as do Louise and Emily...oh and your Em too will surely want a key. Great news about Harper, isn't it? Louise heard prior to me coming here that Annabelle and Morgan are going to be the flower girls. They are taking the job seriously and have already begun to practice. Tess has a couple of adorable princesses there. I wonder if Tyler and Tess will be in the wedding."

"Oh, I haven't heard. They'll be beautiful. I bet Tess and Tyler will; Samantha and Dylan may well be too. We'll just have to wait and see how the planning turns out. How is Leigh handling the news?"

"Oh, she covers up pretty well. Anytime kids or grandkids are mentioned, I know there is a sting in her heart—mine too truthfully. It's one thing not to want kids and be without, but to want them and watch others... it's difficult, but still very joyful too. We are blessed in other ways. I am certain Leigh will publish a touching story about Harper and Isabel's wedding in the paper."

"She's probably already started writing. It will be an article they cherish years down the road. Leigh will undoubtedly describe every nuance and capture the essence of their special day."

"How are the plans for Wilmington progressing?"

"We leave Sunday after the rush in the store is over. It may be quiet as holiday week will be over and tourists go home. Emileigh will be here; she is going to stay next week while we are gone. We'll only be gone till Thursday. Guess I'm a homing pigeon; can't stay away."

"Speaking of Em, where is she?"

"Well, we'll find out when she arrives. I'm guessing she had a very good Fourth of July."

"TMI, Tah, TMI!"

"You sure aren't one of the girls."

"Nope, just a guy who knows I'll hear all about it soon enough anyhow. I'd better get these locks on before customers get here."

"All righty, I'm gonna call Louise and see if she knows any other plans for the wedding yet."

"Ian, I've got to get to work; Mama is probably over there, binoculars in hand just speculatin' on what we've been up to."

"And she'd be right. Before we go, you'd best hand over the rest of those blueberry pancakes and bacon. I've got to keep my strength up around you, lass. My morning swim with the lads has never been so stimulating. You keep that up and—"

"And what, Ian? Seems to me it takes two to tango, and you weren't exactly protesting."

"Protesting? Are you kidding? Not the word I would have thrown about. Saluting, aye, now there is a much better word."

"You are going to make it difficult for me to walk into the store looking innocent, ready for business as usual."

"There is nothing innocent about you or the way you walk, and as for business as usual, I too will have a difficult time focusing on the task at hand."

"Hmm, you didn't several times last night or this morning."

"Loving you is one thing; work seems to have lost its appeal."

Ian is more relaxed and self-aware than I've seen him. Moose and Bear are worn out, and it's only 8:30 in the morning. I have more energy than I've had in a long while, but I am sure once Ian drops me off at the store, the glow will wear off and the long, passionate night with no sleep will catch up to me. I hear Bessie's engine come to life. Ian is calling the dogs. It's time to head out across the water, back to reality.

"Morning, Emily. Y'all up and at 'em already? How is the store doing this week?"

"Good day to you, Leigh. Dylan is getting packed to head home, so we've been up for a while now. The store is doing great. I suspect it to start slowin' down startin' today."

"Are you going to seek out new items to see while we are in Wilmington?"

"I hadn't thought about it. I would really just like to forget about the store for a few days and enjoy my girlfriends."

"Me too. I'm sure Louise will want to relax some too before getting all geared up to help with wedding arrangements. Lord, we all know Tah needs a break. When I think about the week and what Tah and Em have gone through, it's mind-boggling."

"Not for Em. She seems to be finding love fast. Ian sure is a lot of man. I just hope and pray he doesn't disappoint her. What a pillar of strength Tah has been. I don't know how she did it."

"We mustn't think negatively about Ian. I tend to worry too. The reporter in me looks at the glum side of situations; too many years in the business and so much bad news to report, but you shouldn't worry so."

"It's my nature to worry about those I love. My Lord, you know that, after all these years. Are you thinking about retiring? You sound as if you're tired of the newspaper."

"There is a laundry list of things I'd like to do before I dry up and turn to dust."

"Oh what a bright sentiment; you're a long way from dust. I'd like to hear what you're contemplating pursuing. Good conversation for the beach with wine in hand!"

"Why wait for the beach. Let's get Louise to bring the party barge over to Tah's tonight after dinner and take a spin with a glass continually filled to the brim."

"We certainly have kept the glasses full this past week. We seem either to be celebrating or escaping. Think Em will come?"

"If she does, she'll be spillin' the beans about Ian to us."

"Then we must convince her if she ain't with him again tonight."

"MacDougal residence, who is calling please?"

"Is this the lady of the house to whom I'm speaking?"

"Yes, Maggie MacDougal. Who is asking?"

"You don't recognize your own son, Mum? I heard you came home. Is everything all right with you?"

"Ian, son, where on earth are you? I came home expecting to find you about. Stuart told me you are off gallivanting around the States."

"Mother, I hardly think what I'm doing qualifies as gallivanting. I'm certain Stuart didn't describe it as such."

"Well then, what are you are doing instead of tending to the estate?"

"Mum, I am tending to the estate the best I know how. It has turned around tremendously since I've come here and made some investments. Mother, you've got to stop changing what I have set up. I wish I had known you were headed home."

"Would you have come straight away if you had known?"

"I don't know. I have dealings in progress, but what I really want to tell you about is Emileigh."

"Who is she? Some temporary shelter?"

"Hardly, she is the woman who has stolen my heart."

"Tell her to give it back. I'm serious, Ian; those girls in the States are all the same."

"Oh good grief, Mum, you been reading trashy magazines? Trust me to fall in love with someone who has my best interest at heart and who is a woman of substance, like yourself."

"How long have you known this...this person?"

"I have known this beautiful woman for a short time, but we are madly in love. Mother, if you cannot be happy for me, then I am afraid we don't have anything more to discuss."

"Obviously, you have been taken in by her charms. Where are you, Ian?"

"I'm in Moravian Falls, a very small speck on the map in Western North Carolina."

"I'm unsure of where North Carolina is on any map. You are sure this woman is someone who is really and truly in love with you, not just your position?"

"Mother, she had never even heard of a laird. She is unlike any other woman I've ever met. I'd like for you to meet her sometime."

"How long are you in North Carolina?"

"I'm headed to New York come September. I'll be going there for a week soon."

"And is this woman going with you?"

"She is going with me for the weeklong trip. After that, we'll have to see."

"So you are both in love, but you aren't looking past August; is that what I'm hearing?"

"You might be hearing those words, Mother, but my heart is saying something entirely different. Emileigh and I haven't worked out our future; we really are enjoying each other in the moment."

"Well, I have to say, you sound self-assured and happier than I've heard you in a very long time, and if Emileigh is responsible, then I do want to meet her, and soon."

"My happiness is only partially fulfilled by Emileigh. God had a lot to do with bringing us together not only by manipulating my situation, but by softening my heart to a place where I'm able to accept her love, and return it."

"Those are powerful words. We'll talk soon. I love you."

"I haven't heard those words in a long time from you, Mum. They sound good. I love you too. Have a good day. Oh and, Mum, hands off the estate. I am the laird. Sink or swim, let me do it my way."

"Aye, son, you sound like the laird. It's yours to run. Good-bye, Ian."

We haven't been focusing on the store. If we didn't have Ely to help re-stock, we'd be in dire straits. Mama must be dying to inquire about my night with Ian, but so far, she hasn't said a peep, which is not like her. Truthfully, I haven't fessed up either. There is a line with Mama I am not comfortable in crossing. Talking candidly about my sex life is way on the other side of the line. Now the Suggettes, they are another story entirely. I reckon I ought to come clean with Mama before the others start popping their heads in here. Oh, at least I am saved for the moment; Dylan is here getting some gas.

"Morning, Dylan, you filling up to head back to Charlotte?"

"Oh hey, Em, yeah. Salina has an appointment today, and she wants me to go with her, so we're leavin' early."

"You coming back for the weekend or just gonna stay in Charlotte?"

"Since I've run into you, got a minute?"

"Sure, let me get some coffee, and I'll meet you down at the dock."

"Hey, Ely, do me a favor? How about washing my front and rear windows and topping off the windshield washer fluid? The washer fluid is in the trunk. If you don't mind, park the car for me. Here's five bucks for your trouble."

"Thank you, Dylan. Sure am glad Ian is teaching me how to drive. Anything I should know? Sure is a fancy automobile!"

"Take it easy on the gas; she's a peppy one. If you don't want to, just let her sit; I'll only be a couple of minutes."

"I'll be all right."

Of course Mama doesn't say a word to me about arriving home on Ian's boat this morning after being gone all night, but she is mighty curious about Dylan asking to speak to me. Dylan and I are pretty much cousins; he is a bit younger, but we grew up together. Once upon a time, Mama thought we would get hitched. Who knows? It might have been, but the Suggettes, including Mama, were way too pushy. Dylan and I felt like we were being thrown into an arranged marriage. No romance ever sprang up, but we're great friends. I believe secretly Mama and Emily were pretty disappointed when Dylan and I began dating other people.

"Hey, Dyl, what's up? Everything with you and Salina all right?"

"More than fine, Em. I've been here all week and with the goings-on haven't been able to spend one minute with you. It has been really hard to stave off Mama from finding out. She has been thinking Sal and I are on the outs; nothing could be farther from the truth. Sal found out about six weeks ago she's pregnant. Today is her first appointment with the doctor. She should be about three months along. Neither one of us wants to say anything till we know for certain everything is going along fine. She's had a couple of miscarriages, and we announced her pregnancy way too early. Sal had a difficult time afterward, so we chose to wait until at least three months."

"Oh, Dyl, everything will be fine. I'm so happy for you! You don't want anyone to know? Did you tell Sam? When are you going to tell everybody?"

"Well, if everything is fine, we are going to come back tonight and surprise Mom and Dad, and then of course everyone else tomorrow. I couldn't tell Samantha; she can't keep anything a secret, but you can keep it quiet, eh?"

"Of course, you know better than to ask. Please call my cell phone and let me know the minute you and Salina have the news. I'll be on pins and needles until I hear the phone ring. You do know we are all having dinner again down at the dock, so if you tell Grayson and Emily, it won't be tomorrow when everyone finds out; it'll be tonight, most especially since it's their first grandchild."

"Yeah, I figured the moment I said 'tomorrow' it was a stretch. Anyhow, that's my news. How about you and Ian? What's up there?"

I can feel my cheeks turning rosy just thinking of Ian. Our night together instantly conjures up feelings which I am certain Dylan can read at a glance. "Judging by the—excuse the expression—pregnant pause, it must be a pretty hot time between the two of you."

"One could say that. There is no one I've ever met who makes me feel the way he does. I don't know where we are going, but so far, it has been pretty exciting."

"I'm so glad to hear good news from you. You've been through a lot, and always loyal to your mother. I hope to continue to hear good news as your relationship grows. Right now, I've gotta fly. Sal's appointment is at one. Love you, kiddo!"

"You too, Dyl. I'll be thinking about you. Remember, call me, first thing, promise?"

"You got it! Hopefully, we'll see you later."

"I'll be here with bells on."

"Ely, son, watch the store for a minute, will ya? I've got to catch Em before she finishes her coffee and heads back."

"Yes'm."

The screen door opens and slams shut. Hightailing it down the stairs is Mama with a drink held high above her shoulder in one hand and a piece of toast in the other. She must have grabbed those in an effort to disguise her true intention. "Mama, could you be any more obvious? Honestly, sometimes I wonder if your curiosity is a disease!"

"Hush, baby girl, I've got you to myself for the first time. With Ely lurkin' around, I haven't had a second to talk to you. What did Dylan have to say? Emily is a bit upset he is leaving so early; it's only Friday. She thinks he and Salina are having trouble."

"Dylan and Salina are fine. It just didn't work out for them to be here longer. Y'all really need to focus on being more positive."

"Ha, the pot is calling the kettle black. So, he didn't have any news?"

"Oh, not really, he needed to get back for a meeting. We didn't have any time together, just the two of us, all week, which is unusual, so he wanted to say hi."

"Hmm, now about last night, you left in a boat and came home in a boat, but there is somewhere around eleven and a half to twelve hours missing."

"Really, Mama, you counted the hours? Yep, it's definitely a disease, a serious chronic case of curiositosis or some such ailment."

"Baby girl, you are beatin' around the bush, and I am feeling all giddy inside for you. Did y'all have a good time?"

I debate for a moment whether or not to answer Mama with some coy little platitude, evading her question or simply dive in and give her enough of the hot, sordid details she'll have to look away as her cheeks turn three shades of red. Not having seen my mother blush in a long time, if ever, I decide the line which has been drawn between us discussing anything of a sexual nature must be erased.

"By good time and since I went AWOL for a period of...what did you say, eleven and a half to twelve hours? I assume you are asking by beating around said bush, ahem, if I enjoyed making love with Ian?"

"Well, I never came out...umm...well, did you?"

"Mama, he touched me in secret places so secret I never even knew I had them! Ian made love to me with such passion and experience, I climbed to levels of pleasure previously I didn't know existed. Each time he pursued and rose to the occasion, it was better than the last."

Mama sits quietly. I am sure she has more questions frantically bouncing around in her brain. She lifts her glass to her lips. It's probably a good thing she has ice water; anything hot and she would have scalded herself as long as the glass hangs to her lip. Finally, she lowers the glass and demurely states, "Well then, Emileigh, baby girl, sounds like you enjoyed yourself."

"Mama, is that all you're gonna say? I have plenty more details to reveal concerning the passionate night Ian and I spent together. Don't you want to hear more? You simply say I enjoyed myself. Mama, you are the queen of understatement. I know you have more to say. I never have had a night like that in my lifetime, have you?"

"Oh, I recall a few right up there. Not with your father, before he came around. I take it you and Ian are in love?"

"Yes, Mama, we are. After what life has thrown at both of us, there is a connection I don't think I'd have with anyone else. He is quite a man in all respects, not just in bed."

"Well, I see how good he is for you. I hope the two of you will have a long, happy, and yes, my dearest, *passionate* romantic relationship. I don't need to hear any more of the details of your night. I am thrilled for you, Em, and I do like him—a lot. Since hearing how he is in the sack, maybe he is dating the wrong Suggs after all!"

"Oh, Mama, that's just gross to think about."

"Hi, Ian, you finding a property of interest this morning?"

"I'm missing you at my side, but I'm trying to look at some properties with Beth. So far, we haven't come across anything I want to part with the money to buy except the land on Traverse Hill. Do you know of anything someone maybe interested in selling that isn't listed?"

"I'll have to give it some thought. We see a lot of people. Grayson may know of some property; he is building for folks and probably hears rumbles long before anyone actually acts."

"I'll have to give him a call. Really, I just wanted to hear your voice. I did call my mum and told her a bit about you."

"Oh, what did she have to say?"

"Lass, like I told you, she is a hard nut to crack. By the end of the conversation, she actually said she wants to meet you. Did you just feel a cold chill run down your spine?"

"No chill, but when and where will this happen?"

"Who knows with mum? Could be a week or a quarter century. Her attention span isn't the best, as you may have guessed."

"Since we are talking about mothers, mine heard about our night."

"What does Tah think? Is she ready to kill me for pouncing on her baby?"

"She thinks you're dating the wrong Suggs."

"Oh, lass, what did you tell her? No, I don't want to know. I'm having dinner with you all tonight. Sure hope we'll have plenty of scotch on the menu so I can face everyone, because what Tah knows so shall the girls."

"You'll have a bottle of your very own. Bring the puppies."

"Weasy, is that you?"

"Sure 'nuff. What can I do for ya?"

"Well, just wondering if you would look into your crystal ball for me?"

"Usually you are the definition of a skeptic. What's goin' on?"

"Dylan left this morning. I have a feeling something is going on between them. At first, I thought it was trouble; now, I guess I have a gut feeling they're expectin'."

"You mean my old pal Emily Dupree had an epiphany? Stop the presses! Let me call Leigh. They'll put out a special edition for this bit of news!"

"Knock it off, Weasy. Are you gonna see or hear or whatever the hell you do?"

"You sure you want me to, Em? I mean it may not be good news or I may be wrong."

"Louise Tromble, I'm going crazy as a loon over here. Grayson is off with Cook golfing, and Samantha is with some boy from school by the pool.

I'm alone, and my imagination is consumed with thoughts. Your visions can't be any stranger than what I'm thinking. I know you think I'm an old stick in the mud with regards to your visions, but not really; I listen and wonder. It's just difficult when I think of you getting all this knowledge and I don't hear squat. Ain't fair, is it?"

"Don't know about fair or unfair. I'm in your life for a reason. Maybe you can't see, but I can be your eyes, leastwise in this situation. While you were lamenting about being alone with your little epiphany, I was able to tap into Dylan and Salina's energy. I'd say, Grandma, you're right on. A baby is in the oven, and because you'll ask anyway, it's a boy…let's see, I feel like December 26 will be his welcome into the world celebration."

"Holy crap, Weasy! I didn't expect…really? Oh now how can I keep this under my cap?"

"You don't have to. I know too, silly head. But let them be the ones to tell."

"Oh, Weasy, I hope you're right. Thank you, sweetie; you've made my day. Look, my feet aren't touching the floor!"

"I can't see everything, Emily, especially on the phone. Congratulations, everything is going to be just fine. See you for dinner; I'll give you a big ole hug then."

"I'll give you my bill!"

Cook and Grayson arrive and start to put together the food for dinner. Cook is up to yet another of his specialties. Harper and Isabel are hanging around the water. What is it about engaged couples? They act like they are forming a pack, always touching, circling each other, completely and utterly oblivious to the rest of the world. Tyler is helping Tess with her youngins as they play by the beach. Samantha is in the glider with a book, looking like she has lost her best friend. She is rather a pouty girl, always has been. Sometimes I just want to shake her. If she'd only engage in conversation with the rest of us! She is twenty-seven and a lot younger than her brother, Dylan, who is forty. Who knows? Maybe she doesn't feel like she belongs. I know how that feels. Sam and Tess usually hang out together, but Tess, having two girls less than a year and a half apart, doesn't have time to stroke Sam's needy ego.

"Hey, Dyl, thanks for calling to tell me your news. I have been thinking about you all day."

"Got those bells of yours on, Em? We are expecting, and everything, just as you said, is going very well. They gave us a due date of January 17."

"Oh, Dyl, I want to jump and scream. Everyone is gathering already. I am so happy for you both. What a blessing! Are you on your way back to the lake?"

"We are almost back. Are Mom and Dad there?"

"Your daddy is here; your mama is still at the store."

"Would you please ask Dad to go back home for a few minutes? We are literally about ten minutes from the house. I'd like to talk to the two of them together, Sam too, if you can get her to go."

"Okay, but I can see Grayson's expression now...I'll make up something for him and everyone else." "Thanks, Em. We'll see you in a little while."

"Can't wait to see y'all, Dyl, and congratulate you in person."

"Hey, Grayson, can I see you for a moment?"

"Sure you can, Em. You all right?"

"I'm more than all right. Will you do me a favor and not ask questions?"

"I guess, for you. What is it?"

"Make an excuse to go to the house and take Sam with you if you can pull her from the glider. Go get Emily; take her home. Tell her to close up the shop even if you have to wrestle her. Then sit and wait. You have a surprise coming, but you didn't hear it from me, nor can you relay it to anyone. And, Grayson, bring back the good scotch for all the guys, especially my Ian."

"Boy howdy, Em, since you've been dating skirt boy, you have become somewhat of an international woman of mystery, but I'll bite. Anyone who looks as radiant as you while asking a favor, a man would be insane not to follow orders!"

"Sam, up and out with me. We've gotta get your mom and pick up some stuff at the house for dinner. How was that, Em?"

"Perfect."

"Hey, Louise, when are Steve and Leigh getting here?"

"Oh, I don't rightly know—whenever they stroll down, I suppose. Why?"

"How about driving the party barge up to their cottage and picking them up?"

"Em, you got something going on we should know about?"

"No, just taking over getting the party started with everyone present and accounted for."

"Now, girl, you sent Grayson and Samantha outta here, and now you're gettin' rid of me. What is going on?"

"Use that third eye of yours, Louise, and do as I ask this once."

"Well, reluctantly, I shall, but mark my words, Em, we ain't makin' this a habit."

"We'll see, Louise. I hear Ian's boat, so I'm gonna run up to the store and get Mama. She hasn't even had her first glass of wine yet. Hurry back, Weasy, no lollygagging; remember the Rileys."

"Well, now I know something is in the air. You and skirt boy engaged or something?"

"Yes, Weasy, after less than a week, we are getting hitched. Does that sound like me, you nut job? Remember your gift and use it."

"Ayah, maybe not an engagement but there is a lot of sizzle in your energy today."

"I'll give you that. Now get going!"

I probably have given everyone except Tess and her children reason to believe I've gone over the deep end this afternoon. Dylan and Salina's news is so wonderful, and it rides on the coattails of Harper and Isabel's engagement. Life in Moravian Falls has taken a wonderful turn for all of us, even amidst the stress of a robbery attempt and Peter Barbour's behavior, which all seem like they happened ages ago. And then there is Ian, who is just now docking Bessie. Rocking the boat are Moose and Bear, begging to romp in the water with Morgan and Annabelle. Leaping into his arms, I whisper Dylan's news. He squints and whispers back, "Maybe that'll be our news someday."

"Oh, Ian, I'm too old to even dream."

"You are never too old to dream. Stranger things have happened, lass. But this isn't our day; it's Dylan's and Salina's."

"Not a word, Ian. No one knows."

"A kiss may keep my lips sealed."

"Not from what I've seen; a kiss sets you off."

"Aye, for other devilish endeavors."

"Grayson, I don't understand why you made me close the store and now the three of us are sitting here staring at each other. What on earth are you doing? Are you okay?"

"Is it so strange for a husband or a father to want to spend a few minutes alone with his wife and daughter?"

"Daddy, you aren't leaving us, are you? I mean, you are acting kinda weird, even for you."

"Coming from you, Sam, I'll take that as a compliment. Fathers do act weird, according to daughters, from time to time. Here, a glass of wine for y'all; it may make things a bit easier."

"Well, if you ain't leavin', you must be dying or sick. Who just pulled into the driveway, Mama?"

"I don't know. I'll go check and see. Why, it's Dylan, and Salina is with him. Did you know they were coming back, Gray?"

"No, sure didn't."

"Then how...?"

"Dyl, Salina, this is a nice surprise. Come on in. You want something to drink?"

"I'll have what he's having."

"And, Sal, can I get you a glass of wine?"

"A ginger ale would hit the spot."

"Y'all, we've got some news—"

"Oh Lord, not bad news? I knew something was wrong."

"No, Mama, it isn't bad news; we couldn't wait to come home and share it with you. Sal just had her first doctor's visit; we're going to have a baby!"

"Oh Saints be praised! When is the baby due?"

"They gave us January 17 as the due date."

"Really? It isn't December 26?"

"Mama, what? Did you know or suspect?"

"Don't pay attention to me; I don't know what I'm thinking. I'm just so very happy for you both. Grayson we are finally gonna be grandparents, and, Sam, you'll be an aunt."

"Son, I'm proud of you. Sal, you are going to make a beautiful mother. Let's go tell everyone."

"Oh, Grayson, maybe Salina would like to rest for a bit; they've had a long drive."

"I'm fine. Let's see everyone and tell them together. I especially want to meet Em's new beau, Ian. I hear he's hot, and Dyl tells me they're quite a couple."

"He is hot for an old guy."

"Oh, Sam, fifty-something is the new thirty-something, don't you know?"

"That would make me about eight."

"Yup, right where I'd put ya."

"Okay, kids—Dylan, you're going to be a father, best grow up."

"Yeah, Dyl, grow up."

I thought I'd never see the five of them walking down the path to the dock. They're strolling along with dreamy smiles plastered across their faces. "Is everyone already here? Y'all act like something is up. Dylan, has something he'd like to share with y'all."

"Hey, guys, Salina and I found out this afternoon we are expecting a baby in January."

Happy cheers are sent aloft; a lot of backslapping and toasts commence from there. Ian looks at me with a longing glance. He must feel a like a fish out of water. A few days ago, he had never even heard of any of us. Now he is sharing some of the most intimate of family moments. I would be remiss if I didn't tell him I'd rather just climb aboard Bessie and drift off into the sunset with him, and him alone.

"A large scotch, I believe you ordered, sir."

"Oh thanks, Grayson. Great news for you and your family. Congratulations!"

"Thanks, Ian. Why the long face all of a sudden? Usually, you have more energy than all of us combined."

"Does it show much? Sorry, thinking of the past; it has a way of sneaking up and taking you by surprise from time to time. I have so much more this week than last; it truly is amazing."

"No matter where your travels take you, Ian, you're always welcome here. You have to be here when the baby comes, and then there's Harper's wedding. Maybe you ought to set roots down in our neck of the woods. I'd like that. Come to expect seein' you about, and I know Em would love it."

"Hey, Grayson, you and Ian hoarding the scotch? How's about sharing it with the likes of me?"

"Steve, pull up a glass and have a seat."

"Exactly how many have you had?"

Everyone is reveling in the good news of the day. A new life is on the way to share with us all the love, joy, and hope a precious newborn gives. Mama is oblivious to her cell phone ringing. She and the Suggettes are surely in their divine element. Each of them sits with a large glass of wine clasped in a tight grip, legs crossed and swinging; most are twirling their hair in a hypnotic fashion, fingers pointin' at Ian and me and then over to Harper and Isabel and resting on poor Salina's belly.

"Mama! *Mama*, don't you hear your phone?"

"Oh, baby girl, whoever it is can leave a message. I'll check it later."

"Ooouuwee, did y'all feel the breeze? Clouds are flyin' in over the lake. Looks like we is about to get some rain at last."

"Hey, guys, let's get all our dinner stuff up to the store. It's gonna pour in a little while. Looks like we finished just in time."

"Ian, you'd better get going, Louise, you and Cook best load and get the party barge home and your grandkids to bed."

"Sweet Jesus, the thunder and lightnin' are comin' in quick. Let's get a move on; there's a storm coming."

Louise is right a storm with many fronts is coming in swiftly and unexpectedly.

"Em, you know who was on the phone?"

"Who? Someone you were expecting to hear from?"

"Not really, baby girl. Your grandmama. She is coming over tomorrow afternoon. She wants to see us."

"Oh Lord, she must have finally decided what to say after last Sunday's rant. Mama, I'm going with Ian over to his house. Okay with you?"

"Sure. Have fun. I don't like you out on the boat in a thunderstorm though. Why don't y'all go. Try to beat it."

"Hey, Tah, I almost forgot to tell you. Your window is gonna be installed tomorrow. Best get some plastic up tonight with this rain coming. You need help?"

"Normally, I'd say no, but if you don't mind, can you and one of the guys take care of it?"

"Hey, Dylan, lend me a hand for a few minutes."

"Lass, you ready to go so soon?"

"Sure am. Mama wants us to beat the storm."

"Just one second, I got a text message. Moose, Bear, in ya come!"

"Ian, I haven't seen that expression on your face. Is it bad news?"

Ian stands at the helm and brings Bessie to life. I cast off the lines, and while he reads the text message, a huge clap of thunder overhead booms loudly. "You sure we're okay to cross? The storm is moving awfully fast, and the wind is picking up."

"Lass, that isn't the only thing coming in fast. My message is from Mum and Fiona. They'll be here tomorrow; they're asking for directions. I want to get you across the lake tonight, so I can have you all to myself."

"Who is Fiona?"

"My daft sister. The wind's picking up; it's headed in from Scotland."

"Great, the perfect storm brewing, your mother and sister along with Grandmama all gathering in one day."

"The perfect storm indeed. Batten down the hatches."

chapter 12

"Louise?"

"I'm sorry, Ian; I know it's early. Do you mind terribly? The dogs barking probably made you think someone was breaking in. I was going to sit on the dock until you got up. Are you sure you don't mind?"

"No, not at all. Come in. Pardon my underwear."

"Don't rush on my account, skirt boy; you look mighty fine as you are!"

"Ian, who was at the—Louise? Is everything okay? Mama, is she all right?"

"She is fine. I didn't realize how early it is. What time...oh my stars, it's only six. I should go."

"Sit down. Whatever brought you here must have kept you up all night. Ian, are you making coffee?"

"I'm on it and some breakfast for us...right after I find my jeans."

"Now, Louise, what has you so worried you came to see us instead of picking up the phone?"

"This is a really nice house, open and airy, a hint of opulence but not overpowering."

"Louise, quit stalling."

"I'm observing, dearie, not stalling. Y'all are gonna think I'm a nut."

"We know you are. What's the revelation you came to divulge?"

"Last night, after everyone dispersed and the storm ended, clearing the night's sky, I kept getting a strong feeling of angst, like a wall falling on y'all."

"Louise, you're going to have to be a little clearer for me. Your feeling sounds frightening."

"Well, to be honest, a wall is kind of strange for me to see. Usually, when one thinks of a wall, it's an obstacle or a dead end. Maybe it's a turning point."

"My mother and sister are unexpectedly arriving today. For them to rush to the States after not seeing me for years is a turning point. It also has me wondering. I'm not certain my love life would be the draw, certainly not for them to suddenly appear."

"Well, that's somewhat of a relief to hear. I'm sure you can handle your family, Ian. I was thinking more of Em and these spells."

"I'm not so sure I am as capable to handle the women in my family as you surmise, but a heads-up is appreciated. As for Em, she is going to see a doctor before we head to New York."

"If your family is coming, we should postpone our little escapade to Wilmington. Tah won't want to miss visiting with your mother and sister."

"Okay, you two, enough of talking like I'm not in the room. I want Mama to get away from the store for a few days. Y'all have plans that shouldn't be interrupted. Besides, we don't know how long Ian's family will be staying. I'm assuming they'll be staying here, right, Ian?"

"There is plenty of room; they probably expect to stay with family."

"Well, whether Tah and the rest of us go on to Wilmington can be decided later. As for you, young lady, when is the appointment with the doctor scheduled?"

"I haven't made one; it'll have to be after y'all get back."

"Not good enough, Em."

"Not for me either. Call today and schedule. We'll make do at the store."

"Today is Saturday; it'll have to wait until Monday, and then the security system is going to be installed. Hopefully, Hannah will be coming in to help, along with Ely, but neither of them know to how run the store."

"Hannah is coming to help? When did this come about?"

"Their phone has been disconnected, so we sent a note home with Ely yesterday asking if she'd be interested in a few hours a week. Emily wants to give her a few hours a week too. Y'all are just going to have to be a little patient. With Ian's family here, the last place I want to be found is the doctor's office."

"I'm afraid it's the first place you should be found. Ian's family, even if everything goes well, is more stress; with Tah gone, Hannah and Ely in training, and this hunk of man keeping you up all night, your body is going to feel it."

"Lass, she makes sense, and we are slated to leave for New York soon after Tah returns."

"As long as we are being quite frank here, um, I know this is a sensitive area, but are y'all using contraception?"

"*Louise*, now you've stepped across the line. Ian is in his early fifties, and I'm in my forties; I don't think—"

"Stop right there, the last thing your body needs is to have a pregnancy, and the very last thing your soul needs is another loss. We don't know what is going on; I doubt the stress of a fetus would be welcome in your womb."

"Weasy, I appreciate your candor, but Ian's swimmers would have a very hard time fertilizing a powdered egg, which is probably what mine are. I'm no spring chicken."

"Ladies, one minute please. You have me crossing my legs talking about swimmers. Louise, you're right; we'll take precautions. I think my mum and sister will be enough of a contraceptive by their arrival. Em, make your appointment first thing Monday. I'll help, or one of the guys will come to the store while you are gone. The last thing you need to do is put more pressure on yourself. Matter of fact, it'll be good for all of us to chip in while Tah and the rest of the ladies are away."

"Anymore sightings in your magical ball, Weasy?"

"No one needs a crystal ball to see y'all are good for one another. I do see something rather enchanting, a quality you don't see in couples, especially during those early days of a romance."

"Oh now you have my interest piqued, Louise. Do go on..."

"You give off positive energy, especially when you are together. Positive energy attracts positive energy, matter building on matter. Many new couples emit negative energy, keeping the positive to themselves, which actually does two things. It repels and disperses matter and tears it apart."

"Well, a psychic reading and a science lesson all before six thirty in the morning!"

"We'll call Weasy the calm before the storm. Now who wants some of my scrambled eggs and toast?"

"I'll have some of those eggs. Got any jam? As for me being the calm before the storm, remember the bigger the storm, the bigger the potential for a multitude of silver linings."

"Far as I'm concerned, you're pure silver. You come over any morning; just knock first."

"Hmm...sounds like you two are settin' up house. Now about the jam..."

"Interesting way to begin today of all days, eh, Ian?"

"Louise has spunk. She must really care to come here so early. It takes courage to come without knowing how I'd react."

"She'd be the first to tell you, light shines brighter through a cracked pot, and I think she sees herself that way. She is courageous. Looking at her, sometimes I wonder if what she has is a gift or a curse. She views it as a gift. I suppose attitude is everything."

"She has attitude. A spunky woman with attitude is bound to get strange looks."

"Speaking of looks, you have any pictures of your family?"

"I may have a small one in my wallet, from when Fiona and I were little. My father and mum are in it as well. Here is the MacDougal clan. No giggles."

"Oh, my gosh, how cute and chubby you were. I see you in your dad, the strong features and gallantry. Didn't expect your mom to be so small. She is tiny, so much shorter than your dad. What is Fiona like now? You certainly have changed."

"I'm a late bloomer in many ways; in my late forties, I lost the baby fat; of course, exercising helped. Fiona is small, like Mum...at least she was. I haven't seen her in years. She married a Lennox and moved years ago. They have a son, Liam. He must be about twenty now. When Molly died and I fell into my wilderness, Fiona tossed her hands in the air and stopped communicating with me. Mum left, and Fiona probably felt a bit abandoned, as did I."

"Maybe this trip is a way to reconcile and rekindle your family ties, Ian."

"Oh, dear one, you are the one guiding me from the wilderness into the promised land. I don't know what to expect from Mum and Fiona, but my heart and mind are open. Now, since the lake is so smooth, how about a dip with the lads?"

"Absolutely, then I must go to the store. What time are we expecting your family?"

"They should be getting in to New York in a few hours and then flying to Charlotte. It won't be till well into the afternoon. Are you coming back here tonight?"

"Let's play it by ear. With Mama leaving tomorrow, I may spend some time with her, giving you time alone with your mom and sister."

"Your scenario won't sit well with Mum."

"Like I said, let's play it by ear."

"Morning, Grayson. Mama know you're puttin' in the window? It looks mighty fancy with the louvers 'tween the panes of glass. You sure it's within our budget?"

"You two are birds of a feather. Tah was out earlier in her bathrobe asking the same question. She thought I'd lost my marbles. The window was a special order someone rejected 'cuz the exterior was the wrong color. We got it for y'all at much less than I could have ordered a window. Mind if I bum a cup of coffee?"

"Come on in. Mama must be decent. Most likely, she'll have a fresh pot brewing. How does it feel, Grandpa, to have a new life coming into your family?"

"Words can't describe it; there's a fullness in my heart. I wish they lived closer. Hey, thanks for all your help last night, getting us home and everyone down to the dock for the announcement."

"I loved it. You ever thought of inviting Dyl to go into business with you? He was telling Mama how he likes working with his hands more than investment banking."

"I've given it some thought. He makes much more than I could ever pay him; plus, Salina's family is near Charlotte."

"You never know till you ask, Grayson. Besides, if he got involved and y'all invested profits wisely, which he knows how to do, you could pay him more. Salina's parents have land here, don't they?"

"They're working with an architect. It'll probably be at least a year before breaking ground. Em, you've given this thought."

"Purely selfish, I love babies, and it'd be nice to see Dyl more often. Can you imagine how flattering to be asked to go into business with your daddy? How proud, loving, and flat-out happy it would make Dyl?"

"I'll talk to Emily. She would like them near, and she'd also like for Sam to settle down and work for her. You talk like anything is possible."

"Anything is, if you believe. Ian says you must dream and then build on those dreams, or you get mired down in muck."

"Those are perfect words for a contractor's ears to hear."

"Morning, Mama. Sure is a nice window Grayson is putting in for us."

"Hey, baby girl. Yes, it is, I feel like I won the lottery. Your grandmama called; she'll be here about three and wants to stay for dinner. Can you stay, or do you have plans with Ian?"

"Oh, Mama, you don't know! I forgot..."

"Forgot what? You will be here to see Mama, won't you?"

"I forgot to tell you, Ian's mom and sister are coming in this afternoon."

"Oh, Em, how could you have forgotten? I'll cancel going to the beach."

"We just found out last night they're on their way. Don't cancel going to the beach. I want you to enjoy some time away with your girlfriends. They're all lookin' forward to eatin', drinkin', and talkin' too much."

"Baby girl, if you hadn't noticed, we do just fine in that department right here. I want to meet Ian's family and spend some time with them."

"*Estranged* family, Mama, they have some issues."

"The man you love has family traveling around the world, and you think I'm gonna leave right after they arrive? Can you imagine how snubbed they'd feel? Besides, I'd rather go to the beach after it cools down a bit and the kids are back in school."

"Your call, Mama, but I don't know how much time Ian's family will spend with us."

"I'll call the girls and tell them I'm out; they may want to go down anyhow."

"Doubt it, Mama. Y'all travel in a pack."

"You get ahold of skirt boy, tell him we are havin' a shindig at his place tonight. I'm sure his family will be tired; we'll make it an early night, and Mama will have to hit the road early anyhow. Think we should have everyone over?"

"Lord, you're on a roll. Why don't you call Ian and propose your idea. May as well overwhelm Ian's family with all of us. Maybe it will turn out to be a fun evening, but let's leave it up to Ian, okay?"

"All right, what's his number?"

Mama gets excited when she contrives a plan. There is trepidation in Ian's voice when he speaks of his family that makes me wonder who is on the way. "Did we give you the day off?"

"Yes'm, you did, but Mama asked me to bring her reply about workin' with y'all."

"What did she say?"

"It's in here for Ma Bell. She wrote her a note. Thought it would be more formal."

"Well then, Ely, what are you waitin' on? An invitation? Run it in to Mama. You may as well grab something to eat if you're hungry."

"Thank you, Miss Emileigh. Um, how is Ian doin'? Y'all still seein' each other?"

"Ian is just fine. I just got a message from him; he's on the way over here. If you hang around, you can see him for yourself."

"Is he driving or in the boat?"

"Now how on earth would I know? Go on, give Mama the note. Hurry up."

Just as Ely scurries into the store, Ian pulls up in the Land Rover. Ely flies out the screen door nearly knocking over two of Grayson's guys and pulls up to a stop right at Ian's side. "Well, what a greeting! How are you this fine morning?"

"I's real good, Ian. You need any help today, like drivin' or something?"

"Aren't you working here today?"

"No, sir, we are tryin' to figure out so I get a couple days off a week. Since I've been here all week, Miss Emileigh told me to take today off and then Tuesday."

"What about your mother? Does she want to start here?"

"I believe so. She wrote it down for Ma Bell. Misriz Dupree and Ma Bell are trying to figure out when to hire Mama. Each just a couple of days a week."

"My mum and sis are due in this afternoon. Why don't you and I take a drive to pick up supplies so they are more comfortable at the house? Throw your bike in the back of the Rover and get behind the wheel. I must see Tah and Em for a few."

"Cool, Ian, I gots breakfast in the store. Mind if I eat first?"

"Get to it, lad. Must keep up your strength."

"He's a good boy, eh?"

"A changed boy, Grayson. What a difference a few days and some love will make."

"Did I hear your mother and sister are coming in today? Here to meet the love of your life, I suppose, and pass judgment."

"Have you heard? Tah wants a party at my place with everyone to meet them, including Tah's mother."

"Nope, news to me. You want this to happen? We can put the kibosh on it."

"At first, I'll admit, I had reservations. My family and Em's checking each other out? But if the shoe were on the other foot, I'd want Em and all of you to feel a warm, hearty welcome to my house. Having it at my place will help. I'm sure they will be tired."

"Have you called Cook and put him on alert? He'll want to cater."

"Good thinking. I should call instead of leaving it to Tah. You may not've heard, the women aren't going to the beach either. Seems my family has got everyone bowing to them."

"Nonsense on the bowing, the girls love to put on a show. Meeting your family from across the big pond…well, that's the stuff legends are made of, in these parts anyhow. I gotta get back to work and get the window installed; evidently, we have another party to plan."

"Good morning, Tah. I'll ask Louise and Cook to load the boat with whatever you think we'll need. Meanwhile, I've called the owners of the house, and the guesthouse is mine tonight, so there is plenty of room for anyone who'd like to stay over. Ely, think you and your mom would like to attend?"

"Oh, I would, 'cept we ain't got a car; the police impounded it."

"We can work it out. After we go by the Trombles' place, we'll swing by your house and drop off your bike. Tah, when Cook comes by to pick up any food he may need, can you put it on a tab and I'll pay for it later? Em, can you pull some wine and other drinks for everyone like you did last Sunday?"

"Yes, sir, my laird, it shall be done."

"Tah, have any suggestions?"

"Yes, but not what you have in mind." Mama glances at him with a playful look in her eyes. "You seem to have things well in hand. If I think of anything, we'll just throw it in for you to pick up on the way back or give it to Cook."

"That's a girl. Em, Sound good to you?"

"Real good. I can't wait to meet your family—all of us can't. Will you be coming by to see Grandmama this afternoon?"

A tiny hesitation suggesting dread is in Ian's voice. "It depends on Mum and Fiona. I don't know exactly when to expect them. Guess I should send directions from Charlotte; they're probably frantic."

Ian sets off with Ely, but not before giving me a kiss smack dab in front of Mama, God, and all of Grayson's men. Before he pulls away, he whispers playfully in my ear: "If no one else takes it, the guest cottage is ours."

Undercurrents of a brewing storm are in the air. Ian is doing his best to keep everyone cool, calm, and collected. Mama is amazed at his stand-up effort at having everyone included, especially Hannah and Ely. I'm anxious, getting a bit nervous about meeting his mother and sister. The angst about Grandmama coming at three has taken a backseat to imagining tonight with everyone sidling up to Maggie MacDougal and Fiona Lennox.

"Hey, Ian, don't forget to invite Beth and Ulysses. As long as you're giving a party, may as well open it up."

"I need to call Beth anyhow. She found a place someone is about to list, and I've asked to be the first to see it. Since Tah isn't going to the beach, when it's arranged, would you like to go with me?"

"I'd love it. Don't forget to text directions to your mom."

"Right, I can do that now since Ely is driving."

I can't help but wonder what his mother and sister are like. If they are anything like Ian, we are all going to enjoy their company immensely.

"All right, Ely, Cook and his family are on board. On to your house and then over to Ulysses's before dropping by my place. You know the way. Drive on, lad."

"You sure 'bout invitin' Mr. Bucknell to your party?"

"Why do you ask?"

"He's crazy."

"And you know this because..."

"Just 'cause everyone I know says so. I ain't met him, but no one goes near for fear..."

"Fear of what? He is a lonely old man. His wife died years ago; they never had children. The man doesn't have two nickels in his pocket to rub together; he is riddled with arthritis, and from what I see, no one cares to even check on him."

"I didn't know. Just heard rumors is all I knowed."

"Then take this as a lesson, son. Notice things for yourself, not what others have to say. After you do, listen to your heart and let God speak to you. You will be amazed at what and who is placed in your life, and even better, what you can do for others. Look at me; a week ago, my life, although more privileged than Ulysses's, pretty much mirrored his."

"No way, I ain't believin' that, Ian."

"I've been alone for over twenty-five years, no kids and my family estranged. I was a miserable so-'n'-so."

"But they's comin' all the way from Scotland to see you!"

"That's true, I haven't seen my mum since I was twenty-something and my sister for many years with barely a phone call."

"Is you nervous 'bout them coming?"

"A wee bit and deep down excited too. Like Emmy said, maybe this is a new beginning for us. A little anxiety is festering as well, I've tried to rekindle our relationship before and had the door shut in my face. Here I am, with all these new friends in my life and Emmy. Granted, it has taken a long time for my family to come together, but some of the responsibility rests on my shoulders too."

"Well then, I surely want to be there tonight. You is right 'bout noticin' stuff. I'da never thought you and Mr. Bucknell would be sharing anything in common. Can I come in with you when you talk to Mr. Bucknell?"

"Sure, he'd probably like to see a young person."

"You absolutely certain you don't want to go to Wilmington tomorrow?"

"Yes, Leigh. Sorry to disappoint you; there is no reason the rest of y'all can't go and enjoy yourselves. I feel I need to be here while Ian's family visits. It wouldn't look right me, being Em's mama, up and leavin' right after they arrive."

"No, no, you're right. But promise me, we will go somewhere before the holidays. I really need something to look forward to. Seems everyone has family things going on and..."

"I know, sweetie, it's hard on your heart. You're family too. If it weren't for you and Steve, I probably wouldn't even be, after that scoundrel of a husband left me. You are coming to the party at Ian's tonight? Oh, please say you are! Wouldn't be the same without both of you!"

"We'll be there. I can't wait to see his house. Always wanted to set foot inside, and look at us, entertaining international visitors! Can you believe it, Tah? It's like a movie."

"With Mama around, we'll have drama along with international intrigue."

"Hey, you reckon the Ramblers would play if they get something to eat?"

"Oh, Leigh, I think they'd be overkill. Besides if they are playin', it may cut down on the amount folks talk, and I for one want to hear everything Ian's family has to say."

"How's the window coming along?"

"Can you believe it? It's already in and so nice. Grayson didn't even charge us for the labor. I was shocked. When you drive by this evening, take a look. Sure is fancy. I almost want to thank Peter Barbour for smashing it."

"Oh now, Tah, that's goin' a bit far."

"I said 'almost.'"

"Okay, Ely, remember what I said about noticing things for yourself? You know where he lives, right?"

"Yes, we's almost there. Mama seemed really excited 'bout being invited."

"You should have said she needed a ride to the police impound lot to pick up her car. Steve was more than willing to jump in and give her a ride there. You saw, all it took was a phone call to ask Steve."

"It ain't easy for us to ask for things. Y'all are doing so much for both of us, to ask more seems, well, you know, kind of selfish."

"Here we are. Just pull her up to the side here, Ely."

"Good morning, Ulysses."

"That you, Ian. Come on in. Who is this young man with you?"

"Howdy, Mr. Bucknell. I'm Ely Stiles."

"Ely! Gracious you have shot up since the last time I saw you. How old you be now?"

"I's sixteen, sir. You've seen me before?"

"Years ago, you must've only been five or so. Looks like you are growing into a fine young man. Keeping good company, I see."

"Ian's the best, sir."

"So what you doin' here?"

"I'm having a party at the house tonight. My Mum and sis are coming, and I'd like for you to join us."

"Me, you're asking me?"

"Wouldn't be a party without Moose's and Bear's friend joining in the fun."

"I don't know, son, a party? Land's sake, I ain't been to no party in..."

"Mr. Bucknell, I ain't never been to a party. We can hang out together."

"Well now, it appears Ely has made an offer I cain't refuse. Oh, Ian, hang on, I've got something for you. Well, instead of me trying to get up out of this ole chair. It may be faster for you to get it. Look over yonder inside the rolltop desk, right in front."

"This, the bag here, is this what you want?"

"Yes, you got it. Bring the bag over here, if ya please. I made this for you, a thank-you of sorts for helping me with the dogs and fixin' the old wreck of a car, not to mention all the food you keep bringin' over here."

"Ulysses, it's magnificent. You did this?"

"What is it, Ian?"

"A beautiful carved figure depicting Moose and Bear. I will treasure this; it's a real piece of artistry, Ulysses. How did you make it with your arthritis?"

"Pain of some sort is always in your life. The exercise is good and helps, but thinking of you while making it...well, that's a gift to myself."

"Oh, mate, here, here, now, no tears..."

"Cain't help it. You're so kind to this old, used-up husk of a man. God smiled on me the day you drove into town."

"You be ready say about five thirty, and I'll have Ely come down in the Rover to pick you up. Is that okay with both of you?"

"Sure is with me, Ian."

"Well, I've got most of the day to peel off some layers of scum and get handsome. I reckon I've got some clean clothes. This mother of yours, Ian, is she single?"

"Ulysses, thank you for the carving. You could make a lot of money with this gift of yours. And, yes, Mum is single, so look your best."

"Oh, I've got tons of pieces made in the barn, years' worth. Y'all ought to take a look-see. Creatin' something is all that helped after my precious Peg died. Passed the time, ya know, while I remembered our years together. So I'm betting your mom is a looker, judging from the likes of you. I'd best get to spiffin' up."

"Mr. Bucknell, you should talk to Misriz Dupree about puttin' some of your wares in her store. She'll be at the party tonight, won't she, Ian?"

"She'll be there, a fine idea. I'll introduce you, Ulysses."

"Oh, I know Emily. Haven't seen her in years."

"Good, I'll have this piece out in a prominent place and make a point of letting her know it's your creation and you have plenty more for her to see."

"Like I said, God smiled and continues to do so. See you tonight, and thank you for thinking of me."

"See you at five thirty, Mr. Bucknell."

"Bye-bye, Ely. See you soon."

"Okay, Ely, on up to my house. Let's give the lads some exercise."

"That wood piece, I ain't never seen nothin' so beautiful in my life."

"It's something, isn't it? Looks just like Moose and Bear. When you pick him up, ask him to show you his barn and some of his other works. I'd be interested in seeing them too, but don't have time. He is truly talented and doesn't even know it."

"I'll do it, Ian. Surely, I will."

Mama is flitting about the store like a crow on speed. Every second the clock ticks closer to three, she turns her antics up a notch. "Mama, what is your problem? Lord, have a drink and relax."

"The kind of drink I want I'd best steer clear of until tonight. If Mama were to smell alcohol on my breath before yardarm time, there would be hell to pay. I do have customers who may take offense as well."

"I was not intimatin' you have alcohol, but even so, it's summer; you've lived a youthful sixty-three years; and your mama should not be ruling your life so heavily. A little joy juice is in order for both of us. Can you imagine Grandmama going on her venting and us sittin' like two birds on a wire with a silly grin plastered on our faces? Ooowee, it's almost worth getting caught."

"Now, baby girl, I'd ask you what's gotten into you all of a sudden, but I think you already told me the answer. You seem self-assured with Ian's family arriving shortly. Ever hear when they're pullin' in?"

"I did get a text from Ian a bit ago. They landed in Charlotte, got their rental car. They should be here around four."

"You gonna try and be over to Ian's when they arrive?"

"I ain't sure. What do you think? Should I give them a few minutes to say their hellos and then go on over?"

"If it were me, I'd ask Ian to call when he wants you to come over, or text or whatever it is y'all do with those silly little phones."

"Mama, you should get one; they make life easier."

"Nothing is easy if you have to strain to read it or use it. I like jaw-flappin', and for some reason, I feel I'm heard better with a real-sized phone. Now, how come you are so relaxed when you are helpin' to put on this party and meeting—what are their names, Magpie and Fionie?"

"Oh, Mama, get it right, please. You'll have me sayin' the wrong names, and I'd be mortified. It is Maggie MacDougal and Fiona Lennox. This party I'm helpin' with, seems to me, it was all your idea. What are you doin' to help?"

"Lennox, like the china people? And, little girl of mine, Ian asked me to pull all this food and stuff Cook wants. You got the drinks lined up?"

"China people, Mama? You think they're Asian or you mean Lennox chinaware?"

"Do you think I'm dumb or somethin'? These folks live in Scotland, a far cry from China, I think. I'm just wondering if she married into a well-to-do family."

"Mama, I think the MacDougals are well-to-do by our standards. I don't rightly know about Fiona's husband or his family. I do know she has a son named Liam Duncan, who attends school somewhere in England."

"Oh my, am I supposed to curtsey or some such shenanigans when I meet the well-to-do MacDougals? Mama ain't gonna go for any of that crap."

"I wasn't nervous about the party before, but talkin' to you the last five minutes has me wondering if inviting y'all was a good idea. Mama, you know Ian; do you think he would want you to treat his family any different than you treat him?"

"Depends."

"On what exactly?"

"If he wants to make an impression or if he wants us to make an impression."

"Mama, just be yourself; that will likely leave a lasting impression."

Louise and Cook arrive at the dock, music blaring, horns a-tootin'. It looks like they are definitely in a party mood. "Weasy, long time, no see."

"Yeah, I'm sorry about this morning. I really didn't know it was so early."

"What y'all talkin' 'bout?"

"I went over to Ian's this morning to talk to them; it was earlier than I thought."

"Oh, talk about what?"

"Mama, must you know everything? Hey, Cook, we've got nearly everything you asked for packed. Come on up and I'll show you."

"She is getting feisty, isn't she?"

"Like mother, like daughter. Speakin' of mothers, when is yours due? I want to make myself scarce."

"She should be along anytime. When are y'all going over to Ian's?"

"Ian called Cook and suggested five. All right if we park here and have a couple of drinks before going over?"

"Sounds perfect. Knowing you are here while Mama visits is comforting. Ain't it nice to have new blood around these parts?"

"New blood, it ain't like we're a bunch of vampires!"

"We ain't the ones from the Old World!"'"Oh hells bells! Mama's here spinning tires in the dirt. Wish us luck."

"Kick some ass, Tah!"

"Hush now, Weasy. Do wish me patience."

Circling my mind is a humorous caricature of Ian skipping around in his kilt, spreading fairy dust to ward off evil spirits. With that lingering vision, I hear Grandmama muttering her usual ill thoughts toward the world as she climbs the stairs. Secretly, I would welcome fairy dust right about now. Grandmama glances at the new window while stretching out her long, thin fingers for the screen door. Cook makes a flimsy excuse about hearing Louise calling him. Beulah Bell certainly has a reputation.

"Mrs. Bell, how are you today?"

"Steve, isn't it? The day finds me as well as someone like me can be, I suppose."

"Well, you take care. See you at the party. By the way, my name is Cook."

"Party, what the hell are you talking about? I'm not about to go to any party."

"I think you're expected. Emileigh and Tah can tell you."

Oh good Lord, nice move, Cook. We wanted to ease Grandmama into meeting Ian and his family and…she doesn't even know about the week we've had. Where is Mama?

"Fiona, why are you stopping? A store named 'From Swags to Witches' hardly sounds like a place we'll be safe."

"We're lost, I'm sure we are safe, Mum. It's just a hillbilly name."

"I've heard about these Appalachian places. Wasn't there a movie?"

"*Deliverance?* You mean that old movie? Mum, your imagination is working overtime. Why did you come if you're afraid?"

"It isn't as if you gave me a choice. Let's just get directions and find Ian."

"Howdy, y'all lookin' for anything special or just want to browse?"

"I hardly thought you'd have such delightful merchandise, given the name of your establishment."

Emily looks at the two strangers moving rather cautiously into the store. "Your accent, are you Ian's kin?"

"Kin? Are you referring to family?"

"You'll have to pardon my daughter; we are Ian MacDougal's family. Do you know him?"

"Sure do, he's a great guy. You needing directions to his place? My family will be over later for the party."

"A party, how quaint, you would be...?"

"Oh, I'm sorry. I'm Emily Dupree."

Emily extends her hand with a warm smile. They peer at her with a harsh stare; her kind gesture ignored. Emily temporarily overlooks the snub. "I own this *establishment*, as you call it. I imagine you're tired after your trip. It isn't difficult to find Ian's from here." Emily finds herself stammering, trying to keep the conversation civil, but anxious to see them drive away.

"Is there a place we can get some petrol—gas. I'm almost on empty."

"Right on the way, you'll spot Suggs General Store. That is Emileigh, Ian's girl, and her mama's store. Gas pump's there."

"Oh, this ought to be fun. Meeting everyone before seeing Ian."

"We all like your son very much; he and Em are a really nice couple."

"Couple, you say? Hmm, we shall see. Thank you for the directions. Perhaps I'll come and shop another day."

"Please do. I'd love to show you around. The place is bigger than it appears. I've collected some fine items, not only locally, but on my travels as well."

"You've traveled? Surprises are found all around, aren't they, Mum?"

"I beg your pardon."

"Oh nothing, my dear, she was just referring to your collection of fine wares."

"Uh-huh, here are your directions. I look forward to seeing you later for dinner."

"Oh, it's dinner too? My, oh my, Ian must have changed throwing such an elaborate party."

"It won't be fancy. We want y'all to feel welcome, and dinners with each other here are normal. We don't much cotton to uppity affairs."

"Mrs. Dupree, we will see you later."

Just as Grandmama sets down her purse and asks for a cool drink, the phone rings. "Suggs General Store, how can I help you?"

"Em, is Tah there? I must speak with her pronto."

"She is, so is Grandmama. Can't this wait?"

"No, absolutely not. Seconds count. Put her on now, Em."

"Mama, the phone is for you. It's Emily; she is in near panic about something, saying seconds count."

Grandmama takes a sip of her lemonade with a sour look, and she places the glass down on the counter rather loudly. She commences tapping her prune-skinned fingers rapidly, demanding attention.

"Emily, what is wrong?"

"Tah, you won't believe who was here."

"Out with it, Emily! Don't play cat and mouse; my mama is here for a visit."

"Ian's mother and sister were just here. They never said their names, but they are headed your way for gas, and Tah, she is a whirlwind, putting on airs and such. Watch yourself—Em too."

"Oh Lord, thanks for the heads-up. See you later. Em, Ian's family are headed here from Emily's; they need gas and then are going to Ian's. Best behavior, Emily says they're something else."

"Who the hell are y'all jawin' about? Ian who and who cares? I've come all this way to discuss Emileigh's words to me last Sunday, and I don't expect to be interrupted."

"Expect or not Grandmama, you're gonna be. These folks have traveled all the way from Scotland not just from Blowing Rock. Ian is the man I've fallen in love with; you'll be meeting him later at a party. The party Cook told you about prematurely."

"Well, I never!"

"Mama, put some vodka or something in her drink. Those storm clouds are beginning to gather."

"Deep breath, baby girl. Deal with this using a sense of humor. You go and meet Ian's mother and sister. I'll stay up here and hold hands with Mama, fill her in on the week a bit, drop some vodka in her drink, too."

"Oh, Mama, maybe I've got time to call and warn Ian. Here comes a strange car. Wish me patience!"

The rental car is shiny new, black, and bold, one of those uppercrust automobiles the likes of which I have never set foot in besides Steve's. I see the faces of two stern, worn-out women shrouded in black; they look shell-shocked by our little world.

"Hi, what can I do for y'all?"

"We need petrol. Fill it up. Do you know someone named Emileigh?"

"Yes, I do. It happens to be me. Are you Ian's family?"

"Word travels fast, doesn't it?"

"It's a small world."

"You pump petrol for a living?"

"I own the store with my mother. We do whatever is necessary; if it means pumping gas, then yes, I pump gas. Ian is looking forward to seeing you both, Mrs. MacDougal, Fiona."

"Properly said, my dear, it is the Lady MacDougal and Lady Lennox."

"Excuse my informality, but you are in the United States; we don't much abide by titles of aristocracy. I hope you understand. Ian didn't explain and hasn't ever mentioned a title to us."

"Just one more reason."

"Excuse me, Fiona? One more reason for what?"

"You don't have a need to know; it's for Ian's ears. Thank you for pumping our petrol. I expect we shall see you later at our welcoming party?"

"Oh yes, I'll be the one at Ian's side."

My buttons were pushed so hard they're popping off—and by complete strangers. Unable to face Grandmama yet, I make a quick escape to the dock while dialing Ian's number. Louise meets me halfway with a full glass of wine, which I swallow like cool water.

"Hey, Ian, your mother and sister were just here getting gas. I met them and want you to know they are a little ahead of schedule."

"Emmy, you sound stressed; they on a high horse with you?"

"You could say the Lady MacDougal and Lady Lennox are...I had no idea I should have referred to them as such, and I probably insulted them on top of not using their title."

Cook is standing next to me rubbing my back as Louise refills my glass. I wink at their kindness and realize I still have my Grandmama to deal with in the store. "Those titles mean nothing outside of Parliament or London any longer. They are showing arse, and in their defense, both are probably weary, wondering where they are and why they chose to come. I'm not even sure they own the title of 'lady.' I'd have to look into it. When you are beside me, I will take care of you and all our friends. Em, I gotta go. Beth just drove up to take Ely home. He has to fetch his mom and clean up."

"Oh, Ian, I really wish I could just blink and today would be over."

"Just remember, none of it matters; lean on those who love you, and most of them, if not all, will be here tonight."

"Thanks, Louise, Cook...Now to hear whatever Grandmama has to say. Guess you heard about Ian's family, huh?"

"We may need to gather a few more bottles of wine for tolerance sake."

"Weasy, send up some positive vibes for us."

"You got it, sugar."

"Mama, Grandmama, I'm sorry for the interruption. Since no customers are here, what can we do for you, Grandmama?"

"Those people in that there fancy car, are they related to your new boyfriend?"

"Yes'm, they are his mother, the Lady Maggie MacDougal, and his sister, the Lady Fiona Lennox."

"Lady? What on earth? Are they living in the Dark Ages or something, girl? We don't follow titles here. We left all that bunk behind. We have a president not a king."

"I know, Grandmama. I said pretty much the same thing to them. They are prim and proper, probably never been to the States before."

"They're in for a rude awakening."

"I think they've already had it. Now getting beyond them..."

"Is your boyfriend—what is his name? Ian, I believe Tah said—is he like them, all proper and throwing titles around?"

"Far from it; you will see tonight at dinner—at least I hope you'll do us a favor and join us."

"You are becoming diplomatic, missy. I'll go just to see what all the falderal is about. Tah tells me about the week's doings. Seems y'all have had a lot to contend with and have done a wonderful job dealing with it. I wish I had known, but then part of me is glad I didn't because I would have been worried to death 'bout y'all."

"You don't know how much I've needed to hear you say those words." I reach out to hug her, but she sidesteps my arms.

"Don't go gettin' all sappy on me, girl. Fact is, y'all had been asking for trouble for a long time by not taking any precautions. I'm just glad you learned. I don't agree with you hiring the very boy who tried to rob you, no sir. Will he be at this party tonight as well?"

"He'll be there, and I explained he was forced into doing what he did. He is really a good soul."

"I'll be the judge."

"No, Grandmama, you won't. Why do you always feel you have to take a contrary opinion? We've lived through a week of extremely high stress, and you just finished explaining you thought we did a wonderful job dealing with everything. Why must you turn sour now?"

"Well, I just thought you might want my view."

"A view is quite different from judging the boy, Mama."

"I think I finally see that you are contrary and obstinate to us so we feel we need you, but really it's so you feel needed."

"No, I don't see myself being needy or needing anyone. Y'all have gotten big heads all of a sudden; remember, we have humble roots."

"I'm sorry you don't feel as though you need anyone. We still haven't come to why you came here today."

"Those humble roots must show themselves now to y'all. Em, you said to me Sunday I despised your husband. The truth of the matter is yes, I did, but not for reasons you suspect."

"What reasons could you ever have to despise someone I love or who loves me?"

"I ask every year about the baby you lost, not to hurt you. I never knew asking hurt you. I was trying my best to remember a soul who I would have loved, who didn't make it into this world before being taken by angels to our Father's arms. Your husband didn't seem fazed by the loss; he shrugged it off and, excuse the expression, he pissed me off royally."

"So you despised Josh because he didn't outwardly show his grief to you?"

"Pretty much, I didn't see him bat an eyelash at the time, and you were going through a lot of emotional pain. I never saw him comfort you."

"Grandmama, did you show me comfort? All I saw was you walking away from Josh, and that hurt me too."

"I didn't think about my actions. I am here today asking your forgiveness for the mess I made where Josh and the baby are concerned."

"Forgiveness is easy, Grandmama. I want you to know, Josh felt the loss of our baby very strongly. In fact, deep down, I believe he felt a little guilty because we didn't change our lifestyle at all during my pregnancy. I didn't drink or anything, but we were always on the go and I obviously have some health issues dealing with stress, which I wasn't aware of at the time. I actually think he was so hurt and grief-stricken it may have contributed to his heart failure."

"Oh, baby girl, do you really think—"

"Yes, Mama, I do. Especially since I've met Ian, and I see how losing his wife and newborn son has affected him for over twenty-five years."

"Em, he lost his wife and son? Oh, the poor, dear man, and now you two are together. What a gift you must be to each other."

"Thank you, Grandmama, for explaining some things long overdue. Now maybe we can all move beyond the past. I can't wait for you to meet Ian. I think you will like him. Mama does."

"Yes, I do indeed. Em, don't you want to get moving and go on over to Ian's?"

"I'll call and see what he thinks. His family may want to rest a bit."

"I don't want either of you to think I'm getting soft or any such foolishness. I'll damn suredly put y'all or anyone for that matter in their place in a heartbeat. Mark my words."

"Grandmama, tonight, I will hold you to your word. Y'all riding over with Cook and Louise?"

"No, I think Grandmama needs to drive. Should we need a getaway vehicle, it will be at the ready."

"I'm glad to hear your voice. How is it going over there?"

"Interesting, neither one even recognized me. Told you I've changed. They walked in criticizing everything in sight. Guess they thought I own the house. Fiona mentioned she met you. Said you pump petrol with the best of the boys back home. Mum has aged, dresses all in black, probably because she feels it is slimming. I don't think they are prepared for the hot, steamy North Carolina summers. You'll love this part, because our party is going to be outside and since they didn't have the forethought to check to see what the temperature is before packing, they are donning my T-shirts which make them look like trolls. The shirts hang below their knees. Won't that make the headlines when Leigh writes it up in the society column!"

"Oh, Ian, I can't imagine."

"You don't have to. Come on over!"

"Your mom has some wicked long hair. It must be down below her waist if it isn't braided."

"It doesn't appear she has cut it since I last saw her. It was short and perfectly coiffed. Of course, you haven't seen Mum stand yet; she is rather vertically challenged, and so is Fiona. Except Fiona is horizontally challenged as well, which I have to say really surprised me. Last time I saw her, if she turned sideways and stuck her tongue out, she looked like a zipper. Tell me, love, how did it go with your grandmother?"

"She surprised the crap out of me and actually asked my forgiveness. I'll tell you about it later."

"Mum and Fiona are taking a nap; they aren't up for much tonight."

Mama slipped into a nice cotton summer dress and put her hair up in a bun. She could pass for royalty in my book. She and Grandmama, after having had one glass of wine, drive off. I need a moment to myself. Earlier, I wanted to be with Ian to greet his family. How plans get ruffled! The store is quiet, nothing but the overhead fans swirling. The money is in the safe; the shades, including the one on the new window, are closed; and for the first time, the door is locked. It's odd being inside the store after all these years knowing I won't be interrupted. The bathroom mirror reveals a new crop of gray hair has invaded my otherwise dark locks. I'm not one for standing before a mirror and scoping out wrinkles. I am what I am, like Popeye used to say to Olive Oil. A cool shower feels like a baptism of sorts. I wash off the day and prepare for a night with our friends and meeting Ian's family. A pair of form-fitting denim capris and a light chiffon top with impressionist flowers splashed across the airy fabric pick up my spirit. Jewelry isn't something I wear much of, but tonight it seems appropriate, especially since I know Ian's family will be observing every detail. The crowning glory, which I usually skip, makeup, provides a mask to hide behind after such a long day. Since I will be one of the last to show up, why not make an entrance?

"Ely, time for you to go pick up Ulysses. Careful now and help him into the car; he has trouble sometimes."

"Yes, Ian. Should I take Mama?"

"No, she's talking to Leigh. Run along now. You'll be back before she notices you're gone."

"Tah, welcome. Come on in. Is this your mother?"

"Hey, Ian, give us a kiss. This is my mama, Beulah Bell."

"It's a pleasure to meet you. What would you like me to call you?"

"How 'bout Lady Bell? That has a ring to it, don't ya think?"

"So you've heard? I'm not a stickler for titles. How about Beulah? We're all grown up."

"Now, you, I could get to like."

"Come on in, I'd like to introduce you both to my family."

"I already see two members I like; they seem to like me as well."

"Moose is the brown one, and Bear is the black. You're getting the best greeting yet."

"Gotta love God's creatures, and dogs are my favorite. What on earth is on your coffee table? It's remarkable. Wherever did you find it?"

"I'm glad you noticed. Ulysses Bucknell made it. He'll be here soon. Ely just went to pick him up. Oh, Emily, I want to show you this too. Ulysses made this. Isn't it beautiful?"

"Ulysses Bucknell made this, that old codger? The detail is very intricate. Does he have others?"

"A barn full. Think you could sell them in your store?"

"Does a duck have feathers?"

"He'll be happy to hear his talent is appreciated by others. My family is outside. Let's go say hello. What would you like to drink?"

"I'll have white wine, Ian, and, Mama, what will you have?"

"Oh something different. What do you suggest, Ian?"

"I'll mix a surprise just for you, Beulah."

"Here are your drinks. I'd like to introduce my mum, Maggie, and my sister, Fiona. Mum, Fiona, this is Beulah and Tahlulah; they are Em's grandmother and mother."

"Interesting names. Wherever do they come from?"

"Imagination mostly. Folks 'round here like lyrical names which sound like a song when you are callin'."

"Works for me. Is your daughter coming to the party?"

"She's closing up the store and wanted to freshen up a bit. Y'all had a long journey today. You must be tired."

"We are weary, but glad to meet everyone."

"I'm sure you're glad to see Ian. How long has it been since you all have been together?"

"Fiona, how long would you say? It's been twenty-some years, hasn't it?"

"Give or take, yes, Mum."

"What? You ain't seen your boy in over twenty years and yet you show up here? Fiona, where do you live?"

"My husband and I currently live in Glasgow, but we're moving to Inverness soon."

"Do you go back to where you grew up much?"

"Skye, no, haven't been there in twenty-five years, not since Molly's funeral."

"Our family ties are different than what you seem to be used to. We've had tragedy in our time."

"Everyone has some sort of tragedy."

"To each his own. Beulah, I think it wise to change the subject. It isn't our duty to be quizzed on family issues."

"Ladies, how is it going over here? Anyone need a refill?"

"Steve, I could use some more wine, with ice please."

"Mum, this is Ulysses Bucknell; he made the carving."

"Howdy. Maggie, isn't it? I'm pleased to make your acquaintance."

"Maggie, it is. I'm certain I look a sight in this baggy T-shirt. Come have a seat here. Your work is very inspiring. Ian says you have more?"

"Yes, I do. Pardon me sayin' so. You and Ian don't resemble each other much, nor does your daughter."

"We don't? Why, I never gave it much of any thought. I guess you're right. Ian looks more like his father, who is deceased."

"I know, I'm sorry for your loss. My Peg passed years ago. Never have gotten over it. Still expect her to show up and cook dinner."

"Oh, really, when Duncan died, I couldn't bear to stay at the house. Never went back until a few weeks ago. Traveled the world and had a score of beaus."

"A lady of fortune, I see. Never been much for goin' places. I figure my little spot is heaven on earth. I'll just wait on the good Lord to take me home. Guess I fear if I move around too much, He may not be able to locate me when it's time to join Peg."

"You're delightful, Ulysses."

"I ain't heard anyone say those words in a very long time. You shag, my dear?"

"That's being forward, isn't it?"

"To ask if you dance? Beach music is playin', don't ya hear it?"

"A shag is a dance?"

"For you, it must mean something much different, which I don't care to know. Come on out to the end of the dock. Let me see if I can give these old arthritic legs a spin and teach you a few steps."

"Well, I am not prepared to…"

"Come on, if we don't do it now, you never know, we may be ticklin' our casket tomorrow. Kick off those sensible shoes, and let me teach you a few steps."

The dogs and Ian are quick to round the corner of the house. He looks very relaxed in tan shorts and a black polo shirt. "Lass, I've been wondering when you would get here. Look at you! Beautiful, simply beautiful! Lads, look! Emmy, my princess, has arrived."

"Stop, Ian. Your flattery is too much. How are things progressing?"

"Wait till you see Ulysses. He does spiff up pretty nice. He is dancing with Mum on the dock. He is teaching her how to shag. They had the same conversation we did over what a shag is."

"Get out! Really? I've gotta see them dancing."

"Okay, but before you run over there, Fiona and Mum are struggling to get along with your mom and grandmother."

"I thought that may happen; we'll just keep them occupied. Ulysses seems to be taking care of your mom."

"Emmy, come here, you ravishing woman. Oh how I've missed you today."

Ian takes me into his arms and kisses me with so much passion I find myself wishing we could sneak into the house unnoticed and make love all night. His roving hands give pleasure to everything they touch.

"Steady, Ian, we've got a party to host."

"Christ, Emmy, I want you. But you're right; let's put on a show."

"We probably just did. I'm going to hold fast to your desires, Ian. Keep that thought till after the show. Somehow, somewhere, I'll have all of you tonight."

"Maybe I do have the right Suggs after all."

"You seem a bit conflicted on which one of us pleases you most."

"No conflict. Come see Ulysses and Mum."

Everyone's eyes focus on us as we hold hands rounding the corner of the house.

"Evening, Fiona. Are you enjoying the party?"

"Not like my mum; she seems to have picked up a local already."

"Ulysses, he is no threat. They look kinda cute out there spinnin' and twirlin' around."

"Get the grease out from underneath your fingernails? Is that what took you so long to get here? My brother has been trying to take care of everyone."

"Fiona, why must you antagonize everyone? Emmy, here is your wine, with ice."

"Ice? You water down your wine? How gauche."

"Fiona..."

"It's all right, Ian. I use ice to keep hydrated and because I like the coolness. I never claimed to be a wine snob. And as for the grease, it's nature's beauty secret. You should try it; perhaps it would help. Oh, and if you're so worried about your brother, you may have spent some time with him over the past quarter of a century. Do we have an understanding here, Fiona?"

"Quite. Ian, may I speak with you in private?"

"Not right now. As you pointed out, I have a party and guests to attend to. Emmy, come walk with me. Fiona, we can talk after dinner."

I am so glad Ian stole me away from Fiona. I could feel her claws digging into my skin. Sitting catlike with her legs drawn sexily by her side, Fiona sips a martini, measuring her next victim to devour.

"Maggie, you sure can kick up your heels. I haven't danced in such a long time. You've done wore me out, woman!"

"Oh how fun. I didn't expect to be dancing at the water's edge with an artist today."

"I don't think of myself as an artist, just a man who likes to whittle a spell while thinking."

"It's art, and I think we should expand your horizons in selling past Emily's store. She and I can come up with a plan. How about it, Uly? You up for becoming famous?"

"Nope, being famous ain't anything I desire. What I do want is a drink. What can I get for you, Maggie?"

"How about a tall gin and tonic?"

"Ouuwee, sounds refreshing. I'll get Cook to mix you one, and I'll be back in a flash."

Louise looks as though she is floating in her white caftan, hair flowing in the gentle breeze. Cook is firing up the grill. He is in his usual party attire—khaki pants, a white shirt, and an apron with "Kiss the Cook" written on the front. Spatula in hand, he's a man in his element. A wide, bright, inviting smile is always present when he's dealing with food.

"Ian, I'm sorry about my retort to Fiona. I know better, but she—"

"No worries, Emmy. Far as I'm concerned, she needs to be taken down a peg or two. She's power hungry, wants to control everyone all the time. It's been so long since I've spent time with her, I'd forgotten her ways. Seems to me time has made her worse."

"Hi, you two! Em, you look beautiful. Ian, the house is gorgeous. You have put flowers and plants all

around. I can't help but see what a handful Fiona is."

"You have any special insight, Louise?"

"Not yet. I'll wander over her way and have a chat. I'll get back to you."

"Weasy, be careful. Make sure your glass is full. Don't put ice in it, or else she'll think you're a lowlife."

"Dearie, I'm too old to worry about what anyone thinks of me. Don't y'all think I look mystical in this caftan?"

Louise twirls around with her best interpretation of a ballerina. "You do. I like it very much."

Beth walks up to Ian holding a book in her hands along with what appear to be listings. "Hi, I brought you the new listing. Thought you may want to take a look at it before seeing the property. Thank you both for inviting me. The party is wonderful, so many folks I haven't seen in ages. We all get busy with our lives and don't seem to have time to share with others outside our little world. Ian, I brought the DMV handbook for Ely, like you asked."

"Hey, Ely, come over here a minute."

Ely stops talking to Dylan and Salina when he hears his name, and seeing it's Ian calling, he picks up his pace. "Ely, do you know Beth?"

"You're Miss Mackenzie's sister, aren't you?"

"Yes, I am. Ian asked me to bring you this DMV handbook. You'll need to study it before trying to get your driver's license."

"Oh, thank you. I reckon I's got a lot to learn before tryin' to get a license, right, Ian?"

"Hey, Hannah, good to see you. Ian has been teaching Ely to drive in the Land Rover. He seems to be doing well, so Beth brought him a book to study. Hope you don't mind."

"No, not at all. Guess it's past time the boy learned to drive. Thank you for helping him."

"Beth, is your sister one of Ely's teachers?"

"She always says how bright he is and such a nice boy. Do you know Jenn from somewhere, Emileigh?"

"I've seen her at the store from time to time. Doesn't she live near here?"

"Just up the hills a couple of miles; her cabin overlooks the lake."

"Why don't we invite her? Think she'd come? Ely would like to see her. I'm sure it would be good for him."

"Oh, I doubt she'd come if I call."

"What's her number? I'll call. We've got more than enough for everyone. Cook makes plenty for everyone to take some home."

Louise floats over to Fiona with a fresh martini in one hand and a large wine in the other. Tess, Harper, and Isabel track her, not obviously for fear Fiona will catch on. Grayson taps Cook on the shoulder, giving him a heads-up; his wife is about to head into enemy territory while his kids flank her for protection. Ian hasn't noticed any of the movement. He is intent on speaking to Beth about the hot new property. Maggie notices Louise drifting spellbound toward Fiona and sees me watching her.

"Cook, how's dinner coming along?"

"Hey, Em, look at you gussied up. Dinner will be ready in about fifteen minutes. Tables are set up over by the pool. Did you notice it looks like something out of *Architectural Digest?*"

"Very nice! Cook, dinner looks fab. Surf and turf, perfect for the end of a holiday week! I'm famished. Mama, y'all behave. I see what's going on. Louise will come back and fill you in. Don't be so darn obvious."

"I'm going in to talk to Ulysses about his carvings, and see when I can go over and pick some for the store. I think a Web site would be a good idea. Maybe Samantha can help me market his works."

"Maggie and Ulysses seem to have bonded quite nicely."

"Where is Grandmama? I haven't seen her in a few minutes?"

"She's inside, probably giving herself a guided tour."

"Lord, no one went with her? Y'all come on now. Mama, find her and set her down somewhere."

The back of Ian's rental property has windows upstairs and down, going from ceiling to floor for an unrestricted view of the lake. Just as Maggie and Ulysses go into the house and step down into the sunken living room, which boasts a floor-to-ceiling stone fireplace at one end, Beulah Bell comes out of the bathroom and sits down across from the two of them. Mama enters the house by the kitchen entrance and walks down to the living room engaging in conversation with them. There is a piece of me that says to run interference for Ian and charge to the rescue, but my feet remain glued next to Leigh. Louise slowly sidles up to Fiona. Ian is heard in the background chortling with Grayson about how they want their steaks cooked and which scotch is best to serve after dinner.

"Hi, Fiona, we haven't yet been introduced. I'm Louise Tromble."

Louise offers Fiona a fresh martini, which she takes without hesitation. "Oh, you're the cook's wife. Are you working here tonight as well?"

"I think perhaps you've misunderstood. My husband's name is Cook; we are all friends here tonight. There are no employees working. Cook just happens to like to cook. I can see how you'd be confused."

"What is it with you people and these odd names? I thought Ian would hire professionals for us."

"I think Ian would find catering a huge waste of money. Besides, in case you haven't noticed, we are kind of in the sticks here. Rest assured, my husband will please you with his culinary skills."

"We shall see. What do you do with yourself, Louise?"

"What a strange question to ask! I dabble in many areas. I live as I choose. How about you?"

"I married well and raised my son. Now I have other horizons I am pursuing, but certainly nothing, which would interest the likes of you."

"I'm not sure why you get off looking down the tip of your nose at me. If you're trying to intimidate me, it won't work. Where is your son?"

"Liam is studying at Oxford. You've heard of Oxford, haven't you?"

"Of course I've heard of Oxford. What is Liam's area of interest?"

"Currently, he is studying international relations and physics, a double major, obviously beyond your limited ability to comprehend academically or to give a casual comment to regarding their substance."

"You know, Fiona, maybe it's our Southern accent, which to your ear sound illiterate, but we've all made our way in this world, some with more change in our pockets than others, some with more compassion, but all with enough brains to know when we are being patronized. Being a guest not only in our area, but our country, you should be more interested making a good first impression. You act like we are the visitors here. As far as I know, we've all tried to be kind to you. What do we get in return? Insults and belittling snipes. I'd say more, but I think I had better wish you a pleasant evening and hope you enjoy my husband's cooking."

Louise storms away from Fiona her white caftan billowing. Watching her retreat, I follow hoping to hear her perceptions of Ian's sister. "Louise, you all right? You left rather abruptly?"

"She is the devil incarnate. Y'all shouldn't be here. She is up to something all right; far as I can tell, it has to do with Ian and him being here. She is a money-grubbing bitch if ever there was one. Thinks of herself highly. I need to bathe and scrape off her energy. My mouth opened up and scolded her, saying things I'd never utter to anyone. What is it about her that brings out the worst in others? I need a drink."

"I'll get you one. Go sit by the pool; dinner is almost ready. Please don't tell Ian this until later. She is putting everyone off. If Grandmama heard you, she'd have her for dinner and spit out the bones."

"She'd fill Beulah up mostly with shit."

"Down girl, let me get you a drink...no ice this time. Here comes Leigh; she'll keep you company till I get back."

"Weasy, you look awful."

"Visit with Satan and see how you look."

"Really, never heard you say those words before. Usually, you find the good in everyone."

"If there were good, I'd have found it. She's the type of person cops would be draggin' the lake for after a mysterious disappearance, and once found, there would be cheers not tears."

"You reckon Maggie is like her?"

"No one is like her. Fiona is seriously ill. Probably the best thing Ian and his mom did was get away from her. I can understand the years apart. Couldn't before. Sure do after a couple of minutes with her. Honestly, I don't know how Maggie traveled all the way here listening to her. Maybe it's why she has attached herself to Ulysses for the night."

"Could be. I hope she isn't leading Ulysses on, poor soul. Weasy, you reckon Fiona is dangerous?"

"Her mouth is her greatest weapon. Someone estranged from the family for a generation doesn't pop up for no reason. Ian is right; he suspects something. I think Maggie is having fun with Ulysses; leading him on or not, this is a good night for him. So we've found one silver lining; his art is another!"

"Sounds more like my Weasy now, finding the good. Here's your wine; Cook's signaling for us to come and get it. I'll run inside to pee and gather who's there."

"Louise, tell Cook we need a blessing tonight. Ask who is up to give it for me, will you please?"

"Sure, Emmy, good idea."

Inside, there is much laughter amidst Louise's ruminations, as she's still spewing about Fiona. If there is a seat near Ian, maybe I can keep his mind off Fiona.

"Since we've all gathered, before we dig in, Emileigh would like for someone to give the blessing. Anyone volunteer?"

"I'll be happy to give the blessing, if y'all don't mind."

"Ely, that's my man! Please go right ahead."

"Thank you, Ian. 'Dear Heavenly Father, me and Mama have so much to be grateful for I don'ts have the time to say it all; you knows already. We is ever so thankful to be invited to share dinner. I be thankful to Mr. Bucknell for being my newest friend. Ma Bell, you saved my life this week and probably the life of my mama too. God bless you. Father, we asks your blessings on all who is here. Bless this food to nourish our bodies. We prays this through your son Jesus. Amen."

"Ely, how are you tonight? I am so happy you decided to say the blessing. You normally shy away from speaking in front of anyone."

"Oh, hey, Miss Mackenzie, I didn't knowed you is here. Sometimes I just feel overcome with thanks lately. Got to let it out. Will you sit with me for dinner?"

"I'd like to. You can tell me all about your summer."

"Yes'm, but really, if I tells you about the last week, it's enough."

"Okay then, one week in the life of Ely Stiles."

Dinner sets off with much laughter. The food is some of the best Cook has ever produced, and everyone, including Maggie and Fiona, remark how delicious it is. Conversation revolves around many subjects, remaining for the most part light and airy. Fiona has uttered few words, and eye contact with her is rare and uncomfortable.

"Can I have just a moment of everyone's time? I'd like to thank everyone for coming this evening to welcome my mum and sister. Hard to believe I've been here a short time and have such wonderful people in my life willing to come and be a part of the family for a night. As you can see, there is plenty of drink, and Steve is making the rounds with a nice scotch for those who dare."

"Oh, skirt boy, you've done well tonight. I think I can speak for everyone: thank you for your hospitality."

"Thanks, Weasy."

"Skirt boy? Is that what you call my son?"

"Maggie, it has become a term of endearment. First time we all saw him, he was wearing a wool kilt on a day you could've fried eggs on the sidewalk."

"I always did like to see a man in a kilt; lets the imagination play."

"He played the pipes too. We got the full treatment early on, and now he is barefoot, in shorts and a polo shirt, all Americanized."

"Mores the pity, I'll have to take him home with me."

"I think you'd have to fight Em, or take her along with you."

"Time will tell."

"What is that supposed to mean?"

"Well, you don't know someone in such a short time; you may be surprised the more you know him."

"And you've been around him how much in the last quarter century? People change; the past is over. From what I've seen, he is a wonderful man."

"Ian, dinner is over. About our private chat."

"Fiona, please, after my guests have a chance to visit and digest. I'm sure anything you have to say can wait a bit longer, if not until the morning."

"Damn it, Ian, listen to me. I want to talk to you now."

"Okay, Fiona, what's on your mind?"

"Really, Ian, you want to do this in front of all these…these subservient fools and your concubine?"

"And they call *her* a lady? Fuck you, Lady Lennox, and the high horse you rode in on!"

"Grandmama, please."

"Please nothing, Emileigh, I won't have anyone calling you a whore in front of your family and friends. Title or not, guest or not, you, Fiona, are a true-blue bitch on wheels, and I won't be seated any longer at a table with the likes of you. You who haven't cared enough about your mother or brother to have visited for how long?…Oh you can't remember exactly because it has been so long. Shame on you for passing judgment on us. I will not stand for your insolence regarding anyone else seated at this table, most especially my granddaughter, who has more of what a true lady is on the tip of her pinky than you could ever possess."

Fiona sits motionless, taking in Grandmama's rant without a change in expression. As Grandmama mentions me, Fiona slightly lowers her head and squints at me while smiling with a rather evil look. Icicles could have shot from her eyes into my heart. Fiona's lips part slightly, as if she wants to say something, as Grandmama ends her tirade. Fiona sits with a fork tightly grasped stabbing the table repeatedly with the tongs.

"Are you finished?"

"Quite, with you."

I am so proud of Grandmama but at the same time a bit embarrassed for our guests. Ian withdraws from the head of the table, walks to Grandmama, and pulls her chair out for her to walk away. He gives her a small peck on the cheek as she touches his shoulder in thanks. Mama is soon to follow. To my surprise, Ian does not utter one word. He walks around the table over to where Fiona is seated, grabs her by the wrist, pulls her chair out with his other hand, and forces her to follow him. She protests, spouting every conceivable expletive. He leads her into the guest cottage, closes the door, and turns on the lights. In an effort to comfort our guests, Steve goes around the table offering drink to anyone still seated. With Mama and Grandmama going back over to the dock, I ask Leigh to see if they are comfortable and attend to their needs. Dividing the leftovers and whistling a happy tune, Cook eases everyone's nerves. Maggie excuses herself, and Ulysses tags along. They head over to more comfortable chairs on the dock.

"Ely, come here."

"Yes, Miss Emileigh?"

"Take the keys to the Land Rover and escort Ulysses home when he is ready. You make sure he gets in the house safely; he has had some to drink. Over by the grill is a bag Cook is putting together. Take it in and put it in his refrigerator."

"Yes, Miss."

"Drive back here, and give me the keys to the Rover. Cook will put some food together for your mama and you. Take it with you, and, Ely, I want you to drive your mama home, understand? She has had too much to drink. You remember to turn on the lights and drive real slow. Do you think you can do that? You've never driven at night before."

"Yes, miss, I'll be fine."

"Oh and, Ely, take my cell phone. Y'all don't have a phone. You know how to use it?"

"Sure do, jus' 'cuz I ain't got one don't mean I ain't never used one."

"Okay, when you get home, call Ian's number and let us know you got there safely. Turn the phone off while you're drivin', and after you call, I don't want someone tryin' to reach me and hear you answer; it would make someone worry. Bring it to work with you tomorrow."

"Yes, miss, anything else?"

"You've been wonderful company; I'm sorry things look like they're going downhill."

"No problem, miss. Thank you, thank you for everything."

"See you at nine, Ely."

"Yes'm."

"Weasy, what you reckon is happening in the guest cottage? It's grown mighty quiet."

"I don't rightly know, but Maggie is looking a bit lost all of a sudden. You think she knows why Fiona is so furious?"

"We can ask."

"Louise, I hate to barge in and interrupt your powwow, but can you both help me put up some of this food for Hannah, Ely, and the kids? Inside the house, there is a pantry with lots of storage containers. Could y'all go in and bring out several?"

Ian steps out of the guest cottage and signals for me to come over to him. Everyone's eyes are riveted to him. His demeanor doesn't give a clue as to what has been happening inside the cottage.

"Lass, I see the party is breaking up. I guess I should have been more attentive to Fiona and maybe her outburst would have been contained to just me."

"We all said it was going to be an early night anyhow, Ian. Those of us who are able will hang around until we know everything is all right."

"Did you send Ulysses home?"

"Yes, he looked very tired. Ely is taking care of him. What on earth is going on with Fiona?"

"Walk with me while we talk. Will you go up into Fiona's room, pack her things, and place the suitcase outside of her room. Make certain to get everything. I don't want her asking to go back into the house. She is not welcome in my home."

"Ian, what happened?"

"I don't want anyone else to hear. Let's go into the office where we can talk."

Ian doesn't say another word. He takes my hand and walks into his office on the front side of the house, quietly closing the door behind us.

"Fiona, in her misguided wisdom has proclaimed by stating to the county magistrate's office on Skye I have abdicated my position by coming to the States."

"What does that mean?"

"It means the estate and all its assets will be withdrawn from my guidance as laird and given to the next heir in line, her son, Liam."

"Can she just by proclaiming it so?"

"No, I find it odd I'm on Skye for twenty-five years and the estate is in ruin because of me, then we turn a profit and *voila* she is figuring out a way to give it to her son, who is only twenty. With as little contact as we've had, I could have had a son who is older than Liam and truly the next heir."

"But Liam doesn't live there. Louise said Fiona's son is at Oxford. I bet he doesn't even know what she is trying to do. Fiona hasn't been to Skye for decades, even to visit. She said they live in Glasgow about to move to Inverness. Did you hear about the move?"

"Maybe Michael is about to move there. I wonder if there are marital problems. Fiona and Liam not having set foot on Skye is my only prayer, along with receipts showing my work here is supporting the estate and my residence and citizenry is still there. She thinks I bought this house for myself and came here with Mum to prove or gather evidence showing I have left Scotland for good. She is probably looking to see if I have a green card or a visa."

"You think your mom is in on this coup?"

"I hope not. Fiona is the type to use her as a pawn, and Mum would have no idea what her true intentions are. Mum is a different person around Fiona. I believe she is afraid of her and crumbles to her wishes. Fiona must love the power she has over her."

"You should lock up all your paperwork and your laptop; it should be somewhere far from Fiona's eyes until she leaves. Do you have a safe here?"

"There is one, but I don't have the combination."

"Pack it up, put it all in my car, lock the car, and I'll place it in the safe at the store. You can come by during the day and use it or take it with you. Just for tonight, let's take a little extra care; she may be desperate and try something to get evidence."

"You know, you are extremely sexy when acting all spy girl?"

"I'll have to remember that for future reference; in the meantime, skirt boy, gather your things. I'll go pack her belongings. Is she staying in the guest cottage tonight?"

"I can't just toss her out in the middle of nowhere; plus Mum would be upset. Did she say anything while we were in the cottage?"

"Not that I heard. She said her good-byes to Ulysses and sat back down. I'm sure she is tired."

"Tired or not, after we take care of this and visit with our guests, she and I are having a chat. Oh, speaking of chatting, I must call Stuart and get him started on protecting my name at the estate."

"Isn't it really late there?"

"Knowing Fiona, she may have an inside person she is calling at this very moment. She must know the estate is in the black again, or she wouldn't want to take over a losing proposition, which means she must have someone, maybe even my business manager; he is relatively new. Calling at this time of night, I can get Stuart to change the lock on the door to the office first chance he can tomorrow and start to go through my things. He's a friend; he'd be upset if I didn't call, no matter what the time."

"Gray clouds are gathering; looks as though the storm prediction is rapidly coming true."

"Now we'll find the rainbow and those silver linings. Get busy; I'll see you outside with our guests after I take Fiona's things to her."

Grandmama and Mama are still sitting and having drinks. Evidently, Grandmama liked the drink Ian suggested because she is still swilling the same brew. Louise, Leigh, and Emily, along with their men, are sitting nearby and undoubtedly chatting about Fiona in front of Maggie. Everyone else has left. Beth and Jenn must have sneaked out at some point as well as all of the others. Can't say as I blame them; I would have too.

"Hey, y'all, how's it going?"

"Em, where is skirt boy?"

"He'll be here directly. Had a call to make and had a couple of other things to attend to."

From the dock, the guest cottage isn't very visible, even though it sits on the water. There is a boardwalk from a covered porch at the far end of the main house to the guest cottage. From my current vantage point, I doubt anyone will see Ian carry Fiona's things out to her.

"Maggie, can we get you anything? I must apologize for the way the evening has turned out; let's try to end it on a good note, shall we?"

"Emileigh, I can see why my son is interested in you. I would like some coffee. Is that possible?"

"Oh absolutely, I'll get you some."

"No, Em, I'll get it, anyone else?"

"Steve, bring some for Ian as well. I'm sure he'd like a cup."

Steve heads down with Cook to the main house to get coffee for almost everyone. I am certain he will bring up something sweet to go along with the coffee. Meantime, Maggie continues without missing a beat.

"It is I who should apologize. Fiona can be a cantankerous woman. I don't believe she knows how her words slice through people; if she does, it's frightening. Ever since she was a child, you never knew when a switch would be flicked. One minute, sweet as sugar, and the next, hurtful words, which damage the soul, come out of her mouth. I've been walking on eggshells around that girl of mine her entire life."

"She does seem filled with piss and vinegar. It explains why y'all ain't around each other much. No one can live like that; it simply isn't healthy for mind or body."

"Emily, I'm sure Maggie has thought about this until she is exhausted."

"I have. I just thought we were coming to see Ian. If I ever thought any of this would have taken place, oh, please know it was never my intention."

"I think we caught your intention tonight, dancing at the end of the dock with Ulysses. Can you teach me some of those moves? Maggie, none of us has seen Ulysses look so happy or so good in years. You did wonders for him tonight, probably changed his world!"

"Oh now, he is a very nice, humble man. I doubt seriously I changed his world in the span of a few hours."

"Em is right, Maggie. He has been a hermit since Peg died, and she has been gone...oh, about fifteen years."

"He's been a creative hermit. Did you see the piece he made for Ian in the living room? Why it's pure magic. Looks just like these two lazy dogs layin' here. He has more, and I can't wait to put some in my store."

"How would you go about pricing his work, Emily?"

"Good question. You have any idea?"

"On the international market, they could draw quite a lot. I have no idea in the States what his craft would go for."

"I think you and I should go over to his place together and see what he has. Maybe we can catalog them, take some pictures, and send them out to contacts to derive a fair price for him. I'd hate to undersell his carvings; he can use all the money they will draw."

"You set it up, Emily, and let me know. I haven't decided how long to stay here with Ian, maybe a week; I have an open-ended return ticket."

Grayson meets Cook, Ian, and Steve at the door to the house. The guys have coffee, biscotti, and Bailey's. Fiona's absence, while welcome, is obvious to everyone.

"Oh, this looks good, chocolate chip biscotti, yummy!"

"Ian, is Fiona coming back to join us?"

"No, Mum, she has decided to retire and spend the night in the guest cottage."

"Would you have room for a wide-mouthed old woman to spend the night?"

"Beulah, I don't know a wide-mouthed old woman. I do have several rooms, one of which is yours if you'd like to skip the drive home and spend the night with us."

"You're so sweet, the Pimm's you made me, is a hit and has a punch as well."

"Beulah, I'm glad you'll be staying; we can spend time over breakfast and chat in the morning. In fact, I think I will take my coffee and head up to get some rest. I certainly have enjoyed meeting all of you and hope to see more of you in the days ahead."

"Maggie, it will be our pleasure. Good night."

"Mum, you need help with anything?"

"I think I can manage, Son."

"Excuse me, y'all. I'll go make certain she gets settled."

"That's my girl, Em. I'm gonna leave shortly too. Sunday at the store is busy, and it's getting late."

"Mama, please don't leave just yet. I need to talk to you first. I'll be right down."

"Okay, baby girl. Where is that biscotti? It is heavenly, and this coffee is the best I've ever had."

Maggie has a difficult time climbing the stairs to her room. As we are climbing, I hear Grandmama coming up slowly as well, asking which room is available for her to use. I put Grandmama in Fiona's old room and gather fresh towels for her bath. Maggie thanks me over and over for understanding where Fiona is concerned. She asks me if I'll be staying the night. I explain I will with my grandmother staying. She smiles sweetly and says she'll see me in the morning.

"Mama, are you leaving already?"

"Yes, you know Sundays at the store are brutal, and tomorrow everyone will be either going home or returning from vacation. It will most likely be real busy."

"We'll have Ely to help too. I want you to take my car instead of Grandmama's."

"Won't you need it?"

"No, I'm going to stay here tonight, especially with Grandmama here and Fiona. Mama, here is the real important part. On the front seat of my car, you'll see a laptop and a few file folders in a bag. Put those in the safe at the store. I'll explain tomorrow. They are Ian's and terribly important. Don't forget, Mama. I locked the store tonight too; there is a key to the deadbolt on my key ring. I'll get Ian or Grandmama to drop me off after breakfast."

"Fiona is alive, right?"

"Last I knew. Good night. Drive safe."

"Night, night, baby girl. See you in the morning. You'll say my good-byes?"

"Of course, I will."

"I see the last remaining partiers are giving up the ghost and heading out across the waters."

"Emileigh, it has been quite a night. We do have some news though before we leave."

"Do tell. We hope it's good news."

"It is, Ian. Emileigh planted a seed in my head about asking Dylan and Salina to move here and for Dylan to go into business with me. I talked to Dylan before coming here; he seemed disinterested. Come to find out he was just preoccupied. Salina told me tonight they are giving it the utmost consideration as Dylan has been dreaming of returning to the area and working with me. She also said her parents will be here soon as well."

"Oh, Grayson, what fabulous news. I am so happy they are even considering it!"

"Ian introduced Salina to Beth. They got to talking about what kind of house and what they could get for their money up here. They just rent in Charlotte, so moving doesn't depend on them selling a place, just getting a mortgage, and they should be fine."

"I actually think we should find land. I could build them a house for a fraction of what it costs to purchase, giving them instant equity, and Dyl could learn by building on his own house."

"Did you tell them?"

"No, it's my deal breaker; if someone had offered us that, I would have gone anywhere. I think Ian may have just the property for them to buy a slice of too."

"Oh, mate, I'd donate a couple of acres to them. We can make this happen and give those two no excuse to stay city dwellers."

"I see silver linings again."

"Weasy, we'd best get you home."

"Hey, Louise, no six o'clock visit tomorrow okay?"

"Nope, the wall has tumbled down."

"Night, y'all. See you tomorrow!"

"Good night. You two behave now."

"Not gonna happen, my friend. Good night!"

The party barge backs up and turns gently around, heading to the western shore. Everything is cleared and cleaned; no one would have ever guessed twenty-five people had just had dinner here. Ian holds me close as we wave to our friends.

"There are my boys! Moose, Bear, you lads are probably going to make Ulysses famous. Just think, Em, his gift to me depicting these two has everyone wanting to see his other work and to sell it. Ulysses couldn't afford to take care of the lads properly; now hopefully, his hobby will bring him comfort. God works in mysterious ways. I think they deserve a treat. Lads, you want to go for a ride?"

The dogs jump to life and head over to where Bessie is docked, tails wagging ninety miles an hour. "Really, Ian, tonight after all—"

"Especially after all, I want you to myself without thinking of your grandmother or my mum being nearby. I want to talk to you, hold you. I don't feel like I've even had a moment with you except to put out fires today."

"I know. Aren't parties odd that way? You want to spend time with those you care about, but I don't feel like I've seen anyone, well except Fiona. She did add spice to the mix."

"She is gone tomorrow. Told me she is headed back to Glasgow. Sounds like she hasn't told Mum. I expect Mum will stay. She seemed to hit it off with Ulysses and Emily."

"I know. Go figure. Two people I would have never expected. I would like to spend time with your mom without Fiona."

"Well then, I will ask her to stay on as long as she wishes—within reason of course. We did have a lot of silver linings from this perfect storm, didn't we, love?"

"Yes, and I'm still counting them. Where are we headed, Ian?"

"Up to the cove where you almost walked the plank."

"And am I walking the plank tonight?"

"Not tonight. We are going up there to search for rainbows."

"I think that is an Irish thing."

"No, lass, they may claim it now, but we gave it to them, as well as all the tales of fairies, leprechauns, and gnomes. The pot of gold at the end of the rainbow...a Scot suggested using the notion to give hope to the people of Ireland due to their ailing economy."

"Ian Duncan MacDougal, I believe you are full of it."

"Hmm, yes, lass, full of something."

Ian pulls Bessie up snuggly into the cove, stops her engine, and then tosses out the anchor. Moose and Bear rush to the ski deck and simultaneously jump into the water with a great splash.

"Now to follow the rainbow, come closer."

"Ian, what, pray tell, are you doing?"

"Oh, lass, my divining rod is pointing the way."

"There are no underwater rainbows."

"Aye, at the end of the rainbow, priceless treasure waits."

Starting with the first thrust under the warm water, there are sensations of unparalleled pleasure. He sweetly whispers, "You, my love, are my lucky charm."

chapter 13

THE FIRST DIM light of a new day reflects on the calm water of the lake. A few wisps of shiny, curly hair fall down over Ian's forehead, giving him the allure of boyish charm. Last night, he was my hero, kissing Grandmama on the cheek after she roared to my defense against Fiona. Moose and Bear know my eyes are open even without me moving a muscle. Their muzzles are propped on the edge of the bed offering sloppy good-morning kisses. Tails are wagging; both are anxious to please and be petted. Tucked snug and warm down beneath the cozy comforter next to a gorgeous hunk, I find myself wanting to lie here bathing in the feeling of being loved and loving. Moose and Bear will not allow the day to begin so lazily, however. Rising out of bed, I place a soft kiss on the cheek of the man I've fallen in love with, being careful not to wake him. "Okay, boys, I know what you want, so let's try and keep it quiet; we've got guests."

Their paws hit the hardwood as they scoot down the hallway, and soon, I hear eight feet gaining momentum. Clumsily charging down the stairs, they jump at the door. In their boisterous opinion, I am not moving fast enough. There is a dim light in the kitchen. Perhaps Ian left it on in case Maggie or my Grandmother came down early. No such luck. Fiona sits at the kitchen table. Her laptop is open, and a large glass of orange juice before her. She is dressed conservatively in a masculine gray pantsuit. There is an intense expression of anguish on her face. Every muscle is clenched tightly, her jaw moving back and forth grinding teeth in frustration. Fiona has yet to notice I'm watching her. With a loud gasp drawing her attention, I confidently enter the kitchen. "Fiona, I'm surprised to see you up so early. I see you've helped yourself."

"Well, I didn't have a choice. Is Ian up?"

"No, is there something you need?"

"Fetch me a large cup of coffee, real cream and two sugars. When do you expect him to come down?"

"I suppose after he awakens. Do you want him to find you...ummm, here in the kitchen? Coffee's on. As for the 'real cream,' I'm afraid we don't have any."

"I don't care where he 'finds me.' We need to discuss some family issues. I'm leaving in a couple of hours."

"Did we say something to instigate your sudden departure? Perhaps you've acquired all you desired. Does your mother know you're leaving?"

"I didn't tell her. I assume Ian did. Besides, what business is it of yours?"

"I wouldn't assume Ian mentioned anything to her, and by asking, you've made it my business. Did you make travel arrangements for Maggie?"

Fiona disregards my questions. She slithers from room to room with her perfectly poised posture and steely glares noting every nuance of the first floor while using the excuse of waiting for the coffee to brew.

"Where is Mum, still in her room? Perhaps I should go up and talk to her, make certain you didn't leave any of my belongings in the room I was supposed to sleep in."

In an effort to prevent my grandmother's embarrassment, I ward Fiona off at the foot of the stairs, corralling her as best I can. "I wouldn't, Fiona, unless you want a shock. None of your possessions have been left upstairs. My grandmother is staying in your old room. I won't have you trudge in and disturb her. You had better finish your juice in the kitchen or go back out to the guest cottage."

"Well, I never!"

"It's well past time you did."

Climbing the stairs with reckless abandon, I'm thankful to escape Fiona's next retort. Altercations aren't my strong point, but I'm getting plenty of practice. Ian's awake and getting dressed. "Mornin', Ian, you're up early."

"Good morning to you. Come give us a smuirich."

"Before I do, you should know Fiona is downstairs looking to speak with you. She says she is leaving in a couple of hours, sounds like she expects Maggie to go with her."

Watching Ian tuck a bright white shirt into his jeans arouses me. Odd that getting dressed has that affect; usually, it's the other way around. Fiona fades from memory. Temptation is too great. I fall into his open arms, and my insides turn to putty as he folds his arms around me. Ian takes my chin in his hand and claims the kiss he asked for. Wanting more, I taste his sweet, full, supple lips. He pulls away. "I never had my chat with Mum last night. She went to bed before we went out in the boat, and then, well, I wasn't thinking about Mum. Let's get this over with, and then I've got to call Stuart. Maybe I should be going home before heading to New York."

"Just a moment, handsome, I haven't finished giving you a good-morning kiss."

"Now, Em, you know…oh hell, come here." We both pull away smiling, looking into each other's eyes with a desire that has to be quelled. Fiona is downstairs doing who knows what. We both snap into the stark nakedness of reality. "I don't even want to think about anyone but you. So much drama and so many pressing decisions have suddenly been placed upon me."

"Wait on any decisions. Talk to your mom and Stuart before going off in too many directions. Best talk to Fiona soon before Grandmama gets up and wants to add her dollars' worth to the conversation."

"I thought the expression was 'two cents.'"

"Not with Grandmama, you always get more than you bargain for."

"Fiona, I thought I made it clear last night you weren't welcome in my house."

"Get a grip, Ian, I'm leaving, and we have some things to discuss in private."

"All right let's go outside on the dock. The sun is up; we can have our coffee there. Hopefully, the view will make you calmer."

Fiona slams her PC shut, gathers her paperwork, and walks outside with Ian. She certainly doesn't like to be told what to do or even have a suggestion made. The office door is ajar. I'm certain Ian closed it and locked the doors to the house. In a generous attempt not to become paranoid where Fiona is concerned, I'll give her the benefit of the doubt. Knowing Fiona was in the house before sunrise, I can't help but think she must have been up to more than simply getting juice. It seems Fiona lost her benefit as doubt sets in.

"Okay, Fiona, what do you feel we need to discuss?"

"I hope you don't want to draw out the decision I've made. Relinquish control of lairdship to the heir apparent, Liam."

"Don't hold anything back, Sis. That is a lot to hope for; it's a wild fantasy. Just exactly why do you think I'd be amenable to this obsessive delusion you've conjured up? Does Liam even have a clue you're trying to seize control?"

"Not an issue. You have no heir, no children, and from what I can tell, until recently, you drove the estate to ruin."

"How would you know I have no heir? Since it sounds like you haven't even discussed your plan of action with Liam, what happens if he doesn't want the responsibility? You say it isn't an issue; I beg to differ with your assumption. Liam is still in school, dripping wet behind the ears. Do you expect to run the estate in his absence? Sounds like you are putting the cart before the horse, Sis."

"All those are side issues. Are you telling me you have an heir?"

"What exactly is a side issue? I'm not revealing anything, Fiona. You have evidently found out I'm making the estate viable again and have set your sights on acquiring it using Liam's name."

"Who do you think you are talking to, Ian? I am not a spent force—in fact, quite the opposite."

"Regardless of what force is with you, at the time of Father's death, you received a sizable inheritance, as did I. The estate money isn't ours to use freely; it all gets pumped back into running it. So if you're seeking a fortune, it's already been handed to you."

"You'll fight this then?"

"Oh yes, with everything I've got. Are you having marital problems, Fiona?"

"Why do you think you have the right to ask such a question?"

"I realize you don't want to admit it, but we are family and you haven't mentioned Michael's name once. I don't expect if you are moving to Inverness he'd pick up stakes and walk away from his family and his position with their business to move to Skye."

"You run the estate from afar."

"Glad you admit I'm running it from here."

"We are done, Ian. Get Mum; we're leaving."

"Got too close to you? Stepped on your new shiny shoes and put a mark on them, eh? I'll waken Mum so you can say good-bye. Isn't the rental car in her name? You'll have to ask her if you can turn it in on her behalf."

"I'm versed in rental cars, brother dear."

"Mum is welcome to stay here as long as she likes."

"I don't want her staying here with you and the likes of that woman you are so caught up with."

"Thinking for Mum or yourself, Fiona? That woman, as you put it, has a name, and I expect you to use it. Mum doesn't even know you are leaving."

"Why didn't you tell her?"

"Not my job to undo your mess, Fiona. You may have delusions of grandeur desiring control over everything and everyone, but, Sis, you're in for a rude awakening. I'm certainly glad you trekked to the States for this wonderful reunion we seem to be having; all it has done is remind me why a continent between us suits me just fine. You've played these games of yours time and time again. When are you going to learn? Our relationship is really a shame, being blood and all. I suppose blood can spew venom as well as anyone."

"Aha, a deadlier venom if you push me, Brother."

"Hey, Em, got coffee on?"

"Good morning, Grandmama. I do have a fresh pot."

"Are those two up to something this early? Fiona looks as nervous as a long-tail cat in a room full of rockin' chairs. Look at her tapping her nails impatiently, a nasty grin mortared upon her pasty, surly face."

"Hush, Maggie might hear you. I don't think Fiona gets nervous, just revenge. They have some family affairs to talk over. Come here. Sit by me."

"I wouldn't want to discuss the weather with the likes of her. I am partial to your young man. Where do you think the two of you are headed? Things seem to be moving along rather fast and furious, which I reckon is fine, if y'all are both of the same mind-set."

"I don't know where we are going. There're a lot of blurred lines, but right now, it's wonderful. We'll work it out if we're meant to be together."

"Do I hear you two talking about my boy?"

"Good morning, Maggie. Coffee?"

"Yes, please, sounds wonderful. Just what this old girl needs. Black, please, Em. Ian and Fiona patching things up or..."

"*Or* is the operative word. She is leaving in a little while."

"Leaving? Where? Why? To go home? She hasn't said anything to me. What am I supposed to do?"

"Ian and I would be very happy if you'd stay on for a while. How about it, Maggie? Let Grandmama and I and everyone get to know you better. We'll get you situated where you are comfortable; if the room you have isn't the best for you, we'll change to another."

"Thank you. I don't know what gets into Fiona's head. She is all over the place with her schemes, always has been. The thought of a transatlantic flight after getting here yesterday is too much for me to consider. Em, do you think it possible for me to stay in the guest cottage? Those stairs up to the rooms aren't the easiest for this old bird. Sleeping next to the water, hearing it lap against the rocks sounds inviting."

"Ian said it isn't being used while he is here. He'll arrange it for you."

"You may just find yourself with company from time to time."

"Beulah, that would be like a kids' sleepover, wouldn't it?"

"We could carry on, and as much as it sounds like fun, I was thinking how you and Ulysses were getting along last night. Is a romance stirring?"

"Stranger things have happened. I never expected to hit it off with a man the first night. Isn't it nice to have a surprise now and again?"

"Did he kiss you, Maggie?"

"Grandmama, hush!"

She is caught off guard by my grandmother's comment, and a bright red blush spreads quickly over her cheeks. She lowers her head abruptly as a guilty smirk appears, leaving nothing for us to ponder. Grandmama and I know in an instant good ole Ulysses still has studly spunk. Maggie stands up all shilly-shally, sputtering nervously. "I'd better go out and say good morning to my children."

Clutching her mug of coffee, she steps outside. Moose and Bear slip past her, and sighting Grandmama, they sidle up to her. Having had a moment or two with Maggie has me looking forward to her staying. Poor Ian, what he must be enduring with Fiona. I'm truly happy to say farewell to her. Fiona's departure can't come soon enough.

"Grandmama, what may I fix for you for breakfast?"

"Let's wait on the others and see what they'd like. You need a ride back to your mama's?"

"Probably. You mind?"

"Not at all."

With breakfast over, Fiona finally gathers her suitcases to leave. The good-byes are artificial. I'm surprised a cheer didn't erupt when she pulled out of the driveway. Grandmama is restless, obviously ready to hit the road to Blowing Rock.

"Grandmama, are you ready to head out so early?"

"Yes, child, as much as I complain about him—and I know it's wrong, as it causes strife—I want to hear the preacher's sermon today."

"You go on; I'll get Ian to take me over. I'd like to stay a while longer and talk to him alone."

"Well, all right, sugar. You take care now, ya hear? Can't say as I blame you for wantin' to stay. I'll be prayin' for y'all."

"Love you. See you soon."

Ian moves his mother's belongings down to the guest cottage. The cottage is cozy, with two large bedrooms. One is a loft. The other spans the side of the cottage with a grand view of the lake from a bay window. There is a champagne bath, which Maggie will enjoy. A small, fully functional kitchenette opens to a quaint living area complete with a stone fireplace. She will probably feel much more independent away from the two "lovebirds," as she calls us.

"Lass, you have a passport, don't you?"

"Whatever would I need one of those for, Ian? I don't reckon trips to the coast or theme park rightly require one for visiting, not yet anyhow."

"Blast, not what I wanted to hear. After talking to Stuart, I should probably make a quick trip to the estate, escort Mum there as well. I should sort out some doings and make nice to the magistrate over Fiona's bumbling efforts to take over."

"When are you thinking of leaving?"

"Soon. I have a couple of things here to attend to and need to see a new listing with Beth. Mum probably would like a few days here."

"Your mother doesn't need an escort, although company is always nice to have on a trip. What is the urgency?"

"Stuart seems to think, as I do, that our business manager is funneling more than information to Fiona or vice versa. If I can find a trail connecting the two, first thing I'm going to do is fire his arse and repair the damage."

"Sounds like a hostile takeover. Are you certain there isn't another reason for heading to Scotland?"

"I'm not sure I understand you. Do you fear my trip has other motivations? The trip involves my sister, and yes, there are a few other things I can attend to while home. I don't want to get into those. You are right; the odds are pretty good something hostile is happening."

"I suppose you asked about my passport situation thinking I may be able to go with you?"

"Yes, but that can't happen this time, can it? Get your application in, though it takes some time to acquire one."

"I will. You leaving so soon, even if it is for a short while, isn't what I want to hear. Can't Stuart do the groundwork for you? Then perhaps you can handle whatever is wrong from right here?"

"Some things are better done yourself. Like for instance, see those dogs begging you to pay them attention? Only you can give them what they want and might I say, me as well. We'd better get you over to the store. Lads, would you like to go for a ride in Bessie?"

"Maybe some things do need to be dealt with in person, but I don't see the urgency. There is a big difference between what dogs want and changing the subject like you have done so smoothly. No one can do anything without you being present, can they?"

"I don't understand the trepidation or your heightened concern over a simple trip home. The estate and everyone within its boundaries are my responsibility. I'm going to abolish the fear Fiona has pushed on me. Please, Em, I really don't need you to question my motives. I already feel insurmountable pressure, worrying about you will only add stress. I may have changed the subject, but it's because we do need to get moving."

The dogs leap with gusto, twisting their torsos midair, exhibiting raw exuberance. I wish I could feel the same excitement today. For the first time since knowing Ian, I sense a bit of secrecy. He did ask me to go in a round-about fashion. The calls he gets and won't answer nag at me, making my inner voice fearful. It is probably insecurity on my part. Damn Fiona and her power-hungry ambitions. Morning usually makes me feel like the day is full of promise—the dew heavy on the grass, all the flower heads pointing toward the sun, a freshness exuding hope of a new day—but today, the brimming hope is as a faded flower. My heart longs for Ian, and he hasn't even left.

"Hey, Tah, how are things going this morning?"

"Oh, Emily, you're here mighty early. Have Dylan and Salina headed back to Charlotte?"

"Dylan's boss called before seven this morning. He wanted to give him a heads-up about his job."

"Oh, this doesn't sound like it has a good ending."

"I think the ending will be fine; it's just bad timing. The company is merging with another investment bank, and the new firm doesn't want to carry over junior executives. Dylan has until the end of July and then he is out of work. Mind you, they gave him a substantial severance package, and when Dylan mentioned he's been offered the chance to go into business with Grayson, well they threw in a relocation package. Even in the face of having to let him go, they are still treating him with a lot of respect. Most folks don't get squat."

"Seems there is a greater hand working magic, don't it? After having talked to Grayson about this and then to have his job suddenly evaporate, it is mighty strange indeed. Did Dyl have a clue a merger was in the works?"

"He knew a buyout was in progress, but the details were not public. Of course, rumor had everyone getting sacked and the top dogs getting filthy rich. Anyhow, once the news struck Dylan this morning, he didn't want to hang around. Salina looked worried, but they'll be fine. Heck, they can live with us until a house is built. Just means we've got to revise the timing."

"Hi, Mama, Emily, looks like another scorcher in the making." I honestly want to slip past the two of them and go into the apartment for a quick pity party. Between last night's party, Fiona's devious personality and now Ian leaving, I've had enough of Sunday, and it isn't even nine o'clock.

Reaching out and grabbing my sleeve, Mama pulls me back to the register. "Em, quite the party we had last night. Whatever happened with Fiona?"

"She's on her way to Scotland, hopefully never to be dropping in on us again. I don't like to speak ill of anyone, but mercy, she is difficult."

"How is Ian?"

"Oh, he is handling it with more class than I would. It sounds like he's going back home."

"Why is he leaving? Is he coming back? I thought y'all were headed to New York."

"I don't know the answers to any of those questions except why he's leaving. Fiona has power on the brain and wants to take control of the estate. It's all complicated governed by ridiculous ancient rites and bylaws, which Fiona is trying to overcome. Ian needs to head her off before things get too far along. I just hope it's the only reason he is going back."

Emily pipes up after holding her tongue, which must have been torturous. "Did he ask you to go with him? What's stuck in your craw to imagine there is another reason?"

"He asked if I have a passport, which I don't, so that ended any conversation. I don't have any concrete reason to question his urgency to leave other than Fiona. As you say, it could just be my imagination. Maggie is here and didn't go back. Are you going to ask her to go over to Ulysses's and take a look at his artwork?"

"I thought about seeing if we could set something up for tomorrow. I'm gonna close my store on Mondays for the rest of the season."

"I'd like to close for a day, but don't see how; people always need something."

"Mama, with Ely, me, and now Hannah, you should be able to take a day or two off a week."

Mama and Emily go off on some tangent about working too much and how time seems to race by now that they've gotten older. I decide to see what needs to be stocked and cleaned so Ely will be kept busy. The alarm system will be installed tomorrow, and the store will need to be filled and stocked before the guys come to begin work. The last day of a holiday week can be either busier than anticipated or slow as molasses in January.

"Mornin', Suggs General Store, what can I do for you?"

"Good Morning to you Tah. Is Em about?"

Oh, hey, Ian, she's done a Houdini and disappeared. Anything I can relay to her?"

"Just have her call when she gets a free moment, if you will."

I heard a bit about what happened last night. Since we met you seems the drama factor around these parts has risen immensely. Most scuttlebutt we had before was that no good husband of mine runnin' off, oh and maybe a bear devouring leftovers after Thanksgiving. Anyhow, I'm rambling. I'll let Em know you called. Oh, Ian, I heard you are leaving us and going back to Skye. Anything we can do for you?"

"Nothing I can think of right now. Word spreads like wildfire, eh? Guess I should ask the grapevine when I am leaving."

"Oh, Ian, it ain't that bad!"

"Mornin', Weasy. That was Ian. You seen Em? He wants her to call him when I find her."

"Did you ask Ian about his sister? Tah, she just ain't right, is she? I ain't seen Em; she is probably down in the stockroom."

"Fiona is gone, left to go back home this morning. Sounds like Ian will be going soon as well."

"Oh really! How is that sittin' with Em?"

"To be honest, she's a bit suspect he's going' over not just 'cuz of Fiona."

"Do tell, Tah!"

"Well, she isn't spillin' any beans, claims she don't know why. Him leaving so sudden without one iota of thought as to how she'll miss him… well, it's beginning to make her wonder. You can read Em like a book; she is in love and missing him already. It may be her mind conjuring up all sorts of imaginings—her way of putting armor on so the absence won't hurt as much."

"Tah, Louise, give it up. You two are embellishing and gossiping about stuff we don't have any right to discuss."

"Emily, what in tarnation are you talking about? Em's my daughter; I just want to protect her and her happiness."

"Understood, but we don't know what if anything Ian is up to besides dealing with that sack of dung Fiona. Besides, Emileigh is bright and strong, a woman who will stand up for herself."

"Uh-huh, I heard that."

"Weasy, you hear everything."

"Ain't it the truth, Emily?"

"Y'all know my gift! I hear more in silence than most do partying in a room bustin' at the seams with kinfolk dancin' and a-swearin'."

"Speakin' of which, Louise will you be able to see what's going on in Scotland from here?"

"Do you really want to know, Tah? It may not be what you expect. It ain't right for me to meddle into affairs of the heart."

"I take that as a yes. Some wine might loosen your tongue."

"It may, but it also may cloud any visions."

"Not gonna believe that one, Weasy. I've seen you too many times swill down radiator fluid men call moonshine, top it off with a bottle of wine, and still have all systems go where spirits are concerned."

"You got me, Emily, spirits for the spirit medium."

"Hang up the phone, too many gosh darn spirits."

"Emily, you're mistaken. There are always spirits, never too many."

"All right, now you're creepin' me out."

"Well, it ain't like I can just hang up the phone, as you suggest. Sometimes I can, but mostly when they know I can hear and see them, those spirits pile up on each other. I know y'all send them to me too." "Can't deny it, Weasy. It's a hoot to see you squirm as ghosts line up impatiently waiting their turn."

"Real funny, like that rabid raccoon chasing you down the driveway."

"Remember Emily screaming and flailing her arms. Well, I bet if raccoons could laugh, that one would have been hysterical."

"Not funny, ladies, it was sick and hell bent to pass rabies onto me."

"A coon with a plan?"

"Oh squat, we were supposed to have Em call Ian."

"Y'all jawin', we lose track of time. Looky there, here comes Ely. Time to get marching I've got a business to run. There you are. Ian called, wants you to give him a jingle. Hey, while y'all are here, why don't we have party on the dock and celebrate Fiona's departure?"

"Mama, that's fine, just don't let Maggie hear, okay?"

"Oh shucky darn, all right. Weasy call Leigh and tell her about tonight. It'll be good to see y'all together after the outbursts at Ian's the other night."

"It wasn't all about Fiona, Mama. Some actually had a good time, and the rest, well, consider it free entertainment."

"Tah, it was just last night."

"Oh for heaven's sake, it feels like eons ago."

chapter 14

"Hi, Ian, it's me. Got your message. I'm here when you get a moment."

"Miss Emileigh, what you want me to do today?"

"Take this list and begin restocking the shelves. I'll check on you in a little while to see if you need any help. Thanks for coming in today; I know it's supposed to be your day off."

"Yes'm, is Mr. Ian comin' by today?"

"I don't have any idea. Better get to those shelves, Ely; they won't fill themselves. Mama, did Ian say what he wanted on the phone?"

"No, sugar, he actually didn't say much. I did most of the talking."

Bright golden sun is reflecting off the placid lake; the sky is the color of a bluebird. It's quiet—not as many boats churning up the water, pulling hollerin' kids around on tubes. A large portion of the tourists have packed and gone home. The season is far from over, though; stragglers will arrive from now until the middle of August when school starts. Many serene weeks are ahead for those fortunate enough to live near the lake. "Hey, Ian, sorry, I missed your first call."

"Emmy, do you have free time today, so we can talk?" His voice is raspy, not upbeat and carefree as usual.

"Lunchtime is free."

"Good, I'll come by and bring a bit to eat. Noon okay with you?"

"Fine. Is everything all right?"

"Out of sorts, Fiona has put a dagger in my plans."

"See you later."

"Looking forward to it, Em."

Our conversation was unusual; Ian was rather formal and uneasy.

"Mama, how do you like the security system?"

"About as much as stepping barefoot on a red ant farm."

"Like it that much, eh?"

"Guess I'm getting more like Mama every day. All these newfangled electronic gadgets ain't my cup of tea."

"Roll with it, Mama, or get left in the dust."

"I'll take the dust. What did Ian have to say?"

"Just that he's coming by for lunch."

Rumbling up the road is the familiar sound of Ian's clunker. His tone changed even before his sister's arrival. For some reason, I'm in a defensive mood; I have been since Fiona's visit. A shrink would probably tell me insecurity is bubbling up to the surface.

"You look fresh as a summer's day." His Scottish accent warms me all over, and his voice is noticeably relaxed and easy. His clothes are rumpled, his unshaven face has heavy stubble, and his hair is tussled. "Rough night, Ian?"

He doesn't take my comment with lightness of heart. "I'd say that's obvious."

"You sound exasperated. What is eating at you?"

"I've been up all night trying to devise a cunning plan to teach Fiona a lesson, at least where the property is concerned. I'm leaving Saturday to go home."

"You should have called. I would have come over to help. Fiona isn't exactly on my top-ten list of favorite people."

"Coming over would have been wildly distracting. I have enough trouble concentrating when thinking of you. Imagine sitting close by; your intoxicating scent wafting in the air; your sweet, tender lips whispering wily ideas in my ear—Christ, Em, I'm aroused just thinking about it. Do you understand it just wouldn't have worked to scheme a plot with me?"

"Leaving so soon? I thought you mentioned going next week."

"According to Stuart, his reliable friends heard rumors Fiona stepped up efforts to take over."

"Will Maggie be leaving with you?"

"I can't be certain; she hasn't mentioned it. Mum has been working with Emily cataloging Ulysses's artwork. They are having fun trying to figure out what pieces go where and sell for how much. I love seeing her engage with new friends doing work she enjoys. Ulysses has a few pieces he wants to keep that have sentimental value. He carved those soon after Peg died. Mum is getting those pieces out of the barn. From what she tells me, he is grateful to have them inside, where they belong."

"What about you, Ian?"

"I don't understand."

"When are you going to have fun again?"

"Oh, Emmy, you of all people should know I've had a lot of fun up until my sister came. First, I have to get things under control at home. I assure you, upon my return, our fun will resume." The glimmer in Ian's eyes fades, and his demeanor suddenly changes. "Em, while I'm gone, I want you to finally go to the doctor and see what your spells are about."

"Get off it, Ian. How is it I lived all these years, taking good care of myself, and you come into my life and within a few short weeks, tell me what I should do? I seem to remember you forcing this subject when we planned on going to New York."

"You make it sound as if I'm mandating this. You're not taking care of yourself. You've been surviving, not living. I came roaring into your life, but damn it, Emmy, I love you and just want you to deal with whatever is going on. It makes me worry, not knowing."

"Why does it have to be while you are gone?"

"Because if I know you're addressing it, I'll worry less about you while I deal with Fiona. Wondering if you are all right will add to my stress."

"So this is really about you?"

"Emmy, don't do this; you sound a bit like Fiona, yer bum's oot the windae."

When Ian's Scottish roots flare up, it's time to throw in the towel. He looks so stern, but I can't help but break out in laughter at the odd-sounding words rolling off his tongue and him all disheveled. "What on earth does that mean?"

"Oh, it means you're talking rubbish."

"I should be outraged, but you've made me laugh as only you can do. I'll go."

"Phew, I should revert back to home wheesht more often."

"I give up. What's a wheesht? Is it what I think it is?"

"What would that be?"

"Bull—"

"No, Em, it means *tongue*."

"Where is lunch? I'm starving. Give me some detail about the plan you've devised to squash Fiona."

"She's not a bug, Emmy. Well, I take that back." As Ian begins to put forth the plan, I pick at my food and don't hear a word; instead, I daydream about meeting him in the store. Squatting down in his kilt, trying to pick out wine, playing the bagpipes on a warm summer's evening as we spy from the boat, our first swim together, and the first time he showed his passion and stirred long-forgotten feelings of primal desire within me. My life has flipped upside down in a short time, and now he has to abruptly leave to fend off Fiona's scandalous attempts. Oh how I wish my passport would come in. I paid extra to expedite the application. "That ought to give her a skelping."

"I'm sorry, Ian, you lost me, a skelping? Don't know that word either."

"A thrashing, don't you think my plan will put her in her place?"

Not having a clue as to what Ian had been saying for the past five minutes, I decide the simplest thing to do is nod and agree. I hope it will all unfold and I can figure it out later. His big brown eyes have begun to brighten with a look of confidence and defiance blended together. He doesn't usually use Gaelic terms; I assume he is now because he's going back home. "I'll be back in a couple of minutes. I need a bit more to drink. You need anything?"

Fiona has underestimated Ian; he's become a formidable force. His phone is ringing on the picnic table; it's from "Sarah." He hasn't mentioned Sarah. My reminiscing is crushed by apprehension.

"Hey, girl, how was lunch with skirt boy?" Louise has been with Mama, no doubt with binoculars, deciphering our expressions.

"You can probably tell me more than I know."

"Don't know about that, but you seem a little off. You okay?" Those simple words slap me in the face.

In a sarcastic tone, an annoyed smirk on my face, I loudly declare, "I've had it up to here with people wondering if I'm all right. I'm fine, hunky-dory."

"Whoa, baby girl, Louise didn't deserve your outburst!"

"I know she didn't. I'm sorry, Louise. It's Ian...oh never mind."

With wide eyes and dropped jaws, they stare at me. Pressing past the two stunned women, I move swiftly into the apartment. Mirrors don't lie. The one in the bathroom confirms my suspicion; I look like a deer caught in the headlights. Ian and I didn't have a fight, barely a simmering hot discussion. The thought of him leaving has thrown me into a tizzy. I still don't understand the extreme urgency, and now I'd seen a call from Sarah. She's probably the one who's been calling, the calls he won't answer in front of me. Everything has happened so fast, and with my past, I suspect everything good has an expiration date. As hours pass, I dwell more on Sarah. It begins to border on obsession. Ely leaves for home, kicking dirt, grumbling about something or other. Peering over the aisle trying to be invisible, Mama is obviously giving me space to wane.

"Hi, Emmy, let's take Bessie out."

"Great idea, I'm ready to get away from the store!"

Somehow, there has to be a way to work Sarah's name into the conversation. If push comes to shove, I'll just have to bring it up. Ian brings Bessie to rest at the dock. Moose and Bear are so excited it's difficult to remain suspicious. With windblown hair, face freshly shaven, khakis perfectly pressed, a shirt clinging tightly to his rippling abs and chest, this dreamboat walks directly toward me, of all the women in the world he could have. Still my inner voice nags at one simple name that's driven me crazy all day: Sarah. "You're not gonna make me walk the plank, are you?"

"It depends, are you planning a mutiny?"

I couldn't help myself, out of my mouth it came, faster than I could retrieve it. "Who is Sarah?"

"Who?"

Oh way to go, Em! Subtlety isn't my forte; it should be placed on the shelf right slam next to being coy. Ian doesn't look guilty or perplexed; his expression never changes. He reaches for my hand to help me into the boat; I avoid looking directly into his eyes. "Sarah, at lunch, I saw a call from her on your phone while you were getting a drink."

"Oh, it's nothing, just a call about some work on the estate."

"What does she do?"

"Emmy, have I ever given you a reason not to trust me? Sarah is someone I will be seeing next week. We have some work to discuss. I have a lot of people who work on the estate or are tenants. Sometimes they call."

"Sometimes? You seem to have a lot of calls. Are those the calls you don't answer?"

"If you must know, when I'm with you, I don't want to talk to anyone on the phone. My time with you is limited, too limited."

"I...I'm sorry, Ian. I didn't mean to pry. I forget how long we've been together. You had a long life before you even thought about coming to North Carolina. We've actually only known each other a very short time. It's been so good, like a dream, and I'm afraid I'll wake up and the dream will be over."

Ian slows Bessie and turns the engine off. He takes both of my hands and ever so softly kisses each. Slowly, lightly, he moves his fingers up my arms. His forefinger runs lightly across my jawline, and his thumb traces my lips, separating them slightly. Looking longingly into my eyes, he melts any doubts I have. "Whist's fur ye'll no go past ye."

"Should I ask?"

"Yes, love, it simply means, whatever is meant for you, will happen to you."

chapter 15

ONE MERE STROKE of Ian's warm hand draws me to a place I reckoned time forgot. I feel as if I have a new life, satiating my innermost passionate dreams, which seem to be evolving into reality. Words, as Leigh would explain, using heady jargon, all have meanings. Feelings don't; they are the result of emotion and years of learned behavior. Unduly, some take the most sincere expression of compassion or empathy and drive it into the ground trying to discern hidden agendas. Until today, her thoughts always befuddled me. Usually, I'm a mere simpleton; I actually believe people's actions or words, taking them at face value. Reading between the lines seems like something someone with too much time on their hands or a suspicious nature would do. Ian's words last night keep pestering the hell out me. "Whatever is meant for you, will happen to you." On the surface, it's quite an innocuous expression, hinting at a divine plan. I can hear Mama recitin' her Bible verses, swearing the good Lord will tend to all our needs if we believe. In God's timing, He will show us a personal plan leading to abundant life. Louise would conjure up haints in her magical crystal ball, who'd loudly wreak havoc using paranormal activity to scare the bejeebers out of folks, attesting to the statement's platitudes and inaccuracies. Emily, caught between a rock and a hard place, would teeter on the brink of fallin' off the fence of indecision. And then there is Leigh, who knows how words affect people. Words are her life; they are meant to sway people away from emotion and convince folks toward her point of view. Leigh writes for the paper, far from the world of romance and love. In the end, like mother like daughter, I lean toward Mama's way of thinking. I believe, knowing Ian, the intention is the same. In the mind lives the bondage of life, it perpetuates and hardens as the years pass. Few have the ability to set thoughts free. I am lucky enough to have four powerful women in my life who do not succumb to the view of the masses. I hope and pray Ian does not as well. If he does, I just may have to forget my Bible-teachin' mama and surrender to reading between the lines wondering what is meant for me and how it will happen. His leaving is making me way too cerebral for my own good. My head is aching with assumption and all about one sentence.

The Suggettes are planning a farewell party for Ian. Louise wants to make certain skirt boy has a fond adieu and most likely read his aura or some such mystical nonsense. I swaney if she pulls out a crystal and dangles it around his neck for luck, well, I'm not sure what my reaction will be, much less his.

"Miss Emileigh, you gots a minute?"

"What's up, Ely?"

"I don't understand why Mr. Ian is leavin' us. Is he done workin' here? Gosh, I hope not."

"No, Ely, he isn't done here, leastwise, I hope not. Remember his sister Fiona?"

Ely shakes his head while looking at the ground.

"I know, she makes smiling difficult for us all. Anyhow, Ian has to go return to Scotland for business reasons. It has to do with her."

"You reckon there is somethin' I can do for him here whilst he be gone?"

"Isn't your time taken between workin' here, home, and Mama's Bible lessons?"

"I gots time, if it be for Mr. Ian."

"That is mighty sweet of you. I can't answer for him though. Why don't you ask him? I think he'll be touched."

"All right, miss, I'll do it. Sure will miss him though, sure 'nuff will."

"I will too, Ely."

Ely walks away, pulling up his shorts, kickin' at the ground, looking dejected and sad at the thought of his friend leaving. Ian has been a good role model for him.

"So, Louise, what have y'all got up your sleeves for the merrymaking?"

Louise has a dubious expression upon her beautiful face, not unlike a fox hunting down prey; she casts it upon me like a spell. "Come on now, my friend, with such a look, I know you are up to no good."

"Hummm, young one, are you reading my mind or expression?"

"Louise, your mind is a cluttered mess, but your face gives up all your devilish doings."

"Well, sweet girl, we are talking about big doin's for skirt boy. I assure you, anything in the works is for fun. You only pick on the ones you love; besides, he is larger than life, so we have to scheme more than usual."

"Just beware, he is under a great deal of tension and might not take your efforts in good humor."

"Lighten up, Em, our fun will lift him above any nervous tension—one might say, *levitate* him above it. You must have plotted to aid in his relaxation."

"Well, if I do, levitation isn't involved. You're the one who performs the parlor tricks."

"Parlor tricks? Are you really going there? I hope for your sake time is allocated for plenty of rumpy pumpy."

"Louise, hush your mouth! Wherever did you dig up that expression?"

"I've got a few of them stored in my noggin. Thought for a good long time I'd never use them on you again."

"Good gracious, do you ever hold your tongue?"

"Not my style."

Louise knows the right words to elicit a dark red, streaming blush. She is spot on; it has been a long time since she's had the opportunity to pick on me in such a fashion. I'm sure the others have had varied parleys on how to send Ian off with a bang. Ordinarily, I sit by, wildly amused by their capers; I hope tomorrow night will prove to be no different.

"Hey, you, everybody is planning some sort of doin's, and they want to have it tomorrow night. I know it's the night before your flight, but everyone wants to bid you farewell."

"Emmy, I want to see you and only you for the entire night and slip out quietly in the morning."

"Not possible to slip out; they will hunt you down if you don't attend."

"Promise me one thing."

"And what might that be?"

"Promise me after all the partying is done, you'll come back here with me, alone."

"Why, Ian MacDougal, is that the best you can do to seduce me?"

"Not seduce, entice, so will you?"

"Sounds a little like beggin'. I don't rightly know; ask me again at the social."

"I see, playing hard to get? Two can play at that game, Em."

"Sorry, MacDougal, you've already shown your hand by pleading for my exclusive company."

The moment the invitation left my mouth, a lead balloon fell on my mood. He is leaving, and I have one day left to be with him, look into his eyes, caress his body, and feel it tethered to mine. Ian has never said how long he'll be gone, except to say he can't put a date on it. For the first time in a great long while, I can't imagine going through the next few days or weeks alone. Mama and the Suggettes are dearly loved, but Ian is the throbbing ache in my heart. He quickens my pulse at a glance. He sends my head spinning, creating warmth and engrossing every part of my being at the thought of his tender touch. My heart grows increasingly distraught as his departure looms. A short time ago, the blink of an eye really, I never would have fantasized anyone like Ian could take possession of my heart and soul so quickly. Being unable to visualize his home, the topography, even the light of a sunrise upon the lake, makes separation unbearable, impossible to endure. Being alone, being without him, will ravage my heart.

"Mr. Ian! Mr. Ian!" Ely is frantic to catch his idol and express his plea to help in any fashion.

"Ely, I've told you, it's just Ian. Forget the 'mister.'"

"Yes, sir, Mister, I mean, Ian. I jess' wants to know, when you be gone, is there anything I can take care of for you?"

Ian looks at Ely standing there in worn, faded jean shorts too big for his slender body, a tied frayed rope around his waist for a belt, a mostly clean T-shirt half tucked in, and bug eyes overflowing with awe, staring at him with nary a blink.

"Can you take good care of the Land Rover?"

"Is you kiddin'? You trust me with the likes of your car?"

"You have your license now, don't you?"

Ely nods his head with a proud look on his young face.

"I would appreciate you making sure Ulysses has rides to wherever he needs to go. Can you do that for me?"

"Yes, sir, course I can do that for you, sir."

"Forget the 'sir' too, Ely. Now, I also need someone reliable to check on Moose and Bear. Mum is going to stay on, but she may need a hand making certain they get exercise."

"Oh, I cans do that do fer sure."

"Don't forget your responsibilities to Tah and your mother."

"No, I won't. Ma Bell won't let me. She done keeps a close eye on the likes of me. I reckon Mama jess' likes me bein' outta the house and not gettin' into no mo trouble."

Ian pats him on the back, showing he is proud of his progress and appreciates his exuberance. "Hey, Ely, you know anything about the soiree tonight?"

"Swear whooi?"

Ian can't help but bend over laughing at Ely's attempt to mimic him. "The party being planned for tonight."

"No, I doesn't. I'll be dare, but seems like it's all hush-hush like, or dem ladies jess' don't truss' me with the plannin'."

"I don't think trust is involved. Maybe they don't even know what they are doing."

Ely chuckles loudly as he stomps the up the stairs to the store, making a halfhearted attempt to tuck in the other portion of his T-shirt while swiping at his unruly hair in a gesture to mat it down.

"One more thing, is your mother coming to the party tonight?"

"Mama said she'd be comin' but later on; she gots stuff to do."

"Good. See you later, Ely."

"Yes, sir—I means Ian."

"Cook, Steve, Grayson, all present and accounted for! Let the shenanigans commence!"

"Miss Leigh, ain't we forgettin' Ian ain't here?"

"True, but the party is starting before the guest of honor arrives. It may not be normal, but neither are we. Let's get those corks a flyin' y'all."

"Guys, we'd best get set up before everyone starts to trickle down to the dock."

The day is spectacular—warm with less humidity. The oak leaves are swaying in the breeze. Squirrels are tossing down pine cones from way atop the trees. They fall to the ground with a loud kabang, looking suspiciously like grenades bouncing around on the ground. Sailboats large and small dot the water with sails full of fresh summer air; movement is swift, almost silent. The water being sliced by the boats and the captains' orders being bellowed are all they hear. Everyone who is anyone is making his or her way down to the dock. Mama put out the message to everyone using the emergency phone tree: "Bring a dish to share; let's send Ian off with an overwhelming urge to come back."

Tonight holds the promise of one of the greatest parties this season. Maybe that's just because it's to celebrate the man I love.

chapter 16

IAN IS FLAGGED down by the police. There's a roadblock set up going each way on the road. Sassafras Lane is between the road blocks; it's a rutted, curvy dirt road heading up the hillside shaded by a forest of trees. "Show me your license and registration, sir."

"What's going on here, officer?"

"Routine check. You been drinking, sir?"

"No, I'm on my way to a party."

"You ain't from around here, are ya?"

"Whatever gave you that impression?"

"You got a strange, queer accent, and what is this here license you handed me?"

"An international license. I'm from the Isle of Skye in Scotland."

"Isle of Skye, ain't never heard of that there place."

"Now, how did I know that?"

Chief Billy Joe Hobbs slowly pulls his mirrored aviator sunglasses lower on his nose, far enough so his beady eyes, which are set too close, can be seen peering over the top. He spits on the ground, wiping what dripped out of his mouth on his sleeve all while sternly staring at Ian. "You sassin' me, boy? Outta the car right now, ya hear?"

"What is it you think I've done?"

"I don't require a reason other than considering you a suspicious person. You up for takin' a sobriety test?"

"I certainly am, especially if it gets me outta here."

Ian takes the exam without further comment. Passing it with flying colors, he assumes wrongly he can hop back into his Land Rover and head to

Tah's party. As he reaches for the door handle, the chief pulls his arm back and shouts, "Tommy, come over here! Give me a hand! We got us a live one."

Flanked by two cops, Ian begins to become defensive and show his Scottish stubbornness. Tommy saunters over to Billy Joe; his forefinger pushes back the sweat-stained official hat of the Moravian Falls Police Department.

"Now, son, where is this here party you was going to in such a hurry?"

"Not that it's any of your business, but Tahlulah Bell Suggs is having a send-off party for me."

"You...ahh...thinking of goin' somewhere?"

"Back home."

"I see. What you think of that, Tommy?"

Tommy moves closer to Ian and looks inside the Land Rover. "I reckon if Mr. MacDougal agrees, a look-see into his automobile is in order."

"Good thinkin', you got any objection?"

"Knock yourselves out."

Tommy opens up the Land Rover after putting on latex gloves. He moves the goods with his nightstick, including unopened bottles of Scotch Ian's taking to the party. "Exactly what is it you expect to find?"

"Don't rightly know, but when Tommy sees it, we'll know."

"Glad you have a plan, Officer."

"Mr. MacDougal, do you know where Sassafras Lane heads?"

"I've looked at property up the road, and an acquaintance of mine lives up there."

"Who might that be?"

"Hannah Stiles."

"And how do you know her?"

"From the general store, she's been there with her son."

"You spend a lot of time at the store?"

"I'm seeing Emileigh."

"Seeing? What does that entail?"

"Now you've stepped over the line; I refuse to answer the question."

"You say you know Hannah Stiles's son, Ely. How do you know him?"

"He, well, he had some trouble awhile back, and I've taken interest in him."

"What does that mean?"

"I'm trying to help him out a bit. Since I'm at the store, I frequently see him and we talk."

"Is he going to this party you spoke of?"

"Yes."

"Is Hannah Stiles going to the party?"

"Ely said she'd be late coming, but yes. She might already be there since you've held me up from arriving."

"The interest you take in Ely, what sort of interest?"

Billy Joe is interrupted by another of his officers at the scene. He comes up to the chief out of breath and sweating. "Billy Joe! Billy Joe!"

"Hebron, what the hell is it? Cain't you see I'm in the middle of somethin' important here?"

"Lt. Champlain of the state police is on the radio lookin' to speak with you. He says it's urgent!"

"Urgent my foot, there's probably a skunk on one of his highways that needs disposin' of, and his people are too good to do the deed."

"I don't think so..."

"You heard what I said, Hebron, not now. Tell him I'll call when available, ya hear?"

"Yes, sir, I hear."

Chief Billy Joe Hobbs turns around and stares at Ian for a good spell. Beads of perspiration cover his upper lip. "Now, Mr. MacDougal, you know what happened up the road here, don't you?" The chief points up the dirt road where the coroner's car and the town's ambulance are headed.

"Not a clue."

"Do you have anyone who can confirm your whereabouts for, oh say, the last three hours?"

"My mum and Ulysses Bucknell."

"Your mum, what is that?"

"My mother."

"A mother would say anything to protect her son, no matter what his age. And old Ulysses is nothing but a crazy drunk, hardly a reliable source. Anyone else of reputable reputation?"

"I spoke with Beth McKenzie, my real estate agent, on the phone for quite a while this afternoon."

"On a cell phone?"

"Yes."

"Well then, you could have been anywhere."

"She was on the road, but I was at the rental house."

"How did you and Beth get acquainted?"

"She showed me the rental, and then we began looking at property I might want to purchase."

"How is it we should think you were at the house you are renting? Where is this house, and whose is it?"

"I've rented the Sutherlands' home for the summer. Beth probably heard Ulysses in the background along with my dogs; they were barking and splashing in the lake."

The authoritative tone the chief has taken on is making Ian nervous, and he is reluctant to share much more information. "Sounds like you got some money. What is it you do in Scotland? Tommy, go over to the Sutherlands' place and have a look around. You okay with that, MacDougal?"

"As a matter of fact, no, I'm not okay with it. If you want to search my home, get a warrant, and don't disturb Mum. You asked what I do in Scotland; I'm a laird of an estate. What is all this about? I demand you tell me or let me go on my way."

"You ain't in the position to demand squat."

The chief looks away while putting a chaw of chewing tobacco in his mouth. "What is a laird?"

"A laird is simply a landowner."

"How much land?"

"A lot, I have responsibility as well, which is why I am required to return home tomorrow."

"You sound pretty highfalutin', more like a king."

"Laird does mean lord but not in a religious sense and certainly not a king."

"Well ladeefuckin'da. I'll tell you what, since you require a warrant to enter the property, I'll be takin' you into the station. In the meantime, I expect this business to be kept quiet, ya hear? Your so-called acquaintance, Hannah Stiles, we suspect has met her demise at the hand of someone other than herself."

"You mean murdered? Dear God, please not Hannah! Who? Where? How did she die? Am I a suspect? Is that why you are taking me into custody?"

"Chief, got another call. The lieutenant is back on the radio. He wants your cell number. He keeps saying it's urgent."

"Hebron, for Christ's sake, tell him I'm in the middle of a serious investigation. I'll be back at the station soon and will contact him then and no sooner. You understand?"

"Yes, sir, he ain't gonna be happy to hear those words."

"I don't care about his happiness, Hebron, now disappear. Don't you dare give him my cell number. Back to you, MacDougal, too many coincidences for me to ignore the fact you may be involved in this heinous crime. I'm paid to read between the lines of what is said and examine the facts at hand."

"You suspect me of murder?"

"You seem oddly concerned about your own welfare when a friend has just been killed. That is one reason at this point of the investigation you are a person of interest, damn suredly a person of great interest. For the record, you are not being taken into custody, just questioning, even if you are a lord."

"Hannah's death is a shock to me. I can't believe you think I, a God-fearing Christian could do such a horrible thing to anyone, especially a friend. You should be out catching the real killer. I do need to call someone and tell them where I'll be."

"No calls, at least not at this time. You said Ely is at this party. Is it over at Tah's place?"

"It is supposed to be down at the dock. He doesn't know, does he? Please, Chief, don't be the one to tell him. Tell Tah or someone and ask them to let him know. Don't let the kid hear about his mom from a law enforcement officer. He has been through enough."

"Oh how considerate of you, MacDougal. You almost sound sincere. I'll oblige this time, but only because I agree. Hebron, get your ass back on the radio call a tow truck here. We need to impound this here piece of shit the lord drives around. And use precautions, we don't want to spoil the investigation by sloppy work."

Ian can't help but retort to Chief Billy Joe Hobbs. "Sloppy work? Seems you've already done that, thinking I could do such a thing."

"Shut your mouth, boy. I don't want to hear another word out of you until we're down to the station."

Since the chief stopped being polite and reasonably professional, Ian thinks it best to be quiet. He also regrets giving so much detailed information to him, but he had no idea he was becoming a suspect in a murder case.

"Mama, you in here?"

"Over here, Em, do they need more vittles down yonder? Never in all my born days would I have expected so many would show up to attend a farewell shindig."

"I'm sure they need somethin', but I am wondering if you've heard from Ian. I thought he'd be here by now."

"No, baby girl, ain't heard the phone jingle, and I've been here a spell."

"I've been tryin' his cell, but it keeps going straight to voice mail. Maybe I should call the Sutherlands' place and see if his mom has seen him."

"I wouldn't do it, Em, you may get her all riled up and worryin' 'bout nothing."

"He's got fifteen more minutes before I send the cavalry after him. I'm going back down and see if everyone has a place to sit and eat."

The Ramblers begin to play some of the crowd's old favorites. Cook has the barbeque flaring up, charring an assorted array of meats. Emily and Louise are acting like the quintessential hostesses. Most folks who don't have a drink tightly grasped in hand are clenching either a fishin' pole or a ski rope. Those brave enough to be pulled around the lake by a maniacal wannabe captain, whose only intention is to see them fall headfirst into a large wave are braver than I. Loud doesn't begin to describe the sound emitting from Tahlulahville. No one except Grayson and Steve notice the squad car slowly approaching the store. Both of the guys look at each other and figure some old fart called the cops complaining about the noise. The two of them skedaddle to the car to make nice. From the expression on the officer's face, they know in a moment more than a noisy party is the purpose of his visit.

"Hey, Tommy, long time no see. Would you like something to eat?"

"No, Grayson, I'm on official business. You two know Ely Stiles?"

Steve turns his head toward Grayson wondering what Ely has gotten himself into now. "Yup, we know him. Is he in trouble?"

"Is there a place to talk that's a bit quieter?"

"Tah is up in the store; she is the only one there."

"Good, she should hear this too."

The three of them walk in silence to the store, up the four creaky steps. "Hey, Tah, you in here?"

"Why in tarnation does everyone keep asking me that question? Oh hello, Tommy. Didn't know you were here and in uniform. Everything okay?"

"No, Tah, it ain't. Got some bad news to tell y'all; it involves Ely."

"Bad news? He has been the kindest boy I know these past weeks. Don't tell me..."

"Well, I um..." Tommy looks down at the floor, unable to look any of them in the eyes. As he speaks, there's a tremble in his voice. Finally, he's able to look up with tears beginning to well. Hannah has been through so many ordeals; we all have prayed for her delivery from her trials. Tommy knew her well. Away from the scene and the chief, his emotions flare up. Hannah was always poor as a church mouse and well thought of in Moravian Falls.

"Tommy, tell us please."

"Y'all know Hannah Stiles?" The three of them nod slowly knowing they are about to hear bad news. "Well, a neighbor went to call on her earlier today...This is hard to say to y'all." Tommy wrings his hands and turns away for a moment to regain some semblance of composure. "She's gone on to be with her maker."

"What? That can't be. She is coming to the party tonight, all excited about being invited. Tommy, you're mistaken."

"No, Tah, I wish it were so."

Steve asks the difficult question, knowing how much she has been through and her obvious bouts of depression. "Hannah didn't...she didn't commit..."

"No, Steve. When the call came in, we went there too. It was quite plain she was violently killed by hands other than her own."

"Do you know who would do this?"

"We have taken a person in to question."

"Who is the bastard? Give us a name."

"I don't think the chief would want me to do that, Grayson, not just yet. I'm telling you this, because, well, it may be easier for Ely to hear the news concerning his mother from y'all."

"Mama! Mama..." Em bounds up the stairs after seeing the police car out front. Fear overtakes her as she mounts the stairs. "Mama, it's Ian, isn't it? He's been in an accident; that's why he's so late!"

"No, girl, it's Hannah. Someone has taken her life."

"Oh dear Lord, who would do such a terrible thing? She'd never hurt a fly. Tommy, who? Do you know who?"

"Miss Emileigh, I ain't supposed to say, but since you're here and know him...the chief took Ian MacDougal to the station for questioning."

The only words Em is able to utter are, "My Ian?" Her heart starts palpitating, and she begins to hyperventilate; her chest heaves spastically. Em's eyes roll back into her head, and down she falls like a sack of potatoes dropping to the floor where she remains motionless. Steve races to her side. Tah screams out her name and runs to get a wet rag. Grayson stands staring at Tommy with a fierce anger cast toward him.

"How dare you come in here telling us about Hannah's death, and then with Emileigh standing right here calmly state Ian is a suspect. Ian is the most upright person you'd ever meet, salt of the earth. In the short time he has been in our area, he has stimulated growth, brought back a sense of genuine pride to our little town...look by the lake. Take a long look, Tommy. See all those local folks? They're gathered to wish him well on his trip. A trip, I might add, we have known about. So if you so-called law enforcement officers think this trip is a cover-up of some sort, forget about it. All those friends and neighbors are showing their invitation for Ian to come back to our little Podunk community. Shame on you, Tommy, and the chief too."

"I'm sure if he has done nothing, he has nothing to worry about."

"Don't accuse him of murder because he is an easy target, an outsider. Don't y'all dare pin this on him without concrete evidence. You better have an ongoing investigation looking for the real murderer."

"You seem so sure of him, Grayson."

"I am."

"We'll straighten this out later. Emmy, you all right? Grayson, go bring Ely up here. I don't know how, but we've gotta make this as easy as possible for him."

"I'm all right, Mama, but I need to get to the police station. Oh Lord, what about Maggie? Should we tell her?"

There is a sense of panic and disbelief palpable in the store. Steve helps Emmy off the floor and exclaims, "I'll take care of that when she and Ulysses get here. Meantime, shouldn't I scatter our guests back to their homes?"

"No, Steve, not just yet. Tell them to quiet down. Get the Ramblers to stop playin'. I don't want sounds of a party going on while he is hearing about his mother. After Ely is aware of Hannah's death, I want you to tell them all about her, and while they are here, pray for Hannah, Ely, and Ian. I'm not believin' this is happening, a true nightmare in the bright of day. Steve, please, ask Louise, Emily, and Leigh to come here."

Once again, Tah has taken on the role of being the strongest force among the bunch. Leigh arrives before the others. Explaining what has happened, Tah is barely able to keep her composure when she sees her dear friend lose it. Struck with an overpowering sense of empathy, Leigh sits down with her hands to her face. "Oh, Tah, what horrible, horrible news! How is Ely going to survive this? And to think this was supposed to be a happy occasion, the party of the season! I was going to announce my final story at the paper. I'm leaving to finally write the novel I've always dreamed about. Now my last story will be about Hannah. Oh, I can't!"

"No one better to write it than a heart filled with compassion."

"Oh, this isn't about me and a silly story. Oh and, Ian, you don't think he did this, do you?"

"Has hell frozen over?"

Steve is down at the docks taking care of business, and Grayson escorts Ely to the store. A hush falls over the guests. No one even has to explain; they sense something has happened. As soon as Ely enters the store, the coroner's truck and the ambulance carrying Hannah's body drive past the store, and all the guests' mouths gape open simultaneously. Cook whispers in my ear, asking what is going on. As I relay the information to him, he takes my arm and opens the car door. Gratitude sweeps over me as I am in no condition to drive, much less walk into the station where Ian sits being interrogated as a murder suspect. As we approach the police station, a small spark of doubt about Ian's innocence flickers in my mind.

"Ely, son, come over here and sit by me." Tah sits for a moment, closes her eyes, and takes a deep breath. She reaches out to Ely, putting an arm tightly around his shoulders. Steve, Grayson, Leigh, Emily, and Louise stand nearby, a look of horror and compassion upon each of their faces.

"What's wrong, Ma Bell? You look real worried like."

"I am, Ely. I am. We've got some very sad news to tell you."

chapter 17

BEULAH BELL'S MINI Cooper can be heard pulling into the store's parking lot and skidding to a halt. She storms into the store and sizes up who is there. "Tahlulah, you should have called me, girl. I had to hear 'bout the news from Maggie. Get me up-to-date."

"Mama, don't you say hello anymore?"

"We ain't got time for formalities. 'Sides we all know one another."

"How did Maggie hear?"

"Police called her."

"Em and Cook are down at the police station. Em says they aren't allowed to see Ian. Ely went home with Grayson. Dylan and Salina are drivin' up from Charlotte and should be here soon. I think that covers everyone."

"Nothing else?"

Eyes drop; they realize more gossip has been going on than planning. "Well then, line up! I'm here to hand out job assignments. I took the liberty of contacting Harper. He is well on the way to the police station to represent Ian. If he ain't been charged, Harper says he'll have him out of there in no time. I'm gonna stay over with Maggie. We'll make the Sutherland house HQ. Tah, you get with Emily and help Ely with the funeral arrangements."

"Mama, back off your high horse a moment. Hannah's body won't be released until an autopsy has been performed, Could be awhile after as well."

"Still, there should be plans in place so it can quickly happen when her body is released. Trust me, it will be easier on Ely this way. Has anyone thought to contact Peter Barbour? He's incarcerated; should make it easy."

The suggestion to contact the snake appalls Louise. He is the last person that'd care about Hannah's demise. "All right, since no one is jumping in to let him know, I will."

"Oh, Mama, you don't have to play the martyr."

"I ain't. We need to present an organized front. Y'all know if Barbour weren't in jail, he would be the first on the list of suspects. Ain't all those sensationalized newscasts usually showing family members being the first to be interrogated?"

"Beulah, Hannah had no one besides Ely and Peter, so we know someone other than those two is responsible."

"Time for me to leave and sit with Maggie; surely she needs comfort. I ain't sure if Ulysses is well versed in such matters. If y'all should hear any news, please call us."

"Sure 'nuff, Mama. You do the same. Night now."

"Emmy, you've gone quiet. A penny for your thoughts, dear."

"There is no way I could be here alone; I feel indebted for your kindness."

"So then, spill it, kid. It has been an awful day, most especially for Ely, Hannah, and of course, Ian."

"How do you think Ely took the news?"

"That's a question you needn't ask. We all know hearing about the death of a loved one is devastating. Ely has no one else; at sixteen, this shouldn't happen, but unbelievably, it has. As for Ian, to be stopped on the way to a party and then hauled in for murder, there are no words. Loss is no stranger to you, sweet pea, or Ian either."

A slight breeze picks up, rustling the leaves above. Cook and I sit on a bench across from the police station. It has been a long, hot summer with little rain. Some of the leaves have died and are now floating to the ground. As they land, the crinkled leaves sound like raindrops hitting the pavement. I begin to cry after hearing Cook speak of the day's events. "I can't believe I'm saying this, but a part of me wonders if Ian is guilty. I love him; I know he isn't capable of such a horrendous crime—at least the part of Ian I know isn't. I can hear Maggie at their welcome party saying I don't know him. When he first showed up, Emily doubted anyone could be so good and questioned his motives. We joked, saying maybe he is a serial killer in a kilt. Now that

I think about it, Ian was the one who started the joke about being a serial killer. I've betrayed him. My head is playing tricks. How can I ever look him in the eye or trust the way I feel again?"

"Emmy, Emmy, Emmy, trust your heart, girl. A lot has transpired, all of it stressful. We all think about what-ifs in situations we are not able to comprehend. Since Ian has arrived, the emotional ups and downs have been unrelenting. Your head must be spinning by news and events of each and every day. Don't beat yourself up, darlin'. When you see him again, the exchange will probably be strained. Put yourself in his shoes—his innocent shoes."

Harper pulls up and scurries out of the car. He looks across the street at the two of us sitting on the bench. A fast wave is exchanged as he bounds over to greet us. "Em, Cook, I'll get him out lickety-split. That's legalese." A smile crosses his tanned face, putting us at ease; finally, someone who can work on Ian's behalf.

"Oh, Harper, please don't spend time with us. Go help Ian!"

"Em's right, Harper. They won't let us inside and haven't said shit about their so-called investigation. Go on, and when you can, give us an update."

"I promise I will. You two go over to the diner and get something to eat. This isn't going to happen fast; give me your cell numbers. Think good thoughts."

"Thank you, Harper. Thank you so much."

Before Cook and I get up to go for a bit to eat, Grandmama drives up with Maggie beside her. Maggie looks like she has been in the Grand Prix, her hair windblown so much it would make any witch proud. Grandmama, as we all are well aware, can be pretty volatile when an event perturbs her. Her driving habits usually reflect whatever mood has possessed her. She spins around and grabs my arm, practically pulling it out of its socket. "Come on, baby girl. We've got ass to kick. Is Harper here yet?"

"He just got here. Have you heard something?"

"Oh, you bet I have. Cook, Maggie, get a move on. We need all the muscle we can get."

Cook looks a little worried concerning her state of mind. "Umm, Beulah, is you planning on breaking Ian out?"

"As a matter of fact, I am, much to your chagrin—legally too."

"That's good to hear."

"Enough chitchat, move it!" Grandmama pushes the door to the police station with such force the hinges bend. "Hobbs, where is your lazy, good-for-nothing ass?"

"Well, if it ain't Beulah Bell followed by her entourage." Chief Hobbs saunters up with a confident smile, sucking on a toothpick. He leans on a desk, putting his hands inside his front pockets and rattling change rhythmically. He exudes pride through his demeanor; he must be thinking he's caught a murderer. "Where is Harper, Tromble?"

"Why, hello to you too, Beulah. Mr. Tromble is with his client in the interrogation room."

"I need to see him, right now."

"Well, I ain't so sure he'd welcome the interruption. I think it best to wait till they's done."

"Ain't you full of yourself? That's okay. If you're unwilling to interrupt, I most certainly will."

Chief Hobbs takes his hands out of his pockets. Standing at attention, he puts one hand on his pistol and loosens the guard on the trigger. "No, this is my place, Beulah. What I say goes."

"Fine, have it your way—for the moment." Grandmama takes my hand, and we go into the women's restroom. "Give me your damn cell phone."

"Well, okay. You're gonna make a call to Harper, aren't you?"

"I knew you were smart."

"Grandmama, what is going on?"

"Just wait, stand guard at the door. That rat bastard, Hobbs, probably has his skanky ear at the door. Harper, come to the lobby right now. I've got news you need to hear before this crap goes any further."

"Beulah Bell, I can't right now!"

"You will, or I'll come get you."

Everyone knows when Beulah talks, we need to jump. Harper charges out of the interrogation room. "Beulah, Maggie, Cook, and Em! Quite a showing. What is so important?"

"We need some privacy other than the bathroom."

Chief Hobbs moves toward the group, leaning his head to the right as if to catch our conversation. Hobbs slyly smiles. "Y'all got anything you want to share?"

"No, we're going out for a spell."

"Okay, probably best if Hebron puts Mr. MacDougal in a holding cell."

"Chief, I don't expect to see any bruises on my client when I return."

"Lawyer time is up in just a few minutes. You sure you want to leave?"

Harper looks at Beulah with a questioning expression. She nods, letting him know with one look they need to talk. "Chief, there aren't hours for attorneys. I am going to speak with these folks, who obviously have an urgent private message for me. I suggest you give my client something to drink in the meantime."

"Son, I ain't used to takin' direction in my station."

"Like I said, my client is thirsty. You don't want to neglect the basic needs of a prisoner, do you?"

Harper escorts us out to the park across the street. "Beulah, this better be good."

"Young man, I assure you it is. Have a seat y'all. I called the county jail in Taylorsville to ask someone to relay the news of Hannah's death to Peter Barbour. They referred me to a prison in South Carolina where he has been extradited. The administrator sounded a little weird when I mentioned his name but was kind enough to give me the number in Charleston. I called Charleston, and guess what? I got yet another number to call. By this time, I figured they were giving me the runaround." Everybody is sitting, listening attentively to Grandmama, with the exception of Harper, who sits sighing at the long story. "Called the third number given; a Lieutenant Champlain answered. Said he's been trying to get Hobbs on the phone since early this afternoon. Peter Barbour was being transported in a van from Taylorsville to Charleston. Not far from North Wilkesboro, there was an accident involving Barbour's transport vehicle. He ran. No one near the accident knew he was a prisoner. All the guards were knocked unconscious. They've had a manhunt out for him ever since. He could have easily made his way here from North Wilkesboro and gotten to Hannah."

"Beulah, I'm glad you're on our side. Do you have Lieutenant Champlain's number?"

"Sure do; it's right here."

"Did you mention Hannah?"

"No, I figured we may need an ace up our sleeve where Hobbs is concerned."

"Y'all chill for a moment; I want to call the lieutenant. How long ago did you find this out?"

Maggie pipes up laughing. "We got here after going through the sound barrier. It took about ten minutes from the time we left till we got here."

"Good, I can probably catch him."

"Chief Hobbs, good to hear your voice finally."

"Who is this?"

"It's your good ole buddy Champlain."

"Bob, sorry for the delay in getting back to you."

"You never did; I just called you. How are those good ole boys of yours?"

"Fine, they've been workin' hard today. I've got a murder suspect to interrogate soon as his lazy lawyer gets back in here."

"I don't think you have a suspect in custody. I just got a call from Harper Tromble, says he represents Ian MacDougal. Mr. Tromble informed me of Hannah Stiles's murder. The urgent calls to you, and I do emphasize the plurality of calls, were to give you a heads-up. Peter Barbour escaped from a transport vehicle involved in an accident just out of North Wilkesboro around one o'clock this afternoon."

"Holy shit! Damn it, Bob! How come you didn't relay this to Hebron earlier?"

"Alert says chiefs only to be informed. You've most likely been focused on an innocent. Unless you've got concrete evidence, better release him."

"Don't be tellin' me how to run my office!"

"Somebody ought to. Besides, I'm just tryin' to help you stay employed. You think Barbour is a threat to anyone else up there?"

"Maybe. I'll give them the news and tell them to be aware of their surroundings."

"If it were me, I'd station some officers outside their residences."

"I don't have unlimited resources like you."

"I'd be glad to send some help your way; all it takes is for you to ask."

"No, not yet, Bob; I've got some crow to eat and get my staff out looking for Barbour."

"Tah, we'd best head out for tonight. You need anything or one of us to stay till Emmy gets back?"

"No, the day has taken a toll on us all. Good thing business was quiet. News about Hannah must have kept most folks with their kin today."

"All the folks at the party probably spread the news. Everyone has seen Ely here workin'. I bet they stayed clear to give y'all some time to grieve and the police room to investigate."

"I only hope they do the same tomorrow, Louise. Looks as if Ian won't be leavin' now, don't it?"

"Don't appear likely he's gonna be allowed to get out of Hobbs's clutches anytime soon. How could Billy Joe think Ian of all people could do such a thing?"

"Emily had her doubts about him at first."

"Oh tish tosh, Leigh, she recanted her speculations shortly afterward."

"You know what they say about first impressions."

"Yeah, but Emily is the only one of us who felt like he was up to no good. All the rest of us were intrigued by him, and, Em, well, she tumbled head over heels pretty darn quick."

"Louise, what you see happenin' to Ian?"

"I see the same as you, but what I know is with the Lord's help, it'll all turn out just fine."

"Your ball got a crack in it?"

"We all know, light shines best through cracked pots. Ain't that our motto?"

"Should be, but you ain't gettin' a hit off this affair?"

"Leigh, it just may be that I do and don't wish to share it."

"Uh ho, the only thing don't pass your lips is bad news."

"No worries, Tah, like I said, with help from above, it's all gonna be just as it should be. Don't forget to set that alarm; it weren't put in for you to look at the pretty lights."

"All right, Weasy, all right. I hope Emmy knows how to turn it off when she comes in."

Louise blows through her lips, a comical sound showing how ridiculous her words are. "Come now, girl, your youngin can work all those new gadgets as if she were the inventor herself."

Chief B.J. Hobbs walks slowly from the holding cell, his head hanging lower than a snake's belly. Chewing tobacco drips down his chin in a dark stream of spit; he'd been workin' it fast and furious. His confidence drained, showing in his slumped posture; his hands are tucked together in front. Hobbs takes his tobacco-stained shirt sleeve and wipes the spittle from his chin as he tells Ian he is free to go. Ian doesn't say a word to Hobbs; he asks Tommy about his Land Rover. "Until we have all the forensics, it stays impounded."

"Are you saying I am still a suspect?"

"You are still a person of interest."

"When it's released, let Ely Stiles pick it up for me." Keeping his words and plans to a minimum, he gathers his belongings and walks to the lobby where Emileigh stands open armed. Cook looks proudly at Em, knowing her doubts. Ian's mom can't hold back her tears; she heads to the door with Harper's assistance. "Em, get me out of this rank place. I hope with God's grace I never set foot in this or any other police station again."

Em looks deeply into his eyes, and without so much as lowering her eyelids, she tosses her arms around his neck, kissing Ian hard and long. Grandmama smiles at the two lovebirds; she remains at the station. She must be saving some choice words for Chief Hobbs.

"Ian, did the chief say anything to you concerning your plans to leave town?"

"No, and I purposely didn't bring up the subject. What is the latest on Peter Barbour? Anyone know?"

Harper looks at me, our attention has been so focused on freeing Ian, the consequences of Barbour remaining at large suddenly strike us. "We should warn Grayson and Emily for Ely's safety. Tah should definitely not be left alone tonight; you staying with her Emileigh?"

"I hadn't planned on it. Can you give us a lift back to Ian's?" Emileigh points toward Maggie and Ian who obviously are weary from the day. "I'm starving, and the two of them have to be famished. I'll call Mama from there. Can you stay for dinner Harper?"

"I'm gonna stay with Mom and Dad tonight. I'll catch a bite there. Do me a favor and call me after you talk to Tah. I have to go right by there and can stop in to check on her if needed."

Tah hears a fumbling at the door to the store. She realizes a light has been left on, and a customer must be rattling the door to get her attention. The constant pushing and shoving at the door hurries Tah to pull on a robe; she grabs her tea as she walks to the front of the general store. A deafening blaring sound emits from the alarm system. As she is mumbling about the alarm, the phone rings, startling her even more. The alarm company is on the other end. "Mrs. Suggs, this is Womack Security. Is everything all right?"

"Well, um, I don't rightly know. I heard a commotion at the front door and then this hellacious noise from your system."

"I know the system is new; most times, it's someone coming in who forgets to reset it. Are you expecting someone?"

"My daughter. Shoot, my friend Louise said she'd never have trouble with the system."

"The police are being called; they should be on the way. Just to be safe, do you think you can look at the front door and see if it remains closed, or if your daughter has indeed come back?"

"Land's sake, all this over Em coming in, and the police too. Miss, the local police have their hands full; can't you call them off?"

"No, Mrs. Suggs, it's procedure."

"Hey, Harper, Mama's line is busy, so go on to Cook and Louise's. Chances are she is gossiping with one of the Suggettes anyhow."

"Okay, Em. If you need anything, you know where to reach me."

"Good night, Harper. Thank you so much for everything."

Grandmama stops bawling the chief out for his inept decisions regarding Ian when the call comes in from the alarm company. "Chief, you got a call."

"Again with the calls, Hebron?"

"Now, Billy Joe, remember what happened last time you didn't take a call?"

"Beulah, I don't need reminding." The chief reaches for the phone. He had been leaning on his desk listening to Beulah chide him relentlessly concerning Ian and Peter Barbour. "Chief Hobbs here, how can I help you?"

"This is Womack Security; we have an intruder alarm at the Suggs General Store in Moravian Falls. I have Mrs. Suggs on the phone. She says the door is open, but she doesn't see anyone. Chief, we just lost our connection with Mrs. Suggs."

"Tommy, Hebron, fast as you can we are going up to the general store. Beulah, you stay put."

"The hell I will! She's my baby."

She scrambles into the Mini Cooper and simultaneously pushes number two on her speed dial. "Em, there is an alarm at the store. The cops are on the way."

"Grandmama, I've been trying to call; the line is busy. She probably did something and goofed up the system."

"Hobbs yelled to me on the way to his squad car. The door is open; no one is in sight, and then the line went dead to the security company. Get there, girl, and bring Ian!"

Tah drops her tea when the familiar voice is heard. "Got ya a security system, eh?"

"Who's there? What do you want?"

"Come now, y'all know'd who this be. I jess' came for my gun. You remember, the one that sorry, good-for-nothin' stepson showed you up close?" The front door slams, and shattering glass can be heard falling from the only lit light. Tah hears ripping paper and the twist of a cap. She knows where he is, over by the beer and wine.

"Since you know I have a security system, you'd best be on your way."

"Not till I gets what's mine."

"You know I don't have your gun."

Tah is panic-stricken; she knows he must be the one who murdered Hannah, his own wife. If he's murdered once, what is to stop him again? "If you ain't got it, then what else you got to take its place?"

Police sirens can be heard in the background getting louder with each passing second.

"Well now, Peter, we can talk about what I've got."

"Don't play me, Tah. I hear 'em loudly as you do. Maybe I'll just take you. You know, as a hostage, so's I can ditch this place."

"You shouldn't have come back here. That was a dumb move."

"Oh, but you know, I have some unfinished business here."

"What you don't know is along with the security system, everyone thought it best for me to get a small pistol. I've been at the shootin' range, gotten a good aim."

"Maybe you did get one, you may even have a good aim, but you ain't never shot a livin' thing."

"You ain't livin'; you're dead to me, Peter."

"I see, you is tryin' your damnedest to muster up courage."

Tah can hear Peter slowly making his way down the libation aisle toward her. She decides to wait for him to speak again and then jump into the cooler at the back of the store; by then, hopefully the police will be storming the door. Peter starts chanting with an evil cadence. "Come here, Tah. You know I'll find you. I'm a lot younger, stronger too. Tah, oh, Tah, come to Daddy. I've got a surprise for you."

Tah manages to get inside the cooler; she looks around and finds a large rack of ribs; she jams the door handle with it. Peter hears her and quickly gets to the cooler. He tries to open it but can't. Frustrated, he beats on the cooler door. Hobbs boldly enters the front door wielding his weapon and yelling, "Police! Come out with your hands up!"

Hebron and Tommy bust down the back door, trapping Peter inside. Peter swings at Tommy and connects with an uppercut to his jaw. Tommy is thrown back into Hebron. Hebron's weapon mistakenly goes off as he falls haphazardly, taking Tommy with him. The two lie on the floor, limbs entangled. Hobbs yells, "Stop or I'll shoot!" Peter jumps over the officers attempting to escape out the apartment door. Hebron and Tommy try to trip him but are unable. Hobbs blindly shoots twice and hears Peter moaning by the back door. Chief Hobbs makes his way past his officers who are still tangled in a heap on the floor.

"I can't believe you shot me! Billy Joe, you shot me!"

"Too bad I didn't kill you. Least this way, Hannah will have peace, and Ely can say his."

Grandmama, Ian, Em, and all the Suggettes along with their kin wait nervously in the parking lot with the exception of Grayson and his family. The gunshots keep them from being able to take another breath out of fear for Tah.

"Tah must be all right. She simply must."

Tommy convinces Tah they got Peter, and she can take the brace out of the handle. He laughs out loud when the ribs fall to the floor. "Is that what you used?"

"Best damn ribs in town—they've always said that; now I believe it."

Tommy leads Tah out of the store. Hebron hits the lights, illuminating not only the interior of the store, but the parking lot as well.

"Mama, Mama, oh Mama! Thank the Lord you're okay."

"There'll be a lot of thankin' going around. I figured you boys had lost your minds when an alarm system was put in, but it just saved my life. Next party, we're havin' ribs. Don't ask; I'll tell you later."

Chief calls for an ambulance and cordons off the store. No tears are shed for Peter Barbour; if he survives his wounds, he won't escape again—that's for dang sure. "Tah, you've gotta spend the night somewhere else tonight."

Ian looks at Emmy. "So much for being alone tonight." He winks and smiles, knowing there is a lot to be grateful for on this night.

Louise, as only Louise can, throws a bit of levity into this situation. 'I could sure use a glass of wine right about now. We've had enough drama; how about that party we were supposed to have?"

"Yeah, how 'bout it? Everybody, over to Ian's! I'm starving."

chapter 18

IAN STARES AT Emileigh where she rests on the chaise beside the pool. Moose and Bear are sitting on either side of her, affectionately begging for attention. Em has on a flowing top of soft lilacs and baby's breath; her white capris are form-fitting, making Ian dream of secret places. She raises her eyes and catches a glimpse of Ian ogling her from a distance. Emileigh suppresses the urge to confess her doubts about him during dinner with everyone.

The evening has turned out to be more of a tribute to Hannah, a celebration of her life. Her killer has been apprehended; recollections of her life flood our memories. There are stories of a troubled life, but many more uplifting, inspiring tales of a woman who may have lost the battle of life but is surely receiving her reward in heaven. Candles flicker on the dock for Hannah. Maggie strolls to the cottage holding hands with Ulysses. Ian and I are left by ourselves. We sit amidst the glowing candles. Water slaps Bessie's side, and a full moon shines, casting a tranquil light across the lake.

"Ian, about today—"

"Shhhh, Emmy, it's over. Let's not focus on drudging up the dirty details. Hannah is gone; it wouldn't be fitting to relive the injustices. We should just embrace the time we had with her. This is the first time I've seen you by myself today."

"You're right, but oh, Ian, I wish...I wish there was a way for me to hold this in, but it would haunt me." Emmy rings her hands together and looks away from Ian staring across the water. "So, here goes...When we first heard the news of Hannah's murder and you being taken in for questioning, the news was shocking—more than that; words cannot describe how I felt. I couldn't believe Hannah was murdered. I was stunned Hobbs took you to the police station. What you must have gone through!" Emmy strokes the side of Ian's face gently with empathy. "But, as time passed, I began to wonder."

"Wonder what exactly?"

"Please forgive me, but I wondered if somehow you could have been responsible. My mind went to places even I can't believe."

"You listened to the devil and actually questioned my innocence?"

"I know how awful it sounds. I love you. All these…these off-the-wall speculations kept nagging me, though my heart screamed to stop the negative thoughts."

"You lost trust in me so quickly?"

"Oh, I wouldn't go so far as to say that."

"I would. You do realize Peter Barbour's innocence or guilt regarding Hannah's death hasn't been established. I'm still a person of interest. Christ, Em, they still have my car impounded. Aren't you afraid, sitting next to me? I haven't been exonerated of the allegations."

"Oh, Ian, don't be silly. We all know Peter killed Hannah."

"And if we didn't, Em, what then? You'd still have doubts. I was sitting in a stark interrogation room, with Hebron and Hobbs spitting smelly brown crap all over me, doing their damnedest to get me to sign a confession. Time after time, they questioned my whereabouts for the afternoon, making my life a living hell. I was unable to focus on anything other than you. Your love gave me strength. I wanted desperately to hold you, make love to you, especially before I leave. And those bastards were taking up my precious moments to share with the one I love. I sat and watched each second tick off the wall clock, knowing each click meant less time to be with you, Em, just you. Now I hear you doubted me! You thought I could actually be capable of hurting her, killing her! Put yourself in my place. How would you feel hearing this?"

"Ian, don't do this, please. I told you because I want you to know everything. The doubt was for a second. I told Cook, and he just put it down to stress. Remember, you asked me to keep no secrets. You're leaving tomorrow; don't let it be like this. I beg you."

"You want me to know everything, except when I ask you to do something, you take offense."

"What? What are you talking about?" Em was now getting defensive. In her mind, she thought her confession was the right thing to do—no, she knew it was the right thing to do. If she waited to tell him upon his return, he'd be even more upset. It may have been bad timing, but he was leaving in a few hours for who knows how long. Ian may have had a horrible day, but so had everyone else. "I'm talking about asking you to simply go get a checkup from the doctor. You went off on a diatribe thinking I was trying to control you, thought my asking was a selfish way for me to cope with my dealings in Scotland, remember?"

"I told you I'd go."

"Yeah, but after coercion, you told me awhile back you'd go too and haven't yet. Em, you don't trust me enough. Trust is a large block in the foundation of a relationship."

"I know; that's why I wanted to tell you."

"I think your mum isn't the only one who has trust issues."

"Ian, enough!"

"If you can tell me you doubted me, let me go on here. You've had to be prodded to trust me ever since we met. Have I ever done anything to make you feel I was untrustworthy?"

"No, I'm afraid; it all happened so quickly."

"It happened just as fast for me. You lost your husband; he died. Is that where your trust died too?"

I put my face in my hands and begin to sob. "It isn't like that, Ian."

"So tell me what it is like."

"Oh, I don't know. I loved Josh, and deep inside, I never thought love would find me again."

"Deep inside, you felt guilty loving another man?"

"Maybe a little. I thought it had passed. I told you I hadn't been with anyone since he died. Josh would want me to love again."

"Maybe you don't feel like you deserve love."

"I...I don't know if that's true."

"I do, because I felt that way for a long time. I'm over it; with God's help, I'm over it."

"It took you twenty-five years to cope and get over it. What are you saying to me, Ian?"

He takes my hands from my face. His forearms are leaning on my thighs pulling me down to his level, holding my hands lightly. He waits until our eyes meet; mine are overflowing with tears. "I'm saying until you can tell me no matter what, you'll always trust me, we need some time apart."

"Ian, I do trust you."

"No, love, not enough for me to go where my heart wishes. While I'm home, maybe we can rebuild our relationship and you can tell me more about what you want out of it."

"Did you have this in mind all along?"

"See, there is another example of how your trust is lacking. And as I recall, you wondered about phone calls from home too."

"Keeping a list?"

"I guess you do too. Maybe love did happen too fast; we got caught up in the romance of wanting, needing to love."

I squirm in my seat. Sitting up, I look at Ian with disbelief at his declaration love may have happened too quickly. I reflect on his revelations. My hope of a life with Ian is rapidly falling to pieces. "I don't deny I want to love and to be loved, but I also can't deny my love for you, Ian. I understand a little more how you feel. Maybe I do need to trust more. I guess that stems from insecurity, and Josh's death really made me feel insecure about life. Happiness in life seems to have a use-by date."

"Death will do that, but knowing the root cause makes the healing easier." His words sting with truth.

"Do you still love me, Ian?"

"You shouldn't have to ask, but, yes. However, I do think you should spend tonight in one of the guest rooms."

"Oh, Ian, I don't want to, please, not when you go in the morning." I plead with Ian, revealing my desire to be close before he leaves not knowing if he will return. I tried to be open and honest with him. My words struck a chord. I see disappointment in his face.

"I need sleep, Em. It's been an exhausting day, and with our discussion, for my sake, it's best."

"What about my sake, Ian? You're leaving, separating from me. Are you reprimanding me for my honesty? Your disappointment, is it in me or in our love?"

"Good night, Em. I'll see you in the morning."

Emileigh tosses and turns all night. Ian dismissed her question. She feels disciplined and sent to bed by a man acting more like her father than her lover. Mentally aware or not, his actions, the sheer power of his words control her emotions. The entire time spent with Ian alone turned her confession of a brief lapse in faith regarding his innocence into a psychological exam of her love for him. Her faith tested, her heart breaking, she rolls over in a futile attempt to sleep. At four, she's had enough. Sitting up, slightly dizzy, she manages to find her way to the bathroom. Looking in the mirror, she sees her reflection reveals swollen red eyes from crying, about Ian and with grief for Hannah and Ely. Nauseated by guilty thoughts, she runs a hot, relaxing bath, hoping it may help wash away sorrow. Tahlulah, not resting any more comfortably than Emileigh, hears water running and realizes someone else is awake. Tah gets up, trudges downstairs, and makes coffee. The aroma of freshly brewed coffee permeates the house. Beulah Bell shakes off sleep. It takes her several tries to get her arms into the bright blue guest robe. It wraps around her slender body nearly two times, so she ties a hefty knot in the belt to keep her modesty intact. Emileigh makes her way down the stairs holding onto the railing steadying her steps. Beulah and Tah are talking about Ely and how they can help him. One look at her mama and grandmama forces Em to take a deep breath, put on a fake smile, and enter the room cheerfully.

"Good morning."

"Em, you're up early. I heard the water running in one of the guest bedrooms; you trying to let Ian sleep? That's mighty sweet."

Emileigh weighs her options of telling them now or later. "That among other reasons. I smell fresh coffee. Can I get either of you anything?"

"Not me, I'm on my second cup. Too dagum early to eat anything. What time does Ian leave for the airport?"

"I'm not sure; we avoided the subject of his departure."

"Really? That's strange."

"Given what happened yesterday, I don't see it as strange."

"Em, pardon me for askin', but bein' your gran, it's my privilege— what's bugging you? Remember, God gave us two ears and one mouth. We probably should listen more than we speak; you know that's difficult for us. So while we're a mind to listen and too sleepy to talk, we're all ears, dear."

"Oh, Grandmama, I'm not looking forward to this day. It's nothing more than Ian leaving and trying to deal with Hannah's death, then there's Ely."

"That's all?"

"For now it is, and that's a lot."

"Have some more coffee, baby girl. After Ian leaves, you should get some rest."

"Mama, we have to get to the store."

"No, we don't. The police have to take down the tape before we can enter, remember?"

"They didn't finish last night?"

Beulah turns on her Blue Ridge charm. "You expect those clowns to do a proper investigation? Hey, look out the window, see that?"

"See what? Them dawgs I let out?"

"No, Tah, flyin' pigs? Hobbs ain't gonna do any investigation, just ain't gonna happen. He should be drawn and quartered for what he put Ian through."

Tah perks up, the lightbulb over her head at full wattage. "Y'all, since Barbour was being sent to South Carolina and broke away from custody outside of Hobbs's jurisdiction, ain't this up to the state police?"

"Tah, they should be payin' us the big bucks 'cuz seems like we've cracked the case long before our famous bumbling purveyors of local justice. You've come up with a great question. I've got lieutenant what's-his-name's number. They may be already in charge, but I'll call and ask."

"Ian must be up. I hear water bein' drawn upstairs."

"I'm going to take the dogs for a walk while it's cool. If Ian comes down, tell him I'll be back shortly."

Tah and Beulah look at each other nodding. Both ladies with their vast and unremarkable male experience see a clear picture painted before their eyes—troubled times are brewin'. Ian comes downstairs smelling fresh and clean. He has a letter in hand for Ely and asks Tah to deliver it. At the base of the stairs are three suitcases and a briefcase. "Coffee smells good. Is Emmy up yet?"

"She sure is. Has the dogs out for a walk."

"I suppose she told you both about our discussion last night."

"No, she didn't say a word. She just mentioned today isn't a day she looks forward to, what with you leaving. What time do you leave?"

"Oh Tah, I should be on my way in a couple of hours. Has Mum shown her face in the house?"

"No, I can go get her up for you to say good-bye."

"I'll go out in a few minutes."

"Best be careful upon entering. I saw Ulysses walkin' hand in hand with Maggie last night. They both went into the cottage."

Ian grins from ear to ear, puts his coffee mug up to his lips, and before taking a sip, murmurs, "Well, good for Mum. Thanks for the warning; I'll knock before I enter."

"Y'all seen Ian?"

"He went yonder." Beulah points to the cottage and shines a quirky smile toward Emileigh.

"I'll let Moose and Bear back out then."

Ian's cell phone rings. "Should we get that for him?"

"Mama, I am not sure of anything we should do for him."

Tah looks at Em as only a mother can when distress is heard in a beloved child's voice. "Em, whatever is going on, answer the phone."

"Hello?" There is heavy Scottish brogue on the other end. Em can hardly discern the words spoken. "Can you repeat what you just said? I didn't understand." Finally, she grasps what the caller is asking. "He isn't here right now. Can I take a message?"

"Is this Emileigh?"

"Yes, who am I talking to?"

As difficult a time as Emileigh has in understanding the brogue, the person calling has equal trouble with Emileigh's Southern drawl. "Sarah Donavan, I work for the MacDougal estate. Is Ian going to be able to travel today?"

"Why do you ask, Sarah?"

Sarah pauses briefly. "Oh the gillie mentioned there was some sort of trouble yesterday and his plans may be interrupted."

Emileigh hadn't heard a call from Stuart yesterday, but while the police had his cell, there may have been a message. "He is scheduled to leave today. I expect he'll be on his way shortly."

She detects a hint of surprise in Sarah's voice. "Ahh, good then, I hope to meet you, Emmy."

"Good-bye, Sarah." Unsure about Sarah's relationship with Ian and her own with him as well, she doesn't feel as though she needs to be cordial. Ian and the dogs are walking over to where Bessie is docked. The powerful engine comes to life, and slowly, the boat moves away from shore. A mist covers the lake. As the sun begins to ascend, the scene is a ghostly and a beautiful sight to behold. Sadness fills Emileigh's heart, seeing Ian go off with his dogs, slowly vanishing in the mist until only the rumbling of the motor is heard off in the distance. The sight makes the pain of inevitable separation unbearable. Emileigh's head drops in despair as she clutches her chest. Her mother draws near, placing a compassionate arm around her daughter's trembling shoulders. Ian's cell phone rings again.

"If that's Sarah again, I don't want to speak to her."

It isn't; a man's cheery voice fills the phone with laughter and kind words.

"Ahh, you must be Ian's new love."

"I am. Who might you be?"

"I'm the MacDougal's gillie Stuart. Is he about?"

"Oh hello, Stuart. Glad to put a voice to the name. Sarah just called; I guess Ian told you about his horrible day yesterday."

"No, I haven't spoken to him since his trip arrangements were confirmed. What's happened?"

"But Sarah…" Emileigh's voice trails off, not knowing exactly what to say.

"Sarah what? I haven't seen or spoken to her in days. I didn't catch what you said about Ian; is he all right?"

"Oh yes, nothing is wrong. Can I give him a message?"

"Just tell him I phoned. Where is the boy?"

"He's out on his boat with the dogs."

"A fond farewell to Moravian Falls, I guess; you should be with him."

Emileigh doesn't care to give details of their unstable relationship. "Well, good-bye, Stuart. I hope to meet you in person someday. Ian thinks the world of you."

"Aye, likewise, my dear, he sounds happier than I've heard in a long, long while—all due to you, I suspect."

"Oh, I can't say I'm totally responsible for his happiness. Good day to you."

"And to you, fair lass."

Emileigh's mother and grandmother see Ian returning and make themselves scarce; using a lame excuse, they troop up the stairs. Shortly after they leave, water is once more heard trickling from the bathrooms above. "Good morning, Ian. How was your ride on the lake?"

"Happy mornin' to you, my sweet. 'Twas a wonderful ride. I should have asked you along, but sometimes solitude is a good way to begin the day."

"After your day yesterday, I certainly understand wanting some time on the lake alone. Can I get you anything for breakfast? Oh, by the way, Sarah called, so did Stuart. I took the calls. Hope you don't mind."

Ian looks puzzled by her timidity. "Em, dear Em, no worries. What did they have to say?"

"It was a bit weird. Sarah called wondering if your travel plans are still intact."

"What's odd about her asking?"

Emileigh sits down at the table looking much more at ease with Ian's tone; she sips coffee from her mug. "Hang on, I'm getting to the strange part. Sarah mentioned Stuart told her about your troubles yesterday. She was concerned you may not be able to travel."

"That's queer. I haven't spoken with Stewy."

"I know. When he called, I mentioned Sarah's call and the fact she'd gotten the information from him. Stuart said he hasn't spoken to you or Sarah since you made arrangements."

"Hmm, you mind making me some eggs and toast while I call him? I've got to leave soon."

"I don't mind. I'll make some for myself too."

Ian walks over to Emileigh, takes hold of her arms, and pulls her up from the chair. "Em, I do love you; always remember those words." He tenderly looks into her eyes. While continuing to gaze into her eyes, his fingers move from her face down her neck and between her breasts. Opening his hand over her heart, he whispers, "Keep me locked in here, my love. I spoke harshly to you last night. The day was extremely stressful for all of us. I still think a break is good for both of us...all of us really. I need time to recover, and so do you. Our love is great enough to last; I pray you feel the same."

Emileigh needed to hear his words, even though they confuse her. Last night, he devastated her, and now so early in the morning, she feels revived, seeing him and hearing his gentle words. Her heart isn't used to taking abrupt turns, and her emotions have never endured such a wild and tumultuous ebb and flow. Emileigh's head begins to swim; she finds herself caught between having her love within arm's reach while staring at his imminent absence and a growing hunger within. "I do feel the same. I just wish you weren't going so very soon."

"The sooner I go, the sooner I'll return to you. Now I must call Stewy. Give me a few minutes."

Emileigh doesn't dare convey her scattered thoughts or the bit of residual, lingering doubt—not necessarily doubt from his dealings yesterday, but mostly because of Sarah's role in his life and the ability he possesses to radically shift her own emotions on a whim. Ian has simply worn her out. The past few days' events and words have taken a toll on her; it's time to make the appointment to visit the doctor.

"Em, it's time. I must go. Steve drove up; he's taking me to the airport. I don't know how to say good-bye to you."

"I could have taken you."

"This is hard enough on both of us without you having to drive back by yourself."

"Before I forget, do you mind if I stay here? I'd like to spend time with your mom and play with Moose and Bear."

"That's a smashing idea. Tah should stay as well. The store and apartment will have to remain off limits for a while. The boys will love having you near. Take Bessie for a ride and swim with the lads. I like that image. I'll replay it on my journey, it's sure to bring a smile to my lips." They stand awkwardly apart, not knowing how to say farewell. Moving closer together, Steve begins to blow the horn. "I'd best go or the neighbors will have my skin—too much noise for this sleepy place. Em, I love you. Not a day will go by when you don't hear from me, I promise."

Emileigh takes a deep breath, and her body shudders as she attempts to hold back tears. "The only promise I want to hear is this isn't good-bye; it's just a blip on the radar."

"Aye, just a blip." Ian takes her tightly in his arms, kisses her softly, and then probes more deeply, inquisitively, hoping she responds likewise. They are lost in the passion of the most intimate and emotional kiss Emileigh has ever had. As the embrace is broken, Ian reaches for his luggage. Emileigh opens the door, waves at Steve, and walks Ian out. "Turn around, Em. Please go back inside. I'm not good at farewells."

"I can't, Ian. I want to spend every last second looking at you. We don't know when we'll see each other again." She stares at him as he loads the luggage into the backseat. Ian pats Moose and Bear on their heads and says good-bye to his lads. Promising them he'll be home soon, he opens the passenger door, puts on his seat belt, and blows a kiss to her. Emileigh catches it and blows it back. Ian is gone.

chapter 19

THE LONG AND arduous train trip finally reaches its destination. Bedraggled and bewildered, Ian picks up the keys to his rental car and begins the journey to the estate. The sights, smells, and sounds of his homeland are a welcome relief. He'd forgotten how much he loves the awe-inspiring landscape the island provides. Around every corner, a new enchanting, picturesque view awaits. Reaching the estate, Ian sees the old, familiar handcrafted Celtic symbol with the lock to the manor cast in the middle of the knot. The lock, stationed generations ago, was placed there to keep man and beast from entering the enormous weathered wooden doors. Ian feels not only the lock move as he twists the key but something within his heart. He is home. Once inside and standing amidst the grand foyer, which has entertained its share of dignitaries and royalty, he drops his baggage and gazes upon a home holding so many memories. Sweet and traumatic memories come pounding back with lightening force, and his head begins to throb. The intimidating oil paintings of relatives adorn the wooden walls; they peer from the triple-width staircase carpeted with moth-eaten Persian rugs and glance at Ian from all angles. Ghosts of the past, they guide the future of the estate with fearsome expressions captured by the artist. Surely looking at the foreboding images pressed Ian further into his depths of depression after Molly and his son died. The judgmental faces took him to lowly places, their voices echoing in his head and making him feel like his life would never measure up to their success. Looking past the eyes of his haunting family on the walls, past the open rooms filled with tattered tapestries and neglected antiquities, he focuses on the rear entrance: bright light is streaming through the solarium windows. Ian looks out upon his favorite view of the entire estate. Massive steps from the loch flow seamlessly up through meticulously tended gardens to the manor. The gardens were his wife's favorite hobby. Ian made certain extra funds were always provided to maintain Molly's gardens. Captivating palettes of mixed hues create the perfect contrast to the dark gray loch beyond. He is delighted the gardens have been so well tended. Across the loch are grassy, high hills spotted with Highland cows grazing beneath the constantly formidable and changing skies of the isle. Dropping from the bright blue sky is a mist. Enraptured by it, Ian stands paralyzed, watching the opaque mist transform into a figure. Mesmerized, unable to utter a sound, Ian watches the figure adopt a form most familiar to him. His heart races; he tries several times to speak but can utter nothing. Mustering all of his strength, Ian calls to the mist with a passionate cry, "Molly." The time between her death and today is erased in the blink of an eye. The mist moves with a tantalizing glide, effortlessly, seductively, floating up each step staring and shooting stars of light and hope into Ian's startled brown eyes. Nearing him, luminescent fingers reach out to caress his stunned, love-starved face. Ian feels the blood drain from his head. Dizzy, he drops to the ground and watches the mist evaporate as quickly as it formed. Shaking his head violently, looking to see if the mist had vanished or moved, he is struck with remorse and fear. Thoughts of going mad enter his mind. After a moment of self-doubt, Ian begins to pass it off logically as jet lag, hunger, or the stress of coming home to deal with Fiona's newest obsession. After regaining enough strength to walk down to the loch, he stares across the tumbling waves, his heart still pounding and mind reeling with what had just happened; Ian's thoughts for the first time since arriving home turn to Emmy. Longing for her, aching for her touch, he reaches down to pick up a flat stone and skips it into the waves, tossing along with the stone a whim and a prayer, wishing she was near.

Long, slow strides take Ian up from the loch into Molly's garden. He can visualize her fondly touching each plant like a child, hoping it would bear flowers upon tender limbs. Meekly reentering the mansion, Ian notices a lack of cobwebs clinging to the ceiling and walls. Running his forefinger along the antiques scattered throughout, he discovers not one speck of dust covers any piece. Before leaving for the States, he had had the furniture covered. Not only has it been uncovered but rearranged as well. The pungent aroma of venison stew wafts into the sitting room, a far cry from the kitchen.

Skipping down the stairs humming a happy tune is Sarah. As soon as she sees Ian, the humming ceases and the joyful skipping halts. Perplexed by her presence inside the house, Ian's questioning expression elicits a response without him saying a single word. With a startled lilt in her voice, Sarah tries desperately not to show her surprise.

"Hi, Ian, glad you're home. I've been doing a bit of cleaning and got a stew simmering for you. I haven't stoked the fire yet."

Ian is struck by her ease and apparent familiarity within the house. Her generosity is welcome, but he didn't request her to do additional duties for his homecoming. "Sarah, I appreciate your help, but really, I didn't ask for or expect it."

"Oh, just wanted to give you a nice welcome."

"May I ask how you got in?"

"Oh, I've been coming in for a while to check on things."

"Sarah, how did you get a key?"

"You gave me one."

"No, I didn't. And the house doesn't smell musty and dank like a house on the shore would after being closed for months."

"Your mother was here for a few days; perhaps she cleaned the house. I seem to remember you giving me a key. Maybe it slipped your mind, sir. I told you I've been coming in once in a while to check on things."

"You keep saying that, Sarah, but I didn't ask and am not paying you to do the work. A place this size doesn't get clean with a mere stop in from time to time. My mum has never cleaned, so I doubt she would take it up this late in life. The only people who have a key besides me are Stuart, my mum, and Fiona. I'll thank you to give the one you have back to me, as I'm home now and won't require your services inside."

"Yes, sir, I'll just pop upstairs for a moment, finish, and then be on my way." She turns away, but not before humiliation shows upon her youthful face.

"Be honest, Sarah, you've been living here, haven't you?"

Sheepishly, Sarah turns from the mahogany stairwell and answers Ian; she hadn't expected him so early, and now she's been found out. Looking down at the floor, she answers back. Her lips tremble, and she stutters ill-chosen words, which reluctantly slip out, "Well, sir, I...ah...yes, we have."

"Sarah, all you had to do was ask me. Has something happened? Did you lose your apartment?"

"No, sir, nothing like that."

"You mind explaining to me why then?"

"Oh, sir, I do...I can't. I'll be on my way. Please, sir, let me gather our things, and I'll be gone. Do you still want me to do my regular job?"

"Yes, I do. You've done a fine job as far as that's concerned. But, Sarah—"

She interrupts him midsentence. "I have? I'm ever so grateful you think so. I know how much it means to you."

"Yes, yes, but before you begin another day's work, you must tell me who gave you a key and why you felt like it was all right to live here without asking me first. Who is the other half of 'we' that's been staying under my roof? When and if you decide to come back, after you answer those questions, we have a few other things to discuss, okay?"

"Yes, sir."

"Your stew smells delicious. You mind having some with me?"

"Really, I'd like to. I'm starving."

"Me too. It was a long trip. I bet there is a good red wine in the basement."

"Want me to go get it?"

"Sarah, you've done enough; it sounds as if you know the house too well."

Ian gathers his bags and begins walking the memory-laden halls to his room. The bedroom has a huge picture window overlooking the gardens and loch. A French door opens to a private stone-paved patio, which partially overhangs the solarium below. Inviting pale yellow hues, the color of faint sunshine, as Molly used to call it, adorn the walls. In the bath, her bath salts and perfumes still remain in their rightful place after all these years. Ian stands for a moment with the doors strewn open looking out at the whitecaps on the lake. He takes note of the difference between the one before him and Moravian Falls. The landscape scenery from Skye is strikingly more beautiful, but despite the magnificent view, one thing it lacks is companionship. Ian realizes he misses company more than ever. Twenty-five-year-old bath salts can't bring companionship to him, and looking at them only stirs heartache from another time in life. In a brave gesture, Ian gathers the salts and perfumes and places them gently in the bottom drawer of Molly's vanity. He shakes off his loneliness and heads down to the wine cellar to select just the right bottle of red wine to share with Sarah over dinner. Walking back from the ancient wine cellar into the dark, cavernous basement, he notices water from stones dripping with dampness collecting in small puddles on the floor. Ian makes his way up to the main floor clutching two dusty bottles of cabernet sauvignon. At the top of the stairs, his forefathers' portraits from days long gone stare at him, disturbing the tranquility home should offer. Ian lifts his head and peers at each of the men. Triumphantly raising his voice, he says, "It's mine, damn you all; it's mine. Time for all you ghosts to stop playing tricks with my mind. The devil is in your stares; your lips whisper lies of inadequacy in my ear. With God's grace, I vow to care for those living within these walls and on the estate not as a heartless laird but using more compassion and generosity than any of you." Ian sees a white mist forming midair at the top of the second floor. Floating slowly, deliberately down the staircase, it glides past the forbidding portraits, moving so closely he reaches to touch it. Suddenly, warmth passes through his body, bringing to life each and every cell with an intimacy he'd never felt before, stirring passion, freeing his soul. Ian is left feeling elated, and thoughts of Molly linger. He feels her love intertwined with and touching his heart, filling his very essence. A strong sense of loss races back, and the flooding remorseful memories leave him drained. Stoking the fire in the dining room, a curious Sarah peeks around the corner observing Ian talking to the walls standing arms outstretched eyes closed and weeping. Thinking Ian has gone a bit daft, she meanders unobtrusively to the kitchen with a dastardly grin.

"Mama, you ready to go up to Grayson and Emily's?" An unseasonably cool and wet morning reflects the mood within the Sutherland home. Rain pours down the gutters rushing onto the burnt grass summer has ravaged. "Maggie, are you coming along with us?"

"No, I'd be in the way. It would be different if I knew Hannah or Ely. I'll stay here with the pups, enjoy a rainy day by reading and sipping my Earl Grey."

Emileigh wishes her day could be spent with tea and a good book as well. Hannah's body not yet having been released from the coroner's office is hampering efforts to make funeral arrangements. Ely previously discussed with Tah and the others how to conduct a proper service for his mother. He's had to grow up through tragedy brought on mostly by his stepfather. He arrives at a difficult conclusion; cremation, although not accepted by all, is the least expensive way to honor a departed one. Most everyone gathering to assist Ely and give him strength agrees, regretting decisions at the most delicate time in life having to consider money. The memorial and religious portion of the service have been delegated into the loving hands of the Suggettes.

"Ma Bell, I's ever so glad to see you." Ely rushes into Tahlulah's arms and nuzzles the nape of her neck. Tah, though she tries to remain calm and collected, can't help but empathize with Ely's misery. She wipes away his tears and her own. Neither of them is able to move, the poignant moment is painfully observed by those gathered. Not long ago, Ely was pointing a pistol at Tah, trying to escape town; now the man he was attempting to escape from has taken his mother forever. Grayson asks if anyone would like a drink.

Tah appreciates the opportunity to step away from the heightened emotion. "Ely, I'm ever so sorry about your Mama. She will be missed by us all."

"Ma Bell, I cain't believe she be gone. They won'ts let me go yonder back home. What does you think I should do?"

"I think your home is with any one of us. Ain't any need in goin' anywhere or to make plans too far ahead. None of us knows where the road leads. And none of us is going to let you go without a home or without plenty of love and food." Tah's words seem to bring comfort to Ely. She knows the future is difficult to envision—futile really; none of us really knows what the future holds.

"Ely, you look real tired."

"I is, Miss Leigh, jess' kinda hit me all sudden like."

"Come on, son, time you take a nap. We'll wake you in time for dinner."

With Ely napping, it gives the Suggettes time to commensurate on the funeral arrangements and steps to help the poor soul. Before they can even sit down, Grayson pulls out a bottle of wine and pours each of them a large glass filled to the rim. He looks at his wife and winks. "Y'all, I know the gracious ladies sitting round this table would be able to come up with a fine plan to help Ely." The Suggettes look at each other with an affirmative nod.

"But, this time, Emily and I have had a few moments alone with Ely and our family. We would like Ely to live with us. Not just for a few weeks, but as long as he wishes, at least until he finishes school. I know he likes construction, and I'd be proud to take him under my wing and give direction. We'd even adopt the boy if he'd like."

The women don't need any time to consult; all of them agree: Ely would have a wonderful home here.

"Grayson, I'm so glad you feel that way. What about Ely? Did y'all ask him yet?"

"Not yet. That's where we need y'all to help us out a mite. Not sure if we should put his doubts about his future whereabouts to rest before or after Hannah's funeral—if he even wants to stay with us."

"I hate to mention this, but Salina is expecting, and with them movin' in, well, ain't that gonna stress the seams of your house?"

Emily and Grayson begin speaking at the same time; Emily defers to her husband. "We'll make do; a full home is the happiest in my book. Besides, remember, I own a construction company. We'll be fine. My concern is what to do if he doesn't want to be here. He loves Tah so much, maybe—"

Leigh interrupts Grayson before Tah hears the rest of his sentence. "I'm doing my final edition next week; afterward, I won't be working. As y'all know, Steve and I want children, but it isn't to be—leastwise not in the traditional sense. We'd welcome Ely. He probably does love Tah the most, but honestly, her apartment is small. Fine enough while Emmy was growing up, but it's hardly the place for a young man."

Saddened by the truth of her living situation, Tah knows what Leigh says is right and shares her own thoughts. "Looks as though Ely is blessed having two homes open their arms to him. As Leigh says, my place is fine for me, but hardly fit for bringin' up a boy. I'd take him in a minute, but it's good for him to know others love him as well."

"As far as when to tell him then?"

After taking a sip of beer, Cook enters into the conversation. "Probably best to go ahead and ask him if he'd like to keep staying right where he is; it'll give him a bit of stability before Hannah's service."

"Ely, son, its dinnertime. Get up, sleepyhead. You need something good to eat."

"Ma Bell, you still here?"

"Course, silly. Before I forget, Ian wrote you this letter before he left."

"Did you read it?"

"No, it's for your eyes, not mine."

Tah sits on the edge of the bed, holding the letter in her hand, looking down at Ely's slim body hardly traceable underneath the covers. "Ma Bell, would you read it to me, right now? Is it true some folks thought he killed my mama?"

"Oh, I don't know if they actually thought that way, but they did need to ask him questions. You know he is home in Scotland, right?"

"He done gone already, but I's didn't get no chance to see him off." Ely sighs as he sinks farther down under the covers.

"He'll be back. You sure you want me to read this letter out loud to you?"

"Yes'm, please." Ely lays his head on the pillow and looks up at Ma Bell. She is the closest thing to a saint he has known in his sixteen years. Tah opens the letter, puts on her readers, and takes Ely's hand.

"My Dearest Friend Ely..."

"Stewy, you old fart. Fine welcome home you gave!" Ian strides up to Stuart as he's saddling a mare for a ride. "Checking on those poachers, eh?"

"Boss, when did your sorry arse show up?"

"I slid in unnoticed yesterday...until Sarah came down the main stairs and saw me."

"What? She was in the house?"

"Aye, mind puttin' off your ride for a while? Let's go into town for a lunch and a couple of pints."

"I'm with ya, mate. Let me just put the old girl in her stall. See how happy you've made her?"

"You ride her too hard. Should use a four-wheeler and visit the twenty-first century once in a while."

Waiting on Stuart to settle his mare, Ian strolls over toward the administrative offices situated in a small white cottage well behind the stables. Walking down the stable hall, he sees Sarah give up trying to enter the business manager's office.

"Hey ya, Stewy? Has payday been changed?"

"Are you looking for money already, Laird MacDougal?"

"Don't try to be funny. Told you years ago, it doesn't work for you. I saw Sarah trying to get into John's office."

"Payday is end of week as always. I told John you were cutting down on expenses, and he's only needed on Friday. I took his key to the office and changed the lock as you asked."

"She's getting around then, isn't she?"

"Who? Sarah? Oh, Ian, she's just a wee bit of a thing. You don't expect her to be up to no good, do you?"

Ian turns around to face his friend after watching Sarah drive down the gravel path to the main road. "You give her a key to the house?"

"Me? Are you accusing me of something, Ian?"

"No, no, she's been living in the house and had a key. Looks like she had an old key to the office as well."

"Got mine right here, boss."

"Hmm, while we're in town, let's buy some new locks."

"Change all of them? You must be joking!"

"Just the ones the main key opens."

"You do suspect her then?"

"I do, and I don't. I just arrived home, but I can sense something, and it smells of Fiona."

"No, boss, I just haven't mucked out the stalls yet."

"Hey, Stewy, you've been working on it; that was this close to being funny."

Ian holds his arms wide apart with a silly grin between.

Ely and Tah go over to his home for the first time since Hannah's funeral. Time has come to sort through his belongings and take some to the Duprees'. "Ma Bell, what is we 'posed to do with Mama's things? Shouldn't we be packin' thems up or somethin'? I mean, it ain't like she's comin' back, and we talked about sellin' the trailer."

"Sure, son, if you want to take some of her special things with you, Em and I can pack the rest for you to sort through after a spell."

Ely respectfully walks through the trailer. When he comes to his mama's room, he pauses and looks back at Tah. "Ma Bell, I jess' cain't bring myself to go in there. Dem police done messed everything up; it don't look the same as when she was here, but it do still smell sweet like her, and I jess' cain't do it."

Somehow, with the loss of a loved one, that person's smell brings back vivid and realistic memories; perhaps, in a way, it brings the departed one back to life. Tah understands and comforts Ely. They both leave the trailer. Ely stands next to the Land Rover with his arms full of clothes. He looks back toward the only home he's ever known. I hope he can feel her presence, as Hannah would really want him to go on and be with folks who love him. Ely has good memories of his mama and painful ones of Peter Barbour not only of him hurting him but hearing his mama being beaten. Leaving may help keep those dreadful moments from being ever present in his mind.

"Louise, you and Cook up for a barbeque tonight over at Ian's? If so, let's get there earlier than usual. Mama decided to close the store early." Since it had to be shut down while the investigation was underway, stock couldn't be delivered, and there was no sense being open full-time. It should be back to normal tomorrow. Louise is poised in a sunbonnet trimmed with floral appliqués that match those in her long skirt, which shows off her delicate form. "It's such a beautiful day. Ely will probably like going over there with us. Four sounds like a reasonable time."

Louise holds her hat as a breeze kicks up. "You heard from skirt boy recently?"

Leigh and Tah arrive at the store just as Louise asks Emmy about Ian. "Hey, Mama, we were just talkin' about havin' dinner over at Ian's. How about it?"

Tah looks at Louise; she heard the question about Ian and decides it's time to pursue. "Sure. We can bring something over. Have ya called Maggie and Ulysses?"

"Not yet. I wanted to see what y'all thought first. Maggie leaves in a couple of days. She tried to get Ulysses to go with her, but he's steadfast in his desire to stay put."

"Poor ole Ulysses, he'll never leave Peg's memory. It just ain't in him, even though those two seem to have somethin' going on."

"Baby girl, when is the last time you heard from Ian?"

Emileigh is uncomfortable with everyone's attention focused on her, especially since she has only vague information to relay. "I hear from him every day, sometimes in an e-mail, but mostly he calls."

"How is he doin', Em?"

"He thinks he is starting to figure out how and why Fiona is trying to claim the estate for Liam, but he hasn't gone into detail."

"That's all very nice, but what about y'all?"

"Oh well. You know how phone calls are." You don't have to be a psychic to realize Emileigh is trying to avert the question, but it helps.

"Let me get this straight: you know a bit about the estate, but there aren't words saying how much he misses you or loves you?"

Emileigh knows trying to bypass questions from the likes of these women isn't going to work.

"Okay, since you have to know: for the first few days, he was really lovey-dovey. Now our calls keep getting shorter; he seems to be distancing himself, avoiding talking about us."

"You said those same words when he was here. Are you reading too much into the situation? He is trying to keep the estate from falling into Fiona's money-grubbing hands. Maybe he is simply preoccupied."

"You asked; I told you. Let's leave it at that."

"Ya know, maybe Maggie can tell us more."

"Leigh, I don't want Maggie being drilled about us; our relationship is ours. No sense in asking her; she'd probably get worried. I have to go. Mama, you okay alone in the here?"

"Yes, girl, Ely will be here for his first day back to work. He needs to keep busy. We may not be open, but there is always cleaning to be done."

"Oh, I'm so glad to hear he'll be working. Tell him I said, 'Hey.' I'll see y'all later."

"Girls, what ya reckon is really going on between those two?"

"Now, y'all know what Em said is true; it *is* their relationship."

"Uh-huh, since when has that ever stopped us from speculating?"

"Not to change the subject, but you think everyone can have dinner together tonight?"

"It's short notice; we'll just get those who can and miss the others."

Leigh stands next to the cooler and suddenly remembers Tah saying the next time there is a celebration ribs are on the menu. "Tah, you got ribs to cook tonight?"

Tah's countenance changes; she laughs loudly and clearly. "Yep, I do, best damn ribs in town."

"Out with it! You look like a scarecrow that's swallowed a pumpkin."

"Y'all remember the night Peter Barbour came here?"

"Hello? Of course we do."

"When I scooted into the cooler, the only object I could find to jam the door handle was a rack of ribs. They saved my skin."

Laughing until tears ran down their faces, they hugged Tah, remembering that horrible day. It's good to have something funny to hold onto. "Back to skirt boy, you think he is all right?"

"Course he is. If I can get his number, I'll see for myself."

"Louise, you could get it from Maggie. Just say you'd like to speak to him."

Louise puts her finger aside her nose, hearing a plan in the making and liking it. "The only problem is Em; she'd be furious if she ever found out."

"Then she mustn't." Tah pushes her sleeves up a bit, assuming a fighting stance, which is laughable because of her gentle soul. "I didn't hear a thing; I'm totally oblivious to this covert operation."

"Yes, Mrs. CIA, you sure it's a covert and not an overt operation?"

"Whatever. It may even be a pervert operation; I ain't a part of it."

"Tah, you sound like a desiccated frittering."

"What the hell is that, some Scottish crap?"

"Tah, I wouldn't let Em hear you say those words."

Interrupting, Emily unloads, "What the fuck is a desiccated frittering, Louise?"

"'Scuse, Tah. I know you don't like anyone to say the f word."

"No, I guess it's the old school in me coming out. Mama always said those who have to curse to get attention lack intelligence and should use the Funk and Wagnalls more often."

"Let me get this straight: you think I lack intelligence?"

"Now, now, don't get your panties in a wad, Emily. I said Mama said it; all it did for me was make me feel like a fool to use it, so I don't. Besides, have you ever really understood how it is used?"

Emileigh returns unexpectedly with Grandmama. "Mama, Emily, what are y'all discussing?"

"Oh, Emily just let loose the f bomb."

Grandmama turns her disappointed expression straight toward Emily. "Mama, those who live in glass houses shouldn't throw stones or ghastly looks."

"Girl, I ain't never used that word, so don't lecture me on what to do."

"Um, Grandmama, I recall you tossing the f bomb and hitting Fiona with it."

"Facing a child of the evil one must have lured me into a freak moment of weakness."

"I understand you think usage of expletives exhibits a lack of intelligence?"

"I could easily give y'all a lesson or two in the importance of choosing…"

"You two go off on your diatribe some other time; we were discussing skirt boy when you went off into never-never land."

"Oh, Louise, why don't you stop sitting on your crystal ball, or fluff up eagle feathers, whatever the hell you do to conjure up someone juicy so it isn't never-never land for me. I think it's the least you could do for an old friend."

"Old is right, Tah, conjuring up someone isn't the problem."

"So what's the problem?"

"You don't trust the opposite sex. This brings us full circle back to Emily and Ian. Before we go any farther, where is the bottle of wine? I seem to have found the bottom of the glass, and that ain't right in our world, even though it's early."

"Ladies, and right now I must use the term loosely, my love life isn't the problem."

"Oh, something happen in the last five minutes to change the fact skirt boy has been ignoring you?"

Emileigh decides it's time to let the Suggettes pursue their own conversation. Once wine is flowing, they get stuck on one subject, imagining all sorts of scenarios. Her love life has become the focal point and most likely will be after she leaves, but at least she won't hear it. "Grandmama, let's go over and see Maggie."

"Is she still shackin' up with Ulysses?"

"What is it with everyone today? Let it be."

Deciding he can't solve the problems of the estate late at night, Ian carefully locks the exterior doors and windows to close up. Throwing open the patio doors off the master suite, he takes a large scotch out to savor while watching the moonlight dance upon the water. His thoughts are haunted by the strange mist appearing to him, leaving him wondering if it's some sort of delusion or angels guiding his movements on the estate. Pondering whether suspicions of Sarah and John are paranoia, he takes a large sip of scotch. Tugging at his heart are two women, one whom he loved and lost, casting his life into years of misery. Then there is Em, who is refreshing, warm, and eager for his love. She's thousands of miles from his touch. Fear envelops his mind; did he quash the one good thing that's happened to him by thoughtless words? Why did he insist on being alone the night before his departure? The questions circle within his mind like rings of cigar smoke. As he is standing out on the patio, a familiar squeak from within the bedroom draws him back inside. Ian's jaw drops; he squints several times, and still it appears the same to him. There upon the green-and-yellow duvet, a bodily impression lays curled up on Molly's side of the bed. Ian takes another very large gulp of single malt scotch straight from the Talisker bottle; he sits on the edge of the bed touching the depression. It feels warm, the same warmth that passed through him earlier. In his limited knowledge of spirits, he has heard they are cold, drawing energy wherever they can. Scared and comforted at the same time, he is no longer secure being alone. Fearful his experiences are hallucinations, he reaches for the phone, dialing a seldom-used number.

Maggie and Ulysses join the party late. They try slipping out unnoticed from the cottage—an impossible task when the Suggettes are involved. Emily jabs her elbow into Tah's side. She lets out a painful whimper. "Emily, why are you jabbing me so hard?"

"Looky over there, Tah! See what I'm seein'? Ouuuweee, since Maggie announced her date of departure, seems like those two have spiced up their romance!"

Leigh drifts toward them with a refueling bottle of wine. She overhears Tah and Emily ruminating about Maggie and Ulysses's love life. "Y'all do know at their age, romance means one of two things: they've got a notion to snuggle—and as you know, it has to be addressed as soon as the mood strikes to come to fruition—or one of them's bout to kick the bucket."

"Oh, that is so wrong, you ole harlot."

"Who you callin' a harlot, Louise? Best I recollect from our younger years—"

"Ladies, no need to go back so far. Look what is happenin' before us."

Louise hears "Born to Be Wild" softly playing in the background. Walking rapidly toward her red-and-white-striped canvas tote, she reaches in and sees the name on the phone. Looking around to spot where Emileigh might be and unsure why he'd be calling her instead of Em, she answers, concern evident in her voice. Hand to the phone, covering her lips, she says, "Ian, that you?"

"Hi, Louise, am I interrupting anything?"

"Funny you callin' now, we are all over at your place havin' a party."

"I see, when the cat is away...Sounds like you've been into the libations, as you call them."

"You know us, Ian. I've had a few. Actually, must be late over there."

"Oh, it's about midnight. I talked to Ely and Em earlier. Wonderful news for Ely! He sounds excited."

"You called me to talk about Ely?"

"No, just breaking the ice. I'm really calling because some strange things are happening in and around the house."

"Oh, so you have strange stuff and you call me? Why, Ian MacDougal, if I were the more sensitive sort, I'd take offense." There is a pregnant pause on the other end. "Just kidding, skirt boy."

Louise sees Emileigh approaching. She turns to the side and strides over to the pool. "So tell me, what's going on?"

"I'm not certain; it may be paranoia on my part. I feel like I'm losing my mind and slipping back into depression."

"I'm not a therapist."

"You are with this. When I first arrived, I saw a mist approach me from the lake. It moved purposely toward me and then vanished."

"Ian, did it feel familiar, or did a name pop into your head when you first saw it?"

"I could only think of Molly."

"Wasn't she your wife?"

"Yes, and then minutes ago, I heard a noise in my bedroom. I was standing near to my room out on a patio. It was a squeak of old bedsprings. The impression was warm to the touch. It lay on top of the bed, looked like an outline of a body, Louise, a body that wasn't there. When I saw the bed, I freaked and knew I had to talk to you. I'm losing it, aren't I?"

"Pretty powerful spirit you have there. Not many are able to appear, much less make an impression. Pardon the pun. Ian, you ain't paranoid; you just had your first paranormal experience."

"I saw the mist one other time. Looking at the portraits of family in the foyer, I rather lost my composure and let them know I'm going to run the estate my way. Once I finished yelling at dead men, the mist appeared to come down the stairs and then, the damnedest thing, it felt like the mist went through me warming me all over and then vanished."

"Damn, boy, I don't recommend yelling at dead men; a few may talk back and you won't like what they have to say."

"Louise, I would really rather hear what to do, or what it is. With everything else going on, you know trying to figure out Fiona's dealings, I wasn't expecting this ghost stuff, if that's what it is."

Sounding desperate to understand, he is relieved to hear Louise's easy tone. "Well, instead of feeling doomed or haunted, which in that huge old house of yours could easily lead to depression, it sounds like Molly is glad to see you return home and she is with you, standing by your effort to keep the estate."

"Can I talk to her, if it's Molly?"

"Sure, I'd ask pointblank, tell her to give you a sign that only you will understand. Something you shared with her. Make it easy, the easiest would be something electrical. Ian you have to look for the sign. Don't pass things out of the ordinary as stress or balderdash. I wish I could be there with you, to help."

"Louise, I wish you were here too, you and Emmy. How is she?"

"She is about thirty feet from me. You want to speak to her?"

"Not right now, Louise. I spoke briefly with her earlier. I don't want her to hear me like this and so far away."

"She's gonna know, Ian. I may as well tell her. Is that okay with you?"

Ian has to think for several moments before answering her. "We said no secrets. Let her know I'm okay, and please, Louise, tell her I love her."

"Sure 'nuff, skirt boy; that's what I like hearing. Call me with an up-date. Nothing to fear, Ian. Molly will keep you safe."

"If it is Molly. Thanks, Louise, I'll call soon, bye."

The bed no longer has the outline of a body on it. He closes the doors and slides onto the bed—remaining fully clothed.

"Emmy, how you doing, dear?"

"Hey, Louise, such a beautiful night, and with everyone here, except Ian of course, it feels good. Ely even looks as though he is able to enjoy din-ner."

Louise touches Emileigh's sleeve and moves to face her. "Em, about Ian, I just had a call from him." Perplexed at hearing Ian called Louise instead of her, Emileigh shoves her hands into the pockets of her khaki shorts. She looks down at the crystal-clear blue pool water not wanting to see Louise in case bad news is to follow. "He...he called you? I spoke with him earlier; it was all about Ely. He sounded happy for him, but different. Oh, Louise, tell me he's all right?"

"He's fine, sweetie. He has a little paranormal activity happening at that castle of his though. We are trying to sort it out."

"What kind of activity?" Shivering in expectation of what Louise may say, she impatiently punches Louise in the shoulder. "Louise, what's going on?"

"Easy there, Rambo! No need to get violent."

"Sorry."

"He's seen a mist a couple of times; sounds like it may be Molly."

Emileigh's eyebrows arch, and then her brow furrows. "Molly? Oh my gosh, Molly? Are you sure?"

"How can I be sure, talking to skirt boy thousands of miles away when he sounds frantic to make sense out of his experiences?"

"Why didn't he call me?"

"I asked him if he wanted to talk to you. Ian was upset; he didn't want to frighten you. He did ask me to tell you he loves you. Em, he needed help—*my* kinda help. You'll hear soon enough from him."

"Yeah, sure I will." Doubt takes a strong hold once again.

Moose and Bear beg for attention, pulling Tah over to Louise while tugging a nasty, ratty rope. Huffing and puffing, Tah drops the rope, and the dogs take off still tugging it. She straightens her T-shirt reading "What happens during the wine tasting tour, stays on tour" and tugs on her shorts, which are giving her a wedgey. "Weasy, what's up with Em?"

"Ian called me. She's jealous, I guess."

"Of you? That's a hoot!"

"She isn't jealous of me, although that shouldn't be laughable; she's jealous because I got the call. Emileigh has been a real pill these past few days."

"My daughter, remember?"

"Just statin' the facts, Tah."

"Well given that her love has gone overseas, a friend has been murdered, Ely's become an orphan, Peter tried to get me...let's see what else? Do I really need anything else? I think she's earned the right to be a pill for a few days!"

"Point taken, I'll lay off."

"How come you got a call from him anyhow?"

"He's got a few visitors from my neck of the woods."

"Are you serious? Have they hurt him?"

"Tah, haven't I taught you anything about spirits?"

"Only that you irk me expecting me to see them same as you. Will you ever learn?"

"It's fun to see your reaction; anyhow, in answer to your question, he ain't hurt, just bewildered."

"He's seen them?"

"It's more like he has seen their presence, not seen them exactly."

"What exactly?"

"A mist, his bed making noise, and then what appeared to be a depression formed like a body."

"Is he on his way back here?"

"Tah, not yet. He still has Fiona to deal with."

"I'd be on the next plane out of there for dang sure."

"Boss, I saw your light on as I was driving home; you still awake?"

"If I weren't, I would be now. What's up Stewy?"

"Just saw Sarah's car parked outside the office; there are two people in the car."

"Meet me there. I'll be down in a couple of minutes. I'll go through the stable. Stewy, load a rifle and wait for me."

Stuart takes Ian's direction. He loads a rifle, quietly pulls his car up to the stable with the lights turned off, and waits. The house phone rings just as Ian is heading down the stairs. "Ian, I just spied through the binoculars a window has been broken, someone is standing on the car climbing through."

"Right, I know someone in Moravian Falls who should meet you."

"Huh?"

"Wait, I'm on my way."

"I've called the police; they're coming, but it's a long way. If we wait, chances are these hoodlums will be gone. Stewy, you don't have to do this. Heather will kill me if anything happens to you."

"Any gillie worth his salt wouldn't let the laird walk into an unknown situation alone."

"Good, mate. Give us the gun now."

"Beggin' your pardon, Ian, but you don't exactly yield a weapon every day. I do."

"Right, you get whoever is in the car, and I'll open the door to see who's inside."

Stuart approaches the car; he only sees one person inside on the driver's side. The engine has been turned off, and the driver isn't alert. Waiting and watching, Ian puts the key into the lock. Stuart stands by before coming too close to the vehicle. The all-too-familiar mist forms between Ian and the door to the office. Ian's adrenaline is pumping. "Oh for the love of God! Not now, go away. I'll be all right."

He fans the mist away and unlocks the door. Just as the door squeaks open, without him touching the switch, all the lights go on. Outside, Stuart points the rifle at the driver's window with his hand on the trigger. Lifting his hands as if to surrender, the driver quickly sounds the horn. Stuart hurls the rifle stock at the window, and with a single powerful blow, the window shatters, sending glass flying down upon the driver's lap. Inside, Ian sees a slim figure with blazing red hair by the computer frantically trying to shut it down. "Didn't expect to see you here. Guess your key no longer works, eh?"

Sarah closes the computer and dashes for the door. Ian simply catches the hood of her sweatshirt. "No need to run, Sarah; your driver's detained as well. Why don't we just sit in here and wait on the police. By the way, who is the lad at the wheel?"

"He's none of your business."

"Oh, but he is. You see, at the very least, he is trespassing on my property. I'm betting he lived in the house without permission, as did you. Obviously, you two are in cahoots, but it can't be just the two of you."

"I had permission to stay, so did he!"

"Are we going down this dead-end street again."

"I saw you, talking to the paintings, acting crazy as hell in the hall. I saw you!"

"Yep, I bet you did. Probably have it streaming on YouTube. Now about having permission to live in my house—"

"You aren't the only one who owns this house, you know."

"Last time I checked, as laird, I am, but I'll be checking again tomorrow with the general register and conveyancing solicitors and consulting with the Highland Council even if I must drive to Inverness to do so. Hey, Stewy, got everything under control?"

"Yes, boss, bringing the son of a bitch in to wait with you."

"Excellent. Sarah, looks as though you have a message on your cell phone. Shall I see who is calling?"

"Keep your hands off my property."

"Oh, that's a fine kettle of fish coming from you. Just going to hold the phone till the coppers arrive. Oh, look here! My dear old sister calling you. Imagine. Gotten kind of chummy have you now? Bet John's number is in the top five as well. You disappoint me, Sarah. I hired you to take care of Molly's gardens. I paid you handsomely. You did a brilliant job. Did Fiona promise you something more? Take it from me, she doesn't keep her promises."

The police sirens are within range, and tires can be heard rushing down the driveway, throwing gravel to and fro. When the cars come to a halt, Ian explains the situation. They realize pretty quickly Sarah and her boyfriend should be cuffed and carted to the station. The computer is confiscated; ledgers must be scrutinized by an independent source to find out if money is being funneled away from the estate accounts and if information is being relayed to Fiona. A burly policeman with a rough, ruddy complexion, probably the result of swilling down a few too many at the local pub, pats Ian on the back. "Nice detective work for a laird." He smiles at Ian and suggests he leave the arresting to those trained. Ian asks for the ordeal to be kept quiet until the books have been examined and he has time to go over all the estate dealings.

"I dunno about that, sir. In this small community, word gets out no matter what."

"You've got to at least make an attempt. I'm certain at least two warrants for arrest will be issued if I can find evidence."

"Beggin' your pardon, Laird, but issuing warrants is our job. You might want to take inventory of the house; some items may have been liberated or sold."

Stuart speaks up on behalf of Ian. "Baxton, give him a chance. Try to keep it quiet. No one knows the workings of the estate better than Ian. If you want an inventory of any missing items, that could take forever. Christ sake, man, he jetted back from the States to check on the status of some trouble we've noticed. It seems this may be bigger than we first thought."

"You're saying this isn't the end of it? Who else do you suspect?" Baxton Healy asks while shaking his head in disbelief.

Ian points to Sarah and asks to step aside where she has no possibility of hearing. "I hate to say this, but my sister Fiona came to the States demanding I turn over lairdship to her son. I suspected someone from the inside had to be giving her information. Honestly, I had no clue Sarah has been mixed up in it. I do expect Fiona has something to do with this and also John, my business manager."

"Liam? Fiona thinks Liam can run the estate? That's laughable. Fine people you hang around with, Mr. MacDougal."

"Stuart here, do you think he—"

"Not for a moment. He's the one who turned me on to this whole thing. Besides, the old gum ball has been at my side since I can remember."

After the excitement of the night has worn off, Ian goes back to try to get an hour or two of sleep before a meeting at the local registrant's office. A perusal of estate documents ought to discern when Fiona's inquiries may have transpired. Topping off his scotch, resting a weary head upon the pillow, he hears Louise's words repeating in his mind. *Ask Molly to do something letting you know it's her; something electrical is easiest.* Adrenaline had been pumping through his veins earlier, so he didn't note when the mist appeared in the office doorway. Ian remembers shooing the mist and as he unlocked the door, the lights, including the lamps came on without so much as him touching the switches. "Molly, sweet Christ in heaven, Molly, it is you!" Taking the glass of scotch, he drinks it all in one huge gulp and then buries his head in the pillow crying Molly's name while drifting off to sleep.

"Mama, I'll be back after a spell. Got an appointment."

"Where you off to, sugar?"

Emileigh stands tall, wearing a frilly, lace-covered floral summer dress. Appearing angelic standing in the early morning light as it softly sifts through the screen door, she says, "I promised Ian I'd see ole Doc Hathaway while he's in Scotland. I'm only doing this for him."

"You ain't had many spells since he's come around, have you?"

"No, a few, but fewer than before."

Tah moves toward her daughter, pulling at her arm and making Emileigh spin around to face her. "You're probably right, Em; stress, loss, and grief may be to blame. What they call it? Oh yeah, post-traumatic stress. I bet that's what ya got."

"Well, since you've diagnosed me, Mama, what's the remedy?"

"Love. It cures everything!"

Emileigh turns around, pushing the creaky screen door open and bidding her mother a cheery good-bye.

"Mornin', Weasy. You heard anything from Ian?"

"No, not yet. Has Em?"

"She didn't say. You just missed her; she's gone to see Doc Hathaway."

"Is she all right, Tah?"

"Oh sure, just finally goin' to see what her spells might be."

"You worried?"

"Naw, maybe a bit, but she seems to be gettin' along better lately."

"I reckon skirt boy might have something to do with it."

Both women look at each other knowing full well Emileigh's health is a concern, but downplaying the situation makes it easier to bear. Emily drives up with Ely. He bounds out of the car, hurtling up the stairs and into the store before Emily even has a chance to close the car door.

"Gracious, son, what's the rush?"

"I gots me somethin' wonderful to tell y'all!" Ely tips his head in a gentlemanly gesture. "Mornin', Miss Louise."

"Tell us, Ely."

"I cain't hardly believe it. You 'member talkin' to me about dem bored angels?"

"Of course I do."

"They ain't bored no more, not since my mama died. I been talkin' to 'em, lettin' be known my needs, prayin' a mite too. Low and behold, theys done worked a miracle fer me."

"A miracle? Pray tell." Tah winks at Louise, knowing about the miracle to which he is referring.

Emily enters the store to hear Ely's excitement. "Mr. Grayson and Miss Emily, theys done asked me to stay with them—I means live with them forever! Can yous believe it? They wants me!"

"Ely, too bad you don't show a little more excitement. We're so happy for you! Looks like you want to stay with them?"

"Sure 'nuff, Ma Bell. I means, you know, I'd likes to be here too, but I still be here workin', right?"

"Absolutely, son! Don't know how we got along without you. Grab yourself a drink."

Ely grabs a bottle of Gatorade, his feet hardly touching the floor. "Miss Louise, you reckon I could tell Ian 'bout this? Sure would like to talk to him; that'd be mighty good."

"Soon as Emmy gets back, ask her. I'm sure she'd like to share your good news too."

"I'll do it. I dang sure will." He scampers off down to the lake. Grief has taken a break, a much-needed break for him. "Well, Emily, seems you have made one sixteen-year-old a very happy camper."

She checks to see where Ely went and then solemnly brings up Steve and Leigh. "I called over to Leigh's this mornin' before we headed here. Talked to Steve and relayed Ely's decision. I feel bad; they were hoping Ely would be living there."

"You mean they weren't happy for him?"

"Oh, they were happy. I get the feeling it was disappointing. You know they've wanted children for a long, long time. Must be hard seein' everyone they know with kids."

"I can see how for the moment they're saddened, but knowing the two of them, they'll quickly pull out of it and count their blessings."

"I hope you're right, Weasy." Emily kicks at the hardwoods acting like something's there; it's a badly camouflaged effort to hide her feelings of guilt.

Emileigh pulls up with music blaring. Ely comes charging up the hill to catch her and tell her the news while begging to call Ian. "Ely, how wonderful! Sure, we should call him. Let's see, it's eleven here so that makes it four in Scotland. I think we should wait awhile, Ely. He's probably in the middle of somethin'."

"What time then, Miss Em? How soon?"

"Well, I usually hear from him long about quittin' time. Think you can wait that long?"

Ely looks at her stunned, waiting until the store closes seems like a lifetime to him.

"Miss Em, that's sure gonna make today a long day. Cain't we do it earlier?"

"We could, but I think you'd be disappointed; if we reach him, he may have to rush, and you don't want that, do you?"

"No, I guess not."

Walking back to the car, Emily shouts out to Ely, saying her goodbyes. "I'll be back to get you later, Ely."

He smiles and waves, standing a bit taller in his sneakers.

Leigh pulls up in her Lexus just as Emileigh walks into the store. "Mornin', Leigh, how you doing today?"

"Oh, fine, I guess. Heard Ely's news?"

"I think all of Moravian Falls has by now. You okay with his decision?"

"It's probably best for him. We're used to just the two of us." Leigh does a remarkable job of hiding her feelings of disappointment. They walk into the store together.

"Em, what did Doc say?"

"Nothing like small talk, Ma. Sorry. I was a trifle longer than antici-pated. I stopped by my apartment to get the mail."

"Anything interesting in the mailbox?"

"My passport came, not that I'll be using it."

"All right then, what did the doctor tell you?"

"Like you said, probably mostly stress induced. He did tell me what vitamins to take to help with stress and told me to drink plenty of water."

Leigh, already not in the greatest of moods, is appalled by the advice she got. "You paid good money to be told to take vitamins and drink water? I always thought Doc to be a quack."

"Hold on, Leigh, before you go giving him webbed feet; he did order some blood work. See, there's the hole the vampire made to get her feed."

"Well, I guess that's better than nothing."

"Doc Hathaway said I should hear real soon if they found anything."

Tah looks at the hands on the clock approaching the lunch hour. "Girls, you want to have lunch? We haven't eaten lunch together in a while."

chapter 20

"EXCUSE ME, SIR. Are you Ian MacDougal?"

Pouring over a file at the register's office, he peers over the top of his glasses to see standing before him a large-girthed short man in a grey suit with a skinny tie. "Aye, can I help you?"

"Ah yes, Stuart Anderson told me where I could find you."

"And you might be?"

"Oh sorry, sir, I'm Axton Bernard of SIS, we used to be MI6.

"Is this a joke? Are you filming a James Bond movie here?"

"I assure you, sir, this is no joke. I'd like to speak with you somewhere more private and secure."

"I'm not sure there is such a place. Why not over at the study table?"

The two men sit down at a very heavy wooden table lit by an ancient bronze and gold chandelier. The late afternoon sun is strobing in and out of the windows aloft. Bernard pulls out his credentials, displaying them to Ian before progressing. Ian's eyebrows lift as he pulls off his readers.

"Mr. MacDougal, the local police put out an inquiry last night into one Sarah Donovan and Chesney Kinney. Mr. Kinney has no prior convictions, Miss Donovan only a drunk and disorderly. Baxton Healy, the copper from last night, also gave us the name of your business manager since we made inquiry about the former. Can you verify a Mr. John C. Riley is your business manager?"

Ian squirms a bit in his chair. Last time he answered questions posed to him by law enforcement, he nearly got charged with murder. "Would you be kind enough to tell me first where this is leading?"

"Of course, it's a long story, so I'll give you the condensed version. Hopefully, you'll be able to fill in a few blanks we seem to have. We've been tracking Mr. Riley's actions for the past year. We have placed him working at your estate for a period of approximately five months."

"Can you at least verify that?"

"It sounds right."

"Do you know where he was last employed?"

"I have his CV in my files, but as close as I can recall, it was for a small whiskey producer in Glasgow."

"Hmm, it may surprise you to find out he actually worked for one Michael Lennox."

"Yes, I'd say surprise doesn't begin to explain how I'm thinking."

"Did you check out Mr. Riley's references?"

"Right now, I can tell you I wish I had. Michael Lennox is my brother-in-law."

"Yes, we are fully aware, and he is married to your sister Fiona, correct?"

"Seems you have the family lineage down pat. Where is this going?"

"What I'm going to tell you, I'd prefer if you didn't repeat. We've followed a very interesting money trail leading from your estate to Michael Lennox through his wife's accounts. At first, we just thought you had heard of Mr. Lennox's financial troubles and were sending money in support."

"Wait, you're telling me they have money woes?"

"Aye, he filed for bankruptcy just before Mr. Riley began working for you."

"I'm beginning to see a much clearer picture of what's been happening and why."

"When the local police told us you suspected your sister and Mr. Riley of some sort of misdoings, things began to click for us as well. John Riley indeed was in Glasgow; he fled very quickly as Michael Lennox knew he'd soon be pinned for embezzlement. You see, Mr. Lennox has been siphoning money from his parents' company using Riley to do so. It was an effort to keep Lennox's ailing personal finances afloat. Mr. Lennox, the senior, contacted us after his money manager noticed funds disappearing from corporate accounts. Mr. Lennox, the younger, had set up Riley to take the fall if it got too hot. Your sister became aware the estate had a position open for a business manager."

"How did she know that?"

"In comes your gardener Sarah Donovan. By this point tracking both Mr. Lennox and Mr. Riley, we monitored all their communications."

"You tapped into their business and personal lines?"

"Yes, I assure you we obtained all the essential permissions. Mrs. Fiona Lennox was heard instructing Ms. Donovan to keep tabs on all estate transactions and events. She told her to live in the house as you were in the States and would never be aware. She also said she'd have duplicate keys made for her. Of course, Ms. Donovan was being paid well for her information. I'm sorry to tell you, but Mrs. Lennox also told her as a gardener of your deceased wife's gardens it gave Ms. Donovan the perfect excuse to phone you and keep tabs on your dealings and whereabouts."

"You already know John sent money out of my estate funds to the Lennox's? I never approved of such transactions."

"We know that now, and with the office computer and your ledgers confiscated, the trail should be much easier to connect the dots on"

"What about the money John stole and sent to my sister and her husband?"

"I suggest you hire a solicitor and freeze all of their funds before the bankruptcy hearing."

"Hired one today, and I'll advise. One thing I don't understand is how Sarah knew I'd been questioned in Moravian Falls by the police the day before I left to come home."

"Aha, wondered when you'd ask. The police chief, Hobbs I think his name is, he called here…well, he had your cell phone while you were being interrogated. Sarah Donovan actually called while you were being questioned. Hobbs saw your contact list, heard a message from her, and called to gain information about you. Sounds like the chief must have divulged more information than he should have concerning your situation. He is a character, isn't he? Hobbs sounds like he's got a mouth full of marbles when he speaks."

"That'd be his chewing tobacco."

"Gads, they let him use that stuff at the office?"

"Yeah, it is part of Hobbs's uniform, literally. You should see his sleeve; he wipes his brown spit all over it."

"Too much information, Mr. MacDougal. Your mum, is she still Stateside?"

"Please tell me she isn't involved."

"Relax, no, from what we can tell she is just an innocent bystander."

"Good, you had me wondering for a moment. She is coming back day after tomorrow."

"I'll need to get a statement from you at some point. Sounds like Healy asked you to take an inventory of household items?"

"Aye, it's a monumental task."

"Hopefully, your mum can assist. Here is my card. Call soon so we can get your statement."

"Thank you, Mr. Bernard, I am awed by your investigation. The timing is perfect for me and your attention to detail impressive."

"All in a day's work, and it's Axton from now on. I wish you good day, and we'll be talking to you soon."

The two men respectfully part ways. Ian feels a tremendous relief. "One more thing, Ian, warrants are served for Fiona's, John's, and Michael's apprehension. Should you see them, use the number on the card and give us a call."

"Will do, Axton. I don't anticipate seeing them."

Before his next heartbeat, Ian is calling his friend and feeling confident the estate troubles may soon be resolved. "Stewy, have dinner with Heather, and if she'll let you, come back to the house for cigars and a lotta scotch. I'm gonna fill your ears tonight."

Ulysses, having a difficult time watching Maggie pack her luggage to return home, asks her in a meek and sad voice, "Promise, Maggie, you'll return to me and until then think of me from time to time."

"Shhh, I shall be back soon, probably with my son. We have a lot of your carvings to send out. Keep carving and give a thought as you do."

There is a silent good-bye between Ulysses and Maggie. Neither can muster up more. Outside, Ely opens the car door and loads her bags; he is taking her to the airport where she'll fly to points beyond. First, the Suggettes meet Maggie outside before she gets into the car. They give her a hardy so long, making certain she is fully aware her new friends expect her back.

With a lot of gusto in his voice, Ian finally has enough time to describe in detail Axton's intricate investigation to Emileigh. Both are relieved and gratified knowing Fiona will this time indeed learn a lesson, albeit the hard way. Ian explains there are still a lot of loose ends to deal with and he feels strongly he should remain home until all charges are filed. Not pleased with his decision to stay on, she bites her lip in an effort not to antagonize him farther. She is relieved to learn Sarah meant nothing to Ian on a personal level. Ian also let Em know he and Maggie have begun working on an inventory of household items.

"Sugar, have you talked to Ian in the last few days?"

"Oh, Mama, I just got off the phone with him; he was able to find an extended length of time to explain in detail what he's been dealing with. I was starting to wonder what happened; it has been several days since all hell broke loose. He said with the help of the authorities, they discovered an investigation by SIS was already underway. Ian found out Fiona and Michael did conspire to take over the estate and were draining its accounts beforehand. Oh, Mama there is Grandmama, she's come to pick me up"

"I'm so glad you're going to spend some time together. Wait one second sugar, you think Ian will be comin' back soon?"

"Fingers crossed, I do, in the very near future. Gotta go. I'll be seein' you soon, Mama. Love you!"

"Right back at ya, sugar!"

Emileigh walks down the four squeaky steps, smiles at Grandmama, and hops into her Mini Cooper.

"You ready for this, Em?"

"Yes, scared but ready. Grandmama thank you for hearing me out and helping me decide what to do."

"You'll explain to Mama, won't you? I've never done anything without her knowing."

"Of course I'll tell her. Sweet child, no matter what happens, nothing can stop me from loving you with all my heart." She punches the gas pedal, and off they speed along the lakefront road out of sight from Tah's binoculars.

The mist reappears on the steps to Molly's garden beckoning Ian toward it. A trance comes over him once again; as the apparition evolves, every fiber of Ian's body is paralyzed. The light white mist floats toward Ian, and he clearly sees Molly holding a child. He's unable to help imagining it's his boy torn from her womb so long ago, his only child who died alongside his mother. Molly takes her gaze off the baby, throwing a brilliant smile in Ian's direction. He is held captive by the sight, and raw emotions of the horrible day such a long time ago come pouring back in one breath's time. Through the mist, Ian hears a familiar languid voice. It isn't Molly's. The translucent being's gaze is fixed on Ian, the vapor begins to disperse. Bewildered at the sight of Molly and the child, the soft voice continues to call his name. Ian is jogged back into this realm; realizing its Emmy's melodic voice, he drops to his knees. Her beauty is radiant as she strolls through the vanishing mist. Emileigh continues to methodically move toward Ian with short, nervous steps wearing a solemn expression; she doesn't know what Ian's response to her unexpected arrival will be. Seeing him on his knees, she is surprised by his emotional welcome.

"You've come back. I have to admit, my sweet Emmy, in my heart, I married you the first moment I saw you standing in the doorway of the general store. My mind has been spinning all the time hoping and praying you're still in love with me."

Emileigh reaches out to Ian. A wide, inviting smile crosses her lips. Remaining on his knees, he puts his arms around her waist pulling her as close as he can. He places the side of his head on her abdomen holding her ever so tightly. "You've made all my dreams come true."

"No, Ian, I haven't yet."

"What do you mean? You've come back to me, haven't you?" Ian can't bear to hear what she has to say, but instinctually listens, raising his head bravely not only to hear but to see her response.

"Do you hear a heartbeat?"

Ian looks at Em's face, with tears filling his eyes, his heart pounding with hopeful anticipation. "You mean...?"

Emileigh, overcome with emotion, is unable to say another word, so she nods. They gaze at one another; hot, salty tears stream down their faces. Ian stands up embracing his Emileigh, ever so gently touching her abdomen as an expectant father does. He moves his eyes up from his hand, and their eyes lock. "Yes, love, all my wildest dreams have now come true."

A faint giggle of a wee child is heard coming from the last of the mist disappearing into the great beyond. Ian, embracing Emmy, lifts his face to the heavens above and whispers, "Thank You."

Made in the USA
Charleston, SC
20 September 2012